Kanone II

Oberkanone

Edmund LeRoy

Published by New Generation Publishing in 2016

Copyright © Edmund LeRoy 2016

First Edition

www.newgeneration-publishing.com

PROLOGUE

25 NOVEMBER 1917

Hysterical screeches rose up out of the darkness with the call of wild lamentations. Demented winds struck the Eastern Tower, making it shudder like a bell. Andrea Harker braced herself against the onslaught, her unbound hair streaming past her face as sea grass does when caught in the flow of an ebbing tide.

She stood upon the top of the tower looking south and, with a fleet of moon-flooded clouds racing ahead of her it was easy enough to imagine that she was a mariner anchored and resolute upon a rolling deck riding some blind storm of black crested waves.

And this is my crow's-nest, my high place from where I look to France.

She could not see it. She could not see anything. The light of a full moon was hidden behind coursing clouds and her dark-widened eyes were night-blinded to everything save for the nearest shapes and shadows.

But she did have her imagination. And with it she tried to hitch her mind upon the migrating storm, using its winds to carry her across the intervening miles, across the English countryside and over the turbulent waters of the Channel to the war torn fields of France.

To a place called Ste Helene.

She knew this place. It was where her husband's squadron was located. She also knew that it was just north of Lens. According to her husband the countryside there was quite lovely even when buried beneath a layer of winter snow. He had promised to take her there after the war.

When the guns fall silent and the birds sing again.

Often when the house was quiet she would go to the bookcase in the living room, take down her husband's atlas and open it at the two pages that showed Northern France. By running her finger south from Bethune and La Bassèe it was easy enough to locate Ste Helene.

I've even drawn a circle around it.

But knowing where to find it on the map wasn't much help in conjuring up an image of what it might look like. All she knew for certain was that somewhere in that circle was an airfield where her husband ate and slept and commanded men.

But hopefully not for much longer.

She'd received news. The best news possible! Her husband was due to leave Ste Helene tomorrow morning. And not just Ste Helene! He would be leaving France and coming home. He would be coming home for good. For him the war would be over. And for the first time in a long time she would have him all to herself.

So why do I feel so anxious?

Why this restlessness and inability to sleep? Was it only the sound of the storm that had kept her awake? Or was it some greater fear that had driven her to climb this tower and stand upon its wind battered pinnacle in nothing but her nightdress? Surely he is beyond all danger now?

But he is a hero. And heroes are never out of danger.

She knew this. She had always known of his heroic qualities even before the war started, even before she had married him. It was one of the reasons she had married him. But a trait can be loved for what it is without wishing for it to be tested.

And the war has tested him again and again.

It had tested him in the skies over France. Day after day it had tested the strength of his nerve. But she had been tested too. Her endurance had been tested. For her every one of those days had been a day of silent torment, a day of dread and uncertainty.

Before going to war her husband had told her not to look at the newspapers fearing she might read something she would find distressing. But news came to her anyway, news of her husband's exploits and with each story her love and pride grew stronger. But with the pride came resentment.

Sometimes I wish I'd married a coward.

Not that she ever spoke to her husband about this, not in her letters or during his leave. She knew how much store he set by his courage and feared that if she cast it in a bad light his warrior spirit would be injured and fate, which had protected him till now, would turn against him.

The wind shrieked and barged against her back and shoulders, almost lifting her heels from the tower and in that moment her heart lightened. She knew that this storm was heading toward France and would soon reach her husband. And when it did all would be well.

Not all storms are bad.

She remembered her husband once telling her that nothing ever flew in a storm. Nothing ever got off the ground. So, raising her face and both her hands to the raging heavens she offered up a prayer and infused it with all the power of her love.

Oh kind winds, keep him safe. Keep him on the ground.

CHAPTER ONE

26 NOVEMBER 1917

Driven by a sudden blow of wind the door to Major Harker's office flew open. Standing framed in the doorway was Colonel 'Prim' Pritchett, his expression drawn and stricken.

'What filthy weather,' he declared to no one in particular. 'Looks like we're in for a bit of a storm tonight.'

Lit with bitter hope his red-rimmed eyes searched the shadowed corners of the office, but the hope soon faded when they fell upon the lamp-lit figure of Captain Parkinson slumped in a chair by Major Harker's unoccupied desk.

Closing the door against the wind Pritchett strode into the office. 'Any further news?'

As if responding to some far off sound Parkinson slowly raised his head and, with eyes dull, lifeless and devoid of recognition, he looked upon the Colonel as if he were a stranger. Like a man gasping for air he opened his mouth to speak but then, thinking better of what he was about to say, stayed silent.

He tried once again and this time found his voice. 'Nothing since battery reported sighting a Camel drop out of the clouds near Oyster Crater.'

This was not what Colonel Pritchett wanted to hear. But he was too much the old warrior, too much the man hardened by daily tragedy to easily relinquish his air of determination and self-control.

He shook his head in disbelief. 'It doesn't make sense. He was supposed to be leaving for home this morning. I told him not to go out and face Buchner.'

Parkinson made no reply and both men retreated into their own thoughts, their brooding silence heightened by the sound of riotous winds. Then Colonel Pritchett, seeming to make up his mind about something, snapped himself into a brisk and business like demeanour.

'Remind me!' he asked. 'What's the name of the German in command of the airbase at Bois de Cheval?'

Parkinson sat blank faced and unresponsive, apparently not having heard or comprehended the question.

'Come on, man!' Pritchett shouted. 'Pull yourself together.'

Parkinson looked up blinking rapidly as if he had been slapped hard across the face. 'Rudolf Hantelmann is the Hauptmann in charge.'

Removing his leather gloves Pritchett grabbed up the telephone from the desk and, tapping the key vigorously, said to himself, 'Right! Let's see what we can do to get Major Harker back.'

****

He should have been pleased. This was the first quiet moment that Major Henry Jameson had enjoyed for days, certainly since the start of the recent Ste Helene offensive and the drive to capture Bois de Cheval.

But as he sat in his office at the F2B airbase at Motte de Gazonville and stared at his desk and what lay upon it he realised that his quiet moment came with a price, one that he'd much prefer not to pay.

Leading a ground attack would be preferable.

It was the sad task of every commander to write 'next of kin' letters. And he had nine of them to do. For his convenience his adjutant had neatly laid out the headed notepaper and the blank envelopes. There was also a list of names. Not that he needed it. He knew all of them. How else could he possibly write words of comfort to their relatives? But it didn't make the task any easier.

God! I feel tired.

At the top of the list were Captain Percy McCall, Lieutenant Geoffrey Farrington, Lieutenant Lawrence Tipton, Lieutenant Wallace Groves and Lieutenant Donald Fox-Russell, the three pilots and two observers who were killed on 22nd November over Trois Risseaux.

Virtually the whole of 'A' flight.

And according to eyewitness accounts the slaughter had not been the result of an attack by a wave of enemy machines but by a single German pilot who had dived out of the sun and ambushed the flight of F2Bs on its right flank.

Three machines down, five men lost and all in a matter of seconds.

And that wasn't the end of the squadron's losses. During the retreat two more F2Bs were shot down resulting in the deaths of Captain Vernon Farnborough and Second Lieutenants Caspar Hardman, Valentine Hughes and Will Shoreham.

All killed by Leutnant Buchner.

Nine men and five machines, nearly half the squadron. As far as Jameson could remember this was the single greatest disaster ever to befall 89 squadron and even though he knew that replacement men and machines were on the way with more to follow he wasn't entirely confident that the unit would ever fully recover.

I only pray that things stay quiet for a while.

There was a knock on the door to his office.

Grateful for the interruption Jameson yelled, 'Enter!'

The door opened and in stepped the round and solid figure of Captain Silk, 'B' flight leader. He had a scrap of paper in his hands.

'You look a bit put out, John. What's up?'

'I've just had a call from Colonel Pritchett.'

'Really? What does he want?'

'He wants us to drop a message on the JGN airbase at Bois de Cheval.'

'What, right now? In this filthy weather?'

'I'm afraid so.'

'Fine! Well, I suppose we'd better get someone up straight away before the wind gets any stronger. Where is this message?'

'Here! I've written it down.'

****

Nothing beats a gale up your arse to speed things up.

Lieutenant Paul Singleton was exaggerating, but only slightly. In normal weather conditions it would have taken his F2B about twenty minutes to fly from 89 squadron's airfield at Motte de Gazonville to the JGN airbase at Bois de Cheval. But the weather conditions weren't normal.

It's worse than flying through an artillery barrage.

The sky was heavy and overcast, visibility was bad and Singleton struggled to keep control of his machine as it was continually buffeted from side to side by a gusting wind of such strength it had grounded almost all other aircraft.

At least the flight's been uneventful.

No one had fired at them or come out to chase them off. And that suited Singleton perfectly. The last thing he wanted was to fight his way to where he was going especially as Major Jameson had sent him and his observer Second Lieutenant Robert Trivers on some silly job.

Dropping messages on Hun aerodromes. Anyone would think I'm a bloody postman.

Thankfully his 275 horse power Rolls-Royce Falcon engine had roared clear and healthy all the way there and continued to do so as they passed low over Trois Risseaux and then the black waters of the River Auburn.

It was here that Trivers tapped him on the shoulder and pointed down to the narrow *Pont Flottant* where many dead bodies and wrecked vehicles crowded the bridge and the waters beneath it.

And that was not an end to the bodies. Like a trail of scattered twigs a long line of them led from the eastern end of the bridge and along the path that ran across the plains of snow-covered grass to the dark skirts of the Bois de Cheval. Then all was hidden from view as they flew over the trackless forest with its endless canopy of lean and leafless branches.

There seemed no end to it. Trees, trees and more trees passed beneath them in an unbroken mass except for some ragged gaps that stood out like bald spots on an almost perfect head of hair.

That's where the bombardment fell on our troops.

Then suddenly the forest ended, swept behind them like the dark sea's edge when it meets the shore. They had reached its eastern boundary and now before them lay the bomb-cratered lower landing field and, at the top of the hill, the ruined chateau of Bois de Cheval airbase, smoke still rising from its smouldering tower.

In the gathering dusk the airbase seemed deserted. Not a single person could be seen anywhere. But Singleton had been in similar situations often enough to know that appearances can be deceptive; there were no guarantees that they were not being observed by unfriendly eyes.

Let's do this and get out of here.

He took his machine halfway up the field then when the wind behind him briefly abated he banked sharply to starboard so that he could circle back and head for home. This was the signal for his observer, Trivers, to drop their cargo onto the field below.

****

Disgusted by the primitive conditions in the new officer's Kasino Fuchs had got up and left, abandoning his drink on the bar. As if sensing his mood the wind outside pushed and shoved him in the direction of the chateau and hurried him around the corner to the old Kasino.

Stopping to light his pipe Fuchs surveyed the damage. It was in a sorry state. The roof and veranda had collapsed. Much of the wood was charred or scorched by fire. It was beyond repair.

We'll have to clear the site and start again.

This thought made him feel better. He had something to aim for, something to work toward. And if he needed a portent of success and good fortune one was duly delivered. A black cat that had been sheltering from the wind came up to him and started brushing itself against his leg.

'Hello there, little kitty.'

Kneeling down he picked it and held it in his arms and, as he stroked its head and back, it purred contentedly.

'I think I'll name you Mimi,' he told the animal. 'She likes being stroked as well.'

Possibly the cat found this name disagreeable or more likely it wasn't too happy with the smell of Fuchs' pipe. Whatever the reason the cat suddenly tensed, leapt out of Fuchs' arms and ran off into the shadows.

He was about to call after it when the cascading winds momentarily ran out of breath and the brief silence that followed was filled with another sound; a low-throated drone that seemed to emerge out of the dark forest ahead of him.

I've heard that sound before.

He had heard it before. It was the same sound that had accompanied a flight of F2Bs when, several days earlier, they had bombed the airfield and wrecked his Kasino. Now they were back. He should have felt afraid, he should be sounding the alarm and running for shelter, but he didn't. He just continued standing there smoking his pipe.

Who goes on a bombing mission with only one machine?

It didn't make sense. And, for some reason he couldn't quite explain to himself, he sensed that those flying the machine were not bound on a mission of war. But the men manning the machine gun emplacement behind him didn't share his view. They were furiously loading a fresh belt of ammunition into the heavy gun, readying it for action.

With a calmness that seemed almost insane Fuchs walked over and told them, 'You won't need that.'

As if thrown into a trance by his words the men stood down. And together they watched the enemy machine burst over the tree tops, a thunderous black winged shape that seemed to slide unsteadily in the wind as it flew up the field toward them.

Fuchs felt no surprise when the F2B started banking to starboard or when he saw a small dark object drop from its side. Puffing on his pipe he waited patiently as the enemy machine circled the field and disappeared back over the trackless forest of Bois de Cheval.

When everything had quietened down Fuchs stepped from beside the machine gun emplacement and strolled leisurely down the field's slope of snow toward the small dark object that now sat like a marker in the frozen desolation. Even the wind obligingly moved aside to ease his passage. But there was really no need to hurry. The dark object wasn't going anywhere.

****

Hantelmann was not the easiest of men to deal with at the best of times. And when the situation was a touchy one he had to be approached with considerable care. The stress of being his adjutant had taught Fuchs this lesson well enough and it was at the forefront of his mind as he entered Hantelmann's office.

But he's still the boss. And this is something he has to know.

Trying to make light of his entrance Fuchs slapped his arms and puffed into his hands. 'Phew! That wind's cold enough to slice ham.'

Hantelmann made no sign that had heard Fuchs or that he was even aware of his presence. Concerned, Fuchs stepped forward to get a closer look at his commanding officer. A single bare bulb lit the narrow confines of the office. It threw off little light and even that flickered whenever a gust of wind hit the outside walls. But it was enough to make out Hantelmann's grey skin, the thin sheen of cold perspiration on his forehead and the feverish glow in his eyes.

Looks to me like his wound has become infected.

'Are you feeling all right, Herr Hauptmann?'

Hantelmann's head lolled drunkenly from side to side as he waved the air with an irritated hand. 'Stop fussing, Fuchs. There's nothing wrong with me that a good stiff drink won't put right.'

Knowing it was never a good idea to press a point with Hantelmann Fuchs backed off for the moment. 'As you say, Herr Hauptmann.'

'What was all that commotion going on outside?'

'An enemy machine dropped a message.'

Hantelmann's glazed eyes struggled to focus. 'Message! What message?'

'This one.'

When Fuchs retrieved the sack from the landing field he found it contained a fist-sized stone. Attached to this was a note. It was this note that he now offered to his commanding officer.

Hantelmann brushed a loose hand across his face. 'I'm sure you've read it all ready, Fuchs. Who's it from?

'Colonel Pritchett.'

Hantelmann shivered. 'Ah, the dear old Colonel. Always a delight to hear from him. Tell me, what does he have to say for himself?'

'He's anxious to give Major Harker a proper burial and asks whether, as an act of military courtesy, we can return his body.'

'Major Harker. The pilot that Buchner shot down?'

Hantelmann was not happy with Buchner. They may have settled their differences to deal with the British, but the reconciliation was always going to be a tenuous one. And now that Buchner had shot down the enemy's greatest pilot Hantelmann's view was forthright.

'They'll be no living with that bastard now.'

'Yes, Herr Hauptmann.'

'Do we have the Major's body?'

'No, Herr Hauptmann.'

'Where is it?'

'Still in no-man's-land, I assume. Somewhere near Oyster Crater.'

'Ah, what a shame.' Hantelmann chuckled with a strange mixture of humour and remorse. 'I suppose you'd better get someone to fly a message back to the Colonel informing him that regretfully we don't have the Major's body.'

Fuchs hesitated. This was the crucial part of the conversation, the part where he had to take the greatest care. 'Rather than do that, Herr Hauptmann, may I suggest another course of action?'

'As long as it doesn't take all day.'

'It will be dark in a few hours.'

'What of it?'

'Well, it occurs to me that we can tell the British we will hold fire on our sector of no-man's-land between say ten and eleven o'clock? That should give them enough time to send out a search party to retrieve the Major's body.'

Hantelmann tensed, giving Fuchs a sharp look. 'And why would we do that?'

In as reasonable voice as he could manage Fuchs said:

'The British were good enough to retrieve the body of Leutnant Neckel for us, and then bury him with full military honours. We'll only be returning the courtesy.'

'That's all very well, Fuchs, but you seem to forget that I am merely a Hauptmann. I might run this airbase but I don't have the authority to arrange cease-fires.'

Sensing from Hantelmann's voice that he was not entirely against the idea Fuchs pressed further. 'If you let me contact High Command on your behalf I could ask for their permission. I'm fairly certain they'd consider such a request favourably.'

****

From their gilt frames high upon the library's panelled walls von Hoeppner's eight male ancestors looked down upon him with dissolute disdain as he busied himself writing a report in the soft light of a desk lamp.

All eight portraits represented three centuries of von Hoeppners. The first Archduke, having fought with Wallenstein in the Thirty Years War, would have been more than keen to read the present Archduke's report about the recent military actions on the Ste Helene Salient.

God! That was a close run thing.

He had just got to the critical part where the British were assaulting the airfield at Bois de Cheval and was about to describe how the intervention by the German Iron Division saved the day when the telephone on his desk started to ring. He snatched at it impatiently.

'Yes. Who is it?'

'Von Abshagen, Herr OberstGeneral. Sorry for disturbing you at this hour, but I thought you'd like to know I've just received an odd call from Bois de Cheval.'

'Odd call? Oh, don't tell me. It's from that idiot Hantelmann.'

'No, Excellency. It was from his adjutant, Oberleutnant Fuchs.'

'Really? And what does he want?'

'He wants to call a cease fire on the Ste Helene Salient.'

Such was von Hoeppner's incredulity his face seemed to expand in size. 'He wants to what?'

'It seems the British dropped a message asking for the return of the body of one of their pilots.'

'Is that normal?'

'Its unusual but not entirely unprecedented especially if the man in question is not an ordinary pilot.'

'And this one isn't?'

'No, Excellency. Far from it. The man in question is Major Harker.'

'Major Harker you say. Mein Gott! Isn't he one of their top pilots?'

'Yes, Excellency, he was.'

'Almost as good as Willi Buchner.'

'In point of fact it was Oberleutnant Buchner who shot him down.'

'This is news indeed.'

'What shall I tell Fuchs, Excellency?'

As von Hoeppner considered his response his eyes fell upon the Seiffert bronze statuette sitting on the desk in front of him, the one of a naked sea nymph being pursued by a leering and grotesquely excited satyr.

Seiffert had used Thetis von Buchner as the model for the sea nymph, and as von Hoeppner reached out to run the fingers of his free hand down the creature's back he thought of her now.

Quite a beauty and one of my best agents.

But she had one major weakness and that was her son, Willi Buchner. It was not so long ago that she had come to him to make a plea on her son's behalf who, at the time, stood accused of insubordination.

And she wanted me to intervene.

Remembering this von Hoeppner wondered what she would say about the British request. Would she demand that it be turned down? Or would she be magnanimous? Then he had an idea and smiled.

'Tell Fuchs that he can have his cease fire but on one condition.'

'What's that, Excellency?'

'He's got to get Buchner's permission first.'

****

With the snarl of a man perpetually flustered by the petty demands of others Oberleutnant Wilhelm Buchner slammed the telephone back onto its rest.

Bloody High Command! Why are they always bothering me?

Needing air he strode angrily to the hut's entrance and wrenched open the door. It was dark outside. He couldn't see much, but he could hear the hiss and rustle of the wind as it roared through the distant treetops like some winged beast trapped in the branches, howling and bellowing in its torment.

The sound touched some deep lonely nerve within Buchner's soul. It called to a part of his nature that was forever groundless, unanchored and drifting, a fanciful part of him that saw the rising storm as not only nature's salute to a fallen hero but also as an accusation.

The Furies are out and they're saying no good ever comes of killing one's greatest opponent.

The thought surprised him. It had a depth and a darkness that would have once been quite untypical of him. There was indeed a time not so long ago when he would have considered the very act of thinking as something unnatural. Always keep one step ahead of your thoughts was his motto.

What has ever been gained from thinking?

Nothing that aided the pursuit of life's pleasures. Life can only be enjoyed when not contemplated. But then something happened, something so shatteringly profound it made him pause long enough for his thoughts to catch with him. And for the first time in his life he was brought face to face with himself.

It was in that moment that he lost his ability to enjoy life. He became sombre when before he would have been triumphant, maudlin when he would have been exultant, moribund when he would have been celebrating. Now he stood alone staring into the darkness when he would have been in the mess getting drunk with the others.

It makes no sense.

How could it? He had achieved something that placed him above all other men, something that singled him out for unequalled fame and glory and yet his success gave him no sense of joy, no sense of pride, no sense of anything. All was dead within him.

How different from yesterday.

Yesterday he had been strafing the khaki-clad English as they retreated pell-mell across the snow-covered fields. He had been spreading panic among them, driving them before his guns like cattle before the savage advance of a red-toothed lion.

They were his sworn enemy. The war allowed him to kill them indiscriminately and without mercy. And he knew that the more he killed the more adulation his countrymen would heap upon him. So his shadowed wings passed over the fleeing troops and death fell upon them.

It was then that I saw the enemy machines.

There were two of them, far off, climbing like two stray sparks into the grey ceiling of clouds. But their distance and the general gloom didn't prevent his keen eye from picking them out as hollow-framed Camels.

His blood was up. Camels were his chosen prey and, unable to pass up an opportunity to add two more to his tally of forty-five kills, he zoomed into the sky after them, pulling away from his murderous pursuit of the steel-helmeted Tommies on the ground.

The cloud layer wasn't so thick.

His swift-winged Pfalz took no time punching through it like a fist through a sheet of wet paper. And all at once his startled senses passed from dismal gloom into the high-walled temple of radiant air where all was dazzle and incandescence.

Beneath him stretched an endless floor of brilliant unbroken white. Over him arched a vaulting dome of lustrous, eye-alluring blue. And the very air itself was bathed in light from an unhindered sun.

But I was oblivious to all of this beauty.

There was no place in his wounded heart. It still grieved for the loss of his friend. It still burned with a lust for vengeance. And the flame of it flickered in his vengeful eyes as they sought out the two Camels he had followed through the clouds.

He found one of them almost immediately. It was no more than a distant speck. And it was alone. Where was the other one? What had happened to it? Had it circled round to surprise him from behind? Wary of a trap he studied every part of the sky but could see no sign of the other machine.

No matter! There was still the one I could see.

It was about a half-mile distant and perhaps two or three hundred feet higher. Pulling on the stick with gentle pressure Buchner lifted the nose of his black-beaked Pfalz into a shallow climb.

Both machines were moving toward each other so it wouldn't take long before they met head on. Indeed, they were soon near enough that Buchner could make out the true nature of his enemy quite clearly.

I was right! It was a Camel!

Then something odd happened. The enemy machine wavered on its course. It would have been imperceptible to most but it was enough for Buchner to sense that the pilot was hesitating, struggling to decide whether he should proceed and engage or turn and flee.

The moment was brief, probably no more than half a heartbeat. Then with renewed resolve the Camel resumed its course. The enemy pilot had overcome his reservations. He had decided to stay and fight.

More fool him.

Neither Buchner nor his opponent fired as their machines met and passed. But as soon as each was behind the other they banked and turned, whipping their hollow-framed machines around into a circle of death so tight it would have been impossible to determine who was chasing whom.

Again, almost together, both machines dipped their port wingtips earthward, tightening the circle of their embrace as a noose tightens about a condemned man's throat.

The fellow certainly had some skill.

They were perfectly matched. Both knew all the tricks. Both could anticipate what the other would do. Each move was met with the correct countermove. The advantage passed to one and then almost as rapidly to the other.

Each could see the other's tail, but could not get it square enough into the cross hairs of their guns to let off a telling shot. And in the whirling duet that followed neither pilot could gain the upper hand.

Almost as soon as they engaged in their spinning merry-go-round Buchner caught sight of the markings on his opponent's fuselage and identified them as those belonging to 63 squadron.

This didn't surprise me.

There were only two Camel squadrons on this sector of the front and 63 squadron was by far the most belligerent, but as Buchner fought to bring his machine nearer he was shaken by an even greater discovery.

He was now closer than he had ever been, so close that the enemy pilot chose that moment to look anxiously over his shoulder. And it was then that Buchner realised that he had seen that face before.

It was Harker! Major Harker!

13

The man who had killed his friend Frommherz. The man after whom he had flown through the skies on an endless quest for revenge, a pursuit that had left a trail of blood and slaughter in its wake.

He had rampaged all over the countryside, killing every Englishman he saw as if by killing them all he would kill the one Englishman he wanted to destroy more than any other. And here was that Englishman no more than half a circle from his gun sights.

It was then that I thanked the gods.

They had answered his prayers. They had put within his reach the one thing he wanted more than anything else in the world. And it was now his for the taking.

But there had been more in that brief moment than just recognition. There had been something about the cast of the Englishman's face, something about his expression that had left Buchner puzzled. What had he seen in that face?

Was it doubt? Was it fear?

But then the Englishman turned away and the mystery remained unresolved. Not that Buchner cared. It was of no importance to him. All that mattered now was killing this man. Maybe then the pain within him would cease.

His gun muzzles were still pointing at the empty sky. Less than half a circle stood between him and Harker's tail, but that half circle felt like an impossible distance to cross.

Every time I let off a burst he pulled away and my bullets passed through nothing but air.

He was being eluded at every turn and the frustration of it stabbed into him like an unbearable pain and, under its impetus, he tried to infuse the power of his anger into the engine of his swift-winged machine.

Oh God! How I willed it to move faster.

The two opponents continued to carve a circle out of the icy sky. They were locked into it and neither of them dared break free. In the ring there was safety. Outside the ring there was only death.

Any attempt to change direction, to fly straight or dive away would spell instant disaster. So they continued on their course, taking turns to fire at each other.

But banking so tightly round and round and for so long loosened their wind-driven grip upon the empty air and slowly, bit by bit, they slid lower and lower.

Soon their port wingtips were slicing closer and closer to the insubstantial floor of cloud that lay beneath them and sinuous tendrils of mist rose up to ensnare them.

My chance of bringing down Harker was slipping away.

In a matter of seconds both machines would fall into the cloud where they would be engulfed and lost to sight.

And Harker would escape.

Buchner fired his guns. It was an act of desperation. He had no expectation of hitting anything. He could no longer even see what he was firing at. Then all was gone, all colour, all sense of place and direction.

I was lost in a sea of grey mist.

Condensation formed on Buchner's goggles, distorting the instruments in front of him. He wiped the lenses clear with the back of his gauntlet, but he was still blind.

He could see no sign of Harker's machine, not even a shadow. It was lost in the impenetrable mist as was everything else.

The whole world had disappeared.

Yet such was his determination that he kept to his tight turning bank, even though there was no longer any point in chasing something that he couldn't see.

And then I realised I was becoming disoriented.

He had no way of knowing where he was in relation to the earth or sky. Was he diving or was he climbing? And how steeply? For all he knew he could be flying upside down.

I had to get out of the cloud.

Trusting to some deep instinct, to some part of him that went beyond reason and thought, he kicked right rudder to level his machine then pushed the stick forward.

The manoeuvre didn't quite work out as he'd hoped. His machine, seemingly as confused as he was, fell headlong into a nauseous spin.

It was then that I burst out of the clouds.

And back into the gloomy underworld. The ground below was a reeling blur and with its fast approach Buchner struggled to regain control.

The natural thing to do was pull back the stick.

But he fought against this. Instead he put his rudder straight then pushed his stick forward. Almost instantly he came out of the spin.

And found myself once again taking in the sights.

At first his view was obscured by falling snow. Then to his surprise he saw that the landscape below was no longer black trees and white fields but the snow-filled craters and desolation of no-man's land.

The explanation was obvious.

While he and Harker had been engaged in their circling fight the wind had drifted the pair of them in a westerly direction to a point somewhere above the lines.

But where was Harker?

The sky beneath the cloud layer was empty. Then he remembered that the Englishman had entered the clouds first so he must have been the first to come out.

He had to be below me.

Putting his Pfalz into a shallow circling dive he looked over the portside of his cockpit and searched the cratered earth. It took a minute or two but he eventually found what he was looking for. Sprawled some yards from the western rim of Oyster crater was the fresh carcass of a British Sopwith Camel.

Its tail was in the air, its nose was buried in the ground and its top wing was missing.

It became clear to Buchner that Harker must have gone into a similar spin when he tried to escape the cloud, but before he could correct it his top wing, weakened by Buchner's reckless gunfire, tore free. The evidence was close to hand, a strange elongated object still fluttering in the air like a seedpod. It was the truant wing.

Harker was dead! Harker was dead!

And he had killed him. The intoxicating thrill of it sang through every part of him, along his arms and along his legs and up his spine and through him it surged into the machine that he flew.

As if sharing in its master's victory the Pfalz zoomed away from the earth like an arrow, soaring upward in unbound triumph to punch through the cloud layer and into the blue heavens above.

And I roared with laughter.

Some of his old carefree spirit burst within him like some mighty display of fireworks. He was his old self again. Frommherz was avenged. He was free of the burden. There was nothing more to be done.

Oh the joy of it!

The thrill of the hunt, the excitement of the pursuit, the exhilaration of being matched against the best. And Harker was the best. He was the best and now he was dead.

I'd killed him. I'd killed the best. I'd sent him to his death and there was no one alive who was my equal.

No one against whom he could pitch his skills. He was alone. And he knew that he would never experience again the intense thrill he had felt in fighting and killing Harker.

And it was then that the sense of triumph emptied out of me.

And with the emptiness came a depth of despair the likes of which he had never felt before even on the occasion of Frommherz's death. And into the emptiness poured a spirit that was not his own. His soul had been dispossessed and claimed by another.

How else could I explain what happened next?

Tears filled his eyes and his shoulders shook with painful sobs. Why was he crying? And for whom? Was it for Frommherz? Was it for Harker? Was it for the many men he had shot down or for the many more he had killed on the ground in his search for vengeance? Or was it for himself?

Even now as he stood at the door to his hut staring into the turbulent darkness, he still did not know the answer. All he knew for sure was that the need for vengeance had died within him. It had died with the death of Harker, his greatest opponent.

Let them look for his body. It doesn't bother me.

CHAPTER TWO

26 NOVEMBER 1917

Oblivious to the screeching wind Parkinson caressed the tip of the small, finely pointed brush over the blob of yellow paint. With great care, he applied it to one of the bronze regimental collar badges, forming a delicate curving highlight against the darker metal.

He paused and stood back to study the entire portrait and the passive immobility of his expression indicated his satisfaction.

I think that's just about done.

Slowly, almost reluctantly, his eyes moved upward, past the khaki tie and its knot, past the throat and raised chin, past the young and sensitive mouth, past the straight and finely shaped nose to the face in half-profile.

Finally he came to the blue-grey eyes. They were fixed on some distant spot off to the left and Parkinson was grateful that he had not painted them staring directly out of the canvas.

Looking at me as if the fault were all mine.

Without removing his gaze from the painting, he laid the brush aside then blindly groped for a rumpled, paint stained cloth that he used to clean his hands, all the while studying the man in the portrait. And, without wishing it, he felt a twinge of anger and resentment.

'Why did you do it?' he asked as he threw down the cloth. 'Why did you have to be the bloody hero?'

Like any man who sees only cowardice in his own makeup Parkinson had thought long and hard upon what it meant to be a hero. Was it there at birth or was it something acquired later? And where did this fearlessness come from?

Yet, despite his efforts, he had not come up with any answers. The best he could manage was a refinement of the concept, a sort of literary device that separated the triumphant hero from the defeated hero.

Allowing me the comfort of regarding my cowardice as just another form of heroism.

But this cynical view of his motives hid a deeper insight. To him triumphant heroism was brash and gaudy, selfish and inconsiderate, a loud and empty gesture. The triumphant hero gained nothing of note from his bravery. He learned nothing of value and was much the same person after the act as he was before it.

Defeat, on the other hand, reflected a truth about the world, a truth that touched most people at one time or another. It was only from the trials of failure and inadequacy that the true hero emerged.

This sentiment was in perfect harmony with Parkinson's dark view of existence. And whereas he could not identify with triumphant heroism he could at least cast himself in the role of the hero defeated.

A role not entirely devoid of splendour.

The sort of splendour he had felt when Harker ordered him to put a stop to Buchner's rampage. He knew that the order he had been given was a certain death warrant. If he took on Buchner there was no hope of him coming back alive.

But the prospect hadn't bothered him as it may once have done. Standing before his friend and commanding officer he knew that he was ready to meet his fate without complaint. He had even felt an odd kind of calmness.

And that feeling stayed with him as he climbed into his flying gear and later as he stood by 'Kallisti', the Camel that had served him so faithfully, waiting for the signal to take off.

All his life he had believed himself to be a coward and there he was devoid of fear, prepared to face a challenge he knew he could not win and that the price of failure would almost certainly be death.

He had no desire to wantonly throw away his life. Like any man who has pondered life's futility, he had toyed with the idea of ending his own existence, but it never went beyond speculation. He didn't have the stomach to carry out such an act.

Nor the lack of vanity needed to turn oneself into a rotting corpse.

But never being free of fear, of always being scared of what the next moment might bring, forever running from the point of danger had taken its toll. It had left him limp and so wrung out that all he wanted to do was to close his eyes and never open them again.

Oh, such bliss!

And Buchner could have given him that bliss. He could have closed his eyes forever. It was what the German did best. He was the swift executioner of the weary. And just as alluring to Parkinson was the knowledge that in his moment of death he would have become what he desired more than anything else; the hero defeated.

'And you took it away from me.'

But the portrait of Harker the hero gave no sign that it had heard. Nor did its noble features show any regret. Like all true heroes it was unmoved by the weaknesses of others. He had ordered Parkinson to his death but then changed his mind.

Maybe he didn't think I deserved a noble death.

Whatever the reason he fooled Parkinson into believing that there was a telephone call about his father.

Fearing the worst I ran to the hut.

But there was no telephone call and by the time he got back it was too late. Harker the hero had taken off. Parkinson could only stand and watch his friend's machine disappear over the trees, feeling for all the world like a man who had been robbed of what was his by right.

And now it seems likely that my friend is dead.

The issue would soon be resolved one way or the other. Only an hour before Colonel Pritchett had informed him that he had succeeded in getting the German high Command to agree to a local cease-fire. It would only last a couple of hours but it was time enough for a couple of men to cross no-man's-land and locate the wreckage of Harker's Camel.

And bring back his body.

Parkinson continued studying the portrait. When he had started it his intention had been to depict the hero triumphant and there had been no small measure of irony in his purpose. He had achieved what he had set out to do, but now that it was complete he could see that something else had crept into the portrait. What he saw now was the hero defeated.

Why should I feel guilty for that? I didn't ask you to take my place.

****

None of this makes sense.

This had been Fletcher's feeling since Captain Baines had told them what they were expected to do. Not that he would normally be worried by a trip across no-man's-land in the darkness. He had done it often enough before.

But this time it's different.

This time they would be traipsing about at a very touchy time. It always was in the aftermath of a great battle. And none came any greater than the recent Battle of the Ste Helene Salient.

I should know. I was in it.

He had witnessed the British push the Germans all the way back to the airfield at Bois de Cheval. He had been there when it was captured. And he had been there when German reinforcements took it back.

That was when the tables were well and truly turned.

With their flanks exposed and no reserves to bring up in support the British were forced into a bloody retreat that only ended when everyone was more or less back where they started with both sides lying breathless and exhausted at the bottom of their own trenches.

But it would have been wrong to assume from this that their eagerness was spent especially the Germans. They had won the battle. The blood that coursed through their veins was still hot with the fever of war. They were still alert.

And ready to shoot at anything on sight.

Having chased the unresisting British across so many miles of snow covered countryside the German soldiers had convinced themselves that they were unstoppable and resented being ordered to halt at their own front line.

Who wouldn't?

This was Fletcher's reasoning but it gave him little comfort as he trudged through the darkness behind his unseen companion, driven forward every so often by the goading hand of the wind. Up until now he'd kept his anxieties to himself, but when the wind abated sufficiently for his voice to be heard he couldn't resist a whisper.

'Are you sure this is safe, Ferry? I mean those Huns are itching to get another crack at us.'

'You 'erd the Captain,' Feriman growled. 'He said the 'uns have agreed to 'old their fire for a couple of hours.'

Feriman's dark form lumbered ahead with sure-footed deliberation, his black hulk detaching itself from the surrounding night long enough to take a step forward before merging with the night once more. Fletcher matched Feriman's pace, pulled along by the stretcher that the two men held between them. But Fletcher had no control over where they went or how long it took to get there.

When the stretcher moves I move. When it stops I stop.

The wind picked up again, pushing them along several yards then hurried off to give Fletcher another chance to voice his concerns.

'If what you say is right then why couldn't they have sent us out during the day when everyone else could see that we're just a couple of stretcher-bearers?'

'Stop your belly-aching.'

Fletcher said nothing more and, as the wind returned he became acutely aware of how cold he felt. His whole body seemed devoid of any warmth but the feeling was strongest in his booted feet. About him lay a carpet of untrod snow. He could hardly see it, but as each booted footfall crushed through its crisp cover, he could feel his feet suck out its cold marrow and transmit it up the long veins of legs.

And as the wind bit into him, cutting through his clothes, he gasped and shivered violently and his breath formed sinuous arabesques about his face like tendrils of cigarette smoke.

God! I could murder a fag right now.

He had a packet of Player's Weights in his tunic pocket, a gift from Home, but they were useless to him now. Lighting a cigarette in no-man's-land would have been an act of suicide. Besides, striking a match would have been nigh on impossible in such raging winds.

But that didn't stop the longing. He was desperate for nicotine and, being starved of it, his tongue thought back longingly to the last time it had tasted smoke.

Seems like an age ago now.

In reality it was only ten minutes since he and Feriman were standing in Curzon Street trench sheltering from the wind and as they waited for the moment to set off on their mission Fletcher had lit his cigarette.

Knowing it might be his last smoke he had stared at the glowing end, taking comfort from the red light and the way it reminded him of his mother's evening fireplace when the parlour was dark and the fire was dying down.

He never got to finish his smoke. Lieutenant Tillings appeared ahead of schedule to give them the off and Fletcher had to grind out his half-finished cigarette on the duckboards beneath his feet. Feriman, who didn't smoke, was already up the ladder and Fletcher passed the stretcher up to him before climbing out of the trench himself.

'Do you know where you're going?' he asked Feriman as soon as they were beyond the coiled fence of their own barbed wire entanglements.

'I always know where I'm going.'

****

Holding an open bottle of schnapps by its neck in one hand and a glass in the other, Menckhoff stared fixedly at the worn pattern on the piece of carpet that lay on the slatted floor of his quarters.

He had brought the bottle from the mess in the hope that it would dull or divert the thoughts that had been nagging at him for days, but he had only poured one drink from it and that was still in the glass.

No one saw it happen.

Every so often this thought would pop into his head. He had been repeating it to himself over and over for hours, hoping it would give him some measure of comfort. But it wasn't working. All it did was remind him of the very thing he would rather forget.

He had done something quite dreadful and the fact that he may have got away with it, that no one beside himself had actually witnessed the deed offered him no consolation whatsoever. It didn't alter the fact that he was guilty of murder.

I killed him. There's no getting away with that.

This was something else that kept popping into his head and whenever it did it triggered an image, a vivid image of Stark's machine appearing out of nowhere. It was flying into his field of view. He could see it out of the corner of his eye.

Within a second it would be between him and his prey. His fingers released the firing lever on his guns. But it was too late. His bullets were already on their way.

I was in a killing mood when I fired.

He was lusting for blood. He wanted to feel the thrill of seeing another enemy machine fall from the sky but all he felt was startled horror as the bullets streaked away.

I wanted to stop them but I couldn't. I couldn't.

They cleaved the air like angry words that cannot be unspoken. They travelled straight, but they could not see where they were going. Menckhoff had been their eyes. Nor did they have intention. They found whatever was in their path. Stark's machine was in their path. And they tore into it. Spars broke, wings collapsed, and Stark's black beaked Pfalz broke up in the air. Its sleek lines became crumpled matchwood with a living man sitting at its centre.

I didn't mean to do it. I didn't.

In the hours and days that followed reaction set in. Horror turned to remorse, a deep gnawing sense of guilt and sorrow that left him shaking and fearful of sleep. He tried to control it. He tried to hide it. But he could not rub away the anguish from his eyes nor could he prevent the shadow of it spreading across his face.

They must see it. They must know that I did it.

While the battles still raged it was possible to cope, to set the burden to one side, even for brief moments to forget that it had ever happened. All that mattered was the need to survive.

But then the guns fell silent.

And now there was nothing left to keep at bay the endless sob of remorse, nothing to ward off the ghostly visitation of guilt and wretchedness, nothing to stop the sights and sounds of incrimination, nothing except alcohol.

For the first time Menckhoff became conscious of the glass in his hand and, with an almost furious snap of his head he emptied it in one gulp. Without pause he upended the bottle and poured himself another measure of schnapps.

How many men have I shot down now?

There were the nine victories he had accumulated while still an Oberleutnant. It had been some months before his first kill, but after that the others had followed rapidly and with comparative ease. Since his promotion to Hauptmann he had added three more to his score; an F2B and two Camels, one over Bois de Cheval and one over the fight for Angriffen. Twelve victories in all.

That makes Stark my thirteenth.

The thought was a macabre one but it was also the harbinger of a change of attitude that Menckhoff would have once considered impossible. Like his compatriots he had never given any regard to those he shot down. But unlike them he never claimed it was the machine he was shooting at and not the man. He knew that when he opened fire he was aiming at the back of the pilot's head.

It's the man I'm after not his bloody machine.

He had never made any bones about the fact that he hated the English. He hated them with an intensity that barely skirted the edge of sanity. He hated them because they had taken away what was rightfully his and they had humiliated him in the process.

Until April he had been commander of *Jagdgeschwader Bronze* then stationed at Ste Helene. He had six Jastas under his control and they had been so successful at clearing the skies of enemy machines it seemed certain that he would take over the new JGN High Command was forming.

The English thwarted his ambitions. They launched an attack along the Ste Helene Salient, pushing back the German lines and overrunning Menckhoff's airfield.

There was nothing I could have done about it.

But his flight in the face of the enemy didn't look too good in official circles and, ultimately, it cost him the command of JGN. It went to Hantelmann instead and Menckhoff ended up as its subordinate commander.

The whole experience had left him feeling bitter and humiliated, the sort of humiliation a man might feel when his beloved wife has been abducted, and ever since he had been driven by two obsessions; getting Ste Helene back and killing every Englishman he encountered.

It was easy enough. They were faceless, nameless strangers. They meant nothing to me.

But now he had killed a man he had liked and laughed with, a man he had trained, advised and felt protective toward, and that single act changed everything. The death of Stark came to represent to Menckhoff the tragedy of all the others he had killed. They were all Starks. And for the first time in his life Menckhoff felt not only shame for all the death he had wrought but also the utter pointlessness of it all.

I'm not so sure I can ever kill again.

This realisation was so profound it shook the very foundations of Menckhoff's view of himself and what he believed himself to be. He was now marooned in a world where certainty had gone and only questions remained. And the one question that troubled him the most, the one for which he had no answer, was what did the future hold for him now?

****

Fletcher and Feriman carried their stretcher through the raging darkness weaving and stumbling their way across no-man's-land in a stooped, crouching shuffle. The crouch was second nature. The rule was never raise your head higher than necessary not even when brass hats safe and snug in the rear had received assurances of safe conduct.

That's the time to crouch even lower.

Normally, Fletcher found it easy enough to handle an empty stretcher. It had little weight and could be manoeuvred readily. But in a storm it was a different matter entirely. For a start there were things lying around in no-man's-land that were hazardous enough at the best of times let alone when the wind was blowing them around.

Worse still was the stretcher itself. In a storm its lightness became a troublesome liability. Sudden gusts kept catching the canvas, ballooning it out like a sail and making it unmanageable. And sometimes the wind was so great the handles were almost wrenched from their grasp.

What we need is the weight of a body.

In his time Fletcher had worked at both ends of the stretcher, but he always preferred carrying it from the rear. He certainly made him feel safer, but his real reason was more sentimental. By holding the two wooden handles in front of him he could close his eyes and imagine that that he was back in Covent Garden, wheeling his barrow of spuds and carrots over the cobbles and bruised cabbage leaves.

Those were the days.

The work was hard but satisfying and it seemed certain that his father would hand him the family business when he retired. He always had a few bob in his pocket and could afford a drink with his friends and watch the football at Arsenal. There was even a girl he was courting.

But then war was declared and the good times ended.

The moment of truth came for Fletcher and his mates during a particularly boozy night in the Rose and Crown. Without warning a red jacketed recruiting sergeant appeared in their midst, his whiskered voice booming like a music hall master of ceremonies.

Appealing to their love of country, their youthful lust for glory and their natural desire for the fleshy adulation of pretty girls he urged them to join the colours. So stirring was his call to arms and so inebriated were all of Fletcher's friends that they all signed up on the spot, joining the venerable London Pals battalion.

'Come with us, Fletch?' they'd urged him as he sat steadfastly at his table pint in hand. 'It'll be a lark.'

'Some lark killing men I've never met.'

He couldn't accept that any cause could be that noble or worthwhile. Nor, unlike his chums, could he accept that it was as worthy as the authorities would have them believe. But such doubts didn't protect him from the shame and isolation he felt when he found himself the only healthy young man left in the market. Nor did they stop his tears from falling when he picked out the names of his chums from the casualty lists.

I became very unpopular in the market after that.

Some men wouldn't talk to him. Others shook angry fists in his face. His relationship with his father became strained and the girl he'd hoped to marry broke off the engagement. Eventually it all came to a head. One evening while drinking in the pub he was set upon and given a black eye. Realising he might not get off so lightly next time he took himself off him to the nearest recruiting office.

'I want to do my bit just like everyone else,' he'd explained to the sergeant. 'And I don't mind being in the thick of it. But I won't do any killing.'

Fortunately the sergeant was a sympathetic fellow and he suggested, 'Why not become a stretcher bearer? It's what a lot of conchies end up doing.'

It seemed like the perfect solution. By carrying a stretcher he would be saving lives instead of taking them and, when all was said and done, it was a darn sight more preferable to being spat upon in the street.

Or breaking rocks in some prison yard.

These were Fletcher's reasons for doing what he was doing. He understood them and they made perfect sense to him. But there was something he couldn't quite fathom out, something that seemingly made no sense at all.

Why's Feriman doing it? He's not a conchie.

At that moment Feriman stopped dead in his tracks and with such unannounced suddenness Fletcher was left with the impression that his silent companion had somehow overheard what he had just been thinking. But Feriman had other reasons. His helmeted head contrasted against the eastern sky with its half-hidden moon, numerous stars and scurrying clouds, he could be seen turning slowly from side to side as if his ears were sniffing the storm for stray sounds.

'Where do you think it is?' Fletcher asked.

'This way!'

It was not an answer. It was a decision and, having made it, Feriman dragged the stretcher off to the right, leaving Fletcher with little choice but to follow. Not that he complained.

Feriman's the reason I prefer bringing up the rear.

Physically he was tall, broad in the shoulder and when positioned at the front of the stretcher his ungainly bulk presented a reassuring shield against bullets and shrapnel. Even under the heaviest gunfire with bullets whistling past them and explosions tearing up the ground Fletcher walked on seemingly immune to danger. Nothing seemed to touch him.

And nothing will touch me if I stay close.

Fletcher certainly felt far safer with Feriman than he had with his previous companions. The first, Frank Acres, lasted no more than a week before being badly injured. The second, Tom Dowling, had been cut in half during his first trip to no-man's-land. Reg Chandler, the third, lost his life during the Battle of Bayonet Ridge.

That's where we're heading now.

Not that Fletcher was paying much attention to where they were or where they were going. Why bother? Feriman, so totally at home in no-man's-land he even referred to it affectionately as his 'rag and bone yard', had an unerring knack of getting to wherever he wanted to be.

And all without map or compass.

In the short time that they had been together they had rescued dozens of injured soldiers and Fletcher happily conceded that most of the credit had to go to Feriman. By any reckoning he was an absolute marvel.

And yet...

And yet there was something about Feriman, something that went beyond his taciturn nature and unsociability that made Fletcher feel uneasy. Little was known about his background although there was talk he had worked in a funeral parlour before the war.

Probably because his got a face like wet weekend.

But it wasn't this that troubled Fletcher; it was something far stranger, something that was altogether hard to explain. It went to the heart of how Fletcher felt about stretcher-bearing and the sense of satisfaction he felt every time he managed to get wounded men back to the field dressing station alive.

Admittedly, what happened to his charges after he handed them over to the orderlies wasn't something that interested him, but at least he knew that he'd given them a fighting chance. The rest was up to the field surgeons.

Some of those he brought in had torn limbs that would have to be amputated. Others had agonising gut wounds, shattered faces or gas-congested lungs. Quite a few died while still on the stretcher such was the awful nature of their injuries, but most of them were still breathing when he set them down inside the hospital tent.

But all of that changed when I took up with Feriman.

It was then that he began to notice that they were delivering more dead soldiers than live ones. At first he shrugged off his concern; when all was said and done there was nothing strange about badly wounded men dying.

They don't always make it.

Then during the retreat from Bois de Cheval they came upon a young soldier who had taken a bullet through the calf. Although strong and vigorous he couldn't walk so they lifted him onto the stretcher and carried him off, Fletcher convinced that all he needed was for his wound to be washed and dressed

And he'd be up and about in no time.

But after a short distance Fletcher noticed the soldier's arm dangling limply over the side of the stretcher. After putting the stretcher down Fletcher checked the soldier and found him to be dead.

It was then that I began to have my doubts.

From then on, whenever they were out collecting injured soldiers, he watched Feriman like a hawk.

Not that I ever saw anything suspicious.

Indeed, other than helping to lift the casualty onto the stretcher, Feriman never made any physical contact with them whatsoever. He never gave them water to drink or a cigarette to smoke. He never looked at them, spoke to them or touched them in any way.

Almost as if we were collecting bundles of laundry.

Finally Fletcher had to accept that Feriman's position at the front of the stretcher was too exposed for him to do any mischief without being seen.

It seems I'm better placed to do harm than him.

But despite this his suspicions remained and, at the end of a particularly bad day, he raised the subject as directly as he dared.

'I say, Feriman, doesn't it strike you as odd that so few of our customers get back to the lines alive?'

Fletcher had expected anger or evasion. What he hadn't expected was laughter. It seemed such a heartless reaction to a question about death. And there was genuine mirth in it.

'You know,' Feriman said still chuckling. 'If I had tuppence for every live one that croaked while hauling him back to the lines I'd be a rich man by now.'

It was a callous remark, but Fletcher had heard far worse and in some strange way it actually put pay to his doubts about Feriman. Clearly this was a man who couldn't care less one way or the other about the men they rescued.

Alive or dead, it's all the same to him.

And if he couldn't care less whether they were alive or dead why would he go to the trouble of killing them? The worse that Fletcher could level against him was that he was a Jonah, the sort of man whose presence alone brings ill-fortune to those around him.

And I've got him at the other end of the stretcher.

****

Much could be said regarding Fuchs' many personal failings and a great deal of it would be true especially concerning his nosiness and gossiping. But blindness to the feelings of others was not one of them.

Some have likened me to a walking weather station.

He had a vane to see which way the wind was blowing, a hydrometer to judge when the tide was turning and a built-in barometer to measure whether the atmosphere was tranquil or blowing up of storm.

And right now it's pointing to a deep depression.

The first sign was Menckhoff's failure to respond when Fuchs knocked on the door. The second was Menckhoff's failure to acknowledge Fuchs' presence after he let himself in. He didn't even look up when Fuchs coughed politely.

Clearly something's troubling him.

It was something about the Hauptmann's hunched posture. The open bottle and glass full of Schnapps were additional clues.

Oh God! First Hantelmann now Menckhoff. What's the matter with everyone?

Sensitive he may have been, sympathetic he was not. As adjutant he'd had enough problems dealing with the temper tantrums, violent mood swings and abject misery of senior officers to last him several lifetimes.

The last thing I need is another one.

Sensing trouble ahead Fuchs considered backing out of the office unnoticed. But this option was denied him when a gust of wind slammed the door shut behind him. Besides, he didn't really have much choice in the matter. Something had happened, a development of such importance that Menckhoff had to know about it immediately.

Who knows, it might even cheer the bugger up.

A floorboard creaked obligingly as Fuchs stepped further into the office. When this failed to solicit a response he said softly, 'Herr Hauptmann.'

Menckhoff gave no sign that he had heard.

Fuchs raised his voice for a second attempt. 'Herr Hauptmann.'

Menckhoff turned in his chair and presented a face that was guarded and careworn. 'Yes, Fuchs, what is it?'

'It's about Hauptmann Hantelmann.'

'What about him?'

'His wound has become infected.'

'Wound? What wound?'

'The wound he sustained the other day.'

For a moment Menckhoff considered this information as if trying to make sense of some complicated equation. Then he asked, 'Have you sent for the Medical Officer?'

'Yes. He came a little while ago.'

'And what was his diagnosis?'

'The Hauptmann is running a fever. The doctor thinks he should have his wound treated in hospital and has sent for an ambulance.'

'Oh, I see. Well, I suppose it's for the best.'

There was something in the way that Menckhoff turned away that suggested an assumption on his part that the conversation had ended. Sensing this Fuchs sighed. There was not only more that needed to be said but probably the most important part.

'Herr Hauptmann?'

Menckhoff turned around and he seemed genuinely surprised to see Fuchs still standing there. 'Was there something else?'

'Yes, Herr Hauptmann. It's likely that Herr Hantelmann will away for some time. Can I assume that you will take over command of JGN during his absence?'

Menckhoff's face took on a bewildered look. 'What?'

'Naturally, you'll wish to get confirmation from High Command, but I'm certain that won't present a problem.'

This was a turn of events that Menckhoff hadn't reckoned on, which was somewhat ironic considering that up until several days previously he had rarely thought of anything else. He had always believed that command of JGN should have been given to him, the better man, and not to Hantelmann. It would have gone to him but for the debacle of Ste Helene. And it was clear to him why it went to Hantelmann instead.

Friends in high places.

Yet Menckhoff had hung on at JGN enduring the humiliation of being Hantelmann's subordinate. He had done so for one reason. He was convinced that one day the command would come to him. And when it did it would have been the day of his greatest triumph.

But not now.

Now the very notion of commanding JGN was abhorrent to him. It was inconceivable. It was intolerable. It was the last thing in the world he wanted. How could he even consider it? He had killed Stark and as far as he was concerned he was not a fit person to command this or any other unit.

Desperate to avoid such a responsibility he struggled to reject it without sounding as if he were rejecting it. 'I'm not so sure, Fuchs. It would be highly irregular to anticipate such a decision from High Command.'

This was not the response Fuchs had expected, but he pressed on in the mistaken belief that Menckhoff was merely following proper form.

'I'm sure there won't be any difficulty, Herr Hauptmann. Would you like me to contact High Command and find out what they plan to do?'

'Don't trouble yourself, Fuchs.'

'It won't be any trouble.'

'For heaven's sake, man! For once in your life will you stop interfering?'

Taken aback as he was, it was at this point that it finally dawned on Fuchs that whatever was troubling Menckhoff went much deeper than he had at first assumed. He didn't know what it was exactly, but the war had shown him enough men broken in spirit to know the symptoms.

Abgeflogene. That's what he is.

It was a tricky situation. Menckhoff needed to see the Medical Officer, but who had the authority to suggest such a thing to him? The only man who could have done so was Hantelmann and he was delirious with fever and about to be transported to hospital.

And who's going to command JGN in the meantime?

It wasn't something that Fuchs could decide, but military procedure did offer him a solution. Taking a deep breath he said: 'I'm sorry, Herr Hauptmann, but I'll have to inform High Command and leave the matter with them.'

'You do that, Fuchs,' Menckhoff said mildly. 'I'm sorry I lost my temper. Can you do me a favour?'

'Of course.'

'Can you let me know how much leave I have?'

****

'Nearly there!' Feriman whispered harshly.

Fletcher became alert yet remained relaxed. There was no need to worry about Feriman's baleful influence. They were out to retrieve not rescue. They were looking for a corpse so no one was about to die on the way back.

Feriman came to another of his sudden halts and Fletcher rammed his groin against the edge of the canvas stretcher.

'Fucking 'ell, Feriman. Watch what you're doing.'

He peered into the near distance trying to figure out what had stopped Feriman in his tracks but he couldn't see a thing; the darkness ahead remained impenetrable. But he could hear something creaking in the wind, a sound hauntingly reminiscent of shipwrecks and the high seas.

Then a green flare rose obligingly from the German trenches. For a brief moment its shimmering light back-lit a hulking shape that stood in their path no more than ten yards distant. Though badly damaged it was instantly recognisable as the wreck of a crashed aircraft.

'That's it,' Feriman announced.

'How can you tell?'

The machine had obviously hit the ground at a steep angle and its tail plane now pointed toward the heavens at forty-five degrees. The under-carriage had collapsed on impact leaving the lower front wing close to the ground. The top wing was missing.

The wreckage was close to Oyster Crater, a distinctive feature excavated by the explosion of a huge underground mine. The Camel's engine and broken propeller were buried in the ground. Such had been the force of the impact the two machine guns had been wrenched free and now stuck out of the snow like two black fingers.

'Good God!' Fletcher gasped. 'No one could have survived that.'

With a grunt Feriman dropped his end of the stretcher and left Fletcher watching his black shape hurry toward the wreck. Then a sharp sheet of wind caught the distant flare and its light was extinguished, plunging both Feriman and the wreck back into darkness.

Blind, Fletcher stood mutely as the light-less void pressed against the surface of his wide-flung eyes. He listened to the wind and the creaking and he realised that the sound was coming from the wreck of the Camel.

After a minute or so there was a tearing sound. In fact there were four tearing sounds, two short and two long. Then silence again. A few moments later Fletcher felt a heavy hand on his shoulder.

'There's nothing there,' Feriman told him.

'What do you mean there's nothing there?'

'I mean there's no pilot. The safety straps are still fastened but the cockpit's empty.'

To Fletcher this was not good news. 'Shit! Are you sure? They'll never believe we came out here if we've got nothing to bring back.'

'Well, they'll believe this.' Feriman held up a scrap of something.

'What is it?' Fletcher asked and, although he couldn't see Feriman's cunning leer he sensed it.

'Something from the fuselage. Proof that we've done our job.'

'Good! Now let's get the fuck out of here.'

CHAPTER THREE

27 NOVEMBER 1917

Kept awake by the storm Parkinson didn't get to sleep until the early hours and when he did it was only to suffer a short, intense dream that had him wandering across no-man's-land, staggering from shell-hole to shell-hole frantically searching for something that he had lost.

Though I had no idea what it was.

Nor did he have any notion where he was or in which direction he should travel. He was standing at the centre of a circular wall of fog that reduced how far he could see to about fifty yards. It even blocked out the sky.

I was completely encircled.

While he stood still the wall of fog remained where it was, but whenever he advanced toward it the wall retreated and at almost the same pace. Not that there seemed much point in moving at all. The retreating fog revealed nothing but more and more craters.

There was no end to them no matter how far I walked.

Even more unsettling was the stark emptiness of this dream landscape. It seemed even more desolate than the real no-man's-land where one might at least expect to find a corpse or a rat scurrying about. But here there was nothing but shell holes, endless shell holes.

And they were all the same size and shape.

They were uniform in depth and diameter and equally spaced one from the other, dispersed across a terrain that was grey, without deformity and as flat as a table-top.

Like the cups in a metal cake-baking tray.

The craters were also all filled with the same amount of red-stained water. And they seemed to stretch off in every direction. No matter which way he turned fresh ones kept appearing out of the mist.

Then he was overwhelmed by a morbid sense of being lost, of being trapped in this place forever. Panic seized him and he started dashing about like a man in a burning building who has no idea where to fine the exit. His mind could take no more and he woke with a start.

What was that all about?

****

Pale light seeped into the recesses of the hut, giving outline to the objects around him, and Parkinson knew that it was dawn. Not that he considered it any cause for celebration. In his own fastidious way he had always regarded sunrise as a rather distasteful spectacle.

Suitable only for farmers and ascetics.

It made more sense to him to greet the day at a much later hour when it was well and truly established. But it looked as if it would take a lot longer today. The storm had not ended with the passing of the night. Strong winds still rattled the windows and battered against the door.

I should be thankful. There'll be no flying today.

He had no jobs this morning either and the bed felt too comfortable to abandon but whether he liked it or not he was obliged to get up early. He was a flight leader and it was his duty to set some sort of example.

But where is my cup of tea?

Duty or no duty he had a right to expect his cup of tea. And he wasn't going to move until he got it. He was going to stay where he was and nothing was going to shift him even if he had to wait all morning. Then the door to his hut opened of its own accord and in walked his orderly.

At last! My cup of tea!

But there was no cup of tea; the orderly was empty-handed and as well as looking fly-blown he had about him the air of a man on an urgent errand. Seeing this Parkinson propped himself up on his pillow and asked:

'What's the matter?'

'Beg your pardon, sir. Lieutenant Lawns sent me over. He said I was to summon you to the office.'

'What for?'

'He wouldn't say.'

Cringing against the bitter cold, Parkinson dressed as quickly as he could and hurried over to the office. There were pendulous icicles hanging from the eaves like trails of frozen mucous, glistening and brittle. Parkinson broke one off as he entered.

Lieutenant Ambridge Lawns of 'A' flight was sitting at the adjutant's desk totting up mess bills, one of his duties as orderly dog. But when he saw Parkinson he stopped what he was doing and picked up the telephone.

Pressing his ear against the apparatus he said, 'He's just come into the office, sir. I'll let you speak to him now.'

'Who is it?' Parkinson whispered.

Lawns covered the mouthpiece. 'General Pritchett.'

Taking the telephone Parkinson sat on the edge of the desk. 'Good morning, General. Captain Parkinson here.'

'Good morning, Parkinson. I'm at Calais on my way to a conference in London, but before departing I thought you'd like to be brought up to date regarding Major Harker.'

'Yes I would, sir.'

'Well, last night we sent two men into no-man's-land to locate the wreck of his machine. They found it.'

'Are we sure it was Harker's machine?'

'Yes! They brought back a piece of the fuselage. It had 'Briseis' on it. And here the mystery deepens.'

'How so, sir?'

'The cockpit was empty and there was no sign of his body in the vicinity.'

'Could he have fallen out before the machine crashed?'

'I wondered that myself, but the men reported finding the Major's safety harness still fastened up.'

'But he can't have just disappeared.'

'I agree.'

'Could the Germans have retrieved his body from the wreck and taken it back to their own lines?'

'It remains a possibility, I suppose, but I feel certain that they would have notified us. Besides, they dropped a message on 89 squadron's airfield at Motte de Gazonville denying they knew anything about it, and I can't see what they would have to gain by lying.'

'So what happens next?'

'Well, without Harker's body we can only post him as missing in action.'

Parkinson fell silent, his mind ensnared by the inexplicable. Thousands of men had gone missing on the western front, their disappearance a mystery that would likely never be solved. Though most were soldiers some were airmen, but their machines usually went missing with them. Parkinson could never recall a single instance where a downed machine was found without its pilot.

'Are you still there, Parkinson?'

'Yes. Sorry, sir. I'm still here.'

'Before I go can you give me an idea of squadron strength?'

'Two in 'A' flight, two in 'B' flight and four in 'C', which includes myself.'

'Eight out of eighteen. What a disaster! Not that the other squadrons in your sector are in any better shape, but I'll send what replacements I can soon as possible.

'Thank you, sir.'

'We'll see about getting Hammer and Milton their captaincy so that they can command 'A' and 'B' flights.'

'Shall I tell them?'

'Yes. Do that. And one other thing, Parkinson.'

'Yes, sir?'

'Major Harker's replacement has been posted elsewhere. So for the time being you're in charge of the squadron.'

****

'How is Martha?'

'Fine! She has taken the children for a visit to her mother in Dusseldorf.'

Passing through a broad open doorway the Baroness Thetis von Buchner and Hermann von Hoeppner entered one of the lofty, well-lit assembly halls of the *Flugzeugwerke*. It wasn't Thetis' first visit to the factory in Essen nor was it the first time she had taken Hermann's conducted tour.

The entire building was a monument to modern architecture. Its structural design derived from its purpose. All lines were horizontal or vertical, all walls stood at right angles, all unnecessary detail had been eliminated, and everything spoke of clarity and simplicity. Even the girders supporting the ceiling were visible.

The entire place was a hive of concentrated activity. In the fitting and woodworking shops men in straw hats and long white aprons sawed, chiselled and hammered mainplanes, tail units and hollow-bodied fuselages. In the sewing and covering room pony-tailed women in skirted overalls stretched canvas fabric over ribbed wings and other pre-assembled parts.

'You seem to be busier than the last time I visited.'

'Yes. We are trying to make up for the losses suffered during the recent British Offensive.'

'What about JGN?'

'They have suffered more than most. They are not only desperately short of machines, but of pilots as well.'

'Will you be able to meet the demand?'

'No. But then we might not have to?'

'What do you mean?'

'I've heard that if things go well in the east we may soon have all the pilots and machines we need.'

As was her want Thetis made a mental note of this information. But she had not endured a long and stormy trip on her birthday just to pump Hermann for intelligence. She had crossed Germany for a very special reason. He had done her a great favour and she had come to thank him in person.

After *Angriffen,* her son's prized Pfalz DIII, was destroyed during the British retreat from Bois de Cheval Hermann had built him a newer and better warplane. This had not only got her son back into the air it had also helped to revive his fighting spirit at a time when he was still grieving over the death of his close friend, Frommherz.

'So this is where the DVIII was built?'

They were now in the Final Assembly room where various aircraft were receiving their final fitments. As this was Hermann's favourite part of the factory he stopped and, with a proud and jubilant smile, turned to Thetis.

'Yes. And I'm sure it comes as no surprise to you that Willi hasn't wasted any time in making good use of it.'

Thetis returned the smile but her large violet eyes were enquiring. 'How so?'

'Oh! Heavens!' Hermann was suddenly excited. 'You mean you haven't heard the news?'

Thetis shook her head. 'No. I have been on the road for the past day. What is this news?'

'Your son has become famous.'

'He has?'

'Yes. A couple of days ago he shot down England's greatest fighter pilot.'

****

With Hermann limping beside her it seemed to Thetis that it was taking them forever to get to the telephone in his factory office. Then it seemed to take another age to get through to the airbase at Bois de Cheval.

'Hello, Willi!'

'Hello, Mother.'

'What's all this I hear about you shooting down this famous Englishman?'

'It was nothing special. I'm not even so sure I actually shot him down.'

'How can that be?'

'We dived through some clouds and his top wing came off. My bullets may have weakened the struts holding the wing, but I can't be certain.'

'I think you're being far too modest. What does your commander say about all this?'

'Hantelmann has been taken to hospital. Infected wound or something.'

'So Menckhoff is in charge?'

'Not really. He's gone on extended leave. Fuchs tells me he's suffering from some form of nervous exhaustion.'

Her mind in motion, there was the briefest pause before Thetis asked, 'So who will be taking over JGN?'

'I don't know.' And it sounded to her as if he didn't care. 'It will probably be Reinhard when he gets back.'

Her eyes flashed with excitement. 'So he's not there?'

'No. He is away with Röth on convalescent leave.'

****

For the last couple of years Thetis had been leading a double life. Not the one she led as one of von Hoeppner's agents, an agent who was actually working for the English, but the one she led as an English spy who happened to have a son who flew for the Imperial German Air Force.

A situation that has given me many sleepless nights.

And on this occasion her call to her son had left Thetis more worried than usual. It wasn't just that he showed so little enthusiasm for his latest victory, an occurrence in the past that would have undoubtedly resulted in wild celebrations; it was the emptiness in his voice.

He sounded like a man hollowed out.

She had hoped that by now he would have started to recover from the death of his friend, that his rampaging quest for vengeance would have driven it out of his system. But that seemed not to be the case. If anything it sounded as if his mood had worsened.

Thetis feared that in such a frame of mind he was in greater danger than he had ever been. But she was not without hope. Her conversation with him had revealed that JGN at Bois de Cheval was without a commander and that the position was still vacant.

Here was an opportunity to ensure his safety. As she saw it if she could get him the command of the airbase his chances of avoiding death in combat and surviving the war would be greatly increased.

Commanders have duties that keep them on the ground.

But her desire and determination to get him the post was one thing. The practicalities were quite something else. How could she possibly bring it about? It was clear that she would need help, powerful help and she knew of only one person with the necessary standing and authority.

The Archduke OberstGeneral Maximillian von Hoeppner.

And therein lay the problem. It wasn't all that long ago that she had sought von Hoeppner's help and on a matter just as critical to the interests of her son, who, at the time, had got into an argument with his commanding officer and stood accused of insubordination.

Hantelmann was threatening him with a court martial.

So Thetis went to von Hoeppner and made a plea on her son's behalf. On that occasion she succeeded. Playing upon his ego and his sentimentality she persuaded the Archduke to put pressure on Hantelmann to drop the charges.

But can I expect him to do me a second favour?

If this hurdle wasn't difficult enough there was one other that seemed impossible to overcome; her feelings toward von Hoeppner. She detested him. She detested and hated the sight of him and found the very idea of asking him for help revolting.

I would rather cut my own throat first.

This hadn't been a problem when she first sought his help. But while making her plea some chance remark triggered a memory she had long suppressed, a memory of a wrong that he had done to her when she was still a young woman. It all came back. How he had posed as her benefactor to gain her trust and then had abused that trust in a manner so terrible she wiped it from her memory.

How I got through that evening without killing him, I'll never know.

And she was convinced that she wouldn't be able to control herself a second time so going to him directly for help was out of the question. But getting Willi the command of JGN was too good an opportunity to miss. There had to be another way.

Maybe I don't need to deal with him face to face.

She thought of sending him a letter instead, but quickly discarded that idea. It would take too long. She needed to strike while the iron was still hot. Any delay, even by a couple of days, could rob her of her goal.

If she was to act she had to act now. But she was at a loss as to what action she should take. Again she set her mind to the task of finding a way to engage the Archduke's help without having to do it face to face. There had to be a way one and it didn't take her long to find it.

I need someone close to von Hoeppner who can argue my case for me.

Such a person existed. And as the name Rittmeister Heinz von Abshagen came into her mind she smiled. Of all the people she could think of none was more suitable or more perfectly placed. As von Hoeppner's adjutant he had the Archduke's ear and his trust. He listened to von Abshagen and respected his opinion. But there was one reason above all others that made him ideal.

He owes me a huge favour.

When she first met him several years earlier she was struck by his good looks and she considered seducing him. It would have been fun and she would have acquired another source of information concerning von Hoeppner. But then she made a discovery.

His tastes lean more to my chauffeur than to me.

And herein lay the answer to her present problem. Two summers ago von Abshagen was in a rather disreputable nightclub in Berlin flirting with a young soldier when the police raided it. He was arrested but being in civilian clothes he was not immediately identified. Discovery would certainly have meant disgrace and an end to his military career. In desperation he asked Thetis for help.

Fortunately the police chief was once my lover.

And von Abshagen was freed. But Thetis was not one to call in a favour lightly. She would only ever do so when the situation demanded it. And what she wanted was not too much to ask. All von Abshagen had to do was persuade the Archduke that her son was the best man to take over command of JGN.

But where is von Abshagen?

He could be almost anywhere. The only thing she knew for sure was that wherever he might be he was bound to be close to von Hoeppner. And the one person likely to know the whereabouts of von Hoeppner was his son Hermann.

'Where is your father?' she asked.

Such information was highly sensitive and Hermann wouldn't normally have disclosed it to anyone. But knowing that Thetis was one of his father's agents and seeing no reason for withholding it from her, he checked his watch and said:

'Well, at this late hour he should be settling down for the night in the Imperial Suite of Breslau's Excelsior Hotel.'

'Breslau!' This was interesting. 'That's on the rail route to the Eastern Front, isn't it?'

'Yes, I believe it is.'

'You wouldn't happen to have a telephone number for the Excelsior Hotel, would you?'

****

'Who was that?' von Hoeppner called from the bedroom.

In the well-appointed living room of the Excelsior Hotel's Imperial Suite Rittmeister Heinz von Abshagen stood staring at the telephone that he had just put down, his mind racing.

'Who was that?' von Hoeppner called again.

Quickly running the question through his mind von Abshagen finally came up with a credible lie. 'Oh, err; it was only the front desk in the lobby, Excellency.'

'What did they want?'

Squaring his shoulders, von Abshagen walked over to the door to the bedroom. 'They asked if you were ready for your supper to be sent up.'

Von Hoeppner's servant had already divested him of his heavy uniform jacket with its many decorations and medals and was now loosening the top button of his shirt.

'More than ready. Are there any other outstanding matters I need to attend to before I dine?'

Von Abshagen quickly rifled through the documents contained in the leather portfolio he held in his arms.

'Only a couple, but if you are feeling tired I feel sure they can wait until after breakfast.'

'Splendid!' Still sitting on the edge of the huge bed von Hoeppner stretched out a leg so that his servant could pull off his boots. 'Maybe you can send up that pretty little maid with my supper.

Von Abshagen bowed his head. 'Of course, Excellency.'

'What is the matter with you? You look distracted. What's on your mind? Out with it!'

Von Abshagen tried to hide a smile of gratitude. In his gruff way von Hoeppner had provided him with the cue he needed to raise a matter hoisted on him by the Baroness von Buchner. 'Well, there is something that needs attention.'

Von Hoeppner looked alarmed. 'I thought we were going to leave everything till breakfast.'

'This won't wait, I'm afraid.'

'Oh, very well. What is it?'

'*Idflieg* needs to know who will take over command of JGN at Bois de Cheval.'

'What! I thought we'd decided to give the post to that fellow Reinhard? He's by far the best suited.'

Reinhard was best suited. Von Abshagen knew that, and to argue in favour of someone else, as he had to do now, would be not be easy. But even as he began to speak the words he needed started to come together.

'Yes, Excellency. On paper he is by far the worthiest. But it occurs to me that worthiness might not be the paramount consideration here.'

'What other consideration is there?'

'Well, there's the matter of public expectation.'

'Oh, I see. This isn't about Reinhard. It's about Buchner, isn't it? You're saying Buchner is the hero of the moment.'

Von Abshagen was always amazed at the speed of the Archduke's mind. With only a hint he had jumped straight ahead to where von Abshagen was attempting to lead him.

'Yes, Excellency.'

'But I thought we had him and Röth earmarked to give those lectures on combat tactics?'

'Neither of them has been told yet so it would be a simple matter to send Reinhard with Röth instead.'

Von Hoeppner shook his head in doubt. 'I still think Buchner's far too young to bear such responsibility. He's not even twenty yet.'

'His age will not concern the nation or the nation's newspapers, Excellency. They will only wonder why the man who has just shot down one of Germany's greatest enemies is passed over for command.'

Von Hoeppner nodded. 'A good point.'

It was. Von Abshagen's argument was smooth and compelling. But then his arguments always were. Yet in this instance von Hoeppner wasn't entirely taken in. Instinct told him that there was more going on here than mere national interest.

I sense the hand of Thetis behind all of this.

He had good reasons for this belief. He was aware of his adjutant's sexual preferences and how in the past they had got him into all sorts of trouble. He was also aware that Thetis had helped him out of a very awkward situation, one that could have ended his military career.

He owes her a big favour. And she's calling it in.

But, even knowing all this von Hoeppner couldn't ignore the fact that what was being proposed made a lot of sense. Giving command wasn't always dictated by military necessity. Sometimes it was a matter of politics.

Besides, this is sure to get up Hantelmann's nose.

'All right, you've convinced me. Now send up that pretty maid with my supper.'

****

He was in his black-beaked Pfalz, the one with the mad-eyed gorgon painted on its fuselage, diving, hurtling toward the exposed flank of a line of unsuspecting F2Bs. The distance between him and the enemy machines was small and getting smaller.

43

Again that sense of total disengagement from what was taking place. It was not him but someone else who throttled back the engine. It was not him but someone else who lined up on the first Bristol Fighter. It was not him but someone else who opened fire.

The attack lasted no more than five seconds.

Three short bursts.

Less than a dozen bullets!

It should have been over in the blink of an eye, but as the F2Bs moved across his line of sight like ducks at a fairground he felt himself suspended in an endless moment; a moment in which he stood outside the passage of time and its wanton brevity.

Faster than thought his eyes beheld the world in all its working parts. Every jolt of his guns as they hammered each bullet from their belts. The twin flashes as the bullets erupted from the muzzles. Their swift passage between the slow turning blades of the propeller. Their lethal impact upon tissue and vital organs.

Three machines destroyed! One after another! An amazing feat of marksmanship! But triumphant exhilaration turns to terror. The fourth machine is only yards away. Need to pull away. Had he left it too late?

Instinct kicks rudder bar! Desperation yanks stick hard over. And the mad-eyed gorgon screams its silent scream. *PULL OUT! PULL OUT!*

Hantelmann woke with a jolt.

Where the hell am I?

Disorientated he looked about him. It was dark but he could see enough to know that he was lying in a bed, a hospital bed, bound into it by the inflexible neatness of sheets and blankets. Recovering his sense of time and place, he turned his head slowly from side to side, taking in the chateau's long hall that had been converted into an officer's ward.

There was a row of beds along each wall, the beds in one row facing tall, draped windows, the beds in the other row spaced between them. The drapes at the windows moved delicately as draughts from the storm outside sneaked their way through gaps in the window casements.

All the beds were occupied. Like Hantelmann, the patients were constrained by their bedclothes into a recumbent position that forced them to sleep or stare longingly at the ceiling. It was darkest night and turbulent. Rigid shadows stood guard upon the beds, boxing them into casket-shaped cubes of forlorn stillness.

At the far end of the ward a nurse sat at a desk reading something in the light of a green covered lamp. Somewhere a clock ticked out black seconds, a man snored, another whimpered timidly. Hearing these sounds Hantelmann ground his teeth.

I need to get out of this place.

In an effort to escape his misery he thought of going back to sleep, but then he remembered the dream. It clung to him like the reek of smoke from a strong cigar. Vestiges of it echoed within him, flickering against the background of his mind as a candle might throw shadows across the walls of an empty room. He didn't need to review it. He knew it as one might know the details of a habit. It was more a recollection than a dream.

That damn dogfight over Trois Risseaux.

He had survived the encounter so why should the dream leave the outcome unresolved? Was it suggesting that he shouldn't have survived? Was it suggesting that he should have collided with that fourth machine and died then and there? Then something even stranger occurred to him.

Maybe I am dead.

He examined the possibility. Could it be that instead of pulling away at the last moment, as his memory seemed to suggest, he had actually collided with that fourth machine and plummeted to his death?

But what about all that has happened since?

Was all of that, the continuance of his life, the air battles, the meals and conversations, the wound that had brought him to the hospital, nothing more than mere illusion, a final dream constructed by a dying brain?

Is this the afterlife?

He had to admit that he was feeling strange, sort of disembodied as if his body and spirit were no longer a perfect fit. He was aware of the back of his head pressing against the pillow, but that was about it. To reassure himself that he still had a body he sought out the only part of him that he could see; his hands. They lay palm down on the counterpane and, in the attenuated light from the nurse's lamp they looked bony and spectral.

Like the hands of a cadaver.

Needing a demonstration of life, his life, Hantelmann lifted both his hands and let them hover several inches above the counterpane. Holding them there he contemplated them with a degree of satisfaction.

Could a corpse do such a thing?

Only one answer was possible. He was still alive. But although this proof dealt with one concern it reawakened another. The problem was his right hand. Whereas the left held its position with perfect poise the right hand trembled uncontrollably. It was something he had noticed since his encounter with the F2Bs at Trois Risseaux. And it seemed to him that all the terror he had felt at the moment of imminent collision had concentrated itself into his right hand.

He tried to make it stop by closing the fingers into a tight fist. This seemed to work for a while but it wasn't long before the effort started to cause the wound in his arm to throb painfully.

Fuck it!

Defeated, he relaxed the fingers and let his hand drop back onto the counterpane. It should have all passed away by now, swept clear by the joyous relief of continued life, but it hadn't. The experience had left its mark and it was as visible as any tear in his flesh.

CHAPTER FOUR

28 NOVEMBER 1917

'I've been put in command of JGN.'

Bowski smiled. 'Well done, Willi. Or should I say Herr Hauptmann.'

'Don't get too worked up. It's probably only until Hauptmann Hantelmann gets better.'

Bowski's face fell. 'So we won't be celebrating in the Kasino tonight?'

'Not this time, I'm afraid.'

'Can I tell the others?'

'I don't see why not. It's official.'

Buchner walked Bowski to the door and let him out.

'And you can also tell them that for the time being you're taking over my Jasta.'

'As long as we're still calling it Jasta Buchner.'

'Of course. Unless you have any objections?'

'None at all.'

Buchner closed the door and walked to the office's small, grubby window. The emergency airfield was basking in the sun now that the storm had moved on. But even through the narrow window Buchner could see that the violent weather had left a trail of destruction in its wake.

The telephone rang.

'It's Fuchs here, Herr Hauptmann.'

'Where are you?'

'At the hangars.'

'How are things?'

'Not good. One of the hangars has been blown away. We've no idea where it's gone. And the machines that were inside it have been badly damaged.'

'How many?'

'Four.'

'Anything else?'

'A tree has fallen across the emergency landing field. I've got some men trying to remove it. Besides that tents have been uprooted and the approach roads are blocked.'

'Very well, Fuchs. Keep me informed.'

Putting down the telephone Buchner sat back in Hantelmann's chair. And as he placed his hands on Hantelmann's desk and looked around Hantelmann's office he was struck by the thought that for him the command of JGN would likely turn out to be a poisoned chalice.

God! What have I got myself into?

Despite the cheery mask put on for Bowski's benefit the very idea of being in charge of such a large unit was anathema to him. His mind rebelled at the prospect of being stuck in an office and already he was beginning to feel like a chained beast.

This is nothing but a glorified Drückposten.

Admittedly, his promotion was only temporary. He would have to relinquish it as soon as Hantelmmann returned to duty and as far as he was concerned the sooner the better. But all the same running one of Germany's largest fighter groups on the western front went against his temperament. It called for qualities that he knew he didn't possess. He was fire and spirit and impetuous courage.

The sky is where I belong.

That was where he best inspired men. That was where he led them into battle. Not on the ground. On the ground he had no real interest in them. In fact, on the ground, he had little real interest in anything.

This is my mother's doing.

He was sure of it. Von Abshagen's telephone call to confirm the appointment was all the proof he needed. It was part of her plan to keep him out of harm's way. She had intervened on his behalf before, using her influence to get him off a charge of insubordination.

She's always interfering in my life.

Now she was at it again. And he knew what she was after. This time she was using her influence to keep him safely on the ground. She wanted him to survive the war, to settle down and get married, to have children.

But he wasn't interested in any of these things. These were things ordinary men desire. And he was not like them. He was not ordinary. He wanted to make his mark upon the world, a mark so indelible it would give him immortality even if it didn't give him a long life.

Only glory can give me this.

Glory was the sun at noon sitting high in the sky. It was the fire of his youth, the joy that made him laugh, the air that filled his lungs, the wings that held him aloft. It was an affirmation of life and he revelled in it. His lust for glory was the same as his lust for life.

Glory is pure gold.

To him it had been more precious than gold. But the death of Frommherz had changed all that. By some strange process of alchemy his grief had transmuted the gold into bronze. What had been warm and radiant was now sombre and lustreless. But it was still glory.

And without glory I am nothing.

There had been a time not so long ago when for Buchner glory would have been important in and of itself. As far as he was concerned it needed no other justification. But now the nature of its importance had changed. It was still important, but for an entirely different reason. Now it was important because it was all that he had left.

But glory is an expensive luxury.

It had cost the lives of countless men. It had cost the lives of the forty-five men he had shot down. It had cost the life of his friend Frommherz. And it had cost the life of Harker, his greatest opponent. Death had come for them all.

And one day it will come for me.

****

With a cessation of hostilities expected to take place at any time fighting on the ground around Dvinsk had more or less come to an end. The poor quality of the average Russian soldier, his low morale and lack of food and ammunition as well as the Bolshevik turmoil had seen to that. There was even talk of mass desertions.

But the war in the air continues.

And Leutnant Volker Burgmüller certainly wasn't going to let his guard down, political developments or no political developments. He still had his duties to perform and they involved patrolling the skies and shooting down Cossacks wherever he could find them.

While at the same time trying to stay alive.

Today he was leading a kette of three machines on a routine patrol along the east bank of the river Nemen between Olita and Kovno. With him on the patrol were two other pilots from Jasta 87; Leutnant Frank Dessau and Leutnant Joachim Abendroth.

They were good, reliable men, eagle-eyed, cool headed and not averse to getting into a scrap even when the odds were not always in their favour. Burgmüller had flown with them many times and he felt safe having them at his back.

It was mid-morning. The sky was crystal white and the freezing wind from out of the north was stiff but steady. They were about halfway through their first patrol of the day flying in a northeasterly direction at a thousand feet.

And so far we've seen absolutely nothing.

That was always the way when covering such a large area and everything in Russia was large; the trackless pine forests and the immense open spaces of flat valleys, flat hills and endless plains. It all seemed to go on forever.

The only thing that isn't large is Russia's Air Force.

And recently it had become considerably smaller. Only the other day they had been on a deep offensive patrol and en route had flown over a Russian airbase, which appeared to be abandoned.

For the most part the skies remained as devoid of human activity as the ground beneath them. There were no machines in the air because there were no machines. There was no traffic on the roads because there were no roads. And there was no movement in the villages because there were no villages.

God help me if I'm ever forced to land my crate around here.

Being lost and on foot was Burgmüller's main concern while on patrol. He may not have seen any men on the ground but looking down through the trees he often saw packs of wolves moving sleekly and sinuously across the snow. This was why his attention was always fixed on the sound of his Mercedes engine. Its strong and steady note was a source of comfort and reassurance.

And long may it stay that way.

Burgmüller tensed. He had spotted something through his starboard struts. Two machines. Black specks against the oyster-white sky. He couldn't quite make out what types they were but if he had to make a guess he'd say that they were a couple of Duks-built Nieuport 17s.

This was a rare sight indeed. Burgmüller could only ever recall seeing such types several times before. But he knew quite a bit about them. The little Nieuport 17 was a popular mount among the elite of the allied pilots including the likes of Albert Ball and Guynemer.

It was powered by a 110-horse power Le Rhône engine, could reach 110 miles per hour at six thousand five hundred feet and had a ceiling of seventeen thousand four hundred feet. It was armed with a single synchronised Vickers machine gun placed in front of the pilot, had an excellent view from the cockpit, and was highly manoeuvrable.

Nifty and climbs like a witch.

He could have chosen to ignore them. After all, the fighting would be over for good in a few days. But he was the leader and the men behind him would be watching. If he turned away what would they think?

Besides, this was too good an opportunity to miss. His bag so far was a couple of Farmans and an ancient Morane Saulnier.

Hardly machines worth pitting one's skills against.

Burgmüller stabbed his finger in the direction of the two Nieuport 17s. He repeated the gesture three times to make sure that Dessau and Abendroth got the message. He cuffed his stick over and kicked his rudder bar. Wires pulled hard. Ailerons rose and dropped. Burgmüller's snow painted Pfalz rolled onto its side as it banked to starboard.

The N17s were also travelling in a northeasterly direction. Burgmüller wanted to get behind them. He held the banking turn until his machine pointed south. It may have looked at this point as if he was flying away from the enemy in the opposite direction. But he wasn't. He was merely getting himself into a position to attack.

When he finally decided that he was where he needed to be he reverse banked, throwing the controls over so that his wings levelled the banked to port. The nose of his machine now rapidly scanned the sky from left to right, from south to north.

The pilots in the N17s were not slow on the uptake. They had long since figured out what their German opponents were up to. They took evasive action, banking round to face south. The two groups were now flying toward each other.

The distance between them narrowed rapidly. Burgmüller could now see that both N17 fuselages were banded with a series of red vertical stripes. He identified them.

Twenty-second Corps Aviation Section.

The two groups of machines rushed past each other, separated by a gap of no more than sixty feet. As with all such encounters they passed, they turned and they engaged.

Burgmüller instantly latched onto the rear of one of the N17s that happened to have the double-headed eagle of the Russian Imperial family painted on its tail rudder.

Dessau and Abendroth split away and chased off after the other N17, which happened to have a skull and cross bones on its tail.

Burgmüller's N17 was no slouch. It zoomed, rising into the sky like a rocket. Burgmüller pulled back his stick and followed.

The N17 stood on its tail, fell onto its back, barrel-rolled then banked hard to port.

Burgmüller did the same, matching him move for move. But the N17 outpaced him. And got onto his tail. The Russian opened fire. An interplane spar splintered.

Christ! Who is this fellow?

Burgmüller dived, rolled and pulled vertiginously into a banking climb. The N17 clung to his tail. Fired another burst. Burgmüller flipped onto his back, Immalmanned, hard banked and got himself behind the N17.

He had the Russian in his sights. Yet Burgmüller held his fire. He always held his fire. He never pulled the firing levers until he was absolutely sure. The N17 wriggled and writhed in front of him, but this time Burgmüller was determined not to let him slip free.

Then came the moment, the moment when the Russian pilot's instinctive sense of manouevre deserted him. For the merest instant he hung suspended on a thread of uncertainty. Should he bank to port or to starboard? He decided but his decision came too late.

Burgmüller opened fire.

Bits of the N17 broke free. A trail of debris scattered across the sky. Something vital was hit. The machine went down, a slick of vaporous smoke streaming behind it.

Burgmüller followed it down, watching the stricken machine as the pilot tried to regain control. He did a bit, but the effort was hopeless.

Burgmüller could have finished it off. It was within his power to do so. But he didn't. It wasn't mercy. It was curiosity. He was conscious of having just fought a worthy opponent and he was keen to know whether the Russian would make it.

They were now down to the level of the trees. Unable to gain or maintain height the N17 went amongst them. But there was not enough room for the width of the wings. Those on the portside were snapped off and the rest of the machine disappeared amongst the branches.

Burgmüller flew on for about a quarter mile then circled back. He returned to the spot where he had seen the N17 go down. There was no wreckage, but he did spot a lone figure standing in a clearing hand raised in salute. Burgmüller's mouth cracked into a smile of pleasure.

Well, I'll be dammed. The bastard's made it.

****

'So what happened to yours?' Burgmüller asked his two companions as they trudged through the snow from the hangars to the office.

'He gave us the slip,' Dessau admitted sheepishly.

'How can that be? There were two of you.'

'You've no idea,' Abendroth explained. 'He was all over the place.'

'And he seemed to know just how to position himself so that that if either of us fired we risked hitting the other.'

'He must have been a much better pilot than the one you shot down,' Abendroth added.

Burgmüller laughed. 'He only seemed better because he had you two after him.'

Reaching the door to the office Dessau pushed it open and walked in. It was called the office because the Hauptmann occupied it. In reality it was a peasant hut that its former occupants abandoned at the start of the war.

It had a straw roof, an earthen floor and shuttered windows and on warm days the interior gave off the rank smell of bovine manure. All in all it was a thoroughly unpleasant abode that only the military would find useful.

Hauptmann Emil Sternhoffer sat at his desk smoking one of the hundred or so cigarettes he consumed every day in an attempt to fumigate his surroundings. With him were four other officers of Jasta 87; Leutnants August Wülner, Gustav Cruger, Theobald Braumfels and Gerd Anders.

The sight of all these pilots packed into such a small space made Burgmüller, Dessau and Abendroth halt in the doorway.

'What's this?' asked Burgmüller. 'Someone's birthday?'

'Come in you three,' Sternhoffer said, motioning them to enter with a sweep of one of his bear-like arms. 'We've been waiting for you.'

'That sounds ominous,' Abendroth muttered as he pushed Dessau ahead of him.

'No! No!' Sternhoffer assured them. 'There's nothing to worry about.'

Burgmüller, the last in, closed the door and joined the group of officers standing close to the heat of the smoking fireplace. With them all now together Sternhoffer rose from behind his desk, stubbing out his cigarette as he did so.

'I have an announcement to make.' He paused long enough to light a fresh cigarette. 'One that affects you all.'

From his tunic pocket he took out a crumpled piece of paper that he spent a moment uncrumpling. Despite the brown coffee stain the assembled officers could see that it was an official communiqué.

'This is a message from Idflieg. It reads:

Recent developments in this part of the world have brought about a cessation of hostilities on the Eastern Front, which will take effect in a couple of days.

Sternhoffer paused again, allowing time for the meaning of his words to sink in and also for him to look and see what effect his words were having. But they were German officers and their faces though young and eager were stony and unreadable. He resumed reading the message:

Your job here is finished. And what you have done should make you proud. But your service as fighter pilots is not over. It is now needed elsewhere.

53

The situation on the Western Front hasn't yet brought us victory. The entry of the Americans into the war could start to swing the balance against us.

Germany needs to act decisively while it is still at the height of its strength. Your skills and prowess are crucial to the success of the fatherland.

Sternhoffer crumpled up the communiqué and put it back into his tunic pocket. 'Well, that's it.'

'But what does it mean, Herr Hauptmann?' Dessau asked as perplexed as his comrades.

'It means that you're being shipped back to Germany and from there to the Western Front. You have been reassigned to *Jagdgeschwader Nord* at a place called Bois de Cheval.'

The seven young officers stood staring at each other, not sure what to say or think. But Sternhoffer, never a man at a loss for words, took the cigarette out of his mouth and barked:

'What's the matter with you lot? You should be over the moon. This is what you've been after all along. You should be celebrating.'

'The Hauptmann is right,' Anders declared. 'The first round of drinks is on me.'

****

'It's so good to get out of that place even if only for a day.' Reinhard turned to Röth who was sitting beside him driving the open topped staff car they had borrowed from the hospital. 'Don't you agree?'

Röth nodded his head vigorously. 'Absolutely! But should we be spending it visiting a sick relative?'

'Somebody has to. And if we don't then who will?'

Given the nature of the person they were visiting this exchange struck them both as quite amusing and they burst out laughing. When they finally quietened down Röth gave Reinhard a few sly looks then asked:

'Tell me, are you ever going to get together with that Princess of yours?'

'Oh, you've reminded me, it's her birthday soon.'

'Really! Hold old will she be?'

'Nineteen, I believe.'

'A lovely age. And is there to be a party?'

'Some sort of costume ball.'

'Will you be going?'

'How can I? You know we have other commitments.'

'Surely you will at least send her a gift.'

Reinhard laughed. 'I already have.'

'What is it? Diamonds? Pearls?'

'No, nothing like that. She wrote to me telling me what she wanted.'

'Really! There are no flies on her. What did she ask for?'

'Well, her costume for the ball is a flying officer's uniform. She wanted something to go with that.'

'Not your trousers, surely?'

'Very amusing. No. I sent her my pilot's badge and Iron Cross.'

Röth was so startled he momentarily lost control of the motor car and Reinhard had to cling on for dear life as it skidded from one side of the country lane to the other. But Röth was a skilled driver and he quickly brought the vehicle back into a straight line.

'You didn't!' he finally managed to gasp.

'I did.'

'Such sacrifice! It must be love. It must be! It can't be anything else.'

'Don't be a fool. It was only a small offering. Besides they were only a couple of spares.'

Further discussion of the subject was terminated when Röth jerked the steering wheel and turned the car through a gated entrance that had appeared on the left. After barely missing the brick posts on either side he drove at full speed up the gravel drive.

'Does your foot ever touch the brake?' Reinhard asked.

'Brake! Does it have a brake?'

Hardly bothering to lower his speed Röth skidded the open topped staff car with reckless precision into a narrow space his front fender barely missing the hospital wagons parked on either side. With the front wheels spitting gravel he brought the vehicle to a screeching halt and with only inches to spare between the large headlamps and the Chateau's grey brick facade.

'Is it safe to open my eyes now?' Reinhard murmured.

'Stop being an old ninny.'

After climbing out of the staff car the pair spent a minute straightening their uniforms.

'Wouldn't do not to look our best,' Röth remarked as he lifted from the back seat the bottle of champagne and box of Havana cigars they had brought as gifts.

Clutching these as well as a bundle of newspapers and magazines that Reinhard had brought they bound up the stone steps of the entrance into an echoing lobby. Here a severe looking nurse sitting at a desk greeted them coldly.

'Can I help you, meinen Herren?'

'Yes. We're here to see Hauptmann Hantelmann.'

****

55

Feeling hot and irritated Hantelmann moved his aching legs beneath the bed sheets trying to find a more comfortable position. He had only just woken up or rather he'd only just been jolted awake out of a bad dream.

The same bad dream.

He had it every time he went to sleep. And it not only began at the same moment, the moment when he began his attack on the line of F2Bs, it also ended at the same moment, the moment when he was about to collide with one of the machines.

Why? Why does the dream always stop there?

Why didn't it go on to show him banking away with only inches to spare? He couldn't find any explanation for it. All he knew for sure was that it was taking its toll. Every time he woke from it he felt drained, as if the very vitality of his bones was being sucked out of him.

And despite all the sleep he'd been having he still felt dog-tired. His eyes felt sore and heavy and even now all he wanted to do was close to them again and drift off. But he was afraid to give in to the temptation. He knew what awaited him if he did.

I need to stay awake

But that was easier said than done. To stay awake he needed something to occupy his mind. And there wasn't a lot to do in a hospital. He had considered writing a letter to his wife, Annaliese, not to convey his affections but to forestall any attempt she might make to rush to his bedside.

No doubt to bask in the limelight as the dutiful wife.

The thought of his self-absorbed, high-pitched wife making a grand entrance was more than his weakened constitution could support. He had to prevent it at all costs.

I'd rather she stay where she is in the arms of her lover.

He looked to his bedside cabinet where his pen and paper lay and was about to reach for them when it occurred to him that he would have to ask the sharp-faced nurse to prop him up in bed. And that meant suffering her clucking disapproval at being diverted from her other duties.

Strange how that woman reminds me of Annaliese.

With a sigh he let his eyes stray back up to the ceiling, tracing the outlines of the plasterwork and cornices. While doing this he tried to remember the names of all the officers in *Jagdgeschwader Nord*, but the task proved beyond too taxing and he soon gave up.

Dammed if I can remember who's dead and who's alive anyway.

Then he hit upon the idea of trying to list all his 'kills'. His first attempt was not a success; he started with the two victories he made as a

Jasta commander but when he came to the victories he'd acquired as commander of JGN he mistakenly included the RE8 he'd taken from Buchner.

The one I was forced to give back.

It followed an attack that Buchner and he had made on an RE8. Afterwards a heated dispute arose between them as to who had the right to claim the kill. Angry words and insults were exchanged.

The impudent bastard even called me a thieving, cheating, gangrenous little shit.

Hantelmann took the kill and put Buchner under arrest. But later, under pressure from High Command, he gave the kill back and after the death of Frommherz the two men were reconciled. But Hantelmann knew he would never really warm to Buchner. He had disliked him from the start seeing him as nothing more than a puffed-up, undisciplined jackanapes, an impulsive maverick who did as he pleased and got away with it because of his connections.

High Command's Golden Boy.

With a curl of his lip Hantelmann dismissed both Buchner and the RE8 from his mind and turned his thoughts back to how many kills he now had. Even without the RE8 he still had a total of seven. By anybody's standard it was quite a respectable score the more so when one took into account the fact that five of those victories had taken place on the same day.

And three of them within less than a minute.

Once again Hantelmann found himself confronted by his dream. Despite making a concerted effort to divert his mind onto other things it seemed that those very diversions were leading him back to the very place he wanted to avoid. He rolled his eyes in frustration.

I can't get away from it no matter what I do.

Irritated he decided to turn his attention to something a little more mundane. He might not feel in the mood to write to his wife, but there was nothing to prevent him from sending a line to his daughter, Sophie, letting her know how he was faring.

After getting himself into a sitting position he reached over and retrieved his notepaper and pen from the bedside cabinet. Staring at the lined paper he spent a moment considering what he should say. Not wishing to worry his daughter unduly he decided on a cheery tone. But as soon as he laid the nib of his pen against the paper his hand began to tremble violently.

In desperation he tried holding it still with his left hand, but he only succeeded in making them both shake. Alarmed and angry, he was also puzzled. Why should this be? His temperature was back to normal and his wound was beginning to heal nicely.

So why won't my hand stop shaking?

Even the doctors treating him seemed at a loss. All they could come up with was that he was probably suffering from nervous exhaustion, assuring him that after an extended period of quiet and bed rest the shaking would go away of its own accord.

What the hell do they know?

Hantelmann had his own theory, one that was far simpler and didn't involve nervous exhaustion. What he was suffering from was a reaction to a close encounter with death. That was why he was having the same bad dream every time he went to sleep. Something deep within him knew that he should not have survived that encounter. The gods decreed that he would die that day and he didn't.

Well, there's nothing I can do about that.

With a sigh he put the pen and notepaper back onto the bedside cabinet then sat back to contemplate the rest of the ward. Nothing was going on. All the other patients were lying in their beds. One of them raised his hand as if to catch his eye but Hantelmann ignored him. Not in the mood for idle chit-chat he decided to pretend that he was asleep, but even as he started to close his eyes his attention was caught by some activity near the entrance to the ward.

Thinking it might be a doctor he turned his head in that direction. Two men had entered the ward but neither of them appeared to be medical. In fact they were both in uniform and it seemed that they were walking in his direction. Recognition came a second later.

Röth! Reinhard!

****

'So here it is,' Röth announced grinning expansively as he and Reinhard advanced toward Hantelmann's bed. 'The renowned home for retired and aging airman.'

'Oh, God!' Hantelmann moaned, trying unsuccessfully to hide his sheer delight. 'That's all I need. A visit from you two jokers.'

Reinhard pulled up a chair so that he could sit close to the bed. 'You don't fool us, Herr Hauptmann. We know you're pleased to see us.'

Hantelmann arched an eyebrow quizzically. 'Am I? I wouldn't be surprised if your appearance doesn't set back my recovery several weeks.'

'What's all this?' Röth asked as he too brought up a chair to sit on.

'What's all what?'

'These flowers and cards.' Röth rose from his chair to smell the roses. 'I didn't know you had so many admirers.'

'Nor did I.' Hantelmann sounded less than overwhelmed. 'This stuff keeps arriving by the hour.'

'Who's it from?'

'The cards are from my son and daughter. The fruit and the saucy card are from Fuchs and those flowers are from Hedda von Hoeppner.'

Reinhard cocked his head to one side. 'The ArchDuchess! You certainly have friends in high places.'

'High places, yes. But friends I'm no longer so sure.'

Röth shook his head regretfully. 'Well, I'm afraid we couldn't get you any flowers, but we did bring you these.'

Lifting both his arms he revealed the box of cigars and the magnum of champagne.

'Thanks. Much appreciated.'

'And we've also brought you the latest editions of today's newspapers.' Reinhard unrolled them on the bed sheets. 'As you can see you're on all the front pages.'

'Am I?'

'Yes! You're exploits shooting down those three F2Bs has made you quite the celebrity.'

'Is this your photo?' Röth asked seeing Hantelmann's stiff expression. 'It's not very flattering, is it?'

But having noticed that Hantelmann was carefully keeping his right hand hidden under the bedclothes Reinhard sensed that there was something else amiss. Rolling up the newspapers and putting them to one side he asked:

'When are they letting you out of here?'

Hantelmann frowned. 'That's the big question. And I can't get a straight answer out of the doctors. One moment they say I'll be here a few weeks then the next I'm told I might need a couple of months to recover.'

Röth pursed his lips ruefully. 'As long as that?'

In an effort to lighten the mood Hantelmann perked up. 'Anyway, what about you two? I can't say when I last saw you both looking so fit. Surely you must be fully recovered.'

Putting on a sombre voice Röth said, 'Appearances can be deceptive, Herr Hauptmann.'

'But you can't be that bad if they let you out to visit me.'

'We've been discharged from the hospital,' Reinhard said. 'But we're under strict orders not to return to active duty until after Christmas.'

'Christmas! But what will you be doing with yourselves in the meantime?'

An eager smile swept across Röth's face. 'We've both been assigned to the Jasta Schule at Valenciennes.'

'Doing what?'

'Teaching combat tactics to the new boys.'

Hantelmann shook his head. 'God help them.'

'God help us you mean.'

'Well, keep an eye out for my boy, Gerard. He's doing his pilot training there. He might welcome a friendly face.'

Reinhard nodded. 'We'll do that, Herr Hauptmann.'

'When do you start?'

'Not for a couple of days. We thought we'd use the time to see you and then pay JGN a quick visit just to see how they're getting on.'

'A splendid idea. Give my regards to Hauptmann Menckhoff. Tell him not to ruin the place in my absence.'

Röth and Reinhard exchanged an anxious glance that Hantelmann didn't fail to notice.

'What's wrong?' he asked.

It was Reinhard who answered. 'Hauptmann Menckhoff's not there.'

'Not there? Where the devil is he?'

'Fuchs telephoned me the other day to tell me that on the day you fell ill Menckhoff went on leave.'

'So who's in charge?'

Röth and Reinhard exchanged another anxious glance, but this time there was no need for Hantelmann to ask its meaning. He was already one step ahead of them.

'Oh, no! Not Buchner.'

CHAPTER FIVE

29 NOVEMBER 1917

As Hantelmann lay in his bed troubled by thoughts of his nemesis being in charge of JGN midnight passed unnoticed as did the strengthening of the wind outside. In a last display of might it barged blindly into the night, trampling across the French countryside, shaking the trees of Bois de Cheval and scouring the deserted streets of Senlis to rattle the gates and backroom windows of Mimi's *Estaminet* demanding to be let in.

It also fluted a draught of hissing air down the chimney causing the logs in the parlour fireplace to crackle and pop, fanning the fire's red heat into the intense and baleful glow of a smelter's forge. In a half dream Fuchs stretched his unshod feet indolently toward the warmth of the fire. In his hand was a glass of Burgundy. On his lap was Mimi, a bare arm draped about his neck.

'Have you moved your stock yet?' she whispered into his ear.

Fuchs shifted his weight uncomfortably. 'I've decided to leave it where it is for the moment.'

Having sprung loose Fuchs' stiff collar Mimi started playing with his top shirt button. 'But that means trotting all the way over to that cellar every time you want a bottle of something.'

Ignoring Mimi's fingers Fuchs stared fixedly into the fire. 'I can't keep my stock safe at the new mess. The raid may have reduced the chateau to a ruin but its cellars are solid rock. Besides I might not need to move anything.'

'Why not?'

'I have plans.'

Mimi sat up. 'Really? What plans?'

A smile appeared on Fuchs' mouth, the smile of a man who looks into the future and sees welcome things. 'I plan to reopen the old Kasino.'

'You'll never do it.'

'Oh, I'll do it. Don't you worry on that score.'

'But it'll cost a small fortune.'

'Not as much as you might think.'

The love of money was part of the reason why Mimi and Fuchs were attracted to each other. Both of them liked acquiring it but, whereas Mimi held onto hers with an iron grip, Fuchs was quite prepared, when necessary, to put it to the good use of acquiring more. Mimi didn't approve of such speculation but she did find it exciting.

'How much have you got now?'

Fuchs stirred at this indelicate question. 'Enough.'

Like a man moving in his sleep Fuchs turned to Mimi and, hooking out the low collar of her peasant blouse with a speculative finger, peered down into the softly rounded shadows.

"Hey!" She slapped away his hand. "Always poking your nose about where you shouldn't."

"You've never complained before."

Not convinced her protests were serious he placed his head against her shoulder and made a second attempt on her blouse. Again he was rewarded with a slap on the hand.

'What are you looking for?'

Fuchs looked up with an idiot smile. 'Forgetfulness.'

'Well, you can forget about that. I'm too tired.' Mimi pushed away Fuchs' encircling arm and climbed off his lap. 'Anyway, isn't it about time you got back to the airbase?'

The cheer went out of Fuchs' face. 'Do I have to?'

Mimi smoothed down her skirt and blouse. 'I thought you enjoyed it there.'

'I did once, but things have changed.'

'How?'

'Oh, I don't know. It's just not the same. It used to be full of Esprit de corps. Now it's full of ghosts.'

'It can't be that bad. You've got that young fellow Buchner in charge. Surely he's got to be far better than the one you had before. What was his name? Hantelmann.'

'You would think so, wouldn't you? But Buchner's the perfect example of what I'm talking about.'

'How so?'

'Well, he's a national hero. He's killed England's greatest fighter pilot. Yet instead of strutting about like a turkey cock he just mopes about the place. I tell you I'm beginning to miss the sound of Hantelmann barking orders.'

'How is he? Is he still in hospital?'

'Yes. I might visit him if I can. It won't be easy to get away though not with Buchner needing someone to hold his hand all the time.'

'What about your friends Röth and Reinhard? Will you be visiting them?'

'No need. They've been discharged.'

'I like Reinhard. How's he getting on with that Princess of his?'

'Princess! What Princess?'

'The one he gets telephone calls from.'

'How do you know that?'

'You told me.'

'Did I?'

'Yes, you did. You can't keep anything to yourself. You're a worse gossip than the village washerwoman.'

'Yes. I suppose I am.' He paused for a moment then said, 'Look, can I stay here tonight?'

'What, and ruin my reputation?'

He felt like laughing out loud but smiled instead. 'Seriously, I don't feel like returning to the airfield tonight, especially with this storm. Let me stay'

'All right! But on one condition.'

'Name it!'

'Treat me like Reinhard treats his princess.'

****

Why am I still knitting this scarf? William won't be needing it. Not now that he's coming home.

Andrea felt a thrill of excitement, a feeling of tightness in her chest that made her want to spring from her chair, the one facing her husband's, and pace about the room. But she concentrated harder on the scarf knowing that she had to finish it no matter what.

He can use it for pottering about in the garden.

It would have been the second scarf she had knitted him during his service overseas. He was still wearing the first, but on his last leave he had revealed that he had worn it on so many flights, wrapped around his neck, the wool was beginning to unravel.

And I did promise to knit him a new one.

She remembered how grateful she had felt at having something to occupy her time, something that would help her husband while away at war. She would knit him the best scarf ever, one that would protect his neck from the harsh elements while out on patrol.

But it had taken longer than expected to get the wool. So long that on the day it finally arrived in the village shop she received a letter from her husband, the one telling her that he had been assigned to Home Defence and would soon be home for good.

That had been wonderful news.

Too wonderful to keep to herself. This was news that had to be shared. Still clutching the letter she found herself rushing about the house telling the servants and telephoning her mother and her husband's mother. She even sped off down the lane to tell everyone in Antley village including the Reverend Forsythe at All Saints rectory and Miss Acres the postmistress. And when she eventually got back home she told her baby son Douglas.

Not that he understood a word, but he knew his mother was happy.

He had been fed an hour ago and was now safely with his nanny in the nursery, fast asleep. And as Andrea worked her needles she drew some contentment from the knowledge that it wouldn't be long now before he would rest in the arms of his father.

As will I.

In that same letter, the one telling her he was coming home, he had set out his plans in detail. She knew that he would have set off from Ste Helene late on the 26th November and, by using her imagination she was able to travel with him. She saw him being driven to Bethune railway station then sitting in an empty carriage reading a book as the train carried him to Calais.

Finally she saw him standing on the upper deck of the ferry leaning against the rail, smoking his pipe as he gazed across the calm waters of the English Channel. In his letter he had not thought to describe the waters of the channel as being calm, but she wished it so.

I want nothing to delay his journey.

By his own estimate he should have arrived in England late on the 27th November. Andrea had hoped that he would then come straight to her at Widdings, but that was not to be. He wasn't officially on leave so his first duty after stepping ashore was to report to his Commanding Officer. Rather than staying in the camp he would spend the 28th November with his mother who lived in a cottage near the coast and then drive up to Widdings the following day. Today!

Hopefully, he should arrive around mid-morning.

The past few days had been a frustrating time for Andrea, but as there was nothing she could do about it she stuck rigidly to her usual daily routines, attending the baby, supervising the preparation of meals, keeping up to date with her correspondence, knitting the scarf. She even chaired a meeting of the Parish Council.

Organising Christmas comforts for the troops.

It had not been easy. All during the meeting she was distracted by thoughts of her husband's imminent arrival, knowing that he was so close yet seemingly beyond her reach. Such was her distraction that she couldn't remember a single thing that was said or what was finally decided.

Did we settle on socks or belaclavas?

She was struggling with the same problem now. And the clock on the mantel wasn't helping matters. In fact it was making it worse. Normally it ticked away in a lively enough manner. Now it was releasing each second with all the grudging reluctance of a slow drip from the kitchen tap.

If something doesn't happen soon I'll scream.

This reaction surprised Andrea as she had always prided herself on her patience, her ability to wait calmly no matter how eager or anxious she might be feeling inside. But now her rock hard endurance was turning to plaster and even that was beginning to crumble and crack.

This is torture. Surely he won't be much longer.

The clock on the mantel ticked on. It had become such a commanding sound that Andrea stopped knitting and stared at the hands. Was it her imagination or were they in exactly the same position they had occupied five minutes previously. She forced herself to think of something else.

When he comes up the southern road I'll be able to see him from the top of the eastern tower.

The thought became an impulse and the impulse became irresistible. She had to look. She had to. But she forced herself to stay where she was. After all, what would be gained by flying about the house in a fluster? But then her resolve collapsed when the sound of a motor vehicle came through an open window.

It's him! It has to be!

Throwing her knitting to one side she dashed from the room and out of the door just as the motor vehicle pulled into the drive. Uncertainty slammed into her like a fist. She faltered and stood stock still.

That's not William's car.

The driver, a man in uniform, got out and opened the door to the rear passenger seat. Another man, a tall thin-faced man, exited the vehicle. He was also in uniform, but it was clear from the red band on his cap that he was an officer of senior rank.

'Mrs Harker?' he asked.

Andrea suddenly felt herself imprisoned within a great reluctance to admit who she was. She could only stand and watch mutely as the senior officer walked toward her.

'I am Colonel Pritchett, your husband's commanding officer.'

There was deep sorrow in his eyes that Andrea was unable to avoid. It spoke to her and with such clarity that there could be no doubt as to its meaning. And the meaning was so overwhelming it robbed her of her senses and brought darkness to her eyes. Like a seed that has lost the support of its branch, she fell to the ground.

****

How affectionate should I be?

That was Anthea's dilemma as she struggled to compose her letter to Oberleutnant Reinhard. The intention behind it was clear enough. She wanted to express her concern for the injuries that he had sustained during the recent actions over the Ste Helene Salient.

And wish him a speedy recovery.

There was nothing wrong with that, but as she put the words down on paper it became clear to her that there was a fine line between concern and an expression of deeper feelings. It would be easy enough to stray over that line. The choice of words was critical.

Not that my mother would approve either way.

The Princess Anthea von Hoeppner was aware that throughout her entire life she had been a cause of considerable concern to her parents, but most especially to her mother. The Arch Duchess Hedda von Hoeppner, a woman with pretensions of artistic and cultural sensitivity, could never understand her daughter's tomboy tendencies or her single-minded preoccupation with all things military.

From a very early age Anthea had preferred toy swords to embroidery and skipping ropes and instead of dressing dolls and arranging tea parties she was more likely to be seen knocking down lines of tin soldiers with spring-loaded artillery. She also took to creeping through the secret entrance into her father's library where she would seek out his leather-bound history books and fire her imagination with stirring tales of ancient battles.

Mother hoped I would grow out of it.

And for a while it appeared that she might. As a teenager Anthea turned to other things. She became not only a crack shot but also an accomplished skier, fencer and horsewoman. Although these activities were still far too masculine for her mother's tastes, some of them at least had the virtue of being more attuned to her daughter's proper station in life.

But then the war started.

And Anthea's military obsession returned with a vengeance. But the world portrayed in her father's books had altered. Warfare now had a new dimension; the air. Where before her heartbeat had quickened to the march of vast armies it now beat to the tempo of Germany's Imperial Airforce, its pilots, its machines, its tactics and its capabilities.

Her rooms became a packed storehouse of aeronautical paraphernalia from goggles, gloves and leather jackets worn by pilots to propellers, joysticks and camouflaged tail rudders most of which were gifts from her brother Hermann. Even the cosmetics on her dressing table were pushed aside to make room for spent bullets and other trophies, and the walls were covered with maps, photographs and propaganda posters.

The latest poster showed women looking wistfully toward a pale blue sky as a rather inaccurately rendered biplane flew by overhead. In large Gothic script was the exhortation: GERMAN WOMEN! SUPPORT OUR GALLENT AIRMEN. But for her the message in the poster held a quite different meaning. In her imagination she did not see herself as one of the woman.

I'm the pilot in the biplane.

And she had good reason to see herself from this unusual perspective for unlike the women in the poster and almost every other woman alive she actually knew how to fly. Her brother had given her secret lessons when she was seventeen. It then became her ambition to get an aircraft for her eighteenth birthday. When her mother got to hear of it she put her foot down adding that no daughter of hers would be seen zooming about the sky like a circus acrobat.

Of course, the ArchDuchess' injunction conveniently ignored the fact that she herself could fly and that she had an Albatros BI two-seater with a fan-tailed peacock painted on its fuselage for her own personal use. Not that Anthea would have been deterred anyway. She did the one thing she always did when faced with her mother's opposition, she turned to her father.

In common with his wife, the Arch Duke Maximillian von Hoeppner could not understand how it was that he had come by a daughter who was so impulsive, headstrong and unladylike. Naturally, he wanted to see Anthea settle down and get married and was keen to exploit the dynastic opportunity such a marriage presented. But unlike his wife he wasn't in any particular hurry.

Why would he? I'm the apple of his eye.

As far as he was concerned she could do no wrong and even when she did he always indulged her. And, unlike his wife, he was amused by his daughter's single-minded preoccupation with all things military. In truth the Archduke secretly wished that his bookish son Hermann could be more like her. Indeed, he had always felt vexed that providence had been so cruel as to give him a mild-mannered son and a war-like daughter.

For these reasons he had readily agreed when she asked him for an aircraft for her birthday. Her mother, by contrast, went through the roof, and for days the high-ceilinged halls of the Residenz had reverberated with the sound of her wrath. But Hedda's anger, like all her emotions, could only concentrate on one thing at a time. It was soon diverted, as it always was, by rumours that her husband had embarked on yet another extra-marital affair.

Rumours that I supplied.

Once again Hedda's energies were bent upon the all-consuming need to expose the guilty parties, both husband and lover, and this left the field free for Anthea to get her aircraft. It was specially built for her at her brother's factory in Essen, and the day of its delivery was probably one of the happiest of her life.

But Anthea's obsession with flying was not without its feminine side. She took a womanly interest in the brave heroes who fought the nation's enemies in the skies above the trenches, the *Flugkanonen* and *Oberkanonen*. From first thing in the morning to last thing at night her every waking thought was devoted to the *Fliegertruppen*. She had to know everything about them, their careers, their scores and exploits, their likes and dislikes, their lives and deaths. They even populated her restless dreams.

And I fell passionately in love with several of them.

The first to enthral her had been Oswald Boelke. She had been instantly struck by his manly good looks and for weeks after his death in a mid-air collision she had been inconsolable. Shortly after that she fell for Allmenröder but he too was killed in action.

Now my heart belongs to Reinhard.

It was his Sanke postcard that she now held in her hands and studied adoringly with her large flashing eyes. How glorious he looked in his grey uniform; the very epitome of a German warrior. And the fact that he had been wounded in battle made him seem even more dashing.

A true German hero. Not like that mummy's boy Buchner.

She was pleased to hear the news that a few days earlier Buchner had shot down Major Harker, the top English flying ace, but even this accomplishment did little to alter her low opinion about him as a man or diminish her high regard for Reinhard.

He will always have my heart.

Yet all this love and longing, all this long distance adoration and hero-worship, hid a much deeper and more abiding obsession. She may have found these men exciting but she was more excited not by who they were but by what they represented and that was best summed up by the German Air Service medallion they wore upon their breast.

To her it was a talisman of her true desire. She didn't just want to love German fighter pilots she wanted to be one. She wanted to wear their uniform, to share their jokes and stories, to mix with them in the kasino, to fight beside them in the skies and shoot down Germany's enemies.

Oh God, if only.

This was her one abiding dream and it captivated her completely. It punctuated her fevered sleep and dogged her every waking thought and its unattainability was a constant blight on her ambitions and sense of self. To her it was not only unjust but also totally absurd that being a woman should prevent her from doing what she knew she was capable of doing. After all, she had her own machine.

And I can handle it better than most men.

But as she gazed upon Reinhard's photograph she knew that her dream was an impossible one. Loving men such as Reinhard was about as near as she was ever likely to come to realising it. Not that her mother saw it that way. She was encouraged by these infatuations. She saw them as a sign that Anthea was developing a normal female interest in men and hoped that it might soon lead to marriage.

'Who are you writing to?'

Her mother stood in the doorway and it was clear from her stiffened expression that she had spent some time standing outside steeling herself against the distasteful things that would greet her eyes when she made her entrance.

'I'm writing to Oberleutnant Reinhard, Mother. I am wishing him a quick recovery from his injuries.'

Hedda's matronly figure glided further into the room. 'I'm not sure I approve of you writing to this man.'

'You forget, Mother, this man was a great help to you not so long ago.'

'That's as maybe, but you have never met him.'

Anthea smiled with her eyes. 'I might do one day.'

Hedda continued approaching her daughter, resolutely determined to avoid looking at the maps, the scraps of canvas and all the other aeronautical odds and ends that hung upon the walls. But her eyes, having a will of their own, inevitably strayed toward them.

'Oh, Anthea,' she moaned, her sensibilities offended by such brutish things. 'It's like an aircraft hangar in here. It even smells of castor oil. Why must you have all these horrors on display?'

"They are not horrors, Mother," Anthea explained with carefree defiance. "They are tokens of affection sent to me by all my admirers."

"Why can't they send you flowers or jewellery?"

"They send me what I ask for."

Hedda shook her head in despair. She knew it was an argument she was never going to win but, being a mother, she also knew that she would never give up trying. But for the moment she thought it best to change the subject.

'It's only three days till your birthday. Have you decided what you are going to wear for the costume ball?'

Anthea's eyes flashed and her face lit up with genuine excitement. 'I have, Mother. I ordered it some days ago and with any luck it should be delivered today.'

'What have you chosen?' Hedda was also excited. The ball was to celebrate Anthea's nineteenth birthday and she felt confident that here was something that even her daughter couldn't spoil. 'A figure from history perhaps? Maybe Cleopatra? Or Marie Antoinette?'

A sly smile crept over Anthea's mouth. 'Well...'

Hedda's face darkened. 'On, no. I know that smile. You've ordered something military, haven't you? Something outrageous like Boudicca or Joan of Arc?'

Anthea was spared the need to reply by the arrival of Helga, her lady-in-waiting. She was holding a large white flat box and above it her face beamed with excitement. "It has come, my Lady."

"Ah, my costume." Throwing down Reinhard's photograph Anthea sprang to her feet. "Bring it over here, quickly. I must see it straight away."

Running to Anthea's bed, Helga placed the box upon it. It was four inches deep and about two feet along each side. "Shall I open it, my Lady?"

Anthea turned to her mother. 'You don't need to stay.'

Chin thrust out, Hedda took a step toward the bed. 'I think I shall.'

'Oh, Mother,' Anthea protested. 'You'll spoil the surprise. You'll see it soon enough.'

For a moment Hedda stood her ground then she seemed to have second thoughts. Taking a deep breath she left the room calling out, 'It better not be anything military. That's all I shall say on the matter.'

Helga waited for the door to close then asked, 'Shall I open it now, my Lady?'

"Yes! Yes!"

Helga giggled with excitement as she took hold of the lid and lifted it away from the box. She then parted the protective layer of tissue paper that covered the contents. When Anthea's eyes fell upon what lay within she was transported with delight. She turned to her lady-in-waiting and almost hugged her.

'Help me out of my clothes, Helga. I must try this on straight away.'

70

****

'Careful, Leutnant!' Feldwebel Ernst Kressinger called out as Leutnant Volker Burgmüller catapulted headfirst along the entire length of the carriage containing the baggage and air mechanics.

Having stood panting idly in the depth of the forest for over an hour the two-engine thirty-carriage train with its skirted snowplough and tall, stove-pipe stack had chosen this moment to shudder into life.

God! I hate trains.

It wasn't trains that Burgmüller hated. He felt the same about cars and boats and other forms of transport. What he really hated was being a passenger. He felt trapped and helpless and the longer the journey the more these feelings intensified especially when the conveyance in question kept stopping and starting every few miles.

I'd cope better if I were up front driving the damn thing.

But he wasn't. And the fact that the train kept stopping and starting only added to his sense of powerlessness. Not that being in motion actually helped matters. The endless clicking of the wheels made sleep impossible and his constant restlessness forced him to wander back and forth along the carriages.

'How much longer will this bloody journey take?' he muttered as he passed through the connecting doors.

Entering yet another carriage full of snoring soldiers Burgmüller reflected that he and his six companions had already been on the train nearly a whole day. In that time the seven freight trailers carrying their fragile machines, wingless and crated, and the seventeen carriages full of troops had barely covered a hundred miles.

They had set out from Dvinsk bound for Warsaw early that morning, but had suffered delays right from the start. Part of the problem was they had to share the rail network with hundreds of other troop carrying trains also westward bound. That would have been bad enough, but what was really slowing their progress to a crawl was the snow. The drifts became so bad that by the time they reached Vilna they found themselves diverted to Minsk.

Burgmüller tried to shake off his despondency as he re-entered the smoke-filled car occupied by his fellow pilots. They were gathered round a small folding table playing the same game of *Vingt et Un* they'd been playing when he'd left them earlier.

His friend, Leutnant Frank Dessau looked up from his cards. 'We're underway again. How many times have we stopped so far?

Burgmüller shook his head. 'I've lost count.'

'Don't worry,' Leutnant August Wülner the optimist told them. 'When we reach Germany the delays will stop.'

'Little good that will do you,' Leutnant Gustav Crüger the pessimist said as he sorted through his cards. 'We're heading straight to the Front. So don't expect any home cooking on the way.'

'Well, at least the conditions will be better there than in Russia,' Leutnant Theobald Braumfels observed ready as ever to find the bright side.

'What a dreadful place,' declared Leutnant Gerd Anders a man given to regard the past with disdain.

'And the women as ugly as sin,' Crüger added. 'Every one of them with a face like a ferret.'

Braumfels regarded his companions with a cheery smile. 'I don't know about the rest of you but I'm quite looking forward to this new place we're being sent to.'

'I wouldn't get your hopes up too much if I were you,' Crüger warned him.

'Why not?' Braumfels asked.

'Well, those English pilots are no pushover. Not like the Cossacks.'

'Oh, for God's sake!' Having run out of patience Leutnant Joachim Abendroth finally decided to assert his presence. 'Are we playing this game or not?'

Braumfels sat forward. 'Fine! Give me another card!'

'There!' Abendroth threw down a queen of clubs.

'Damn it!' Braumfels slammed his cards angrily onto the queen. 'I've bust.'

Braumfels looked at the others. 'Anyone else want a card?'

'No.' Dessau's eyes searched the carriage. 'But I'm in need of a drink. Who's got the bottle?'

Burgmüller, who was still standing by the connecting door, spotted the bottle of Schnapps by his feet. He picked it up and handed it to Braumfels who in turn passed it over to Dessau.

'Thanks.'

While the game continued Dessau joined Burgmüller at one of the facing seats. 'What do you know about *Jagdgeschwader Nord*?'

'It's supposed to be one of the biggest set ups in the German Air Force.'

'Who's in charge?'

'The Hauptmann is called Hantelmann.'

'I've heard that name,' Crüger called out.

'And what have you heard?' Dessau filled his glass.

'Not a lot. But a man I flew with says he has a reputation for claiming other pilot's kills.'

Wülner looked shocked. 'I don't like the sound of that. It's hard enough getting a kill in the first place without the boss stealing it.'

'It's only a rumour,' Crüger assured him.

'Yeah, maybe. But there's never smoke without fire,' Anders pointed out.

'It doesn't make sense,' Dessau said. 'This outfit is an elite unit. It doesn't get to be that by being a den of cheats and thieves.'

'Who else is in it?' Anders asked.

Braumfels, now resigned to the fact that card playing was taking a back seat to speculation, decided to play his ace. 'I hear they've got an *Oberkanone* called Buchner.'

'Buchner!' Wülner was delighted. 'That's wonderful.'

Anders looked dubious. 'What's so special about him?'

'We trained together and served for a while in the same Jasta. He's a superb pilot and great company. I tell you, if he's in JGN there'll never be a dull moment.'

Without warning the train jerked and ground to a screeching halt. The lights in the carriage flickered and went out and Burgmüller cursed in the darkness.

'This God forsaken country doesn't want to let us go.'

****

Once again Buchner bent back his head to stare at the ceiling in exasperation.

'How much more of this is there, Fuchs?'

The pair of them had been at it all day and it looked as if they'd still be at it well into the evening. Buchner's chances of a few stiff drinks in the kasino were diminishing by the minute.

'We're nearly at the end, Herr Hauptmann.'

Buchner had heard that one before. He didn't believe it when he first heard it and he didn't believe it now. But as there was little to be gained from arguing the point he lowered his head and said, 'Okay. Carry on.'

'Well, as I was saying you'll have to look at the tables showing usage of aviation fuel on a daily basis. And that goes for ammunition as well. I'll check them before hand but you'll have to authorise them.

Then there are individual officer's Kasino bills. Those are dealt with fortnightly usually on a Friday. Again I'll check them beforehand and only draw your attention to any irregularities. Mondays are important. That's when...'

As Fuchs' voice droned on Buchner was transported back to his school days. Even as a child he found it impossible to concentrate on his lessons and he was struggling with the same problem now as he tried to focus on the seemingly endless business of running a *Jagdgeschwader*.

But although his mind was incapable of taking in all that he needed to know it was beginning to open up to one painful realisation; till this moment he'd had no idea just how difficult and involved a job it was to be a Hauptmann.

I'm gaining a respect for Hantelmann I never thought possible.

He had to write next of kin letters, deal with matters of discipline, authorise stoppages of pay, demotions and promotions, recommend citations and the award of medals. He had to sign off the combat diary for each of the Jastas, attend briefings and meetings with other *Geschwardern* Commanders as well as hold regular meetings with his own Jasta commanders.

He had to check the sick book and read the Medical Officer's weekly report, counter sign casualty reports, organise funerals and authorise the distribution of weekly pay. He had to check the armoury key book, check supply indents for fuel, food and ammunition, read the Chief Mechanic's Daily report and give authority for damaged aircraft to be struck off the roster.

He had to contact the air park for replacement pilots and aircraft, interview new pilots, organise their training and Jasta assignment, regularly review their progress and manage airfield repairs and construction.

Realising that his adjutant was still describing the things he had to do Buchner looked at him beseechingly. 'Surely you'll be doing most of this stuff, won't you?'

Fuchs gave his new commander an encouraging smile. 'Of course, Herr Hauptmann. But you'll still need to keep abreast of all that's going on. What if High Command needs to know something? They'll ask you not me.'

Buchner clapped his forehead in despair. 'Oh God! I'll never get the hang of it.'

Seeing his anguish Fuchs lent closer and adopted the persona of a father speaking to his son. 'That's exactly what I thought when I first took over as adjutant.'

'You did?'

'Yes. I hated the paperwork and all I wanted to do was get back up in the air. But in the end I got used to it. And, trust me, Herr Hauptmann, you will too. You may even grow to like it.'

This was not the sort of encouragement Buchner had hoped to hear. 'Get used to it! Grow to like it! Are you mad? That's the last thing I want. I don't want to get used to it or grow to like it. I'd sooner spend the rest of my days in an English prisoner of war camp.'

CHAPTER SIX

30 NOVEMBER 1917

After a day of intense tutoring Fuchs decided to turn theory into practice by scheduling the early morning for Buchner to look over some construction work being carried out on the lower airfield by a group of pioneers.

So as well as everything else I'm now an Inspector of Works.

Under some rigged lighting one body of men was on the path clearing away the broken glass and damaged timber and whatever else was destroyed during the recent British advance. In the field behind them another body of men was digging away the deep snow, uncovering the bomb craters gouged out of the earth by a flight of F2Bs. The pioneers were making good progress and it was hoped that the Group's machines would soon be able to land there once again.

Standing in the pre-dawn light beside Hauptmann Julian Achtstaten, the officer in charge of the pioneers, Buchner watched with little interest as men brought in fresh timber to lay wooden floors for the new huts they were erecting. But his thoughts were not on bomb craters or landing fields or wooden floors or even new huts. They were on the vagaries of friendship and popularity.

When von Abshagen first offered him temporary command of JGN Buchner's initial reaction was to turn it down. The very idea appalled him. He knew instinctively that he was not suited for such a role and as far as he was concerned it would have been worse than a slow death.

It took all von Abshagen's powers of persuasion to finally get Buchner to accept the post and then only on the firm understanding that when Hantelmann returned to Bois de Cheval he would resume his command and Buchner would take back his leadership of Jasta Buchner. But then the other officers got to hear of his promotion.

And they were full of praise and congratulations.

They told him that he would make an outstanding commander, a far better one than Hantelmann. They also told him that they trusted his judgement completely and that under his leadership JGN would rise to even greater heights of glory, becoming an elite unit with a score unmatched along the entire Western Front.

The backslapping was incessant.

And it culminated that first evening with one of the rowdiest celebrations ever held in the Kasino. All of the unit's remaining officers attended and once again Buchner found himself everyone's best friend, a position he had not occupied since before his argument with Hantelmann.

But it didn't last.

The change took place virtually overnight. And during the course of the following day Buchner found that their attitude toward him had cooled considerably. It wasn't just the normal distance one would expect between officers of different rank. There was a reluctance to approach him at all.

And a decided frostiness when they did.

At first this sudden reversal puzzled him but then it occurred to him that their former adulation had been motivated not out of regard for him, but by the fear of having some stranger foisted upon them, someone possibly keener on discipline than Hantelmann.

Better the devil you know. And I'm the devil they know.

There was a time when this would have bothered him. Even as a child being popular had been important to him and later as an officer he had thrived on the loud and raucous bonhomie of the Kasino. Part of him knew that it was all meaningless and superficial but, somehow, living in a world of ready smiles and harsh laughter had enabled him to maintain the illusion that those around him were friends.

Then came the clash with Hantelmann.

And all that he had believed about himself was thrown into doubt. But it was the death of his friend Frommherz that fundamentally changed his view of the world. Now he no longer regarded it as a place where everyone he met was necessarily on his side. Indeed, it seemed to him that he had never been quite as popular as he had imagined himself to be and that those he had considered his friends were nothing more than empty grins and mindless guffaws. And there was one realisation that hurt more than most.

If it hadn't been for Frommherz I wouldn't have had any friends at all.

The same applied to the popularity he had basked in and had come to believe was his own. It had been Frommherz' popularity.

But now he is gone I can see how this came about.

It had started with his clash with Hantelmann. At the time he had believed that he had the sympathy of the other officers. But he sacrificed it on the altar of his stubborn and inflexible nature. Despite good advice he would not relent nor would he compromise even when the military situation demanded it. And in the end he found himself held in equal contempt with Hantelmann.

Why should I be troubled?

He didn't need anyone else. He had never needed anyone else. All he had ever needed was a crowd of on-lookers to marvel at what he did. Yet there was something that was troubling him more than his lack of popularity or even his command of JGN. From an early age he had revelled in the knowledge that he feared nothing; not danger; not injury; not death. His fearlessness was part of the reason why he was such a consummate killer in the air.

It enabled him to size up a situation in an instant, to anticipate an opponent's every move and countermove, to act decisively and without hesitation, to kill without mercy and without remorse. And being a consummate killer was what separated him from everyone else. He took great pride in it. The death of his friend hadn't altered that. If anything it had, for a while, intensified his man-hunting skills into a frenzied and murderous spree.

He had killed and killed and it seemed that no amount of bloodletting would ever sate his appetite for vengeance. But now his wings had been clipped. Any opportunities of doing the one thing he excelled at had been taken away from him. A call that morning from von Abshagen had informed him that as a national hero he was far too precious to risk losing in a dogfight.

From now on I have to stay on the ground.

Having seen enough Buchner and the officer in charge of pioneers walked up the slope to the devastated chateau. Here a third body of men was restoring the noble building and the officer's kasino attached to it. The fact that this particular work was being carried out at all was down to Fuchs. He had argued vehemently with High Command that having a warm and friendly place for pilots to drink and unwind should be considered top priority. And he had the backing of every pilot on the base.

'How much longer will all of this take?' Buchner asked in a disinterested voice.

'Hard to say,' Achtstaten replied. 'I've had to split the men assigned to me into two groups.'

'These are not all of them?'

'No. I have a similar number of men repairing the air base at Trois Risseaux. It's in a worse state than this.'

'Given that the Kasino and chateau are not top of your list how long before we might expect to see them reopened?'

Achtstaten gave a show of doing some mental calculations before finally saying: 'Maybe four weeks for the Kasino, but the chateau could take much longer. We have to make sure it's structurally sound. Don't want the roof falling in on your officers while they're asleep, do we?'

'Quite.'

Buchner made an effort to sound concerned but inwardly he felt uninvolved and not in the least bothered whether his men's quarters were warm or not. He wasn't bothered whether the new huts went up or not. His inclination at that moment was to turn away and leave the whole matter in Achtstaten's more than capable hands.

He clearly knows what he's doing.

But then he remembered that Fuchs had told him that Achtstaten would regard his presence as a courtesy from one officer to another. With this in mind Buchner turned to him and said:

'Your men are doing wonders, Herr Hauptmann.'

'Kind of you to say so, Herr Hauptmann. Who knows, if all goes well we may have your airbase fully operational sooner than you think.'

'Splendid! Come! Let me buy you a drink.'

Hauptmann Achtstaten was somewhat startled by this invitation. 'A bit early, isn't it?'

'I was thinking of a coffee,' Buchner assured him.

They were making their way toward the huts clustered on one side of the upper field when the birds and the tranquil air were disturbed violently by the unmistakable roar of aero engines bursting into life. Warplanes were about to take off. And at the sound Buchner paused as he always did. It was the only thing that could still get his somnolent heart racing. But his heart was heavy with the knowledge that he could not take to the air with them.

****

Muffled and proofed against the cold the three pilots opened up their engines and took off in the early light when the sky is lucid and the ground still night dark. Three silver-bodied Pfalz climbed from the ice crisp earth, their black-beaks rising up to the sleeping clouds. And there they stayed as the broken chateau and the trackless forest of Cheval slipped into the shadows behind them.

But it wasn't long before the hidden world below began to respond to the intrusion of the sun. Attenuated cloud, stretched and pearl-pink, hung across the sky like chapped flesh. Frigid light infused the air and evaporated the ground shadows. Far below them frozen fields glared and sparkled and the River Auberne, its dark waters still choked with bodies, meandered across them like a deep fissure running through the surface of the snow.

Beyond the river lay the tree-enclosed clearing of Trois Risseaux where men laboured to repair the damage of war. Some miles further on stretched the sunken defences of the Western Front. Winter lay over it like a sheet of fine linen, masking its lineaments and softening its harsh edges. Even the hundreds of shell holes that scarred the earth's natural complexion for as far as the eye could see were now masked beneath a cleansing layer of white.

With this vista in view Leutnant Otto Bowski, leading the kette of hollow-bodied Pfalz, gently banked his machine to port and headed south, following the crenellated line of the German trenches beneath him. This was the start of the patrol. It would last some ninety minutes. During that time they would fly up and down the line ready to intercept any enemy machines bold enough to fly across no-man's-land.

Not that it seems likely.

Fuchs had warned them before they took off that enemy activity in the air would probably be non-existent. It was the same warning that he had been giving them for a number of days now. Besides, even if they spotted anything they were under standing orders not to engage.

We have too few machines to risk losing any more.

Despite this Bowski and his wingmen Leutnants Ulrich Staats and Fedor Bock, remained alert and watchful. Their training ensured that. And the cold air streaming into their faces kept them awake even though all they could think of was their warm beds back at the base.

It took ten minutes to reach the southern limit of their patrol. The point was marked by an L-shaped gully that cut through the trenches at an oblique angle, and here they turned their black beaks north and headed back along the same line of trenches. After fifteen minutes they reached the northern limit, which was marked by a battery of light artillery to the east. Here they turned south and headed back along the same line of trenches.

And so it goes on.

Each time they changed direction they turned their faces west, looking across no-man's-land to the enemy's front line. On a clear day like today it was possible to see British *Drachen* swinging in the breeze. Otherwise the western sky remained empty except for the salmon-streaked clouds. The bleak beauty of the view and the monotony of an uneventful patrol soon reduced the pilot's watchfulness and sense of danger.

Time to change the pace and shake things up a bit.

Sensing his own struggle to stay sharp Bowski threw his machine into a steep and sudden dive. He knew that Staats and Bock would follow, grateful for the break in routine. He continued diving, listening to the wooden frame of his machine creak in protest and the wind scream through the wires. The ground expanded in growing detail. The boards in the trenches could be seen and the faces of the sentries looking up in alarm. When satisfied that he had caused sufficient consternation, Bowski pulled back his stick and sent his Pfalz zooming back into the sky.

I bet that woke everyone up.

When he eventually levelled out at patrol height he reached out and touched the butts of his machine guns, reflecting wistfully that it had been so long since he last fired them that the bullets in the ammunition belts were probably frozen solid

Or they've become rusty like me.

To warm the barrels he jerked down the cocking levers and fired a short burst from each of the guns. Staats and Bock did the same with their guns. It was as well to make sure that they were functioning properly in case they should ever be needed.

Not that I've seen an enemy machine in days.

The skies had remained strangely empty so empty in fact that it seemed almost possible to imagine that the war had ended and that no one had bothered telling him. But he knew that this wasn't the case. The enemy was out there and in his frustration he looked to the west and shouted.

'Come on! Where the hell are you?'

But as no one appeared to meet his challenge he banked his machine and led his patrol back in the opposite direction feeling all the world like one of those palace guards who struts back and forth in a feathered helmet and operatic uniform.

With no other purpose in life than to look decorative.

Bored, he glanced at his watch. Still over half an hour to go. With a sigh, he looked over the side of his machine and tried to see what was going on in the trenches. From his current altitude it was hard to make out anything clearly. Not at first. But as he continued looking he began to discern movement, a man walking along a trench or a group of men talking or sharing a cigarette.

Oh, God, I wish Willi was leading us.

Life had been more exciting and unpredictable with Buchner as Jasta leader. Things happened! He made things happen. Even when the skies were empty like they were now he always managed to find the enemy no matter where he might be hiding.

Why did High Command put him in charge of JGN?

Bowski just couldn't understand the reasoning. It didn't make any sense. Buchner was a fighter and always would be. He was a fighter not an office Walla. Bowski could have told them that.

But when does anyone ever ask Bowski anything?

And clearly the change of role had not been good for Buchner either. Everyone could see that the burden of responsibility was beginning to weigh upon him. He was starting to show signs of becoming more remote and out of touch. The other officers were commenting on it. Why had he stopped joining in the celebrations at the kasino? And why was it that when he was seen he was wandering about the airfield.

As if lost in a dream.

Approaching the northern end of the patrol Bowski looked again at the Western sky and seeing it still empty he wondered what the enemy were up to not just in the air but on the ground. Had they all moved out of the area?

A strategic withdrawal to straighten their line?

Maybe all the troops were gone and their trenches were deserted. It seemed unlikely, but the thought was a compelling one. The truth of the matter lay not that far away. And all he had to do to settle the matter was turn to starboard, fly over no-man's-land and take a look. He glanced at his fuel gauge. The needle was twitching at the low end. Enough fuel to get him back to base but not enough to carry out a reconnaissance as well.

Time to turn for home, I think.

****

Having managed to extricate himself from Achtstaten's company Buchner lingered in front of the ruined chateau long enough to watch the approach and landing of three silver skinned Pfalz. Fuchs had insisted that he read that day's operational roster so that he would know what patrols would be out and who would be flying them. But Buchner didn't need a roster to know the names of the three pilots now coming in to land.

Bowski, Staats and Bock!

They all belonged to Jasta Buchner, his Jasta; although he wasn't so sure that it was his Jasta any longer. He hadn't flown with them since the death of Frommherz and he was expecting to get a call from High Command ordering him to hand leadership to someone else.

Feeling a pang of remorse he watched as the three machines descended out of the sky. And such was his deep affinity with the joys of flying every muscle in his arms and legs twitched and tensed as if it were him and not the three pilots bringing the machines down and landing them on the field of snow with whispered precision.

As the wheels of the three machines rolled to a halt he was suddenly tempted to stroll over and ask Bowski for a report. It would have been an excuse to chat and talk about familiar things. But even from where he stood he could see that there wouldn't be anything to report. All three machines were undamaged. Not a single bullet hole marred their pristine silver bodies or fragile canvas wings.

Another quiet day.

Part of him knew that this was as it should be. Every battle had to be followed by a period of calm and reflection, a time to bury and mourn, a time to take stock and plan. And there had been more than one battle recently. JGN had played a major part in all of them from the battle of Bayonet Ridge where the German attack had been thwarted, the battle for the forward airfield at Trois Risseaux where Hantelmann had shot down three F2Bs to the battle for Bois de Cheval itself.

Where Frommherz lost his life.

They had followed each other in such rapid succession High Command now referred to all three as the battle of Ste Helene. But that didn't alter the fact that the struggle had exhausted both armies to such an extent that there was, for the moment at least, no fight left in them.

Overcome by a feeling of weariness, Buchner turned his back on the three Pfalz taxiing across the landing field and wandered absently toward his temporary office, which was located amongst the various huts and tents that had been erected to the south east of the chateau. It wasn't much of an office but as he approached it he hoped it would be empty. All he wanted now was a quiet moment to himself.

****

When the sound of Bowski's patrol coming in to land reached Fuchs he went to the office window to check that all three machines had returned safely. It took no more than a glance to confirm that they had. He then turned away from the window and found himself once again regarding the problem that had been confronting him all morning. The office was in a mess. It had been for days.

And it's about time I started sorting it out.

Accepting that it was a chore he could not put off any longer he took in the general disorder that lay all around him. Most of it was stuff rescued from the old office that had been bombed out during the last British raid. There were a couple of blackboards that needed nailing to the wall and a map that needed hanging. There were also a number of large packing cases in the corner that contained personal files as well as records.

This office isn't much bigger than the packing cases.

Not that he had regarded the previous one too favourably. That had also been cramped. But at least it had the virtue of being orderly. This one was a mess and he hated sorting out mess.

Where does one begin?

Half-heartedly, he prised open the lid of one of the packing cases. Much to his surprise it wasn't full of files as he had expected, but miscellaneous odds and ends such as an ashtray, a pipe rack, a cigarette box, a glass carafe and various other non-military items. But what caught his attention were two pictures, a small one set in a silver frame and a much larger one in a heavy wooden frame.

I think I know what these are.

Slowly and carefully he lifted out each of the items surrounding the pictures, freeing them up sufficiently to remove them safely from the box. The smaller one came out first and Fuchs regarded it with mixed emotions.

Annaliese!

It was the sepia-tinted photograph of Hantelmann's beautiful but inconstant wife, the one that had stood on the former Hauptmann's desk, the one he had smashed during a particularly violent outburst.

Maybe I should send it to him in hospital.

Putting the framed photograph to one side Fuchs lifted the larger picture from the box. And as he did so he took on the look of someone greeting an old friend.

Ah, there you are. I thought I'd lost you for good.

It was the stern and forbidding portrait of his Excellency Generaloberst Maximillian von Hoeppner, the one that used to hang behind Fuchs' desk in the old office until the English buried it beneath a pile of wooden boards and corrugated metal. But to Fuchs it was more than just a portrait of one of Germany's highest general officers; it was a talisman, a good luck charm that he turned to whenever it looked like he might need a helping hand.

And I could certainly do with your help right now.

With a fond smile Fuchs recalled a time not so long ago when he turned to the Generaloberst for assistance such as when Hantelmann went out on patrol and Fuchs would stand before the portrait and offer up a prayer that the Hauptmann's return might be delayed indefinitely.

Now I'd give anything to see that bastard come through the door.

Holding the large portrait with due deference Fuchs looked about the office trying to decide where best to place it. He looked at each wall in turn and was still trying to make up his mind when Buchner walked in. For a brief moment the two men regarded each other in total silence. Fuchs' face remained neutral but it was clear from Buchner's expression that he was far from pleased to see his adjutant.

He never is these days.

In an attempt to give his presence some value Fuchs rested the portrait against a wall and snatched up a couple of letters from his desk.

'Ah, Herr Hauptmann.' Fuchs thrust them in Buchner's direction. 'These were delivered a short while ago.'

Eyeing them suspiciously Buchner asked, 'Who are they from?'

Choosing the one he thought might lift Buchner's mood Fuchs held out a white envelope. 'Well, I think this might be from your mother.'

The stratagem failed dismally. If anything Buchner's mood darkened as he took the letter and, without even troubling to glance at it, stuffed it into his pocket.

'And the other?'

No longer so sure that anything could raise Buchner's spirits Fuchs examined the second letter, which was in a brown envelope.

'It's from the Convalescent Hospital in Hecksau.'

'Hecksau!' Buchner's eyes opened wide, and for the first time they were lit with a spark of interest. 'Isn't that the hospital where Hauptmann Hantelmann was sent?'

'Yes, I believe it is.'

Snatching the letter from Fuchs, Buchner tore it open, barely able to restrain his growing excitement. If this was what he hoped it might be, if it was indeed a message from Hantelmann, it could well contain news that he was now fully recovered and would be returning shortly to resume his command at Bois de Cheval.

The envelope contained a single sheet of notepaper, which he unfolded. It was indeed a message from Hantelmann, but the two short hand-written paragraphs didn't contain good news. Although Hantelmann was on the road to recovery his doctors had advised him that it might yet be another month or so before he could expect to be fit enough to return to his duties at JGN.

Shaking his head despondently Buchner muttered, 'I'm not sure I can wait that long.'

'I'm sorry, Herr Hauptmann. What did you say?'

'Nothing, Fuchs. I was just talking to myself.'

'Can I get you anything?'

'No. Just carry on with whatever you were doing.'

Sensing Buchner's need for solitude Fuchs tried to think of some task he could offer as an excuse to get out of the office. But in the end he was saved the trouble. At that moment the door opened in a most dramatic fashion and the day lit entrance was filled with the bulk of two officers, their greatcoat collars raised against the cold.

In the half-light and with their faces in shadow it was difficult to make out who they were, but there was something undeniably familiar about them, something that demanded recognition. Not waiting for an invitation they both marched smartly into the office making no effort to disguise their limps. Then, beaming like Cheshire cats, they snapped to attention, clicked their heels and cut the air with a sharp salute.

'Oberleutnants Röth and Reinhard reporting for duty, Herr Hauptmann.'

****

Buchner could hardly contain his joy.

'My God! Kurt! Albert! I never thought I'd ever be so pleased to see anyone as I am you two reprobates.'

Röth turned to Reinhard, his face full of mock indignation. 'Do you hear that? Reprobates he calls us.'

Reinhard matched Röth's offended air. 'And to think of all the trouble we took to get here.'

Feeling in better spirits than he had for days Buchner wanted to catch up with the two men straightaway, but the telephone intervened. Fuchs answered it and after a minute of listening he put his hand over the mouthpiece and addressed Buchner.

'It's Hauptmann Achtstaten, the officer in charge of Pioneers. He says they've struck a problem with the chateau and he wants to speak to you before proceeding.'

Buchner cursed then thinking better of it told Fuchs, 'Oh, all right. Tell him I'll be there in a minute.' He then turned to his two friends. 'I shouldn't be too long. Would you rather wait here or in the Kasino?'

Fuchs put the phone down.

'Leave them to me Herr Hauptmann. I'll take them to the Kasino. I'm sure they'd welcome a cooked breakfast.'

The matter that the officer in charge of pioneers needed to discuss was more complicated and time consuming than Buchner had imagined and it was a good hour before he finally got back to the Kasino.

'Fuchs!' Buchner called out as he entered the large double hut that now acted as a temporary mess for the officers. 'A bottle of your best champagne.'

As usual Fuchs had anticipated his commanding officer's wishes. A bottle of champagne was already sitting in an ice bucket and four glasses were standing ready. Not only that but he had also managed to dig out a box of the finest Havana cigars. Chairs were pulled up and soon everyone was settled cosily.

Buchner raised his glass. 'To the old crew!'

'The old crew!'

The glasses were emptied then quickly refilled.

'So what have you two been up to?'

Röth smiled. 'Besides chasing nurses?'

Buchner laughed, delighted to be in the company of old friends. 'Well, there are no nurses here, but there's plenty of Sopwith Camels. Both your Jastas will be delighted to see you back.'

It was Reinhard's turn to cast a searching glance. He looked toward Röth then back to Buchner.

'Well, we're not exactly back as such.'

Buchner frowned and looked at each of them in turn. 'I'm not sure I understand.'

Reinhard continued. 'We're out of hospital but we won't be cleared for active service until we've completed a period of convalescence.'

Buchner started to look anxious. 'How long is that going to take?'

In a quiet voice Röth said, 'About a month.'

'A month!' Buchner nearly sprang out of his chair then he fell back looking utterly crestfallen. 'But you can't just kick your heels for a month.'

Röth brightened. 'Oh, we won't be. We've been assigned to the Jasta Schule at Valenciennes to show the new boys how it's done.'

'How what's done?'

'Combat tactics and all that stuff.'

During the exchange Reinhard had been watching Buchner closely and what he saw troubled him. Clearly something was not right. Changing the subject seemed the best way of getting to the bottom of it.

'Anyway, old friend,' he began. 'What's it like being in charge?'

It was the right question to ask. It made Buchner wince and his face visibly tightened. After knocking back his second glass of champagne he screwed up his face and shook his head.

'Ah God!' he lamented as he recharged his glass. 'High Command made a terrible mistake when they put me in charge. It should have been you Reinhard. And the other officers would have preferred you to me. I know it.'

Reinhard shook his head and smiled. 'Nonsense! You have as much seniority and experience as I do. Besides, the preferences of the other officers are not the point at issue. You're here to lead not win a popularity contest.'

'But that's the point. I'm not suited for command of a unit as big as JGN. It's just an endless round of censoring letters, holding Pay Parades and inspecting the men's quarters. I hate it.'

'It's still early days. Give it a chance.'

'I don't want to give a chance.' A look of desperation came into his eyes as he turned them upon Reinhard. 'You've got a much sharper brain than I have, Kurt. All of this paperwork would suit you down to the ground.'

Reinhard scoffed. 'Thanks for the complement.'

'Why not tell all this to High Command, Willi?' Röth suggested.

'I did! I spoke to the Generaloberst's adjutant. I told him that I didn't want command of JGN. All I wanted was to be given back command of my old Jasta and get on with fighting the war.'

'And?'

'And nothing. He told me that after shooting down Harker I had become a national hero.'

'We know,' Reinhard said. 'We've seen the newspapers.'

'That's all well and good, but von Abshagen told me that being a national hero means that I'm too precious to be risked in combat.'

'For a while maybe. But you know how these things work. The novelty will soon wear off.'

'He also told me I may well be called upon to tour Germany and other air bases giving speeches and pep talks.'

Röth nodded sympathetically. 'That does sound awful.'

'It is awful. Bloody awful.'

Buchner fell silent and the others followed suit. Then he thought of something more to say. 'You know, after I told High Command it would be all right for the English to search for Harker's body a strange notion came to me. It occurred to me that it's always a bad idea to kill one's greatest opponent. I'm only now beginning to realise just how bad it can be.'

CHAPTER SEVEN

2 DECEMBER 1917

Having worked like a dog over the past couple of days making sure that JGN could get along without him for a short while Fuchs at last managed to find time to visit Hantelmann in Hecksau Hospital. With all that he'd had to do he hadn't been able to telephone ahead. He could only trust to luck that once he got there his visit wouldn't encounter any unforeseen difficulties.

The first sign that his visit would be less than straightforward came when he pulled the staff car into the Hospital forecourt and found it already packed with motor vehicles. After parking around the side of the building he walked back to the entrance and was about to put his foot on the first of the stone steps when the hospital's main doorway suddenly filled with a crowd of people.

What the hell's this? An evacuation?

He quickly discarded this idea. As well as being orderly the crowd appeared to be quite unhurried. Their movements were leisurely and their conversation though animated was for the most part jocular.

Quite the Sunday promenade.

As Fuchs stepped aside to let them pass he began to distinguish between them. First down the steps were the journalists and reporters. They were followed by a coterie of military and civilian officials. Fuchs recognised von Abshagen among them. But he only truly got an inkling of what was going on when the rear of the group appeared. Centre stage was Annaliese Hantelmann, tall and elegant and wearing a hat that nearly didn't fit through the door. Male admirers surrounded her, but her lover took pride of place. Hantelmann's daughter, Sophie, stood behind Annaliese.

Looking lost and bewildered.

Knowing what was expected of her Annaliese posed for the photographers at the top of the steps. Obviously a man of discretion her lover removed himself some distance away so that he would not appear standing beside her on the front pages of tomorrow's newspapers. Camera flashlights exploded, Annaliese's practiced smile was captured for posterity and finally the gathered assembly dispersed to their waiting motor vehicles. With the way ahead clear Fuchs climbed the stone steps and entered what was now a comparatively quiet hospital.

I wonder what the Hauptmann has to say about this.

****

The gods are cruel.

And as he lay in the aftermath of what should have been his greatest moment Hantelmann pondered in awe just how intricate that cruelty could be. Its latest expression began that very morning when the telephone was brought to his bedside and an official voice informed him he was to receive the Iron Cross.

And not before time.

But any sense of entitlement he may have felt lasted less than a minute for in the next breath the unseen voice told him that the ceremony would be performed later that very morning and would take place at Hantelmann's bedside. This was intolerable. How could anyone think it right that a war hero should be subjected to such an undignified proceeding? Not willing to take it lying down so to speak Hantelmann protested loudly and vociferously.

But I might as well have saved my breath.

He was told that the matter had been considered thoroughly by those at High Command with a special concern for public relations. It was their opinion that the German people felt greater sympathy for their heroes when they saw them lying in a hospital bed recovering from their wounds.

So that was that.

With the imminent arrival of the presentation party and the press there was no time to waste. Hantelmann barely had time to draw breath before three hefty nurses appeared as if by magic. Without ceremony they bundled him out of his bed, washed him, shaved him and dressed him in a freshly pressed uniform.

The bed was remade and I was told to lie on it.

Shortly after that the press burst into the ward, disturbing the patients as they set up their photographic equipment. Then three senior officers arrived; they were the presentation party. To Hantelmann's annoyance von Hoeppner was not among them. He had sent his adjutant von Abshagen to perform the ceremony in his stead.

The bastard couldn't even be bothered.

But the cruelty of the gods had only just started. They still had something rather special up their sleeves, something that was guaranteed more than anything else to cause Hantelmann maximum horror and embarrassment.

My adoring wife Annaliese.

She entered the ward a minute or so after the presentation party and did so in such a manner as to give everyone there the impression that they were there for her benefit and not Hantelmann's. But how was it that she was there in the first place?

Someone must have tipped the bitch off.

There being no other explanation Hantelmann vowed that he would establish the identity of the guilty party if it was the last thing he ever did. But therein lay a problem. Most people would have had only one or two suspects to choose from. Hantelmann, by his very nature, suspected almost everyone he knew.

Behind Annaliese stood her latest lover, a heavyset man whose cast of features was distinctly bovine. And behind him at a respectful distance stood a number of her other male admirers. But for Hantelmann there was one bright spot in all this gloom.

The sight of my daughter.

He gave her smile and she smiled back and then the presentation ceremony began. It was mercifully brief. Von Abshagen read out the citation and after that he pinned the Iron Cross to Hantelmann's uniform tunic. There then followed for Hantelmann a moment of exquisite humiliation.

I had to shake hands with him.

Throughout the entire ceremony Hantelmann had kept his right hand out of sight. He even refused to lift it to help von Abshagen when he was having difficulty pinning on the medal. And for a moment it looked as if he might get away with it. But after the medal was securely in place von Abshagen extended his hand. Hantelmann was thrown into an excruciating dilemma one made even worse by the fact that the cameras were now poised to record the solemn moment. What was he to do? He couldn't refuse to shake the man's hand. It would be a terrible show of bad manners.

But if I did shake it the whole world everyone would see my trembling hand.

In the end he accepted that he didn't really have any choice. He seized von Abshagen's hand and shook it with all the force of a cobra throttling its prey. The cameras flashed. Hantelmann withdrew his hand and the matter was done. There only remained some questions from the press, a few remarks from von Abshagen and a parting smile of sweet insincerity from Annaliese. Even his meeting with Sophie was brief. They barely had time to embrace and exchange a few words before Sophie's mother called her away.

Within minutes I was alone with my Iron Cross.

He removed the medal from the breast of his tunic and put it back in its presentation box hoping that the cruelty of the gods had ended. But they weren't. What he couldn't yet know was that they had saved their most tender mercy till last for it was at this moment that Fuchs appeared.

****

'Fuchs! What a sight for sore eyes.'

And as far as it went the sentiment expressed was a genuine one. Hantelmann was delighted to see his old adjutant if for no other reason than he was a valuable source of information about what was going on at Bois de Cheval. Fuchs, for his part, was somewhat taken aback by his former commander's welcome. He wasn't entirely sure how he would be greeted but he certainly hadn't expected to be treated like a long lost friend. Somewhat cautiously he approached Hantelmann's bedside.

'Don't just stand there, man. Take a seat!'

Fuchs obeyed. Then as he sat there Hantelmann stared at him expectantly as if waiting for some important disclosure. Feeling his discomfort increasing by the second he finally blurted out:

'And how are you, Herr Hauptmann?'

'I'm fine,' Hantelmann responded somewhat defensively. 'Why? Do I not look fine?'

'No, quite the opposite. Seeing you as you are I was wondering why you're still in hospital.'

'Really!' Hantelmann gave Fuchs a dubious look, suspicious that his former adjutant might be 'taking the piss'. Only when he had satisfied himself that he wasn't did he finally relax. 'Well, Fuchs, I keep asking myself the very same question. And, to be honest, being stuck in this bed is sucking the strength out of me.'

'Have you told the doctors this?'

'Till I'm blue in the face. I tell them it's a waste of time keeping me here and that I'm only taking up a bed someone else might need more than me. In fact, only the other day I threatened to get dressed and walk out.'

'What did they say to that?'

'They told me that I could do as I wished, but that they wouldn't clear me as fit for active duty.'

'Sounds worse than prison.'

'I suppose it does.' Hantelmann sat pensively for a moment then made an effort to buck up. 'Well, how are things with the unit?'

Knowing Hantelmann was bound to ask this Fuchs was on his guard. 'Oh, quiet. There's been little activity on the front.'

'What about your new commander. How's he getting on?'

Here was the heart of Hantelmann's interest. He wanted to know how Buchner was coping with his new command. He was hoping also to hear that he was making a complete hash of it.

'He's only temporary commander, Herr Hauptmann,' Fuchs said, hoping that this reply would kill two birds with one stone; it would flatter Hantelmann whilst at the same time divert the conversation away from Buchner. 'He's only filling in till you get back.'

The flattery worked, but Hantelmann was not entirely mollified. There was something he'd been itching to say for ages and by god he wasn't going to hold back any longer. 'Whatever possessed High Command to pick that idiot?'

Fuchs, ever the diplomat, decided that he could safely treat this question as if it was a rhetorical one and thereby ignore it. 'At the entrance I saw the press and some senior officers leaving. Am I safe in assuming that they were here to present you with the Iron Cross?'

'Yes, they were.' Without enthusiasm Hantelmann turned his head toward the medal sitting in its box as if indicating to a nurse the bedpan he had just finished using. 'And there it is.'

'You must be very proud, Herr Hauptmann.'

'You would think so, wouldn't you? After all, it's not every day that a man is awarded such a medal.'

Struggling valiantly to find a lighter topic of conversation Fuchs almost blundered into the error of mentioning that he had seen Hantelmann's wife. Skidding clear of this particular pothole his wheels found firmer ground. 'I saw your daughter.'

Hantelmann brightened. 'Yes. She's growing into quite a beautiful young woman, isn't she?'

Fuchs smiled. 'It must have cheered you to see her.'

Hantelmann's face darkened. 'At least she made the effort to be here unlike some I could mention.'

'I'm not sure I understand, Herr Hauptmann.'

'When one is honoured with an Iron Cross one would have expected the Generaloberst to come and present it.'

'Oh, I see. Well, that may have not been entirely his fault, Herr Hauptmann.'

'What do you mean?'

'Today is his daughter's nineteenth birthday. I rather think he may be attending that.'

'Maybe,' Hantelmann replied, but he was clearly unconvinced. He knew that von Hoeppner had little time for him and that any excuse would have sufficed for not attending the presentation.

At this point Fuchs began to wonder whether it was time for him to leave. He had done his duty. He had visited his former commander and a thoroughly draining experience it had been. But being the man he was Fuchs was determined to depart on a high note by saying something encouraging.

'Well, what is done is done. All you need concentrate on now, Herr Hauptmann is making a full recovery. The sooner you are back at JGN the better. And I'm sure you're eager to get back into your cockpit and shoot down another brace of English.'

****

Hantelmann didn't say a word as Fuchs departed. He wasn't even aware that Fuchs had gone. But his parting words had left Hantelmann with plenty to ponder. It was what he had said about climbing back into his cockpit and shooting down another brace of English. Those words had struck a chord within him. They touched upon a vision of himself that he had been playing over and over in his mind for the last few days.

It had begun as no more than idle musing. Confined to his bed as he was, with little to occupy the endless hours, he had tried to while away the time by daydreaming on past times and activities he found pleasant. As love and sex were not things he set great store by he was left with flying as the only activity capable of exciting his sluggish passions. So it was that when the ward fell silent he would lie back and close his eyes.

Being a methodical man he would start his fantasies at the beginning. He would form a picture of himself dressed in his flying gear striding manfully across the landing field toward his black-beaked Pfalz, the one with the Gorgon's head painted on its silver fuselage. And as it was his fantasy he had all the other pilots in JGN form a sort of hedge of honour, saluting and cheering as he made his way to the canvas hangars.

All went well until he reached his machine. Here he did as he always did; he put one foot on the edge of the lower wing and reached up to take hold of the cockpit's leather collar. Tensing the muscles of his body he prepared to lift himself from the ground.

But for some reason nothing happens.

Hantelmann thought nothing of it the first time it happened. He put it down to a change in mood, a sudden desire to think of other things, which is what he did. But when it happened again he found that he could not dismiss it so easily. And when it happened again and again he knew that there had to be some reason for it.

And what made it worse was that at such moments a sense of unease crept upon him, a feeling of dread and nausea that was as alien to his nature as it was repellant. And try as he might he could not get his imagined self to rise from the grass and climb into the cockpit. In the end he avoided the daydream all together, fearful that fate was playing him another dirty trick.

The gods are cruel.

Crueler than he suspected. For sure they had given him what he most desired. They had given him fame and standing among his peers. They had replaced his unwelcome reputation with one of tenacity and valour. His name was now one to be reckoned with. His bedside table was strewn with flowers and letters from well-wishers and admirers. Dignitaries and journalists had visited him and his face adorned the front pages of magazines and newspapers.

All of this the gods had given him. They had been more than generous, but he should have known that one never gets something for nothing. Everything has a cost and in this instance it proved to be something far more terrible than a trembling hand. At the very moment of becoming the hero he knew himself to be, at the very moment of his apotheosis the gods took away his courage. And they lifted it from him with such deftness that he still had no idea it was gone.

Some men might have faced up to the possibility that something was seriously amiss, that their nerve had gone and they were no longer able to face danger, but Hantelmann was not that sort of man. His entire life rendered him incapable of admitting to weakness of any sort, to himself or to anyone else. Instead, whenever such thoughts stole upon him he brushed them aside as one might brush aside a troublesome insect.

His frustration turned to resolve. Why was he still lying there? His wound was healed. It was time for him to stop playing the injured hero and get back to his command at Bois de Cheval. He had tasted glory. He was eager for more. But he wouldn't get that in hospital. And now that High Command had put Buchner in charge he had an added reason for wanting to return to his command.

****

Ah! Here we are again. This is becoming a bad habit.

Just over two weeks had elapsed since her last visit to the Residenz and for the Baroness von Buchner the sense of déjà vu was palpable. Everything was exactly as she remembered it. The only noticeable difference was the motor traffic filing up to the entrance. It was decidedly more youthful.

As well as the usual stately Cadillacs, Mercedes and Lancias there were also spritely two-seaters such as a baby Peugeot, and an emerald green Prosper-Lambert, a blood red Opel Doktorwagen, a caramel brown Delahaye and a light blue Le Zebre Phaeton with ribbed red leather upholstery.

As Erich, her manservant brought the petrol blue Daimler TC45 with its silver radiator and eagle mascot to a halt in the snow-covered drive outside the building she pondered yet again her reasons for returning so soon to this place, a place she detested above all others.

Nor do I have much love for costume balls.

Even with all its tall windows ablaze with warmth and enticement and its grounds packed with the gay laughter of guests trailing their way excitedly up the stone steps she now saw the Residenz differently. She alone knew that behind its flat stone façade lay a secret long suppressed, a secret so terrible it made her shudder whenever she thought of it, a shudder of fury and revulsion.

I suppose I could always burn the place down.

When she first got the invitation her inclination had been to tear it up. But then later her British handler contacted her and ordered her to attend. It appeared that the information she had provided about von Hoeppner's movements close to the Eastern Front set off alarm bells.

Seems he may have been on his way to Russia.

This on its own was of minor consequence but when added to the growing suspicion that Germany was negotiating an Armistice with the Russians it could be of vital importance. Such an Armistice, if it came about, would allow Germany to release a vast army of men from the east to reinforce their forces on the western front.

So again I'm to sniff around the Archduke's library and find out what he's up to.

The prospect was not an enticing one. At the very least it was highly dangerous and she would certainly face a firing squad if caught. After all, she was meant to be one of von Hoeppner's agents spying on the English not a double-agent spying on him. But in the end her decision to attend the costume party had nothing to do with espionage. If for no other reason an evening's mindless distraction might help take her mind off her troubled son, Willi.

His life recently hasn't been a happy one.

It had started with that business with Hantelmann, his commanding officer. On that occasion he got arrested for insubordination and only by her intercession had he avoided being court-martialled.

Then there was the death of his friend Frommherz.

He was inconsolable and for a while it looked as if the depth of his grief would unhinge his mind. But Thetis knew what would relieve his torment. Combat! He needed to take to the skies and seek vengeance.

So I got Hermann to build him a new machine.

But then an opportunity arose to help her son a third time and here she got it badly wrong. Calling in favours she got him the command of *Jagdgeschwader Nord*. But in doing this she had consulted only her own desires and not his. She wanted him safe. He didn't.

Now he is refusing to speak to me.

But distraction and espionage weren't the only reasons for her presence at Anthea's costume ball. Those were the reasons she brought with her. But as a footman opened the door of the Daimler for her to get out Thetis felt something more primitive stir within her. The feeling was not a new one. It was the same feeling she had felt during her last visit to the Residenz. And the feeling was not a feeling. It was a pulsing need for revenge.

Maybe that's the real reason I'm here.

Even the heavy and elaborate costume she had chosen to wear seemed to suggest that she had come with some darker motive. It was the tunica talaris and blue dalmatic of a tenth century Byzantine Empress, in this instance the Empress Theophano.

Notorious for poisoning her husband Emperor Romanus II.

She had taken great care to be as accurate as possible with the pattern on the scarlet paludamentum, the jewels on the blue, green and gold tablion, the pearl-sewn edges on her scarlet shoes and the double string pendant pearls hanging from her pie-shaped crown. She had even dressed her hair appropriately, parting it from the centre and turning it back in a roll on either side of her face.

What I hadn't bargained on was how difficult it would be to get in and out of a motor vehicle.

It was a struggle indeed and, in the end, Erich and a footman had to each take an arm to pull her free. Despite the indignity of her entrance, however, as soon as she was standing in the cold night air she looked every inch an Empress, her manner haughty and indifferent. She put on the mask Erich handed her but before she began her ascent of the circular stone steps to the entrance she paused to look up at the elevation of the building looming above her and there was a hint of sardonic humour to her mouth and eyes.

Didn't someone once say that criminals always return to the scene of the crime? So why not the victims?

****

97

Now that Thetis had accepted her heart's true impulse, the real reason for her presence at a place she hated, the thought followed her up the stone steps and into the building. And it stayed with her as she crossed the floor of the Grand Foyer with its three crystal chandeliers and recently installed sculpted figure of Aphrodite pouring water into a stone bowl.

It was still with her as she ascended the broad carpeted stairway to the wide gallery above and stepped through the black marble columns and over the white tiled floor of the Empyrean with its mosaic of an eagle clutching a double-headed axe in its claws. And now that her heart was set on vengeance in one form or another she actually felt quite excited by the challenges she faced.

It reminded her of the days when she was undertaking some mission on von Hoeppner's behalf. Often it involved seducing some foreign general or diplomat before searching for state secrets while he slept.

Only now I do it for the British.

This reminder was timely. She was there on a mission not a personal vendetta. And as she reached the balustrade overlooking the Grand Hall she concluded that when all was said and done there was little she could do anyway. She was not armed with any sort of weapon and although the idea of killing von Hoeppner in front of his guests appealed to her sense of drama it had little else in its favour. But then the thought of doing him some harm just wouldn't go away.

And a little bit of mischief might liven up the evening.

Slowly descending the stairs into the crowded Grand Hall she knew that whatever she chose to do she had to be careful not to leave any clue that she was the perpetrator. She had to appear innocent of any involvement. It was also prudent not to target von Hoeppner directly. He was too wily not to sniff out any plot against him. And there was little point going after his small-minded wife Hedda.

He would probably help me himself if he knew she were the target.

She discounted von Hoeppner's son Hermann. He was her friend. But his headstrong, ungovernable daughter Anthea was a different matter entirely. She was the apple of her father's eye. Any harm to her would cause him untold grief.

Anthea it shall be then.

Having made her decision, Thetis paused halfway down the staircase and surveyed the gathering, trying to single out her potential victim from the rest of the guests as they mingled in the Grand Hall.

Nothing much has changed since I was last here.

The orchestra was situated at the northern end of the Hall. But now its position had been elevated from the floor of the hall to the newly reopened Minstrel's Gallery. At the southern end of the Hall was the buffet table.

Serving the same food.

The crowd was not a large one, but as this was a costume ball to celebrate Anthea's nineteenth birthday the guests were generally younger.

Much as it was on my nineteenth birthday party.

Setting aside all thought of that ill-fated occasion she cast a critical eye over the assembly and was struck by the variety and flamboyance of the costumes on display. At the last ball she had attended the Hall had been a sea of stiff-collared uniforms and epaulettes, bosoms and feathered hats, glinting medals and iridescent gowns. Now all she could see was a pageant of fashions across the ages from Ionic Chitons to gowns with bustles and under-skirts.

There were leather corslets, purple mitres, Corinthian helmets, Phrygian caps, purple edged togas and silk stolas, gilded cuirasses, linen wimples, lavender-blue doublets, coral-pink bodices, gauze ruffs, Spanish farthingales, tricorne hats, pompadour wigs, muslin gowns with puff sleeves and flowered bonnets.

Some were dressed as bishops others famous courtesans. There were notable figures from history, fiction, fantasy and mythology. There were two Cleopatras; one escorted by Caesar the other by Mark Anthony. There was Alexander the Great and his wife Roxanna, a New Kingdom Pharoah, a Teutonic warrior, an Assyrian King and Queen, a North American Indian Chief and a Roman gladiator.

Spotting Anthea amongst all this isn't going to be easy.

And the task was made that much harder by the fact that, as well as exotic costumes, everyone had their eyes covered by a mask. But it was not impossible. Not for Thetis. She was a keen observer of those singular human traits, voice, gesture and movement that set one person apart from another. Another vital clue was choice of costume.

What would Anthea wear? Who would she come as?

Anthea had a nature that was martial and belligerent. Whatever she chose it would definitely be war-like.

A warrior queen or maybe some spear carrying Amazon.

CHAPTER EIGHT

2 DECEMBER 1917

Staring at herself in the full-length mirror, Anthea could barely contain her excitement. She was in the process of getting into her party costume and now wore a collar-less white blouse, which, with the binding of her breasts, gave her figure a more masculine outline. Her slim legs were encased in soft grey breeches held up by braces and tucked into a pair of highly polished black leather boots. The ensemble was coming together, the transformation was taking place.

'How do I look?'

Helga giggled. 'With your hair cut so short, my Lady, you look like a young teenage boy.'

'Bring me the tunic.'

Helga lifted the Prussian officer's red-piped field grey tunic from its hanger and holding it by the shoulder boards brought it over to her mistress. Extending her arms behind her to receive the garment, Anthea pushed her hands through one sleeve and then the other until they appeared again out of the turn-back cuffs. Helga settled the tunic on Anthea's shoulders, taking care not to disturb the shoulder boards with their silver piping and gilt metal propeller insignia.

She then walked round to the front of her mistress and did up the seven silver buttons that fastened the tunic from its waist to the black-piped stand collar that bore silver double *Litzen* on each side of the throat. Lastly Helga wound a silver and black brocade dress belt around Anthea's waist fastening the round clasp over the lowest of the tunic's buttons.

'Not so tight!' Anthea complained. 'I don't want to draw attention to my hips.'

'I'm sorry, my Lady.' Helga made the adjustment then stepped away so that her mistress could once again admire herself in the mirror.

'Bring me the cap.'

'Here it is, my Lady.'

Helga handed over the soft red-piped field cap with its grey crown, black band and grey visor. Anthea placed it carefully on her short blonde hair making sure that the black, white and red button cockade on the crown was in line with the black and white button cockade on the band.

Fully clothed Anthea took a step back from the mirror. 'There! How do I look now?'

'The uniform fits your slim figure to perfection, my Lady. But there is something missing.'

'Missing?'

'Yes. I think you need to put something down the front of those trousers.'

'What do you mean?' Anthea crackled.

'A bulge, my Lady.'

'A bulge? What sort of a bulge?'

'A man's bulge.'

'A man's bulge. Why would I want such a thing?'

'Every man has one, my Lady.'

'Nonsense! No one will notice whether I have a bulge or not.'

'The men might. They always glance down there.'

'Really? Do they? How odd. Well, I'll just have to risk it. What do you think? Could I pass myself off as a pilot?'

Helga giggled. 'An extremely pretty one, my Lady.'

'Silly girl!' Anthea frowned. 'I'm not supposed to look pretty. I'm supposed to look handsome.'

'You do! You do look handsome.' Helga rushed over to brush away some lint from the back of Anthea's tunic. 'Like one of those heroes we hear about. And that cap sits upon your head so rakishly all the fine ladies will want to take you to bed. And all the men, especially when they see that adorable bottom of yours.'

'Don't get carried away, Helga. My only purpose this evening is to fool people into believing I'm an airman. I'll be happy if I succeed in that.'

'You will, my Lady. I have no doubt.' Helga raised her fingers above Anthea's high collar and touched the hair at the nape of her neck. 'But it's such a pity that you had to get your beautiful hair cut so short.'

Wrenching her head away, Anthea turned to face Helga. 'And how may I ask would I ever pass myself off as a member of the German Air Service with hair hanging down to my waist? You talk such nonsense at times, you really do.'

'I'm sorry, my Lady.'

'Make yourself useful. There's a blue box on my dressing table. Bring it to me.'

While Anthea continued assessing her appearance in the mirror Helga scurried off to fetch the box. She found it beside a small crystal dish in which Anthea kept her jewellery.

'This is a lovely box. Is it a gift?'

'It is. Bring it here.'

Helga carried it over to her mistress as though it were a sacred offering. 'Who is it from?'

'Oberleutnant Reinhard.'

Helga opened the box and gasped. 'A pilot's badge.'

'That's right.'

Helga's eyes shifted to the other object in the box. 'Will you be wearing this as well, my Lady?'

'Wearing what?'

'This Iron Cross.'

'Of course I will. I need to wear both of them if the effect is to be convincing.'

Even if you haven't earned either.

But Helga kept this thought to herself as she lifted the badge and the medal out of the box and carried them to her mistress.

'Pin the badge on my left side an inch or so above the tunic's waist. Just there will do. Good. Now place the medal about an inch above the badge. A little higher! Careful with that pin! Good! Good! Now how does that look?'

Helga stepped back. 'Oh, my Lady. I would doubt that even your own mother would recognise you.'

'Splendid!' Jerking down the hem of her tunic, Anthea pulled back her shoulders and lifted her chin above her high collar. 'I think the time has come to make my entrance.'

****

'I'm going to look ridiculous in this.'

Surrounded by servants Maximillian von Hoeppner stood before his wife's full-length mirror and what he saw there pleased him not at all. His tall and corpulent frame was covered from ankle to shoulders in a flowing white robe. As if this wasn't bad enough he had sandals on his big feet, a voluminous wig of golden curls, which made his large head look twice as large, and a long, broad beard of similar makeup. Perched on top of the wig was a golden crown.

'Who am I supposed to be?'

'The god Jupiter, dear. And I'm your wife Hera.'

Hedda's outfit was almost identical in every detail to her husband's differing only in its feminine touches and lack of beard. The reason for this striking resemblance between the costumes was because she had chosen them, a fact that was not improving von Hoeppner's disposition.

'Really! Then I'll look like an idiot and you'll look like the wife of an idiot.'

'Not at all, sweetest,' she said with a smile of calculated affection. 'You'll look magnificent.'

Von Hoeppner hadn't failed to notice his wife's high spirits, something so rare he was determined to find out what was causing it.

'You're being particularly joyous.'

'Am I dear?'

'Yes, you are. You're up to something.' Then he had an amusing idea. 'You haven't got yourself a lover, have you?'

He wasn't being serious, but he did hope that his outrageous suggestion would force her to confess the real reason behind her happiness. But in the end it proved unnecessary. He knew her too well. He knew that there were only a few things in life that gave her happiness. One of these was her children and her greatest desire with regard to them was to see them married and settled. As Hermann was already married that left Anthea.

'You've arranged something, haven't you?'

Hedda tried to look perplexed. 'What do you mean?'

'It's one of your matchmaking schemes. You've invited someone to the party; someone you hope will take a shine to Anthea. That's it, isn't it?'

Hedda's look of puzzlement turned instantly into one of determination. 'It's about time she got married.'

'Who is it?'

'Count Oscar von Gessendork, plenipotentiary to the Court of Austria. A most suitable match.'

'And you think he's up to the task?'

'Of course he is.'

'Maybe. But I can't say I've been overly impressed by any of your previous choices.'

'We shall see.'

Von Hoeppner struggled with his robes. 'Whose idea was it to have a costume party anyway?'

'Anthea's. After all, it is her birthday.'

'And what is she wearing?'

'I don't know. She's been keeping it a secret.'

'Well, whatever it is I hope it doesn't involve a robe and silly wig. Then we'd really look like a family of idiots.'

Before Hedda could comment a liveried servant in purple tailcoat and white breeches entered the dressing room. A small silver platter was finely balanced on the upturned fingertips of his right hand. Lying on this was a card.

Turning away from the mirror von Hoeppner took the card, but as he read it he frowned. 'I wonder what she wants.'

'Who, dear?'

'The Baroness von Buchner. I've been informed that she's in the Grand Hall. I had no idea she'd been invited.'

'Not begging on behalf of her son again, is she?'

'Now don't start that again.'

Hedda gave every appearance of having more to say and an argument may well have developed if their son Hermann hadn't limped into their presence. He too was dressed in robe and sandals. But his wig was dark and in his hand he held an anvil hammer.

'Oh no,' von Hoeppner groaned. 'Not another one. What is this, the gathering of the gods? Which one are you meant to be?'

Hermann smiled. 'Hephaestus, Father, Smithy to the gods.'

'Good for you,' von Hoeppner commented sourly.

Hermann was used to his father's acerbic moods and barbed comments and found that the best way to cope with them was to pretend they never happened. 'Shall we go down individually or together?'

'Oh, let's go together, dear,' Hedda pleaded, anxious as ever to give a show of family unity.

'If we must,' von Hoeppner conceded. 'Just be careful where you're swinging that hammer.'

****

After spending time moving unobtrusively among the guests trying to catch sight of Anthea, Thetis became aware that her own actions were becoming a matter of growing curiosity. Eyes turned toward her and whispered comments were being exchanged. People were starting to wonder who she was and what she was doing walking about unaccompanied. Normally this would not have bothered her, but in this instance it suited her purpose to remain incognito.

I need to find a companion.

One was soon forthcoming. She spotted him immediately. He was dressed in a Regency costume, standing aloof in periwig, mole-coloured velvet sloping coat with stand-up collar, neck cloth and shirt frill, pale oyster breeches and silk stockings in buckled shoes. But it was not his outfit that took her interest; it was the fact that he was not wearing a mask like all the others and, like herself, appeared to be taking stock of those about him.

Settling a companionable smile upon her face, Thetis came at him obliquely. 'Let me see. From your dress I would hazard a guess that you are the revolutionary leader Robespierre, are you not?'

Lifting his quizzing glass the man regarded her with an expression of glacial indifference. 'That is correct. And I would guess from yours that you are the Empress Theophano.'

Thetis was at once both amazed and impressed. 'My compliments, sir. I felt sure that I would pass the evening without being recognised.'

'It is not so startling. I once made a study of Byzantine history. Though, I have to say, I never thought it would ever prove useful.'

'I am glad that it has.' Thetis removed her mask. 'I am the Baroness von Buchner.'

Bowing at the waist he took her hand and kissed it. 'Enchanté. And I'm the Count Oscar von Gessendork, plenipotentiary to the Court of Austria.'

Here the Count took on a thoughtful look as if wondering whether he should raise a matter that some might consider indelicate. He decided to take the risk. 'May I ask, Madam, are you German?'

Thetis smiled in surprise. 'That's an odd question.'

'Forgive me. It's just that your accent has something in it that I can't quite place.'

Thetis smiled. 'My parents were Scottish.'

Revealing her origins in this fashion reminded Thetis that she had once had a childhood, a childhood of magic in which her greatest joy had been riding her horse freely across the windswept glens of Scotland. It had been a life without artifice and she was surprised to realise that there was a part of her that still looked back upon it longingly.

Unaware that he had caused such deep feelings in his companion von Gessendork smiled with joy and relief. 'Ah, Scotland. A beautiful country. Then meeting you is an especial delight.'

Quick to detect undercurrents, Thetis appraised von Gessendork directly. 'Does your delight stem from me being Scottish or does it stem from me not being German?'

A storm cloud passed across von Gessendork's face. 'Don't talk to me about Germans! A brutish people. No delicacy. No finesse.'

'Really?'

'There is a joke in my country. Why do German troops wear the Pickelhaube?'

'Why?'

'Because it perfectly fits the shape of their head.'

While the Count guffawed at his own playground humour Thetis could manage no more than a strained smile. Not that the count noticed.

'Yet ironically,' he continued still spluttering. 'They still consider themselves superior to everyone else.'

'How can you say that? They are your allies.'

'Yes, they are, aren't they. But in truth they have nothing but contempt for us. They see us as a liability and a burden in this war. Yet they choose to ignore the vital part we are still playing on the Italian front.'

Seeing that von Gessendork was getting worked up Thetis chose to tease him into tranquillity. 'Is that why you are standing alone?'

It worked. He looked at her in surprise then smiled. 'No, not really. I'm afraid my solitude may have something to do with my choice of costume.'

'I don't understand.'

'Nor did I at first. But it seems that dressed as I am I more closely resemble one of the servants than a bloodthirsty tyrant of France. By standing here I at least avoid being ordered about.'

Thetis laughed. 'But I guessed correctly.'

'Yes, you did.'

From his grizzled hair, heavy jaw and fleshy face, Thetis judged that von Gessendork was in his mid-forties. He seemed to have a sensitive nature, but his pettiness and readiness to take offence spoiled what could have been an amiable personality. And, despite the generally encouraging start to their meeting, Thetis was soon to realise that the Count's range of conversation was limited to hatred of the Germans and the convoluted intricacies of protocol at the Austrian court.

'Imagine my horror,' he intoned righteously. 'At how these hallowed traditions of Imperial procedure are giving way to a pernicious wave of growing familiarity.'

In any other situation Thetis would have quickly made her excuses and left, but on this occasion von Gessendork was proving to be the companion best suited to her needs. His presence if not his charm was providing her with the cover she needed. Within minutes the curious glances began to subside. Of equal importance the Count's self-involved monologue released her from any obligation to contribute to the conversation beyond providing the occasional nod.

Leaving me to free to keep a lookout for Anthea.

Thetis scanned the Grand Hall, her ever-attentive eyes moving back and forth not once but continuously as she scrutinised closely each and every guest. But, after ten minutes of doing this, she was forced to the conclusion that Anthea was not present. Not that she was downhearted. She knew her quarry would have to make an appearance soon.

This is her party after all.

And her patience was rewarded though not immediately. Loud applause broke out on the other side of the Grand Hall and when Thetis looked in that direction she saw two men and a woman who were very much the centre of attention. All three were dressed in long robes. Both men sported long curly beards, one dark, one fair. The younger of the two men held a hammer with a long wooden handle. The older man and the matronly woman who stood beside him wore crowns.

They've come as Greek gods.

Thetis had seen others dressed in similar costumes and for a moment she wondered what all the fuss was about. Why they were receiving such rapturous attention? Then she realised that these three were not just a party of newly arrived guests but were in fact the hosts; the Archduke Maximillian von Hoeppner dressed as Jove, his wife the ArchDuchess Hedda von Hoeppner, and their son Hermann von Hoeppner dressed as Vulcan.

The King and Queen of the gods! How ridiculous they look. A fat old man and his red-faced wife.

Thetis laughed a laugh of disbelief. And, although the sight of their buffoonery didn't quite disarm her of her hatred toward them it was comic enough to cool her burning desire for vengeance. But she had no wish to be seen by them so she pulled her mask back over her eyes. It was an instinctive action. She knew that it was unlikely they would have recognised her at that distance, but having words with von Hoeppner was the last thing she wanted.

Especially under the eyes of his malicious wife.

It was then that her attention was drawn to a young officer coming down the stairs. What caught her eye was his uniform. It wasn't a costume. It was a proper uniform. And as the young man descended the final steps to the floor of the hall Thetis noticed something else.

He's wearing a pilot's badge.

Thetis' heart missed a beat and she became giddy with excitement. A pilot! Here! Was it possible that this young man belonged to *Jagdgeschwader Nord* at Bois de Cheval? Might he possibly know her son? Might he have news of him? She had to know. Letting motherly concern overcome discretion she muttered some excuse to the Count then headed toward the young man as he stepped off the stairs. With other guests turning toward him Thetis quickened her pace, fearful he might be diverted before she could reach him.

'Young man!' she called out, still several yards from her objective. 'I am the Baroness von Buchner.'

Startled, he turned toward her and his eyes smiled through his mask. 'Delighted to meet you, Baroness. I am Leutnant Anton Strasser at your service.'

'Forgive my forwardness,' Thetis said breathlessly. 'But I couldn't help noticing that you are a pilot in our Air Service and it occurs to me that you might well know my son, Willi Buchner.'

'Why yes, of course I know Willi. A splendid and courageous gentleman. All my fellow officers at JG Nord hold him in the highest esteem.'

This confession couldn't have made Thetis any happier and she was about to thank Leutnant Strasser for his kind words when something about the young man made her hesitate. She wasn't quite sure what it was. It could have been the timbre of his voice, the size and intensity of his eyes, the shape of his face and mouth, but whatever it was it was compellingly, overwhelmingly familiar.

'Good God!' Thetis exclaimed more loudly than she'd intended. 'Is that you?'

****

Anthea's smile lit up her face. 'Yes, it's me.'

'You've come to your party dressed as a pilot in the German Air Service?' Thetis still couldn't believe it.

'I have.' Anthea beamed at the success of her masquerade. 'Were you convinced?'

Thetis wasn't entirely sure how to respond. Growing within her was a feeling of indignation. To her Anthea was little more than a spoilt brat aping the appearance of brave and valiant men such as her son, Willi, men who risked their lives day after day.

While she amuses herself by dressing in their clothes.

Indignation turned to outrage and the need for vengeance, the need she had put to one side, re-entered her breast. Her immediate impulse was to slap the stupid girl across her grinning face, a feeling that only intensified when she saw the Iron Cross pinned to Anthea's tunic. Thetis knew she was being unreasonable maybe even irrational. She knew that in her own strange way Anthea was only trying to show her respect and admiration for these men. She knew this but it didn't matter. Nothing mattered, nothing but the need to strike out.

Only her training as a skilled agent prevented Thetis from acting on her impulses. Only her years of experience presenting a mask to the world enabled her to bite down hard on her true feelings and offer up a smile sweet enough to fool the wariest observer.

'Totally! I was totally convinced.'

'Were you?' Anthea pressed her. 'Were you really?'

'When I saw you coming down those stairs I thought to myself who is that handsome young pilot and I'm certain everyone in the hall was thinking exactly the same thing.'

This was music to Anthea's ears. 'Do you think so?'

With the heightened awareness of a gifted observer Thetis began to sense the true desire that burned within the heart of the young princess standing before her and with this insight she saw a weakness that she could exploit to her own purpose.

'I have no doubts whatsoever, your Highness. I'd go further. If you visited one of our airfields unannounced, dressed as you are, I'm convinced the other pilots would accept you as one of their own.'

This notion, as absurd as it was, so matched Anthea's own dreams she took pause to consider it. And, as she lowered her eyes in thought, Thetis watched her with satisfaction as the impossible idea she had planted began to take root. She would have worked on it further if she hadn't been interrupted at that moment by the arrival of von Gessendork driven, like any lonely man befriended by a beautiful woman, not to let her out of his sight.

Not for one instant had his eyes left Thetis since she excused herself from his company and now, resenting her absence and seeing her in the presence of a younger and more attractive man, decided that this was the moment to intervene. 'I feared you might have forgotten me.'

Hiding her annoyance, Thetis smiled graciously. 'Nonsense! How could you possibly think that?'

Von Gessendork's eyes moved from Thetis to Anthea and, seeing not a beautiful young woman but what he took to be a handsome young hero and one who might easily use his charm to cast a spell upon Thetis, the ambassador's expression became one of uttermost disdain. 'Who is this person?'

Thetis didn't need any magical powers to sense his animosity. It was obvious for all to see. Sensing an opportunity for mischief by stoking the fire beneath it, Thetis made her move. 'Count von Gessendork, may I introduce Leutnant...'

As quick-witted as any, Anthea saw immediately that Thetis was providing her with a cue to keep up the pretence she herself had started and, feeling obliged to play along did so gleefully. 'Leutnant Anton Strasser at your service Count.'

'Yes, Leutnant Strasser,' Thetis confirmed turning back to von Gessendork. Then, to undermine the Count's masculine pride by heightening another's, she added, 'A hero of our illustrious air force and as you can see a recipient of the Iron Cross.'

Anthea stood expectantly, allowing the Count the time he needed to make some suitable expression of admiration. But Thetis knew that what was about to come out of his mouth would be nothing of the kind.

Raising his chin to a height from which he could look at Anthea down the full length of his nose, von Gessendork observed dryly, 'Iron Crosses are all well and fine, Leutnant Strasser, but this is a costume ball. Coming to such an occasion in uniform and not even a full dress uniform hardly seems fitting.'

Amongst his many failings von Gessendork possessed a voice that, when roused to an indignant pitch, captures the attention of everyone within earshot. And it seemed that every mask in the Grand Hall was now turned toward them. Anthea, on the other hand, was conscious of nothing but the Count and his sour expression.

After examining him with studied slowness from stockings to powdered wig, she called out mockingly, 'More fitting than a servant's garb, I think. Besides, I'm proud to wear the uniform of my country, which is more than can be said for the men of Austria. Tell me, Count, is it just a rumour or is your new emperor actually negotiating peace with the French?'

The severity of the insult triggered an audible gasp from the other guests. As for von Gessendork, the blood drained from his face and his mouth and cheeks underwent a series of violent contortions, contracting and stretching as if invisible fingers were manipulating the flesh.

Then finally his thin lips burst apart. 'Do you know who you're addressing?'

'No! I don't.' With an arched expression Anthea turned to the gathering and asked them: 'Does anyone else?'

'Why you young...'

But his rejoinder came too late. Anthea had already marched off into the embrace of the applauding crowd, her popularity as a war-hero now enhanced by the ruthless savagery of her wit. And von Gessendork, the victim of that wit, could only watch in impotent rage as the person he still believed to be a young man moved from one group of adoring admirers to another, basking, as he saw it, in an adulation that was as misguided as it was undeserved.

****

Hiding her satisfaction behind a mask of astonishment Thetis watched von Gessendork storm across the hall, roughly pushing aside any guests who happened to be standing in his way. Such was the depth of his humiliation Thetis fully expected him to exit the Grand Hall but, for some odd reason, he merely retreated back to the very spot beside the buffet table where she had first found him.

There he planted himself and, with a look of murder in his eyes, observed Anthea as she progressed triumphantly across the floor until she finally reached the loving arms of her family. If Thetis had been watching she would have observed that only the father and the brother greeted Anthea lovingly. The mother, having witnessed her matchmaking plans once again reduced to ruins, was not in a loving mood. But Thetis was not watching this. Her eyes were on von Gessendork.

It seems to me that the Count has unfinished business.

Her plan to sow mischief in the von Hoeppner household was beginning to bear fruit, but it would need further tending before it fully ripened. Needing to act quickly but carefully she assessed the situation. Von Gessendork had not only been insulted but it had been done in front of a large assembly of German nobility. This was not something he could or would ever forgive. His status in society and his loyalty to his country demanded that he do something.

Thetis knew that her task now was to help him to decide what action he should take. She would have to guide him along the proper path. Infusing her expression with all the sympathy she could muster, she once again positioned herself beside him.

'You look angry, Count.'

With eyes fixed unblinkingly on the object of his fury von Gessendork growled, 'Of course I'm angry. That young man has just called not only my honour into question but also the honour of my country and he has to pay.'

Knowing that the one sure way to stoke the fires of a person's anger was by appearing to take the other person's side, Thetis suggested, 'I'm sure he didn't mean to.'

The ploy worked better than she could have been hoped. Turning to Thetis he boomed, 'Didn't mean to! Didn't mean to! How can you say that? He deliberately insulted me in front of all those people. If I do nothing now my family name will be held in contempt.'

'But what can you do?'

'I shall call him out.'

This was a turn Thetis hadn't anticipated. 'Call him out? Surely you don't mean to challenge him to a duel?'

'That's exactly what I mean to do.'

'But you can't.'

'Can't I? What's to stop me?'

'Well, I think there's something you need to know.'

'What?'

Thetis sighed. She had hoped to keep Leutnant Strasser's true identity and Anthea's masquerade a secret for a little while longer, but von Gessendork's ardent determination to shed blood left her with little choice but to reveal all.

Speaking against the backside of her hand in order not to be overheard, Thetis told him, 'According to one of the other guests Leutnant Strasser is not quite what he seems.'

Von Gessendork's brows knitted together. 'What are you telling me? He's some sort of an impostor?'

'Well, perhaps not in the way you might mean. You see, it appears that the person you and I know as Leutnant Strasser is in fact the Princess Anthea von Hoeppner.'

The count's mouth fell open and his eyes popped out of his head. 'What!'

Thetis nodded. 'It's true. The uniform she is wearing is nothing more than her costume for the evening.'

Von Gessendork stood rooted to the spot, struck dumb with disbelief. The idea was just too absurd, but as he brought to mind every feature of the young officer's face it began to dawn on him that he had blinded himself to the truth. There were those large cat-like eyes, the small but sensuous mouth, the luminous, unblemished complexion and the boyish register of the voice. All of these factors finally coalesced into one shocking conclusion.

'Good God!'

'Yes. I couldn't believe it at first myself.'

'But that doesn't alter anything.'

'Really!' She studied the Count's face and saw that indeed nothing had altered. His expression was still just as fierce and unremitting. 'I don't understand. How can you possibly retrieve your honour by killing a woman? Besides, the Princess is a fencer of considerable skill. She might end up killing you.'

He waved a hand indignantly. 'What do you take me for? I don't duel with women. But I am determined on one thing and on this I will not relent. I'm going to get an apology from the Princess.'

'An apology?'

'Yes. And I'm not leaving until I have one.'

Breathing easily once again, Thetis smiled. 'Yes, yes, an apology. Given the circumstances anyone would consider your demand an entirely reasonable one. And knowing the Princess to be a young woman of considerable sensitivity I feel certain that she will be only too happy to comply.'

Like a man impelled by forces beyond his control von Gessendork started to move forward and only by sheer luck alone was Thetis able to restrain him.

'Where are you going?'

'Where do you think I'm going,' he replied perplexed. 'I'm going to get my apology.'

Thetis was flabbergasted. 'No, no, not now.'

'Why not?'

For a moment Thetis was unable to give an answer, not because she didn't have one but because she was so amazed that a man who took such pride in Austrian court etiquette appeared completely ignorant of how such things were done. But then she sighed and shook her head and gave her reply.

'Look, I know the Princess and I'm sure she is ashamed of what she said and would welcome the opportunity to apologise but if you force her hand in front of her guests she will only insult you again and have you thrown out.'

Von Gessendork threw up his hands. 'Fine! Then what do you suggest I do?'

'Hold on to your anger for now. Leave the matter till after the party has finished and everyone has departed. In the meantime, let us get a drink and I will tell you what I have in mind.'

CHAPTER NINE

'Where is that girl with my hot water?'

Anthea sat deep in her white, porcelain bath with only her head, knees, shoulders and long, elegant neck above the gently swaying brew of soft water and foam in which she lay submerged. As she luxuriated in the soft candlelight and the heat coming from the nearby blazing fire, feeling it play across her face and arms, she looked upon the officer's uniform now lying across the back of a chair, a smile of pleasure upon her cat-like features.

What a wonderful day it has been!

The costume ball celebrating her nineteenth birthday, which had ended with a magnificent fireworks display, had been a great success. She not only got to wear the officer's uniform for the entire evening but had also managed to fool all her guests into believing that she was actually a pilot in the service of her country.

And when my true identity was revealed my popularity only grew greater.

Admittedly, not everyone was pleased. There had been some notes of disapproval from her mother who had been upset by her daughter's high-handed treatment of the very man she had set up as a possible love-match.

That great oaf von Gessendork.

Anthea couldn't fathom how he could have come to a costume ball dressed as he was and then criticise her for what she was wearing? The impudence of the man! But he didn't get away with it. In fact he got more than he bargained for. She paid him back. She paid him back and left him speechless. She had left the whole assembly speechless.

It doesn't pay to cross swords with me.

With a self-satisfied smile she recalled the look of dark anger on von Gessendork's face. Never before had she seen anyone in such a towering rage except for maybe the Archduke her father. It could have turned ugly and spoilt the ball, but it didn't. Indeed, as far as Anthea was concerned humiliating the Count had been a highlight of the evening, one she would certainly savour for ages.

An almost perfect birthday all in all.

And there were other pleasures to ponder. One such was an idea one of the guests had put into her head. What with all the fuss with von Gessendork she wasn't sure who the person was but the idea itself was so in tune with her own way of thinking it had left her wondering why she had not thought of it before.

What an amazing notion! Infiltrate an airfield.

Of course, she accepted that whoever had said it had meant it as nothing more than a light-hearted compliment to her and the ingenious nature of her disguise. There had been no expectation by either party that it would be taken seriously. And Anthea was certainly no fool. She fully appreciated the monumental gulf that lay between pulling the wool over the eyes of guests at a ball and attempting to do the same with personnel at a German airbase.

But there's nothing to prevent me from daydreaming.

And that's exactly what she did. Closing her eyes she imagined herself sitting in the rear seat of an open topped staff car passing through the gates of the airfield at Bois de Cheval and then being feted in the officers' Kasino surrounded by a group of dashing young pilots. Then her fantasy delivered Reinhard. He stood before her and together they shared a bottle of champagne, laughing and joking with the sort of open camaraderie that only develops between those who have fought side by side and experienced the same dangers.

For Anthea these musings formed a well-trodden path. They were pleasurable enough, but they were no more than the prelude to the darker side of her desires. And it was easy enough for her to reach down and awaken the devil within. The Kasino was gone. Reinhard was gone. She was in the midst of a furious dogfight. Enemy machines everywhere. She had one in her sights. And it could not evade her guns.

Lips parting, cheeks burning, nostrils flaring, breath quickening, her fingers sought the trigger. They tightened. They squeezed. Her guns came alive, jumping and rocking as they released the ceaseless flow of her firepower. Trailing smoke and fire the enemy plunged to destruction, followed by a second and a third and a fourth and a fifth. And as they fell from the sky one by one the frenzy within her became almost unbearable. She knew it could not end. Not until the ammunition in her guns was spent.

****

As the costume ball drew to a close and the guests started to leave Thetis grabbed von Gessendork by the sleeve and, slipping out of the Grand

Hall beneath the musician's gallery, she led him to a small utility room that was unlocked and empty.

'Wait here,' she told him. 'I won't be long.'

Although she tried to leave the Count with the impression that she had matters in hand in reality she had only the barest idea how she was going to help him resolve his problem with Anthea. But for the moment that would have to wait; she had something more pressing to deal with, the matter that had brought her to the Residenz in the first place, the matter concerning what von Hoeppner knew about any proposed treaty between Germany and Russia.

Moving without a sound she returned to the Grand Hall and, hidden from sight, watched patiently as the servants cleared away the flotsam and jetsam of the party. Moving efficiently they were soon done, and with their departure the lights were extinguished. As all became still Thetis emerged from her place of concealment. Moving on bare feet she glided through the darkness to von Hoeppner's library. She turned the door handles and although it came as no real surprise to find them locked she still felt irritated.

Dammit!

All was not lost. There was another way in, a secret way, one that she had taken many years before when, as a young woman, she had been a guest in the house. She remembered it well, a secret entrance somewhere along the wall of a corridor that ran beside the library.

All I have to do is locate it.

She found the corridor soon enough and, fortunately, there was enough light from the candle brackets for her to search the wall and the several niches that ran along its length. In one of them was a hidden catch that would open the secret door. She had anticipated a long and tricky search but by blind luck alone her fingertips fell upon the catch almost immediately. Not that she felt any joy at its discovery. What she was doing was dangerous. She knew that.

If I'm caught the penalty will certainly be death.

But it wasn't the mortal risk that prevented her from springing the catch. As she stood there she realised that her reluctance to enter stemmed not from fear of danger but from fear of the library itself. There were ghosts in there, ghosts from her past. In there was the dark chamber of her nightmares, the place where the course of her life had been wrenched from normality into a clandestine world of lies, suspicion and fear.

But she had an even deeper reason for wishing to stay where she was. Entering that library meant confrontation not with her past but with herself. There was a truth within her that she would avoid at any cost. If she listened to it that truth would tell her that the life she so abhorred, the life she believed had been forced upon her was the life she was always destined to lead, the life she would have chosen if she had been given the choice. It was in all respects the one best suited to her nature.

Why bother searching anyway? I won't find anything.

This was her justification and the argument was not totally invalid. Von Hoeppner always placed sensitive documents in his hidden wall safe. She didn't know where it was and even if she did she didn't have the combination or the skills to open it.

But there still might be something useful in there.

Something useful to intelligence such as marks on a blotter, a diary entry or a discarded carbon copy. She now stood there immobilised by indecision. She didn't want to go in nor could she just walk away. What was she to do? Then she heard the sound of approaching footsteps. They were coming her way. She could have fled, but this ran the risk of arousing suspicion. Instead she decided to do confront the person and brazen it out.

She didn't have to wait long. A female figure holding a candlestick in one hand and a large jug in the other appeared around the end of the corridor. The jug made her think it might be servant but in this she was mistaken.

'Helga! What are you doing here?'

'Fetching hot water for my mistress.'

Thetis smiled sweetly. This was a fortunate turn of events. She had been trying to figure out how to get the Count up to Anthea's apartment unchallenged. Now, quite by chance, Helga had provided her with the means. Thetis had mistaken her for a servant. Servants were invisible. They passed in and out of rooms unnoticed. And Von Gessendork had already suffered the indignity of being mistaken for a servant. Indeed, Anthea had thrown the insult in his face.

How fitting that as a servant he will find redress.

'You can leave your jug with me, Helga. I'll make sure the Princess gets her hot water.'

****

Not at all happy pretending to be a servant, von Gessendork set off, carrying the jug of hot water before him like a ceremonial offering as he followed Thetis' directions to Anthea's apartment. With him safely on his way Thetis lingered for a moment wondering what she should do next. There was the outstanding matter of von Hoeppner's library and the secrets it might contain. Despite her reluctance she still needed to get in there and have a look around. Then she had a better idea.

Erich's better at cracking safes. He can do it.

Besides, there was something far more exciting than blotters and carbon copies on offer, the next stage in the continuing drama between Anthea and von Gessendork. This was a piece of mischief she had set in motion and the outcome promised to be explosive. As far as Thetis was concerned the temptation to witness for herself what might transpire was irresistible.

To hell with the treaty!

Removing her scarlet shoes with their pearl-sewn edges Thetis' bare feet whispered along the carpeted by-ways of the house, moving along its sleeping corridors and up its shadowed stairways as she followed the very route that she had given to von Gessendork. Running on tip toes like a ballerina she soon caught up with the Count and only just in time for he was now in the very corridor that led to Anthea's apartment.

Keeping out of sight she watched with excited eyes as he strode forward and with such single-minded determination he appeared unaware that he was being observed. Still holding the jug of water before him he paused before the door to Anthea's apartment as if gathering his thoughts. Then he turned the handle and let himself in.

****

Anthea was still submerged in her bath when the door opened and closed behind her. But she heard nothing; such was the intensity of her half-dream, such the transporting pleasure of moistened soap and aerial dog fighting. Only the agitated flickering of candlelight upon her eyelids alerted her to the fact that someone had entered the room.

Ah! Helga! At last!

'And not before time. My bath is almost glacial.'

Footfalls crossed the carpet. There was a pause followed by a noisy stream of fresh water mixing with the water already in the bath. Anthea felt the warmth of it coil about her limbs like a liquid snake.

Shifting her body as if responding to an invisible caress, she murmured, 'Mmm! How delicious. This is such heaven I could just lie here forever.'

'I am glad it is to your liking,' intoned a voice that was not Helga's.

Anthea's eyes flashed open charged with anger. She saw the jug, but the person holding it was not her lady-in-waiting. It was von Gessendork.

'Leutnant Strasser, I presume,' he said looking down upon her with mild amusement though the smile on his face was not a friendly one.

'What are doing here?' Despite the vulnerability of her position she remained defiant. 'You have no business in my rooms. Get out now before I call the servants.'

Von Gessendork placed the empty jug calmly onto the carpeted floor beside the bath and just as calmly lit himself a cigarette. 'Call if you wish, but I fear no one will answer.'

'Why not?'

He looked up from his cigarette and peered at her through the smoke with hard, implacable eyes. 'It seems there's been an emergency.'

'An emergency! What emergency?'

'A fire in the kitchen,' he said, telling her the lie that he had formulated on the way to Anthea's apartment.

'A fire!'

'Well, not a real fire, just a cigarette discarded in a laundry basket.'

'And you went to all that trouble just to catch me in the bath?'

The humour dropped from his face. 'I have no time to waste. I am leaving for Austria within the hour, but before I go there is a matter between us that needs settling.'

Generally Anthea considered men quite simple creatures so simple that when she first saw von Gessendork standing before her it came to her that his intention was to drag her from the bath and ravish her before anyone could come to her aid. But there was nothing in his speech or manner to suggest a man intent on seduction, violent or otherwise.

Feeling more in command, she snapped, 'And what is this matter?'

'One that concerns my honour.'

Suddenly it all made sense and Anthea smiled, nodding slowly. 'Ah, I see. This is to do with our exchange of pleasantries, isn't it?'

Her mockery brought the blood to his face. 'If you had been a man I would have demanded satisfaction. Indeed, so convincing were you in that uniform of yours I almost called you out there and then.'

With all of her natural imperiousness, she told him, 'This is all very interesting but, as you can see, I am out uniform now and enjoying my bath so unless there's some point to this I would suggest that you leave this instant.'

'Not before I get an apology.'

After the merest pause her mouth opened wide and she burst into laughter. 'You must be mad.'

'Mad or not I'm not leaving until I get one.'

Anthea's laughter ceased and her cat-like features took on a savage look. 'How dare you talk to me in such a manner. How dare you stand there looking down upon me as if I were no better than a scullery maid.'

Enraged beyond modesty she grabbed the sides of the bath and hauled herself bodily from the perfumed water, rising amid a cascade of foam and spray like a slick-skinned dolphin bursting through the dark surface of the sea. And there she stood, covered in little more than dripping clouds of soap bubbles, the skin of her arms, long legs and slim hips copper-glinted in the fire-light.

Breathing defiance, face flushed and eyes blazing she raised her hand and, with remarkable speed and strength, struck von Gessendork across his face. Although he could have prevented the blow he made no move to do so. Instead he slowly wiped away the soap from his face and, with great stillness studied the creamy substance as he worked it between his thumb and fingertips.

Convinced that she had von Gessendork's measure, Anthea raised her other hand. 'Get out or you'll feel this against the other side of your face.'

The Count looked up. 'I had hoped to settle this matter quietly and in a mature manner but as you appear determined to behave like a child you leave me no choice but to treat you like one.'

Her hand lashed out, but this time, as her arm swung toward him, he snared it by the wrist.

'Was fällt dir ein,' she hissed. 'Let me go!'

But his encircling fingers held her with the grip of an iron manacle. Turning on the spot he dragged her after him. Forced to follow, she lurched out of the bath almost tripping over the side but as soon as her feet were on the carpet she fought like a wildcat, kicking and scratching.

Seemingly oblivious to her struggles he found a high-backed chair, pulled it close to the fire and, still holding Anthea by the wrist, sat on it. Then, in one fluid movement he yanked her, still kicking and hissing, face down across his knee.

'What do you think you're doing?' she called out, her voice edged with a rising note of uncertainty.

'Something I should have done earlier and in front of your guests.'

Wet and slippery, she heaved and pushed and squirmed, but his strength was greater than hers and as he slowly restrained her, pinning her arm into the small of her back, she had her first inkling of what was about to happen.

'Drecksau!' she cried out in alarmed disbelief. 'You wouldn't dare! I am a Princess, a von Hoeppner, the daughter of an Archduke.'

Pulling up his sleeve and raising his open palm to its highest elevation, the Count looked down upon the intended target now exposed and glistening in the firelight and announced with solemn amusement, 'Then it seems to me that I'm about to strike the very seat of the family's power.'

****

As soon as she saw the Count disappear into Anthea's apartment Thetis left her hiding place and tiptoed swiftly along the corridor to the door. On reaching it she pressed both hand and ear against the polished surface, holding her breath to catch the slightest sound. At first there was only a strained silence. Then there was the sound of pouring water. This was followed by Anthea's voice, sharp with anger, followed by von Gessendork's, low but menacing.

Thetis couldn't make out what was being said, but the exchange was brief and was terminated quickly by a cracking sound like a rifle shot and it was so loud it made her step back from the door.

My God! She's slapped him!

With her ear pressed to the door once more Thetis heard splashing water, Anthea protesting, footsteps across the floor, a chair scraping, more loud words, a brief pause, a resounding slap, a yelp, another resounding slap, another yelp.

'My father will flay you alive for this,' Anthea yelled.

If she had hoped that this threat might have brought an end to her suffering she was to be sadly disappointed; the effect was quite the opposite. Instead of deflecting von Gessendork from his task it merely spurred him to even greater efforts; the resounding slaps increased both in volume and frequency.

For Thetis the sound of Anthea's chastisement was the sweetest most delicious music. As far as she was concerned the punishment was not only richly deserved it was also long overdue, and her smile grew broader and broader as each smack struck home.

If I could only see it for myself.

Not daring to open the door she bent her head to the keyhole. This manoeuvre was not without difficulty. Her voluminous costume gave her little freedom of movement and only by breathing in sharply and leaning at an acute angle was she finally able to get her eye to the opening.

The room beyond was illuminated by nothing more powerful than the glowing logs in the fireplace. At first this presented Thetis with a shifting pattern of red and black shadows that made no sense whatsoever. But as her vision adjusted she could just make out the count's head and shoulders. He was looking down. His mouth was grim but from the light in his eyes it was clear that he was taking more pleasure from what he was doing than seemed entirely appropriate for a man set on reclaiming his honour.

And why not? He's serving my purpose as well as his own.

Of Anthea and her ordeal Thetis could see nothing, but she heard the Princess eventually call out, 'Stop! Stop! You're hurting me.'

The Count had raised his hand to administer further punishment but, on hearing the contrition in Anthea's voice, he held it there. 'Do you apologise?'

'Yes, yes, I apologise.'

There was a pause as he considered the sincerity of her words. Satisfied, he lowered his hand, unceremoniously dumped Anthea onto the carpet at his feet, stood up, stepped over her body and walked toward the door. At his approach Thetis jumped to her feet and sprang back from the door. She was some feet away when it opened and von Gessendork emerged, the knees of his breeches wet and darkened with bath water.

Reversing course and moving forward as if she had just arrived upon the scene, Thetis smiled politely and asked, 'Did you get what you came for?'

'Yes, I got what I came for,' was the Count's curt response, and with nothing further to say he marched off.

After watching him disappear around a corner Thetis turned back to the open door and, without compunction, entered the fire lit room. Anthea was still lying on the floor where the Count had discarded her like some travel rug, but she had recovered enough to prop herself up on her forearms and even in that dim light it was easy to see that her eyes were filled with tears and murder.

'I'll kill him! I'll kill him,' she raged then, sensing that someone else was in the room, she looked up and, seeing Thetis, told her, 'I'll kill him.'

'Who, Your Highness?' Thetis asked disingenuously.

'That swine von Gessendork. Who else would I be talking about?'

Thetis glided further into the room. 'Why? What has he done?'

'He...He...Never mind what he did. I'll kill him. I'll tear that bastard apart. I'll have his head on a plate. Get me a gun.'

'A gun?'

'Yes! A gun!'

'I, err...'

'Why are you just standing there? Get me a gun.'

'I wouldn't know where to look.'

'My father's library. He has one in his desk drawer.'

Thetis hesitated. Anthea had just presented her with a valid reason for not only being in von Hoeppner's library, but also for searching through his desk. But then she realised that searching for a gun wasn't such a valid reason after all.

'Highness, consider your situation for a moment. Gun or no gun you can hardly give chase as you are and by the time you are dressed the Count will be long gone.'

'Aaaargh!' Anthea clawed the carpet in frustration.

Looking suitably anxious Thetis asked. 'Maybe I should get your mother or Helga.'

As Thetis expected this suggestion produced a look of genuine horror on Anthea's face. 'No! No one!'

The very idea that knowledge of her humiliation might become the subject of general gossip was unthinkable. And she was in no doubt that many at court would derive great pleasure in discussing and embellishing the details of her ordeal.

'No one must know about this. And you have to keep it to yourself. Do you understand?'

'Of course, Your Highness.'

Anthea held Thetis with a hard look. 'I'll know if you haven't.'

'You can rely on me entirely. But what can I do to help?'

'Fetch my robe.'

When the garment had been located Anthea climbed stiffly from the floor and turned around so that Thetis could help her into it. And it was at this moment that Thetis caught sight of von Gessendork's handiwork.

My God! Her arse looks angrier than her face.

'Perhaps you should sit down, your Highness,' Thetis suggested struggling to suppress a smile.

'Yes, perhaps I should.' Anthea ambled slowly toward the chair, but then she hesitated. 'On second thoughts I think I'll just remain standing for the moment.'

'As you wish, Your Highness.'

Anthea's lips drew back in a snarl. 'The bastard! I'll kill him. Even if it takes me forever I'll kill him.'

At that moment Anthea finally burst into tears. 'God knows what he might have done if you hadn't been here.

'There, there, child!' Thetis said in a soothing voice as she put a comforting arm around Anthea's shoulders. 'Everything's going to be all right. I'm here now.'

CHAPTER TEN

4 DECEMBER 1917

'Are you sure this statement is long enough, Fuchs?'

A somewhat nervous Buchner held up the single sheet of paper containing the short address he had been rehearsing since the previous day.

'It doesn't need to be any longer, Herr Hauptmann. It's just the right length.'

I should know. I wrote it.

Given Buchner's state of mind and loathing of pen and paper Fuchs had offered to put together a short address, one that he could deliver to the replacements when they arrived. As well as being short and to the point it had to avoid anything high-blown. These were experienced fighter pilots, men familiar with the business of war not bright-eyed trainees. They didn't need sabre-rattling speeches.

They've probably heard it all before anyway.

'I'm sure you're right.' Buchner put the sheet of paper down then glanced at his wristwatch. 'They're late. Do you think there's been another hold up?'

'It wouldn't surprise me.'

The seven new officers should have arrived two days earlier, but their train journey across Russia and Eastern Europe had been slowed by persistent delays. The last update on their progress reached the office the previous evening. It said that the replacements had just reached Valenciennes and that as soon as their machines were assembled and checked out they would be flying to Bois de Cheval early the following day.

'Have we been given their names yet?'

'Yes.' Fuchs started to search the papers on his desk. 'The *Flugpark* gave them to me earlier. Here they are.'

'Read them out.'

'There's Volker Burgmüller, Frank Dessau, August Wülner...'

'Wülner! I know that name from somewhere.' Buchner sat silently for a moment wracking his memory, but without success. 'It'll come to me. Carry on. Who are the rest?'

'Gustav Crüger, Theobald Braumfels, Gerd Anders and Joachim Abendroth.'

'And they're all experienced pilots.'

'So I've been told. Most of them have scored at least one or two victories apiece while patrolling the Eastern Front.' Fuchs paused to check his watch. 'Would you like me to contact Valenciennes and see if they've taken off?'

'No, Fuchs. Give them a while longer. But you can take a look outside if you wish.'

At the time Fuchs had gratefully accepted any excuse to escape close confinement with Buchner but now, ten minutes later, standing on the path beside the airbase's northern field he was beginning to regret the decision.

At least it had been warm in the office.

As he watched some soldiers shovelling sluggishly at a fresh fall of overnight snow his teeth began to chatter and he felt the cold begin to seep through his greatcoat and the fingers of his leather gloves. He patted his pockets, hoping that he may have brought his pipe and tobacco pouch with him. He hadn't. Instead, he dug his hands deep into the empty pockets and hunched his shoulders.

The path was straight and on a normal day it was possible to see to its far end, but today there was a lingering mist that closed down the distance to about a hundred yards. The trees off to his right stood at the edge of the mist and were visible as darkened shapes.

Come on! Come on! Where the hell are they?

Irritated and miserable, Fuchs did the one thing he always did when his situation was a less than happy one; he considered his position at JGN. And as usual his thoughts crystallised into one question.

Should I put in for a transfer?

It wouldn't be the first time. He had submitted three applications so far all of them during Hantelmann's tenure as Hauptmann.

And the bugger turned each and every one of them down.

Would Buchner act any differently? Fuchs thought there was a good chance he might. And he wouldn't need any persuading. He was so distracted most of the time he didn't know what he was signing. Fuchs could just slip the application under his nose and that would be that.

But then where would I be?

Fuchs thought about this and for the first time it occurred to him that the only reason he only kept putting in for a transfer was because he knew that Hantelmann would always turn him down. Maybe he didn't really want a transfer at all. Maybe deep within himself Bois de Cheval was exactly where he wanted to be.

So what's so great about this place?

There was Mimi of course. She was the sort of woman he liked; blowsy and uncomplicated. But she wasn't unique in that respect. There were women like Mimi everywhere. But there was something about Bois de Cheval that set it apart from most other places, something he might not find elsewhere and that was the lucrative little set-up he was running out of the Kasino. He was making money hand over fist and with Buchner in command there was every chance of stepping up the scope of his activities

Especially when I finally get the old Kasino reopened.

How different to when Hantelmann was in charge. He used to watch Fuchs like a hawk, and although he never discovered anything incriminating he remained suspicious that his adjutant was up to something. But Buchner was an entirely different kettle of fish. Most of the time he had no idea what was going on.

To hell with this!

The cold had finally become unbearable. And it seemed stupid to just stand there and freeze to death when there was a nice warm stove in the office. Besides, it seemed unlikely that the replacements would fly in such adverse conditions. Fuchs remembered from his own flying experience that on days such as this everything would be grounded.

They're probably still in Valenciennes.

Deciding to go back to the office and check Fuchs was about to turn away when he noticed that the soldiers had stopped shovelling and their pose seemed to suggest that they had stopped to listen. Then they stood up and moved to one side of the path.

Something's coming!

Fuchs could hear the muted sound of engines in the distance and although he couldn't quite make out what it might be, he was pretty sure that what he was hearing was the approach of the replacements.

****

It feels good to be back inside my machine.

And for Burgmüller the trip from Valenciennes had been a joy. They were flying in two groups. Burgmüller led the front group with Dessau and Abendroth behind him. Braumfels led the rear group with Anders, Wülner and Crüger behind him. Their take off had been hampered by ground mist and the two groups nearly lost each other while trying to form up in the air. But as soon as they were together they climbed steeply out of the mist until at a thousand feet they emerged into a glorious early morning sky.

The seven pilots then turned the beaks of their white-dappled machines toward the west. Burgmüller had hoped that the mist would soon disperse, but it didn't. It kept with them the entire journey blanketing out all sign and feature of the ground beneath it. There were occasional breaks here and there especially over higher terrain.

But hilltops help little in determining location.

Burgmüller's map was of little help either. It showed the significant main roads and town centres, but the mist hid all of this. And it remained that way throughout the thirty-six-mile journey. About half way Burgmüller thought he saw the northern outskirts of Douai, but he couldn't be sure. All he could do was keep to his compass bearing of West-North-West and count off the miles.

With any luck the mist should soon start to thin out.

Then he caught sight of the Canal de la Deûle and he knew they were nearing their destination. But as they had drifted slightly off their course he pulled his stick gently to the left bringing his compass bearing to due west. There could only be about six or seven miles to go now. The mist was still beneath them but it had thinned a bit. Burgmüller considered starting their descent in case visibility might be better at a lower altitude. But in the end he decided to stay at their present height.

Then Burgmuller saw something that made his heart leap. Directly ahead the mist was stained with patches of darkness and as they got nearer he could see that these patches were the trees of a forest. Bois de Cheval stood upon a hill and it was the upper branches of its tall trees that now poked through the mist to welcome them.

Like a beacon on a dark night.

Burgmüller consulted his map. Bois de Cheval was a forest in several parts. One of those parts, the part he could see, was on a hill. From this he could tell that the landing field had to be to the right of the trees. For most pilots attempting to land in such a mist would have been a daunting prospect. But Burgmüller and the six pilots behind him were used to such conditions. Many times their wheels had sought the ground through mists much thicker than this. Throttling down Burgmüller began his descent.

****

Scanning a likely part of the sky Fuchs was rewarded with the sight of a small black shape emerging out of the mist. It quickly solidified into the wings, fuselage and undercarriage of a hollow-framed Pfalz. Two more followed.

My God! These fellows don't lack guts.

The first three machines were already coming in to land when four more machines appeared in their wake, tendrils of mist curling about their lower wings as they dropped into clear air. Now assured that all seven pilots had arrived safely Fuchs hurried back to the office.

'They're here!' he announced excitedly.

Buchner raised his head. 'Who?'

'The replacements.'

'Oh, them. They probably need feeding. Take them to the Kasino for something to eat. I'll speak to them later.'

Feeling that further words would be a complete waste of time, Fuchs closed the door and returned to the landing field. By the time he reached it all seven replacement pilots had landed their Pfalz. One of the pilots had climbed down from his cockpit and was gathering the others around him. It was this pilot who greeted Fuchs.

'I'm Leutnant Burgmüller.'

'And I'm Oberleutnant Fuchs, the Adjutant. Welcome to *Jagdgeschwader Nord.*'

****

'They call this midden a Kasino?' Crüger was not happy with what he saw. But then he never was. 'We were better served on the train.'

'Shut up,' Wülner told him. 'And eat your food.'

The seven officers were sitting where Fuchs had placed them leaving them in the capable hands of several orderlies who brought them food and coffee from the field kitchen. It was plain fare – black bread, cheese and various cold meats and German sausage – but they had skipped breakfast at Valenciennes to get an early start so it was more than welcome. They were about halfway through the meal when Fuchs returned. He gave them a friendly smile.

'Forgive me gentlemen; I had hoped that we could have marked your first day by serving you with something more substantial and in cheerier surroundings.'

'We are used to the rigours of campaigning, Herr Oberleutnant,' Braumfels told him.

'Don't talk rot, Theo,' Crüger said. He then turned to Fuchs. 'Life wasn't easy on the Eastern Front but we did enjoy the extensive accommodations and cellar of a Russian nobleman's palace.'

'A *minor* Russian nobleman,' Burgmüller corrected him. 'And he did do us the courtesy of evacuating the premises before we got there.'

'Well, we have our own palace,' Fuchs began. 'You may have noticed it as you landed. It is the Chateau Cheval and it was our home until the English bombed it. Now we sleep in huts and tents and dine in a wooden pavilion.'

He paused but, seeing he still had their attention, he continued. 'The good news is that our old Kasino should be open for business in a few days. I am planning to hold a gala evening to celebrate the event and all of you are invited as my special guests.'

This announcement was greeted with muted pleasure. There may have been one or two amongst the seven new officers who thought it somewhat strange to be invited to a facility that was essentially theirs by right. But on the whole it was accepted in the spirit in which it was intended and Fuchs was pleased that he and the new arrivals had got off to a happy start.

It was then that the seven new officers sprang to their feet like Jack in the boxes, standing to attention as Buchner came through the door. When everyone was where they should be Fuchs made the introductions.

'Gentleman! This is Hauptmann Buchner, the Commanding officer of *Jagdgeschwader Nord*.'

Fuchs noticed the sudden look of surprise that came over the faces of all seven officers and the reason was immediately clear to him; none of them had been informed that there'd been a change of command. All of them were under the impression that Hantelmann was still in charge.

'Thank you, Oberleutnant,' said Buchner, unaware of any of this as he turned his attention to the seven new officers. 'Be seated, gentlemen. Smoke if you wish.'

They complied.

Buchner cleared his throat. 'In due course I hope to speak to you all individually, but given your numbers and your familiarity with each other as a group it seemed appropriate at this stage to greet you collectively.'

At this point Buchner paused to pat his pocket and assure himself that the address Fuchs had written for him was to hand in case he needed it. As he did so he remembered what Fuchs had told him about the importance of putting across to the new pilots that they were now part of something special and, for that reason, were special themselves. It was this address that Buchner now delivered.

'*Jagdgeschwader Nord* is an elite unit. The pilots that have served within it have been some of the best that Germany has ever produced. During the recent British Offensive in the Ste Helene sector it alone accounted for over forty enemy machines shot down.'

This claim produced a stir amongst the seven new pilots. Some nodded appreciatively. Others exchanged looks of approval. Only Crüger, a man not easily impressed by statistics, whispered to his neighbour, 'Yeah, but how many did we lose?'

If Buchner heard this aside he chose to ignore it. 'Our military record here is an exemplary one. It is one of honour and glory. It will be your task to maintain that record and I have every hope and confidence that in time your actions will add to it.'

Buchner visibly relaxed. He was nearing the end of his address. The worst part was over and he had not tripped up. The rest was easy. 'In due course I will speak to all of you individually but for now I'll let Oberleutnant Fuchs assign you to your individual Jastas and introduce you to your Jasta Commanders. Thank you, gentlemen.'

As Buchner turned to depart and the seven officers once again sprang to their feet Fuchs stood numb with disappointment. He had been confident that his prepared address would set the right tone but all hope of this was lost with Buchner's flat delivery.

He remembered the words; he just forgot to put any life into them.

****

Having only just got back to France the previous day Pritchett instructed his driver to take him on the usual tour of British squadrons in the *Lys* sector. He was eager to get to 63 squadron at Ste Helene, which was third on his list for that morning. Just over a week had passed since the squadron lost Major Harker, its highly respected commander. Forced by necessity Prim had replaced him with Captain Parkinson. He liked the man.

But I have deep reservations about his fighting spirit and qualities of leadership.

Part of his reason for going to London had been to find a suitable replacement commander who could take over the squadron on a permanent basis. But in that respect his journey had been a wasted one. The Cambrai Offensive had taken its toll on the Royal Flying Corps and replacement commanders were rather thin on the ground.

Leaving me with Parkinson for a little while longer.

So it was with some anxiety that Pritchett climbed out of the back of his staff car and headed to 63 squadron's office. But whatever he may have been expecting didn't quite match up to what he encountered. On opening the door he immediately came face to face with the late, lamented Major Harker.

What the devil!

Colonel Pritchett was not a man easily surprised and even when he was he rarely showed it. But on this occasion his face reacted fleetingly to the sight of a face that he never thought he'd see again this side of eternity. And it took him more than a second or so to realise that what he was actually looking at was a portrait of the dead Major, the one that Parkinson had painted, long enough to give the Colonel a nasty turn. What had made it seem so life like was that the frame and the easel on which it stood had been placed in such a way as to make it look as if the Major was sitting behind his desk.

Slowly and reverently, Pritchett walked toward it, until eventually he found himself staring into the face of the man he had come to regard as the son he had lost. And it was such a good likeness that he had to tense up the sinews of his composure. There was the sound of movement behind him. He knew it was Parkinson. Instead of turning he nodded toward the portrait.

'I see that you've finished it.'

'Yes, I have.' Parkinson walked up and stood beside the Colonel and they stood there admiring it together. 'The problem is I'm not sure what to do with it.'

'Well, I don't think it would be entirely proper to hang it in the mess. Sort of goes against the convention, don't you think?'

'Yes, I do.'

'What were you going to do with it originally?'

'Give it to Major Harker.'

'Really!' Pritchett stroked his chin speculatively. 'Well, that gives me an idea.'

'What's that, sir?'

'How about sending it to his widow?'

****

'Would you like any more tea with your breakfast, sir?' asked Private Harry Watkins as he placed a plate of eggs, bacon and sausage before Colonel Pritchett.

The Colonel looked up from what was for him a very late breakfast and smiled contentedly. 'Thank you, no. One cup is more than enough for me.'

As Watkins returned to the kitchen Pritchett sliced hungrily through the fried breakfast that had been conjured up for him at short notice. To add to the feast he'd also been provided him with several thick slices of buttered toast.

'Let me tell you, Major, in my book there's nothing quite like a fried breakfast to restore a man's outlook on life.'

'Indeed not, sir.'

Pritchett put a portion of sausage into his mouth, chewed it appreciatively then swallowed it. 'You know, this is a beautiful little spot you have here at Ste Helene.'

'I couldn't agree more, Colonel.'

Pritchett was feeling happier with life because he was feeling much happier with his Acting Major. Even while they were staring at Major Harker's portrait back in the office he had sensed that there was something different about Parkinson. Years of experience had given him the ability to judge men, their strengths and their weaknesses. And that ability was now telling him that Parkinson had changed. He seemed less involved with himself and his own personal concerns.

And more concerned with the needs of the squadron.

The telling moment came during a conversation they'd been having earlier about the state of the front in their sector and the strength of the squadron. Pritchett had been the first to raise the matter.

'Recent intelligence has come up with some interesting facts concerning our friends at Bois de Cheval. For a start they've had a recent change of command. It seems the fellow who shot down Major Harker is now in charge.'

Parkinson was clearly taken aback by this news. 'I'm not sure whether that's good or bad.'

'Good I think. It seems his own High Command considers him far too precious to risk in combat so this promotion effectively keeps him on the ground.'

Parkinson smiled. 'Much the best place for him.'

'Quite! Intelligence also tells us that Bois de Cheval is in as parlous state as we are. They are short of pilots, machines, the lot.'

Parkinson nodded cheerfully. 'That's comforting to know. A period of peace and quiet is just what we need right now.'

'But we can't say how long it will last,' Pritchett warned him. 'Even as we speak the Germans are transporting men and materiel from the eastern front.'

'I see.' Parkinson became thoughtful for a moment then he rallied. 'Well it looks like I'd best make the most of the time I do have.'

Liking this answer Pritchett decided to probe his acting commander further. 'I hear you've just received the first batch of new pilots.'

'Judge, Lapton and Courtland.'

'Where have you placed them?'

'With Captain Hammer in 'A' flight, sir.'

'Good choice! They've little experience so they'll certainly need his guiding hand. What about Leith and Rycliffe?'

'They're with Captain Milton in 'B' flight. And when Whitworth arrives I'll put him in 'B' as well.'

'Good! Good!' Pritchett liked what he was hearing. 'Whitworth knows his stuff so he won't need much looking after. And you've got another new fellow coming on the eighth of this month. So it looks like the squadron is getting back up to strength.'

'And what about me, sir?'

This question took Pritchett by surprise. 'What about you?'

'Have you got a replacement for me yet?'

Pritchett gave Parkinson a shrewd look. 'Not yet. Why do you ask? Are you anxious to be replaced?'

'Oh, it's not that, sir. It's just that there's a few things I'd like to get underway before I step down.'

Pritchett felt himself relax. 'Such as?'

'Well, for a start I'd like to make sure the squadron is fully up to strength before handing over. And I'd like to organise that quiet time we were talking about to build up morale and training.'

'That sounds fine to me. What else?'

Here Parkinson smiled awkwardly. 'Well, I was thinking about getting a piano for the officer's mess.'

Pritchett smiled. 'Ordinarily I'd advised against starting anything new at this stage, but in this instance I see no reason why you shouldn't.'

And Pritchett was still smiling when he was driven away from Ste Helene airfield. He had arrived there wondering whether he had made the right choice about the squadron's new commander. Now he was departing heartened by the knowledge that 63 squadron was in good hands.

****

Ashamed of the inferior quality of JGN's Kasino Fuchs decided to make amends by taking the new officers to Mimi's Estaminet for a drink. Most were too tired after their long journey and plumped for an early night. Only three took him up on his offer: Burgmüller, Dessau and Abendroth. Fuchs drove them to Senlis in Buchner's staff car. The Estaminet was busy as usual, but Mimi managed to find the small group a corner table.

'Here you are.' Fuchs placed the drinks on the table. 'Three large brandies.'

'Thanks, Herr Oberleutnant,' the three young officers responded eagerly.

With his own drink in hand Fuchs joined them at the table, seating himself on the remaining chair.

Raising his glass he called out 'Prost!'

'Prost!' they echoed.

All four took a manly gulp from their glasses then sat back smacking their lips appreciatively.

'How about a nice cigar!' Fuchs asked, looking questioningly from one officer to the other.

'That would be wonderful,' they chorused.

Fuchs held up his hand and Mimi appeared beside him. 'Four of your finest Cuban cigars please, Mimi.'

She left and returned within an instant holding a box of cigars. She lifted the lid and presented the contents so that each man could take one of the smokes in turn. As soon as these were cut and lit Mimi left them to it. Puffing their cigars and glowing with brandy the four men relaxed, watching their exhaled smoke rise up to the ceiling.

Removing a stray piece of tobacco from the tip of his tongue Fuchs looked upon the young men with an indulgent smile then asked in a matter-of-fact voice, 'During the commander's address was I mistaken or did you seem a bit surprised when he announced who he was?'

'We were,' Burgmüller admitted. 'When we left Kovno we were told that the commander was Hauptmann Hantelmann.'

Fuchs nodded, 'In a way he still is.'

'I'm not sure I follow.'

'Hauptmann Buchner is in temporary command during Hauptmann Hantelmann's absence.'

'Where is he?' Dessau asked.

'In hospital.'

'What is wrong with him?' Abendroth asked.

'He was wounded in combat.'

'How is he?' Burgmüller asked.

'Hopefully making a full recovery.' Fuchs paused before continuing. 'I visited him a couple of days ago and he seemed to be in good spirits. In fact I got there just after he'd been awarded his Iron Cross.'

'Iron Cross!' Abendroth exclaimed. 'What did he do to deserve that?'

'Oh, he shot down three F2Bs in a single sweep.'

'Three!' This was said in breathless disbelief.

'Yes, three,' Fuchs confirmed. 'He's become quite famous. There were many dignitaries at the presentation and he was interviewed by newspaper reporters.'

'We never got to hear about any of this on the Eastern Front,' Dessau lamented.

134

'But we did get to hear about Hauptmann Buchner shooting down Major Harker,' Burgmüller pointed out. 'Was it after that that he took over command of JGN?'

Fuchs nodded reflectively. 'Yes, it was after that.'

'Mein Gott!' Abendroth was enthused. 'Two Hauptmanns and both of them heroes. We've landed on our feet here.'

CHAPTER ELEVEN

5 DECEMBER 1917

Taking a small flask of rum from his pocket Corporal Arthur Steadman fortified himself against the chill night air pressing against the electric-lit sheds, depots, workshops and marshalling yards of Aire-sur-le-Lys.

'All aboard! All aboard!' he called out, eager to get underway.

The Iron Horse stood beside him, docile and alert as he ran an oily rag lovingly over her dark metal surfaces. Before the war Steadman had driven powerful steam engines, but she was nothing like them. She was squat and unlovely and looked more like a square oven on wheels. And, with her 40hp Simplex petrol engine, she could barely reach twenty miles an hour even on good stretches of track. But for all that he had grown quite fond of her, regarding her with the same sort of affection one might feel toward a loyal dog.

Or a good-natured donkey.

Entrained behind her were eight open wagons normally reserved for the conveyance of barbed wire, lumber and ammunition. Now they were being filled with a different cargo; soldiers from 'A', 'B' and 'C' sections of the second platoon, third company, fourth battalion South Sussex Fusiliers; a total of thirty-nine men.

They had just finished their training at Etaples and were now proficient in the art of bayoneting straw dummies and climbing out of trenches, but to Steadman it was clear that the training hadn't included getting aboard cargo wagons. And as the men heaved and pushed each other over the sides Steadman reflected that this was the first time he had carried troops to the front, but he didn't mind.

Makes a change from shells and poison gas cylinders.

The last group of men to clamber aboard was 'A' section of Second Platoon. There were thirteen of them; Corporal McCleod, Lance Corporal Feltham and Privates Hoon, Scuttle, Brinkly, Cokeson, Shorthouse, Heywood, Dibbs, Swain, Hoskins, Entworth and Hutchins.

To hurry them along Steadman put a hand to the side of his mouth like a fairground stallholder and shouted, 'All aboard the ghost train.'

'He sounds cheerful,' observed Brinkly as he swung a leg inelegantly over the side of the wagon.

'Why shouldn't he?' asked Swain as he grabbed Brinkly by his backpack and hauled him all the way in. 'Unlike us he gets to come back.'

****

Without lamps to light the way *The Iron Horse* threaded a blind course through utter darkness. Her wheels and train of eight 'D' class wagons clicked and clattered along the narrow gauge rails in an easterly direction, following the lie of the land by feel alone. The men standing and crouching in the wagons were silent, isolated from those pressing against them by their inability to see a thing. None of them smoked. They had been told not to in case the enemy should use the light to sight their guns.

But it wouldn't have made much difference anyway; it needs at least one hand to smoke a cigarette and they needed both theirs to cling desperately to the sides of the wagons as the train swayed alarmingly into the unseen curves of the track. Disoriented, they peered anxiously into the night, but they were journeying into a realm forsaken by God and only blackness poured into the sockets of their fear-widened eyes.

Travelling at under ten miles an hour the twenty odd mile journey from depot to rear trenches took about two hours. *The Iron Horse* carried no lights and there were no signals along the route to mark the way. But Steadman knew the route like the back of his hand. He could tell by the dip and rise of the tracks, the jolt of the curves and the swish of wheels over points, exactly where he was. Unlike his passengers he knew the places they passed, the places they could not see, the villages and hamlets, the brooks and streams, the roads and footpaths. He even knew when they passed the airfield at St Helene.

Further on they skirted a huge tank park though only Steadman knew the nature of the endless line of strange bulky shapes. One military landmark everyone recognised was a battery of medium artillery in the mid-distance easily identified by the guns' sky-pointing barrels. Their final destination was a cavernous storage depot of stores and supplies and as Steadman gently brought the little Simplex train to a halt it started to snow.

Big and ponderous, the snowflakes fell out of the night sky with such deliberation it seemed as if each one had been pre-assigned a specific spot on the ground to land. Steadman wasn't bothered. Staying in the shelter of his cab he lit himself a cigarette and watched with red and disinterested eyes as the heavily coated soldiers climbed out of the wagons to stand in lines of regimented misery in the white grizzled darkness.

****

'Goodness me!' Private Entworth exclaimed indignantly. 'Am I glad to get out of that awful thing. I think my poor legs are permanently bent out of shape.'

'Yeah,' agreed Private Brinkly as he shuffled about to keep warm. 'Now I know what a bleeding bag of coal feels like.'

'That driver was right,' moaned Private Swain nodding to the empty wagons. 'That thing is a bloody Ghost Train. Every second I kept thinking something nasty was about to jump out of the darkness at me.'

His round and ghostly face peering anxiously out of his Belaclava, Private Hoon started rubbing his mitten-covered hands together. 'Every time we went round a bend I thought the wagon was going to tip over and fling me out.'

''Ere Oon!' Dibbs called out. 'Where did you get that Belaclava?'

Hoon didn't like Dibbs. He found him intimidating. So it was with some trepidation that he admitted. 'Me Mam knit it for me.'

'Oh, did she?' Dibbs weazled. 'Do you think she'd knit me some long johns? My balls are freezing.'

'Me as well, Hoon,' Entworth pleaded demurely through chattering teeth. 'I'm an absolute martyr to my chilblains.'

Like a theatrical villain who appears on stage through a cloud of smoke Sergeant Worcester emerged out of the darkness. 'What are you lot of spotty 'erberts jabbering on about? I could hear you a mile off. This isn't a Sunday school excursion to Margate and you're not on the beach paddling your bare feet in the surf. You're in the Army and this is the Western Front.'

'Please, Sergeant, I wanna go 'ome,' Hoon whined, jerking up and down from one foot to the other as if in urgent need of relieving himself.

Worcester fixed Hoon with a beady eye. 'You'll go 'ome when I say you'll go 'ome, and not a second earlier.'

Second Lieutenant Leighton cleared his throat. 'What's the hold up, Sergeant?'

Worcester straightened to attention. 'No hold up, sir. Just getting the men into their sections.'

'Very well.' He saluted the Sergeant. 'Move them off when ready.'

The Sergeant saluted back. 'Yes, sir.'

With numb noses, watering eyes and ice-crinkled faces bowed against the wind the men formed a ragged column of twos. And, with the snow accumulating on the rims of their tin helmets like deathly halos and on their wilting shoulders like pale epaulettes, they set themselves in motion, a shuffling line of reluctance, trepidation and agitated bowels.

Sergeant Worcester drove them on with his tongue. 'Come on you lot! Stop dawdling! I don't want to see any bunching up.'

Yet despite his harsh voice they dawdled and bunched up anyway. What else could they do? Only by dawdling and bunching up could they enjoy the protection of the man in front, his back and shoulders a break against the wind-driven snow, his closeness a suggestion of shared warmth. The cold was too bitter to keep distance.

Onward into the unwelcome dark they trudged, pinch-cheeked, noses running, uniformly woebegone, dread-burdened and oblivious to the world about them. They were as one in their misery, each man a unit of hopeless dejection, indistinguishable in flattened helmet, backpack, rifle and sodden greatcoat.

But there was one amongst them who stood out. He was shorter and slighter of build than most of his companions, but it wasn't his size that separated him from the rest. It was something altogether different, barely definable yet clear enough to see. It was his eager curiosity that made him distinct. Whereas those around him were hunched against the very presence of the world, his head was high, his face open, his eyes constantly moving about as he absorbed every detail of his surroundings.

Whether it was the descending snowflakes, the state and direction of the trodden road, the broken trees, the moon-lit clouds, the odd glimpsed star and all the shadowed shapes and objects that lay about him, nothing was too inconsequential to escape his notice. He was young as all the rest were young and it seemed that there was a youthful innocence in his face, unformed and unmarked by the cares of the world. But this impression ceased with his eyes. They told an entirely different story.

Like the eyes of a raven they were hard, alert and unwavering. They lacked that sense of wonder associated with unblemished youth. They were eyes that had seen everything. Nothing was new to them. There was no innocence in them. There was only assessment and calculation. Wherever they roamed or fixed their focus they noted distances, elevations, landmarks, cover and places to hide. They did this instinctively, from an instinct born of necessity. It was their way; something they had done for so long it seemed that no other way existed.

At the sloping entrance to the trenches the battalion was brought to a halt. As the men stood and waited for orders their steaming breath fogged about their heads like the smoke from a hundred burning cigarettes. Some rubbed their hands vigorously or blew warmth into them. Others swung their arms back and forth, hugging themselves in a solitary embrace or stamped their boots on the ground to renew the circulation in their numbed and frozen legs.

'I can't feel my fucking feet,' complained Swain. 'What about you, Coaxie? Can you feel yours?'

The young man with the innocent face and hard eyes, the one known to his fellows as 'Coaxie', turned to Swain, but said nothing. Instead he spent a silent moment looking Swain over in a blank and speculative manner. It was as if he was sizing him up, trying to work out his reactions, his determination, his capacity to endure and resist, his willingness to do whatever was necessary, his ability to survive whatever the cost. And when he came to a conclusion he turned away and dismissed Swain from his mind.

'Come on, you lot!' Sergeant Worcester bellowed. 'Get a move on! The quicker we get where we're going the quicker I'll be able to tuck you up bye byes.'

Barely comprehending what was going on the men filed into the communication trench. The entrance had a sort of street sign nailed to it. It read, 'Caledonian Road'. This raised a wry smile from some. But for most of those who passed beneath it there was a sense of descending from one level of hell into another, into an alien place unlike anything they had ever encountered before, a place of filth, stink and discomfort; a world of death, dread and hopelessness.

Their training had not prepared them for this grim and ghastly reality, this waking nightmare nor had the long and slow booted march from familiar streets and grassy hills to camps and barracks acclimatised them to the bare brutality of their new existence. As far as they were concerned they had been transported not to some other part of the world they were familiar with but to some other world entirely, to the lifeless surface of some planet far from the sun, a planet of lurid darkness and stark terrain.

Coaxie felt none of this. As he moved in line with the others along the narrow open trench between the wood-braced earthen walls with its blind alleys and cut-throat corners and breathed in the foetid, pig-sty stench that hung upon the air like a miasma of corruption and disease, he felt perfectly at home. In fact, these trenches, the smell of them and their brutal geometry, reminded him of the home he had left behind. Biologists say that every organism has an environment to which it is perfectly adapted. Coaxie had found his.

✦✦✦✦

'The men of A' section, Second Platoon, third company, fourth battalion South Sussex Fusiliers had finally reached that part of the front assigned to them and it seemed to them that they had come to the edge of the world and were surround by was a bottomless chasm of darkness. They stood in a line with their backs against one wall of the trench.

Facing them was another earthen wall, held in place by wooden fascines and topped with sagging, sodden sandbags. Running along the wall was a fire step with machine gun and mortar emplacements and loopholes for snipers. The names of the trenches in which they stood were the only thing that was familiar to them. Everything else was alien to sight, sound and smell.

Darkness cloaked most of their faces as Sergeant Worcester paced up and down before them like a master at a reform school.

'Right, lads, this is Brewer Street, your new home. It is a fire trench. That over there is the officer's dugout. That over there is your dugout. And that over there is no-man's-land. Beyond it are the Huns. If you need to find the latrine follow your nose. I'll be back in a minute but in the meantime get yourselves comfortable,'

As the line of men dispersed Private Swain peered sourly into the snow-flaked shadows. 'Get yourselves comfortable he says. How do you get comfortable in a ruddy scrapyard?'

All about them lay the detritus of trench life; duck boards, angle irons, shovels, picks, mauls, corrugated iron, sandbags, stakes, rabbit wire, expanded metal, coarse weeds and rank grasses. Strange auroras of light flooded the black horizon, appearing suddenly, fading slowly. Starbursts dazzled the zenith, illuminating faces with spectral surprise. The dark air whistled and crumped. And from somewhere in the distance came a chattering sound like an old and heavy typewriter.

'What's that stink?' Swain asked, sniffing the air.

'Smells like something's died,' concluded Hoon.

The implications of this observation brought silence to the gathering and each man looked about him as if all the yards of darkness surrounding him concealed a graveyard of disinterred corpses.

'I wanna go 'ome,' Hoon whined.

'You'll go 'ome when I say you'll go 'ome,' Sergeant Worcester told him, appearing on cue.

'I'm 'ungry, Sergeant,' Dibbs complained. 'When we gonna eat?'

'You got worms, Dibbs?' Sergeant Worcester asked. 'You 'ad your tea in the reserve area before we set off.'

'I can't help it, Sergeant. It's this perishing cold. All this shivering uses up one's energy.'

'All right,' agreed Sergeant Worcester. 'If you and your mates are so eager to fill your bellies you can 'ave the 'onour of forming our first ration party.'

'Ration party, Sergeant?'

'Yes, ration party. Follow Chapel Street trench and Caledonian Road trench back to the railway line. There you'll find the battalion supply dump and the company kitchen.'

'Ah, Sergeant.'

'Get moving!'

****

With all sense of direction lost in the night-shadowed landscape it would have taken Swain, Hoon, Hutchins, Dibbs and Shorthouse ages to find their way back to the point where they had disembarked from the narrow gauge train. Fortunately they had Coaxie with them. Without saying a word, he led them unerringly across the two hundred yards in under ten minutes. A little to the south of this they found vast mountains of various stores.

But a big-bellied Quartermaster Sergeant stood in front of them, guarding them like a butcher's dog. And as they approached he eyed them suspiciously.

'What do you want?' he growled.

'We've been sent to get rations,' Hutchins told him.

'Well, there ain't no rations 'ere.'

Hutchins was not one to be so easily put off. 'Where are they then?'

'Don't you lip me you, little runt,' the Sergeant threatened. 'Or I'll kick you up the arse.'

Seeing that reasoned argument was not going to get them anywhere with this man the ration group wandered off not knowing which way to turn. Fortunately for them it wasn't long before they happened upon two stretcher-bearers standing by a large stack of crated goods.

'Do you know where we should go to get some rations?' Hutchins asked the taller of the two.

The man seemed reluctant to answer. Instead he turned to his companion. 'Tell them, Fletch.'

The one called Fletch stabbed a finger toward a field kitchen that had been set up in the back garden of a shell-damaged cottage. Standing in the rubble was a cook and his assistant. The cook was stirring something in a steaming tureen whilst the assistant was baking bread in one of the field ovens. It was the assistant who first noticed the approach of Swain and his five companions.

'What d'you want?' he asked sullenly, wiping his hands on a grubby apron.

'We've come for some grub,' Swain explained.

'Oh, 'ave you. Well nothing's ready.'

142

'We only need some tea and a bite to eat,' said Hoon.

'For 'ow many?'

'Just us.'

The cook laughed and shook his head. 'This 'ain't no canteen. Who you with?'

'Fourth Battalion South Sussex. We're Second Platoon, third Company.'

'Right! Well, I'm issuing you with rations for a full platoon. Take that or you go back empty handed.'

****

The grey dunes of the sky pressed low and heavy upon the storm dark waters of the Baltic Sea. And as the waves crashed and battered against the rocky eastern coast of Rügen Island Thetis stood defiant on the edge of the cliff top that jutted out of the Pine forest enclosing her estate.

She loved this part of the world. It reminded her of her home in Scotland. And of her family. They had a castle near the Western Isles, some sheep grazing on the moors and very little else. But they had something greater than treasure, a proud and noble ancestry, one that stretched right back to the Kings of ancient Scotland.

To MacBeth and Robert the Bruce.

And it was this lineage that now gave her the courage to face the danger before her. She dug the toes of her bare feet into the grass and the chalky soil and waited for that moment when the wind gathered its strength and blew hard against her. And when it did she lent into it and let it support her against the fall. Her body was set against the whistle-fierce gusts, her face undaunted by either the terrible height or the raging elements. And as she contemplated the imperceptible edge of the world her hair streamed out behind her like seaweed in the tide.

This was her sort of weather, rough, violent and unrestrained. It exhilarated her. It cleared her mind and left her feeling rejuvenated. It calmed the turmoil that seemed to forever agitate her spirit and left her able to focus on those things that she considered important. And at the moment there was only one thing that was uppermost in her mind. She felt that she had come to a crossroads in her life. Should she continue on her present course or should she break off in an entirely different direction?

From where she stood she could see her yacht *Peleus*. It lay berthed against the jetty, its sails furled, its tall masts swaying into the wind, its well-founded hull, sharp and bone-white, rising and dipping to the rhythm of the swell. Taking the *Peleus* out to sea was one of the few things in the world that gave her joy. She loved standing upon its deck especially when fully rigged and she could feel the thrill of speed as the wind stretched the sails and the prow sliced through the pliant waters.

It was some while since she last felt that thrill and for the moment she was contemplating casting off once moor. But this time it would not be just a cruise around the Baltic. This time she would leave everything behind, possibly for good and set sail across the world.

And why shouldn't I? What reason do I have for staying? The British? Von Hoeppner? To hell with them! To hell with all of them! I owe no one anything.

But her defiance was fleeting. It lasted as long as the wind against which she lent. When it subsided and she stood upright she knew that she had unfinished business on dry land and that it was not part of her nature to just go off and leave matters unresolved.

Besides I'm still having too much fun where I am.

It was some days now since her attendance at Anthea von Hoeppner's birthday costume ball. Now back on her sprawling estate close to the coastal resort of Sassnitz Thetis felt more than satisfied with what she had accomplished during her brief visit.

My opening salvo against the hated von Hoeppners.

Anthea had been the target. In many ways she had set herself up as the target so much so that she left Thetis with the relatively easy task of engineering a trap for the Princess to fall into. But she had done it deftly, taking full advantage of each situation as it arose.

And as a result Anthea's day of celebration had ended in a most unexpected fashion with her suffering an ordeal of outrage and indignity at the hands of the count. Thetis knew she should have felt sympathy for the Princess. After all, twenty years earlier she herself had suffered far worse at the hands of a man. But she didn't have any sympathy for her for that man had been Anthea's father, the Archduke.

So she had to suffer like I suffered.

Anthea's beating had been entertaining and amusing, but it wasn't really what she was after. It was merely a foray, an appetiser. It was not nearly enough to satisfy her desire for vengeance. It was only the first step in a much larger plan. Her real target in all of this remained the Archduke. She had decided to strike at him through his one weakness, his one point of vulnerability, his daughter. But in this instance Anthea's ordeal had had no direct affect on the Archduke.

If only he had got to hear about it.

But he hadn't. He remained totally ignorant of the entire affair. He had no idea what von Gessendork had done to his daughter and that was down to Anthea herself; mortified and embarrassed she was determined to keep it a secret at all costs.

Of course, I could have just told him.

But to do such a thing, even anonymously, would have presented Thetis with enormous difficulties. For a start Anthea would have known for sure the identity of the person who had let the cat out of the bag. She would have known that it was Thetis and that clearly she had broken her promise not to breathe a word about the incident.

And for the moment it's vital I keep her trust.

Losing it risked losing access to the family. Keeping it meant that Thetis had in her possession a secret that gave her considerable power over the Princess. Not only did it giver her the perfect pretext for keeping in touch with the Princess it also ensured that Anthea wouldn't dare risk annoying her by not responding.

Besides knowing his daughter got her arse smacked is hardly likely to cause von Hoeppner any lasting pain.

No! She needed to do something that would hurt him badly and she needed to do it through his daughter. That was the problem Thetis now wrestled with as the northern winds struggled to make her step backwards. Fortunately the costume ball had provided her with the first glimmerings of an idea.

I now know that the daughter has a weakness too.

In her brief conversation with Anthea at the costume ball it had become more than apparent that the young woman harboured a dangerous desire, one that could be exploited.

The silly girl wants to be a war pilot.

Most people harbour fantasies of one sort or another, the desire to be someone else, possibly someone renowned for their courage in the face of danger. Most people with such fantasies are content enough to parade around in the clothes of their heroes without ever wishing to take on the risks that such a role entailed in real life.

But not Anthea!

She would never be happy with just wearing the uniform of an airman. Thetis sensed that deep within the Princess lay a passionate and all-consuming desire not only to play the part of a war pilot, but also to become a war pilot and take part in actual combat. Only one thing stood between her and what she wanted; her sex.

Well, I can help her overcome that handicap.

By any standards it was an insane idea, but Thetis was not averse to mad ideas. They had the charm of originality and quite often they had a better chance of achieving success than conventional ones. And she found this idea more appealing than most.

And the groundwork has already been laid.

It was laid during her brief conversation with Anthea. Though couched as nothing more than a compliment she had suggested that her masquerade as a pilot was so convincing she could easily pass muster at any German airbase.

Now all I have to do is nurture that idea.

And the fact that she had kept Anthea's secret would make her task that much easier. It would mean that she had the young woman's trust. And in time the relationship might become even deeper.

Who knows, we might even become friends.

Fired up by all these possibilities Thetis turned her back on the gusting wind and allowed it to propel her up the grassy slope toward her house with its central light-tower. With her raiment blowing before her like the sails of some seabourne vessel she passed between the billowing curtains of the permanently open French windows. Erich, who was in the study stoking the logs in the great stone-block fireplace, turned at her entrance.

'I want you to return to the Residenz,' she told him as she strode toward her desk. 'I have a letter I wish you to deliver.'

Not wishing to waste a moment in putting her plans into action, she drew paper from a drawer and dipped her pen into the ink.

Your Highness,

I feel compelled to begin my letter by congratulating you for the costume ball you held to celebrate your nineteenth birthday. Without a doubt it has to rank as the foremost event of the season. Everything was arranged with great flair and imagination and the Grand Hall never looked more imposing than it did that evening.

Yet one person, above all others present, stole the evening and no one that was present on that occasion would argue that that person was your Highness. In a company dressed lavishly and beautifully you were the one who stood out. Your costume was a simple one – the uniform of a German officer – yet it had the singular virtue of doing honour to our fighting men.

And, as I said at the time, it was utterly convincing in every detail. If I had not known you for as long as I have I would never have been able to see through the deception. Indeed, when I saw you coming down the stairs I was taken in, entirely, and as you know it was some time before I realised my error.

It is now clear to me that you must have taken great care over every detail of your costume, and by any measure such care does not come by whim alone. It can only come from a deep and abiding interest in everything concerning our glorious Imperial Air Service. I'll wager that if I were steal into your apartment and look in your robing room I would not only find all your exquisite gowns hanging on the rails but also other garments worn by airmen such as a dress uniform and an airman's flying coat.

Here Thetis paused to consider what she was to write next. This was the important part and it was vital that she get it right.

CHAPTER TWELVE

8 DECEMBER 1917

'Now that's something I never considered.'

'What's that, my Lady?' Helga asked as she ran a brush through her mistress's cropped hair.

In the light from the fire crackling in the grate Anthea consulted the letter that Helga had brought her with that morning's breakfast tray. 'The Baroness von Buchner is under the impression that I have an airman's dress uniform and flying coat in my robing room.'

'You haven't.'

'No, I know I haven't.'

Why does that insufferable girl always tell me things I already know?

'But I shall certainly contact Hermann to see if he can get them for me.'

'Why would you want such things, my Lady?'

'Because a collection is never complete until it has everything in it.'

'No, I suppose it isn't. Well, your brother should be able to get them for you. He got you most of the things you already have, didn't he?'

'Yes, he did. He comes across all sorts of things like that.'

Sitting at her dressing table, propped delicately on an especially soft cushion, Anthea contemplated the letter with some puzzlement. Indeed, she had not entirely got over the shock of receiving it in the first place. Her birthday party was now a thing of the past, and as far as she was concerned an event best forgotten, so she hadn't really expected to hear from the Baroness again.

Nor any great desire to do so.

Anthea was uncertain regarding her feelings toward the Baroness. She had never really liked her but that was mostly because her mother didn't like her. But now her own feelings seemed far less precise. After all, there was no denying that she'd been helpful after the von Gessendork incident, and she'd proved herself to be trustworthy by keeping her mouth shut afterwards.

But I'm not sure its enough to change my feelings.

Her first reaction on receiving the letter had been to ignore it. Why would she want to start a correspondence with a woman she didn't really like? But then there was something about the letter that made her change her mind. It wasn't so much what Thetis had to say as it was the way that she said it. The tone and manner of the letter was what one would expect from one friend writing to another and in this respect Anthea found it quite novel. She may have had beauty, wealth and high position but the one thing she didn't really have was someone she could a friend. It was for this reason that she turned eagerly to the next page.

Nonetheless, Your Highness, this interest of yours has left me greatly troubled. On the surface it may appear to be no more than an ardent longing to surround yourself with all the trappings of a noble undertaking. But if you recall your words to me it would appear that you desire to go beyond just wearing the uniform and actually use it to pose as a war pilot and attempt to infiltrate the JGN airbase at Bois de Cheval.

'What!' Anthea sat bolt upright. 'I never said any such thing.'

'What didn't you say, my Lady?'

'Never mind.' Frowning furiously Anthea turned her eyes back to the letter.

Given the gaiety and high spirits of the costume ball I considered this suggestion to be nothing more than the sweet and idle fancy of youth, but now I am not so sure. The look of determination on your face returns to haunt me, leaving me uncertain as to how serious you might be in this purpose.

Forgive my forwardness, but it is only out of my fond regard for you, the fond regard that an Aunt might feel toward a favourite niece, that I write in such a manner. Please, I beg you, give up these ambitions. They can only bring grief upon you and your family.

Yours in honour and friendship
Thetis, Baroness von Buchner

'Stupid woman!' Anthea threw the letter onto her dressing table.

Helga stood back alarmed. 'I'm sorry, my Lady. Am I brushing too hard?'

'Not you. Just carry on doing what you are doing and don't interrupt me when I'm talking to myself.'

'As you wish, my Lady.'

Snatching up the letter, Anthea stared at it, not actually reading it but regarding it with some degree of outrage and bewilderment as if it contained an accusation of impropriety of which she knew herself to be wholly innocent. And as she did this she cast her mind back to the party and tried to remember not only what she and the Baroness had talked about but also the precise words and just as importantly who had said what.

Of one thing she was certain. The conversation between them had been brief, no more than a few sentences at most. She knew this because it would probably have been a lot longer if that swine von Gessendork hadn't decided to poke his nose in where it wasn't wanted. She could recall that the conversation certainly touched upon the JGN airbase at Bois de Cheval. But then why wouldn't it? After all, she was supposed to be posing as an officer operating from that base. And Thetis had asked her if she knew her son.

But I can't believe I suggested something so insane.

Anthea was willing to admit that her interest in the Imperial German Air Service was somewhat extreme, and that most people would regard it as a less than healthy interest for a young woman to be preoccupied with. But even in her wildest imaginings she had never harboured any illusions about getting into an airbase. Fooling people at a party was one thing but an airbase was an entirely different proposition. She'd be spotted straight away.

No, my dreams will have to remain dreams.

'I was thinking, my Lady,' Helga began in a wistful voice, encouraged to speak by the silence of her mistress. 'Now that the party is over there's no need to keep your beautiful hair so short. Don't you think it is time to start growing it long again?'

Still holding the letter, her flashing eyes full of unreadable design, Anthea reached behind her and with thoughtful fingers touched the bare skin where her neck met the base of her skull.

'Oh, I don't know, Helga. I've grown so used to it I think I might keep it just as it is for a little while longer.'

****

As Corporal Soames steered the tender off the road and past the open gate, Lieutenant Cummings crinkled his nose at the pungent reek of pig wafting through the lowered window of his cab. It was a smell he'd encountered earlier that day when he and Soames had driven through a town near the line. On that occasion he'd discretely examined the bottom of first one shoe then the other. But on finding nothing untoward he'd jumped to a different conclusion.

'I say, Corporal, is there a farm close at hand?'

'No, sir.'

'Then where's that smell coming from?'

'From the front.'

'The front?'

Soames had smiled airily. 'Yes, sir. Some say it's the biggest pig-sty in the world."

But now the smell though similar was of a markedly different nature. It carried with it an unmistakable authenticity, one that was healthier, and less sinister. More to the point it came with the sound of squealing pigs.

"Fresh bacon for breakfast, sir."

A large group of scrawny chickens blocked the snow-rutted track ahead, only launching themselves away from the wheels of the vehicle at the last second, screeching and flapping their wings frantically in a mockery of flight.

"And eggs," Cummings said, thinking of his stomach.

"Oh yes, sir. Eggs as well. And cream and cheese! And in the spring when the blossom is in bloom we have fresh strawberries and raspberries and blackberries."

Cummings watched as farm buildings and orchards gave way to bushes and fields and a couple of idle horses, and then the natural world was replaced by a line of Bessoneau hangars and the nostril-flaring tang of castor oil. Craning his neck to get a better view he caught sight of several Sopwith Camels, their round, silvery snouts and wooden propellers poking out of the first hangar. They had an impatient look about them, as if raring to go.

In the next hangar a mechanic in blue overalls stood beside one machine wiping greasy hands on a filthy cloth, the stub of a rolled up cigarette dangling from his mouth as he watched with majestic indifference the tender roll past. Behind him came the sound of hammering as other mechanics busied themselves with repairs and maintenance.

After the hangars came a small wooden workshop and then the swaying of the tender ceased as its wheels mounted a cinder path. Following this the vehicle did a right-angle turn then straightened alongside a neat line of Nissen huts. Realising his journey was about to end, Cummings hurriedly straightened his tie and Sam Brown and made sure his pockets were buttoned down and his 'gor-blimey' cap was properly perched on his head. Brakes squeaking the tender came to a halt.

"Here we are, sir," Soames called out as he climbed out of his cab. 'Home at last.'

Cummings pushed open his door and jumped down onto the cinder path, which had been salted to keep it free of snow. His knees felt stiff from the long journey and he was on the point of stamping his feet to bring them back to life when Soames appeared in front of him.

"You'll find the office in the there, sir." He pointed to a hut with two windows and a Crossley staff car parked beside it. "I'll get an orderly to remove your bags."

"Thank you, Corporal."

After returning Soame's salute Cummings approached the office. The sign on the door said 'Major A. Parkinson – Commanding Officer'. Adjusting the knot of his tie one last time, he prepared to knock.

"Hello, there."

The greeting had come from Cummings' right and turning away from the door he found himself facing a young man wearing an impossibly large grin.

'I'm Whitworth.'

'And I'm Cummings,' he said, shaking Whitworth's hand.

'Just arrived?'

Whitworth was enclosed in a Sidcot flight suit, which made him look like an ungainly Teddy bear; an illusion heightened by the fur-trimmed leather helmet and the black, half-circles of oil under the young man's eyes. He was also clutching goggles and a pair of fur-lined gloves.

'Yes, I was about to report to the CO.'

'I see.' Pulling off his helmet Whitworth scratched a mop of black, curly hair. 'Well, normally an orderly would announce you, but as I don't see one about and as I'm going your way, so to speak, shall I do the honours?'

'I would consider that a great kindness.'

As Cummings stepped away from the door Whitworth pushed it open and yelled, 'Hargreaves! Is the Major in?'

'He is,' was the gruff response. 'Why?'

'There's a Lieutenant Cummings here to see him.'

'Is there?' Hargreaves didn't sound impressed. 'Well, I suppose you'd better bring him in.'

Whitworth allowed Cummings to precede him into the outer office, a gloomy enclosure of creaking boards that smelt of creosote, untreated timber and pipe tobacco. Wooden filing cabinets lined one wall. In one corner stood a hat stand covered in caps, greatcoats and mackintoshes. On a wall was a blackboard with the names of all the pilots in the squadron neatly written in chalk.

Facing the door was a small military issue desk. On it stood a covered typewriter, a blotter, an in-tray, various rubber stamps and an upright field telephone. Behind all of this sat a man with a very young face and fine, prematurely thinning blonde hair. Returning Cummings' salute he stood up. 'I'm Hargreaves, the adjutant. How was your journey?'

'Fine, thanks. Though I fear the roads may have loosened a few of my teeth.'

Hargreaves gave a short laugh. 'Not exactly built for comfort, are they. Got your record of service?'

After taking Cummings' documents Hargreaves turned to Whitworth. 'The lieutenant and I need to complete some paperwork. It may take a while.'

Whitworth, obviously a man who never took a hint, just smiled and said, 'Don't mind me. I've got to scribble this morning's jaunt in the diary.'

Hargreaves turned back to Cummings. 'If you'd like to take a seat.'

Cummings dropped into a rattan chair and waited while Hargreaves sorted through a file that lay open before him. 'You need to enter your details on the unit's Roll of Officers, next of kin register and mess list. And there are some other forms you'll have to complete.'

While Cummings busied himself with this, Hargreaves picked up the field telephone. 'Hargreaves here, Major. I have Lieutenant Cummings with me. I'll bring him through as soon as he's finished the formalities.'

With the paperwork completed Hargreaves rose to his feet and, taking the file with him, went through a door at the back of the outer office. This gave Whitworth the opportunity to inform Cummings, 'You'll like the Major. He's a nice fellow.'

Cummings was about to ask more when the back door opened and Hargreaves re-emerged.

'The Major will see you now.'

'Good luck,' Whitworth called out as Cummings got up. "See you in the mess later."

****

Major Parkinson's office was much the same as Harker had left it. The large, dark brown desk was still there. And on it was the same green-shaded lamp, blotter, bottle of Stephen's ink, upright telephone, wooden pipe-stand, thermidor, glass ashtray and trays marked 'in' and 'out'. Attached to the wall behind the desk was the same framed picture of the king and beside it the same oilcloth map of the squadron's operational area around Ste Helene Salient. Small flags showed the location of neighbouring squadrons.

The only window was not only small and begrimed with dust it was also obscured by the corner of a nearby hut. It admitted little natural light and even on a sunny day the desk-lamp was on, its pool of illumination making the corners of the office even darker.

Pipe in mouth, Major Parkinson lent back in his chair, propping a knee against his desk. This cast his head deeper into the gloom leaving only the glowing bowel of his pipe visible, but its brightness waxed and waned in a manner suggesting deep thought. In reality he was enjoying a break from what had been the burden of daily routine – reading sick reports, signing supply orders, issuing punishments for minor offences, assessing orders from Brigade.

Before relaxing to take a moment and light his pipe, he had been writing a crash report.

Young idiot! Fancy trying to land on a bird's nest.

The pilot had walked away unscathed. The Camel on the other hand hadn't been so lucky. It took a whole day to get it down from the tree and when it was finally back on the ground it was found to have buckled wheels, a cracked propeller and a gaping tear in one of its lower wings.

Sufficient damage to entail reams of paperwork.

Parkinson looked around his office. It was now well over a fortnight since his predecessor Major Harker had sat in the chair he was now sitting in yet Parkinson still found it hard to think of it as his office. In many respects he still regarded it as Harker's.

And I probably always will.

He remembered that Harker had been sitting in this very chair on that fateful day when he had ordered Parkinson to take to the skies and intercept Buchner. Only that wasn't how it worked out. Harker had taken his place and now he was missing and Parkinson was in command.

Strange how things work out.

A knock at the door made Parkinson release his knee from the desk and sit up straight. 'Come in.'

Hargreaves entered and shut the door discretely behind him. 'Sorry to disturb you, Major, but I've brought you Lieutenant Cummings' file.'

Putting down his pipe, Parkinson took the file and extracted several documents, making no movement as he read them other than to absently brush the underside of his thin moustache with the index finger of his left hand.

Lawrence Worcester Cummings... Twenty-one years of age... Two years at Cambridge University studying physics under Moseley. Good God! A scientist!

"Shall I send him in now, Major?"

"Er, yes. Do that will you, Hargreaves." Parkinson continued reading the documents.

Joined up June '17 at London OTS... Applied for pilot training... Took seven months to get certificate... Target proficiency average... Somewhat stiff at controls... First class understanding of flight theory...

What the devil is he doing here? He should be designing these things not flying them.

'Lieutenant Cummings, Major.'

Parkinson stood up. 'Come in, Cummings. I'm Major Parkinson. Welcome to sixty-three squadron. Take a seat, will you.'

'Thank you, sir.'

Pleasant voice. Nice manner.

Parkinson watched the young man cast a brief glance around the office before locating a straight-back chair propped against the left wall. 'Smoke, if you wish.'

'Thank you, sir.'

Cummings was the seventh new pilot that Parkinson had interviewed since taking command of the squadron. During that time he had developed a set routine for putting them at their ease. He had also introduced a number of well-rehearsed pauses into the proceedings. One of these was giving them the time to light up a cigarette. This allowed him the few vital moments he needed to quickly take stock of whatever young man happened to be facing him. Taking several vigorous puffs from his pipe, Parkinson focused his attention on Cummings.

Tallish. Bit thin in arm and leg. More cricket than rugby. Clean shaven. Neat straight hair. Upright posture. Always a good sign that. Somewhat reticent and awkward in manner, but that's probably down to a spot of nerves.

But it was the fierce intensity of Cummings eyes that Parkinson found most compelling. They were lively and alert to a degree that was extraordinary, almost as if the person on the other side of them was in a constant state of observation and analysis. As Parkinson dropped his gaze to look at the documents in front of him, it was Cummings turn to examine the man sitting opposite him. He began by trying to determine the age of his commanding officer.

He had black hair and a neatly trimmed black moustache that probably made him look older. And the burden of responsibility had undoubtedly also had some effect. His eyes were unflinching and penetrating, but not without humour. And there was something artistic about his mouth and the shape of his hands.

Aware that he himself was being assessed, but not bothered, Parkinson took the pipe out of his mouth and pointed to a spot on the document in front of him.

"It says here you were reading physics at Cambridge?"

"Yes, Major. Second year."

"Hopefully, you'll finish your studies after all this is over. A couple of other pilots are mid-course, so to speak but, I have to say, you're our first scientist. Not that you'll have much time for research here."

Cummings smiled. "No, Major. I don't suppose I will."

Parkinson started to stroke his moustache, a sure sign that he was about to ask a telling question. "I'm curious, Cummings. What made you apply for pilot training?"

Cummings took a moment to consider his reply. "Well, I suppose it just seemed the natural choice."

Parkinson nodded knowingly. 'Better than the trenches, eh?'

'I would say it was more than that, sir. I believe flying is the future. I believe that a day will come when the Flying Corp will stand equal to the army and the navy.'

'An interesting point of view.' Parkinson would have enjoyed discussing the idea further, but with more pressing matters to be dealt with he turned back to Cummings' file. 'You've had eight hours on Camels, I see. Not a lot.'

'No, sir.'

'Fortunately, our sector is reasonably quiet at the moment so you should be able to get a few more hours under your belt before undertaking any serious work. Was that Whitworth you came in with?"

"Yes, Major."

Parkinson lifted his head and shouted, "Hargreaves!"

The adjutant poked his head into the office. "Yes, Major?"

"Is Whitworth still out there?"

"Yes. He's completing his log book."

"Whitworth!" Parkinson shouted again.

Whitworth appeared, looking slightly sheepish despite his friendly smile. "Yes, Major?"

"Take Cummings up for a look around, will you. Show him the sights."

"Now, Major?"

"No time like the present. Unless you need to be somewhere else."

"No. Now is fine, Major."

"Splendid. Well, you go with Whitworth, Cummings. He'll show you what to do. Hargreaves will assign you to a flight when you return. Then maybe we can have a further chat this evening in the mess."

"Yes. Thank you, Major."

After the door closed, the Major sat back in his chair and drew on his pipe speculatively.

Seems a nice enough fellow. But then, don't they all?

The engine note lowered as Cummings eased back the throttle. He applied a touch of right rudder as he did so. In his anxiety not to lose sight of Whitworth he had clung to his companion's tail and, as a result had drifted too close. It wouldn't do to chew off someone's rear end on the first day especially as that someone showed every sign of becoming a good friend.

What a day!

Ever since his arrival at the squadron, barely an hour earlier it had been one thing after another. First there'd been his interview with the CO. That had gone fairly well, but no sooner had he started to relax and contemplate the pleasures of the mess than he found himself preparing for flight. First priority was to change into suitable clothing. In a state of utter confusion he tried to locate his kit bag and the flying gear he'd bought at great expense from Robinson and Cleaver in London. But before he could track it down Whitworth stopped him.

"No time for that. We've got everything you need."

Hanging from hooks and hangers in the equipment hut was a cornucopia of Sidcot flying suits, fur-lined leather helmets, fur-lined flying gloves, fur-lined boots, perplex goggles and leather map-holders.

'An aviator's bazaar,' Whitworth quipped.

As Cummings struggled into a Sidcot it occurred to him that it wasn't new. It had once belonged to someone else. And he wondered what tragic turn of events had parted the previous owners from their gear. He could have asked Whitworth but didn't.

Probably best not to know.

Proofed against the elements, he followed Whitworth across the snow-crisp grass to three large canvas hangars that stood at the eastern end of a flat open field. Two Camels stood waiting outside the first hangar. Whitworth marched up to one of them and, with a heavily gloved hand, stroked and patted the silvered curve of its cowling.

"Isn't she a beauty?" he asked, turning his infectious grin toward Cummings.

Cummings' Camel was fresh from the airpark in Candas and although he was familiar with the type he knew that he would have to treat it warily. Each machine had its own idiosyncrasies and failure to discover them quickly could easily prove fatal. Squeezing his padded legs into the cramped cockpit, he slid his backside onto the wicker seat. Finding the rudder bar with his feet he started fastening his safety straps across his waist and chest. A Sergeant mechanic in greasy overalls appeared at his side.

'Still fine-tuning the wiring on this one, sir. So nice and steady, if you take my meaning. Nothing too steep or extravagant.'

Cummings nodded then pulled his goggles over his eyes. As he started to check his stick and rudder Whitworth appeared beside him.

'Remember, this is just a jaunt to the front. Follow me closely. It's unlikely we'll see any of our friends from across the way, but if we do ignore them. Don't go giving chase. Stick with me and we'll be back for an early tea.'

Cummings smiled weakly then pulled his scarf up over his mouth. There was a brief moment of anxiety as he tried to remember the correct procedure for starting up but this soon passed when the rotary engine roared into life and the machine juddered to the spin of the propeller.

The poplar trees that lined the road were a quarter mile distant, but as Cummings opened the throttle and the Camel began moving forward they seemed worryingly close. Would he rise from the ground too soon and stall or would he leave it too late and end up bird-nesting in some treetop? These thoughts cascaded through his mind.

Taking his lead from Whitworth, who was ahead of him and already several feet off the ground, he waited a second then eased gently back on the stick.

Almost immediately the bone-shaking contact of wheel on lumpy grass disappeared as his Camel sprang into the air like an angry bird. All he could see ahead of him was a looming barrier of tree-trunks and branches. Then the sky pressed down on the trees and he was over the top, banking left as a flock of roosting birds took flight in protest.

Aloft and banking, all he could see was the snow-covered ground on one side and blue sky on the other. Whitworth's machine was fifty yards ahead still banking left, still following the tree line round the airfield. Smiling, Cummings set off in pursuit.

They continued circling the airfield, gaining height until they reached 3,000 feet then Whitworth straightened his machine and headed east. Cummings followed as closely as he dared. To him everything below him was now unfamiliar territory. If he failed to keep contact with Whitworth he felt sure he would become hopelessly lost.

Try to remember landmarks – forests, rivers, roads.

There was also the need to keep a constant lookout for other aircraft. What had Whitworth said on the way to the hangars? 'We'll be keeping to our side of the lines, but stay alert. You never know what might creep up behind you.'

Stretching his neck Cummings looked over his shoulder. But his anxious eyes were greeted with nothing but empty sky. He snapped his head forward. Whitworth was still there, his Camel bobbing gently in the air currents. Then it started a gentle bank to the left and Cummings followed, straightening when Whitworth straightened.

Whitworth throttled down and slowly drifted back until he was flying on Cummings' left. Both pilots greeted each other with a wave and a smile. Then Whitworth pointed a finger toward the ground. Cummings turned his head in the direction indicated.

For a moment he wasn't quite sure what he was looking at. Then he saw it. The front-line! They were flying parallel to it in a more or less northerly direction. Though still a quarter mile distant, at their present altitude it seemed as if they were actually looking directly down upon it.

Easiest to make out were the forward trenches, deeply imprinted lines of darkness that criss-crossed the snow-softened ground like railed shadows. Beyond the front line lay a tangle of barbed wire and beyond that the pitted domain of no man's land, a broad skin of burst boils, their oil darkened waters winking up at the sky like mirror-reflected messages.

What did Soames call it? The biggest pig-sty in the world.

This vista of white desolation was so mesmerising he found his eyes locked upon it in morbid fascination. Thousands had died on this narrow stretch of ground, chewed, jointed and minced into butcher's meat and offal by shell and machine-gun fire. He was too high to see such things, but he knew they were there, the shanks and flanks, the hams and loins, the shins and ribs all buried and preserved from decay beneath mud and snow.

Then he saw the wreck of an aircraft, nose in the ground, wings twisted back like a broken butterfly. It was a British machine; he could make out the roundels, faded but still discernable on the upper wing.

I wonder what happened to the pilot.

Had he made it back to the lines or was he still out there, still sitting in the cockpit dead and skeletal? Quite unaccountably Cummings' arms and legs started to shake, making it hard for him to keep a firm grip on the stick and rudder.

What the hell's going on?

At first he thought it might be vibrations caused by the Le Rhône engine running unevenly or by the prop being slightly out of trim. These possibilities were worrying enough, but the truth, when it finally dawned on him, was mortifying. The shaking was not coming from the machine.

My God! It's me! I'm shaking! My first time out and I'm shaking with fear.

He looked up, fearful that Whitworth might be close enough to see his predicament. But Whitworth wasn't there.

Shit! Where is he?

The sky ahead was empty. Frantically, he looked left and right, panic rising in his chest and throat.

He looked to the rear.

For a second his mouth wrenched open to emit a cry as his eyes fell upon a machine thirty feet behind him.

The enemy! No! The air rushed out of him in relief. It was Whitworth's Camel.

He watched it side-slip from behind his tailplane and draw up beside him. Grinning like a Cheshire cat, Whitworth drew a finger across his throat. Despite a rush of anger, Cummings forced himself to return the smile. Any other response would have been a dead give away. Besides, his anger was misplaced. He was the one guilty of inattention; a fatal lapse given the closeness of the enemy.

Prank or not, I deserved that jolt.

Then he realised that the trembling in his arms and legs had stopped. They were now rock steady. The funk had given way to embarrassment. Like a man at a party who discovers he hasn't properly fastened his fly Cummings felt sure that every soldier on the ground had witnessed his humiliation.

Probably the entire British army.

His eyes strayed down to the trenches. He couldn't see anyone. He was too high for that. But in his imagination he saw soldiers pointing in his direction and laughing. And not just the British. He was convinced that even the Germans across the way were shaking their heads in astonished disbelief that an English pilot could be so incompetent.

God! What a first day!

CHAPTER THIRTEEN

8 DECEMBER 1917

Why did I start shaking like that?

Although it had not returned, the question as to what had caused it to happen in the first place pursued Cummings all the way back to the aerodrome. Only as he came into land did he come up with a reassuring possibility.

Maybe it happens to all new pilots.

He hoped it did. It would be unbearable to think that he was the only one. But hope was all he had. He didn't dare ask anyone. After all, it was hardly the sort of topic one would normally raise in the mess after a drink or two.

Why the hell did I choose the Flying Corps?

The decision had been a logical one. He had no stomach for the trenches or the ocean waves. That left the war in the air. But it hadn't been merely a choice by default. To Cummings the Flying Corps represented the frontier of technology, and he had wanted to be a part of it.

And what could be nobler than swooping about like a hawk high in a bright blue sky?

But as he switched off his engine and climbed out of his cockpit he was no longer so certain. The elements of his dream were now cast in a grimmer and more sombre light. Where before he had seen only beauty in the act of flying he now saw some of its blemishes. With the welcome earth far below him, surrounded by an expanse of hostile sky, alone and enclosed in a machine that offered no protection from either the elements or enemy bullets, he began to doubt the soundness of his reasoning.

Whitworth draped a friendly arm across Cummings dispirited shoulders and guided him toward the huts.

'That was a fine landing.'

"Thanks for the crumb of comfort, but I hardly think my performance was something to write home about."

"Rot! You followed me out and you followed me back."

"And that's all there is to it?"

"No. But you'd have felt even more of an arse if you'd got lost."

"What, more than the arse I felt for being jumped while not paying attention?"

Whitworth laughed without mockery. "Sorry about that. I didn't mean to spook you, but its better the lesson comes from a friend."

"I'm not going to last ten minutes out here, am I?"

"Why should you say that?"

"I still have to think about what I'm doing. And while I'm thinking someone like you, admittedly with a German accent, is going to creep up behind me and shoot me down. For God's sake, you were right in front of me and I didn't even see you slip away."

"I was just like you when I started my war flying and I'm still here."

"And how long ago was that?"

Whitworth concentrated. "Well, including the couple of days I've been with this squadron I'd say about two months in all."

"Two months!"

"Doesn't sound a lot, I know. But you learn fast out here. You have to. I did. And you will too. Have you eaten?"

Whitworth's change of tack made Cummings remember his empty stomach, which, till now, had been lurking fearfully behind his bowels. "Not since breakfast in St Omer."

"Come on then. Tea and biscuits on me."

"Hadn't I better change first?"

"Whatever for? In these parts hungry airmen don't stand on ceremony!"

****

The mess hut's spacious and gloomy interior was filled with a blue-grey haze of tobacco smoke that swayed and curled beneath the arched ceiling. The small, uncurtained windows admitted a meagre amount of afternoon sunshine. The boarded floor was covered with oddments of carpet whose original design was worn beyond memory. At the hut's far end, several tables stood end to end, empty and idle. The slatted walls were decorated with bulletin boards, a faded portrait of the King and framed black and white photographs of pilots posing or standing in cheerful groups.

At the centre of the hut three officers lounged in battered leather armchairs. One was reading *Almayer's Folly*, one was flicking through a battered edition of *Tatler* and the third was scanning the front page of a four-day-old edition of the *Times*. All three looked up as Cummings and Whitworth entered the hut.

Lieutenant William Judge, a chubby faced man with black, slick hair, greeted them. "Hello, Whitworth. Enjoy your ramble?"

"Certainly did," Whitworth replied with his usual cheeriness. "The countryside has never looked lovelier.'

Judge shifted his attention away from Whitworth. 'And you must be Cummings.'

'I am.'

'I'm Judge. The fellow beside me with his nose in a book is Lapton. And the one pretending to read the Times is Courtland. We're all in 'A' flight.'

'Which flight are you in?' Courtland asked.

'I've no idea,' Cummings glanced at Whitworth as if he might have the answer. 'No one's told me yet.'

'You'll probably be in 'B' with Whitworth,' Courtland suggested. 'There's a vacancy in 'B'.'

"Oh, really?" Cummings was struck immediately by an obvious question, but it seemed too indelicate to ask.

Seeing Cummings' pensive expression and guessing the reason behind it, Judge said: 'Ignore Courtland. He's a clot, aren't you, Courtland? 'Vacancy' is not a word we use around here. It tends to have tragic overtones. I'm sure the truth, in this instance, is far more banal.'

'Yes, you're as safe as houses here,' Lapton said with a mischievous grin. 'Nothing to write home about except fresh rashers for breakfast and lots of sightseeing.'

Judge motioned toward a couple of vacant chairs. 'Why don't you join us? Watkins is supposed to be bringing tea.'

'Watkins makes a lovely cup of tea,' Lapton explained. 'His mother's own recipe I'm informed. It's russet-coloured and lines one's pipework with a coating that's not only leak proof but also calming to the digestion."

As Cummings and Whitworth sat down Lapton stretched his neck and yelled, 'WATKINS!'

A door near the tables opened and the gangly form of Private Harry Watkins appeared in all its unkempt and goofy solemnity.

'Where's our tea?' Lapton demanded imperiously. 'We're dying of thirst out here.'

'Almost ready, sir.'

Watkins head was about to withdraw when Lapton added, 'And bring two extra cups.'

****

Watkins' rapid retreat back into the small kitchen ended in a collision with Corporal Soames strutting chest.

'Watch where you're going, lad.'

'Sorry, Alf.'

'None of your Alf. It's Corporal Soames to you.'

'Sorry, Corporal.'

'Anyway, what's all the rush?'

'I'm making a brew for the officers.'

'Well, get on with it then, lad. Doesn't pay to keep officers waiting for their afternoon refreshments.'

'No, Corporal.'

Soames watched with idle amusement as Watkins took a cloth and lifted the large boiling kettle from the stove. 'Do you know what I've just done?'

'No, Corporal.' Tilting the kettle Watkins poured steaming water into a fat teapot.

'I've just taken the post to the office.'

Watkins head jerked round so fast he almost spilt the water onto the table. 'Anything interesting?'

Soames took a cigarette out of his breast pocket and lit it in a casual manner. 'I'm not saying there was and I'm not saying there wasn't.'

Not letting Soames out of his sight Watkins finished filling the teapot. 'Anything for me?'

Pulling on his cigarette, Soames eyed Watkins speculatively. 'I'm not saying there was and I'm not saying there wasn't.'

'Oh, come on, Alf,' Watkins pleaded, too excited to keep up the pretense. 'Don't mess about. You know I haven't heard from Dolly in over a fortnight.'

Shaking his head in disbelief, Soames stuck his cigarette in the corner of his mouth and unbuttoned his other breast pocket. 'For the life of me, I just can't figure out what my sister sees in you.'

But the criticism was lost on Watkins. His eager eyes were fastened on Soames' fingers as they extracted a small, white envelope from his pocket.

'I could get court-martialled for doing this.'

Watkins gave him a goofy smile of glee and gratitude. 'You'll get your reward in 'eaven, Alf.'

Soames handed Watkins the letter. 'I doubt it.'

Not wishing to sully any correspondence from Dolly, Watkins carefully wiped his hands on a tea towel. 'Thanks, Alf.'

'What you doing, you dopey 'aporth? Don't open it now.'

Watkins looked ruefully at the letter. 'Why not?'

'Because the officers are waiting for their tea, that's why not.'

****

'This looks cozy.' Cummings preceded Whitworth into the gloomy hut, sniffing the smell of damp earth and creosote and the sweeter odours of ripe fruit, hair oil, cologne and shaving soap.

'We've tried our best to make it look like home.' Whitworth lingered by the door. 'But there's only so much you can do with what in its basic essentials is little more than a glorified beach hut.'

Cummings surveyed the four beds. 'Which one's mine?'

'The one with your kit bag on it.'

'Who do the other beds belong to?'

Whitworth nodded to the bed near the door. 'This one's mine. A bit draughty I know, but it means I get first tea in the morning. The others belong to Rycliffe and Leith.'

'Where are they?'

'Ferrying a couple of new buses from Candas.'

'What's this?' Cummings pointed to a large glass jar beside Rycliffe's bed that had a few spent bullet casings at the bottom.

'It's a collection Rycliffe has just started. He gets his rigger to dig them out of his bus after every patrol.'

'Why does he do that?'

'The squadron's running a wager on how many they'll be in the jar by the time he goes west.'

Cummings couldn't help but smile at such a ghoulish idea. 'How many are in there now?'

'About four or five, but between you and me I think he got them off someone else so as not be embarrassed by an empty jar.' Whitworth's attention shifted. 'Oh, before I forget, Corporal Ballard is hut orderly. He'll be doing your laundry and such like.'

'Anything else?'

'Well, this basin is for freshening-up and shaving. There's an ablutions hut with shower cubicle but I wouldn't recommend it. The water's always freezing cold.'

'Doesn't the Major notice a lessening in the standard of hygene?'

'It may have escaped your attention, but we share this part of the Earth's lower atmosphere with a herd of pigs. What with that and the constant reek of engine oil, he'd be hard pressed to smell the smoke from his own pipe.'

'The Corporal who drove me here mentioned fresh eggs and bacon from the local farm.'

'Not only that, the Major has hired the farmer's wife to do our cooking. Well worth the few extra sous on one's mess bills.'

'This seems a very well organised squadron.'

'Oh, it is. The Major has plans to organise sporting events with other squadrons, and other things such as lectures and concert parties. There's even talk of a piano in the mess and moving picture shows with Charlie Chaplin.'

'It'll be hard to remember that there's a war on.'

Hands in pockets, Whitworth lent against the doorjamb and looked at the floor with a wry smile. 'Not that hard.'

****

With the hut to himself Cummings decided to get out of his flying gear and into fresh clothing but he had only just started unpacking when a young man with a pleasing and precise manner appeared in the doorway.

'Hello, sir. I'm Corporal Ballard, your hut orderly.'

Cummings turned. 'Hello, Ballard.'

'Can I do that for you, sir?'

'What?' Cummings looked down at the pile of folded shirts he was holding. 'Oh these. That's all right. I may as well finish what I started. Those things on the bed, though, could you return them to the stores for me please.'

'Certainly, sir.'

Ballard gathered up the Sidcot suit, boots, goggles, helmet and gloves and started to leave.

'Oh, and Ballard.'

The Corporal stopped and turned. 'Yes, sir?'

'I've been told I must speak to you about laundry and things of that nature.'

'That's right, sir. If you have no objections, I'll include you in the same arrangements I have with the other gentlemen in this hut.'

'That sounds fine to me.'

'Very well, sir.'

Ballard left with his burdens, but Cummings wasn't alone for long. Hargreaves walked in.

'Oh, Cummings! Just the man.' He consulted a list in front of him. 'You've been assigned to 'B' flight.'

So I will be flying with Whitworth.

Cummings felt cheered by this development, but Hargreaves hadn't finished.

'And your first patrol with them will be ten o'clock tomorrow morning.'

Although he gave no outward sign Cummings found this news far from welcome. He had known all along that he would have to go out on patrol at some point, but he hadn't reckoned on it being so soon. It was an unsettling reminder that from now on his shaky nerves would be tested on a daily basis.

'This covers our operational area.' Hargreaves handed him a map and a leather case to put it in. 'Do you need a log book?'

'No thanks.' Cummings was eager to see the back of Hargreaves and all his operational talk. 'I still have my one from TDS.'

'Remember; if you're forced down in Hunland destroy the map. That goes for your bus as well. Brigade isn't keen on the Huns getting their hands on anything useful.'

'No. I suppose they aren't.' Cummings nodded absently, not at all bothered by Brigade's concerns. Then he forced a cheery grin on his face. 'Anything else worth knowing? What about dress in the mess?'

'This is a fairly easy-going squadron. No strict rules as such, but you'll be expected to wear a clean uniform for dinner.' Here Hargreaves took off his glasses and smiled. 'However, if there's a binge afterwards I'd advise you to hang your jacket somewhere safe.'

****

There was a pleasant stillness to the cold evening air as Cummings and his three hut mates strolled along the path to the mess. Second Lieutenant Benjamin Rycliffe and Second Lieutenant Jeremy Leith had returned from Candas barely half an hour earlier and, after reporting to the office, found themselves with less than fifteen minutes to change.

Naturally, everything had to be done at a rush, including the introductions. The latter had been a comic interlude as Cummings shook hands with Leith who was under his bed looking for a lost shoe and Rycliffe who was hopping about trying to get his legs into his trousers.

"You're not seeing us at our best." Whitworth winked as he offered Cummings a cigarette.

When they were ready all four of them headed to the mess; Cummings and Leith led whilst Rycliffe and Whitworth followed arm in arm.

'Like two pairs of courting couples,' Rycliffe observed.

Leith was a short, plump fellow with burning cheeks and a wheezing gait, but he seemed to have an enthusiasm that outweighed all possible impediments.

"What were you doing in civilian life, Leith?" Cummings asked.

"I was a professional photographer."

"Really? With a tripod and a black cape?"

"Do I note a hint of mockery in your voice?"

"No, not at all. It's just that your answer took me by surprise."

"It does most people. Can't see why. But there you are. And yes, I did have a tripod and a black cape. One has to look the part, you know."

"How did you start? The photography I mean."

"My father. He liked going into the country at weekends to capture the scenery. I tagged along and helped him set up the equipment."

"Turning professional seems a bold step to take."

"Not really. I had no other talents worth mentioning. So a couple of summers ago I took the old boy's gear, drove down to Whitby and set myself up on the seafront taking portraits – mostly soldiers on leave with their girls."

"Sounds carefree."

"It was while the season lasted. But coastal resorts are much less appealing during the winter."

"What did you do then?"

"Father came to the rescue. He couldn't abide the idea of me tainting the family name among bathing huts and penny arcades. So he paid the rent on a vacant shop in the Seven Sisters Road and lent me the money to set up a studio.'

'Was it a success?'

Leith laughed. 'We shall never know. I'd just opened for business when I was afflicted with the mad notion that my country needed me.'

Further conversation was momentarily suspended by the need to enter the mess and make their way through a crowd of noisy officers toward the now open bar. It was while waiting to be served that Cummings took the opportunity to resume his conversation with Leith.

'I'm puzzled. Surely, given your photographic skills, you would have preferred being an observer?'

'Not so loud,' Leith hissed, looking round nervously in case someone might be eavesdropping. 'Wouldn't do for someone in authority to get the wrong idea.'

'I'm not sure I understand.'

'Have you ever seen an RE8 lumbering across the lines with the observer perched in the rear taking snaps of the Huns sunbathing in their trenches? It's a risky business for those poor devils and I have no desire to join them.'

****

With the meal completed everyone rose from the table and headed for the bar, which was immediately besieged by twenty officers. Amid the shouting and jostling drinks were ordered then carried away. The most comfortable seats were quickly taken and Cummings and his three companions had to make do with a table by the wall.

Leith had laid claim to a bottle of whiskey and now, squinting through the smoke coming from his cigarette, he proceeded to fill four glasses.

Rycliffe lifted his glass. 'What shall we toast?'

'To our new hut mate!' Leith suggested.

'To Cummings!' everyone chorused.

This was followed by a manly gulp of whiskey after which their faces grimaced in shocked delight. With a gasp of satisfaction, they placed their glasses on the table and relaxed into their chairs, eyes elevated ceiling-ward as they drew on their cigarettes.

After a pause, Rycliffe turned to Cummings. 'Whitworth tells me you were studying to become a scientist. What were you studying specifically?'

'Inertial frames of reference.'

'Aren't they the sort of reading glasses that perch on the end of your nose?'

Everyone including Cummings laughed at Rycliffe's attempt at humour, and Whitworth took up the theme by pulling a myopic expression.

'Can't see a bloody thing without my inertial frames.'

The laughter doubled, encouraging Leith to pat his pockets and make a show of peering under the table. 'Has anyone seen my inertial frames?'

They knew they were being silly asses, but it didn't matter to them that their humour was absurd. This was the evening and the evening was a time for mindless mirth for tomorrow was likely to be no joking matter.

Leith topped up everyone's drinks. 'Make the most of it. We're on short rations tonight.'

'Why is that?' Cummings asked.

Rycliffe knocked back his second drink then said, 'We've got the ten o'clock patrol and the Major's not keen on pilots with bad heads.'

****

Seeing Cummings weave his way through the smoke-enshrouded throng of loud-faced officers toward the exit, Parkinson called out, 'Leaving us already, Cummings?'

'No, Major. I was just off to write a letter to my sister.'

'Good idea! How are you settling in?'

'Fine, thank you. The fellows in my hut are first rate.'

168

'Glad to hear it. I believe Hargreaves assigned you to the ten o'clock patrol tomorrow?'

'That's correct, Major.'

'Well, forget that. I've arranged for you to come up with me tomorrow at ten-thirty.'

'I see.'

Mistaking Cummings' look of shock for wounded pride, Parkinson quickly added, 'I'm sorry, Cummings. I know you must be eager to get out there, but before my pilots go in to combat I like to make sure that they're as ready as they can be.'

'Yes, Major.'

Parkinson smiled. 'Good! Then I'll see you tomorrow at ten-thirty.'

Outside, beyond sight and earshot, Cummings relaxed his stoical expression into a broad smile and his tightly held breath into a heart felt chuckle.

Wonderful! An extra half-hour in bed and a morning ramble with the Major.

CHAPTER FOURTEEN

9 DECEMBER 1917

'Ere!' Swain called to Dibbs. 'Borrow us your pencil.'

Dibbs snarled. 'What do you want a pencil for? You can't write.'

'I want to draw a picture of your stupid mug.' Swain thrust out his hand. 'Give us your pencil.'

It wasn't much of a pencil. So much sharpening had reduced its length to a stub and one more sharpening would have placed it beyond use. As it was Swain found he had to hold it at its very end to get any purchase.

'What d'you keep this piece of nothing for?'

'It fits snug and out of the way and doesn't bother me like you do.'

Ignoring this jibe Swain rested the tip of the pencil on the small sheet of lined notepaper and started writing.

Dear Mum and Dad,

This is just a line or two to let you know that I've arrived safe and sound. I can't tell you where exactly as I don't really know myself, but it's supposed to be a quiet spot. It's certainly cosy and dry. At the moment I'm sitting with the other chaps round a roasting brazier that's so hot everyone has a red face.

Swain brushed away the flakes of snow that had startled to settle on his piece of notepaper. Then, his body convulsed by a bout of shivering, he took out a crumpled handkerchief and blew his nose. Putting away the handkerchief he pointed the pencil at the paper once again.

You needn't worry about me. We're well fed and the blokes I'm with are a good bunch. One of us is toasting bread on the end of his bayonet while our Sergeant, a very nice fellow, is spreading each slice with a thick layer of butter and a sort of jam us old soldiers call 'Pozzy'. It's supposed to be apple and plum, but we're not so sure.

Swain still had the taste of it in his mouth, a strange metallic flavour that refused to go away even after a good swill of strong tea. It had come in a one pound tin with 'Plum and Apple Jam – TG Tickler Ltd' stencilled on the side. One tin for every six men meant that they'd had to carry nine tins of the stuff back to the trenches.

And that wasn't all.

The cook had also given them sacks stuffed full of loaves of bread as well as three metal dixies containing hot tea, each dixie carried by two men supported on their shoulders by a wooden yoke. In addition each man had to carry his rifle and pack. And after the long and arduous trek back, with their leg and shoulder muscles burning, they had nearly collapsed with exhaustion. It was some while before they found the strength to share in the grub the others were plundering.

Thoughtfully, Swain ended the letter and put it in his tunic pocket. From his other pocket he took out a small note book that he had been using as a sort of diary. He wasn't by nature a diarist nor was he very diligent in making entries. He only committed thoughts to paper when the fancy took him or when there was something worth recording. Opening the note book at a fresh page he whetted the end of the pencil with his tongue and began:

9th December 1917, Sunday

You never know where you are from one day to the next out here. Mud and muck cakes everything. Kit and clothes are always damp and dirty. Rats everywhere. Always scratching. Sleeping's not easy. Kept awake most nights by starbursts and gunfire. Fortunately, the men in my section are not a bad bunch.

There's Lieutenant Leighton. He's about the same age as the rest of us, but looks much younger. He has nice manners and never loses his temper but he is sensible enough to leave the real work to Sergeant Worcester and Corporal McCleod. Word has it that he's the son of country vicar, but there's so many junior officers out here who are the sons of vicars it's become a bit of a...

Swain raised his head trying to search out the word he needed. It was at the back of his mind, but it kept eluding him. Then he spotted Lieutenant Leighton and, as the Sergeant wasn't in sight, called out.

'Excuse me, sir.'

Leighton turned. 'Yes, Swain?'

'You're an educated man, sir. There's a word I once saw in a magazine but I can't quite remember it. It's used to describe something that has been said so many times it has lost all its freshness.'

Leighton smiled. 'I think the word you are looking for is *cliché.*'

'Yes! That's the word, sir. Can you spell it for me?'

Leighton complied then added. 'And don't forget the acute accent over the 'e'.'

Swain thanked the Lieutenant then turned back to his notebook.

Sergeant Worcester is tall and big-boned and was a Sergeant in the Metropolitan Police before the war. It's hard to tell how old he is, but he looks older than all of us. I think it's because he has bags under his eyes and his complexion is somewhat ruddy. One thing is for sure, you don't mess with the Sergeant, not if you know what's good for you, you don't. But he does seem to know what he's going on about and that gives you some comfort in a place like this.

Corporal 'Haggis' McCleod is a right little terrier. He keeps his trap shut when the Sergeant's around, but when he's not he loves to throw his weight around. Think's he's the Commander in Chief. If he weren't Scottish we would probably call him Napoleon.

Lance Corporal George 'Chippie' Feltham worked in a fish and chip shop before the war. Out here he spends most of his time trailing behind Haggis, but he's not a bad sort really. If there's any light duties going he makes sure we get them.

Private Archibald Hoon was a piano tuner's assistant in civilian life. He has a woebegone face and he can be a bit of an old woman at times. We call him 'Prune'. I don't know if that's because it rhymes with his name or because he's always whining and complaining about the food and the smell. He's scared of everything even his own shadow and is always muttering to himself 'I want to go home'. Not that I can blame him. This place is enough to give any man the willies.

Private Harry Brinkly, a plasterer's mate, is a bit of a joker. He's always smiling no matter what's going on and seems to find something funny in almost every situation. He's a bit of a Mickey-taker, but he does it in a friendly manner so nobody takes offence.

Private Joshua Hutchins, one of our machinegun men, also makes us laugh. He worked in a library and I suppose that accounts for him having a much dryer sense of humour than Harry. He's always saying something droll that makes us all laugh, but he manages to keep a straight face no matter what.

Private 'Shorty' Shorthouse was a school caretaker before he joined up. This is probably why he's the troop's resident know-it-all. There isn't a single subject under discussion to which he doesn't contribute some fact or opinion and he never misses an opportunity to correct people when he thinks they've got something wrong. Most of us take it in good part but not Haggis. Shorthouse would never dare correct Haggis but that doesn't stop it getting right up the Scotsman's nose and he challenges Shorthouse at every turn.

'Ow d'ye know that?' he always scoffs.

At six foot three inches Private Leonard Scuttle is probably the tallest man in the entire battalion. They couldn't find a uniform big enough for him so his wrists are always sticking out of his cuffs and he has a real problem getting his trousers to stay in his puttees. Despite his size he is a bit of a gentle giant. He doesn't throw his weight about and he usually has a good word to say about everyone. He was a stable groom on some landed estate before the war. He's a dab hand at brewing tea and cooking up scoff. The Lieutenant has taken a shine to him and now uses him unofficially as his manservant.

Private Isaiah Dibbs or 'Ferret Face' as some of us like to call him, is our other machine gunner. He was a bailiff before he joined up. He's one of those characters who seem to take a great delight in poking his nose into other people's business then souring the atmosphere with his nasty comments and observations. Unsurprisingly he sits alone most of the time.

Private Victor Heywood is a dapper looking man. We call him 'Unmentionable' because he worked in the Ladies Lingerie department of a large London Store. He's fussy about his appearance and hates dirty fingernails, but he keeps us amused with his endless fund of saucy stories about his high-class lady customers.

Private Alistair Hoskins worked in Chapel Street market selling wooden toys. The poor man has stomach problems and is always in and out of the latrine. He passes wind quite a lot for which he constantly apologises. Fortunately for us, situated where we are we are plagued by the sound only. The smell around here is so awful that Windy's effusions don't stand a chance.

Private Lucian 'Lucy' Entworth was a stagehand in a West End variety theatre before the war. None of us are quite sure about Lucy. Some of us have our suspicions, but given our situation most of us have decided to live and let live. All of us except Ferret Face. He was the one who nicknamed Hoskins 'Lucy'.

Of all the men in the section Private Ishmael Cokeson, our bomber, is the strangest. We call him 'Coaxie', but it's not a name we gave him. As far we can establish it was attached to him long before he joined up. Some say that in civvies he worked in the coal and coke trade and that's why he's called 'Coaxie'. Others are putting it about that whatever that work was it was less than legal and I have to say that I lean toward the latter version.

Whatever way you look at it he's a queer cove and no mistake. Sometimes I find him staring at me intently, sizing me up as if he's trying to decide something about me. I tell you, it sends a right shiver up and down my spine. Not that I should feel all that privileged. I've caught him doing it to the others.

'What are you writing down in that book of yours?' Dibbs asked belligerently.

'Just my thoughts.'

'Your thoughts!' Dibb's upper lip curled into a sneer. 'And what's the good of that?'

'What's the good of what?'

'Why bother, that's what I mean.'

'Who knows. Maybe I'll get them published after the war is over.'

'You hope. More likely you'll get killed in no-man's-land and you and your little book of thoughts will rot away into nothing. Think on that.'

Having made his point Dibbs trudged off down the trench leaving Swain somewhat stunned by the whole episode. Of course, he had considered the possibility of his own death. One would have to be silly in the head not to. But he had never heard anyone spell it out to him in such a stark fashion before and it was unsettling.

He stared at his little book and wondered whether Dibbs was right. Maybe there was little point in writing down such things, little point in writing down anything at all. But then just as he was about to close his notebook and put it away he thought of one more thing to write down, one more thing he just had to put on paper and he smiled.

Private Dibbs is a right miserable little git.

****

As Swain was writing in his notebook Cummings was being awakened much earlier than expected. Chairs were scraping, water was splashing and the air was polluted by the sound of fierce cursing. Bleary eyed, he peeked out from under his blanket and, in the half-light, watched three frantic silhouettes scurrying back and forth bumping into each other every so often like a gang of incompetent burglars.

'Has anyone seen my blasted goggles?' Leith pleaded.

'Look inside your blasted helmet,' Whitworth suggested as he wrestled with the inside of his Sidcot.

'Keep it quiet, you two,' Rycliffe hissed, sluicing his razor in a bowl of water. 'You'll wake Cummings up.'

'Too late,' Cummings murmured. 'I'm already awake.'

'Sorry, old fellow,' Whitworth apologised. 'We'll be gone in a few minutes then you can get back to sleep.'

'What time is it?' Cummings murmured sleepily, pulling himself into a sitting position.

Leith consulted his wristwatch, only it wasn't there. 'Has anyone seen my blasted watch?'

'It's on your blasted bed-side table,' Whitworth told him. 'Where you left it.'

'So it is.' Leith checked that it was ticking then said, 'Mine says five minutes past eight.'

'Thanks.' Cummings yawned extravagantly then asked, 'Tell me, Leith, do you lose everything?'

Rycliffe took up a towel and started drying his face. 'He doesn't lose things. They hide themselves on purpose.'

'It's true!' Whitworth stomped his boots to get his feet into place. 'Inanimate objects have it in for Leith.'

Rycliffe buttoned his Sidcot 'I'm waiting for the day when we gather for a patrol and Leith will say, 'Has anyone seen my blasted bus?''

Snatching up his gloves and helmet, Leith headed for the door. 'Well, you comedians had better gather soon or our buses might just take off without us.'

The door slammed shut and silence descended upon the hut once again. Cummings contemplated going back to sleep. The bed was warm and the world around him was cold. But then from somewhere in the distance came the cough and spluttering roar of Camel engines. The squadron was waking up and with all the activity going on around him he knew that sleep was now out of the question. Besides, he was going up with the Major in a couple of hours.

And I'd best be wide awake for that.

****

Casting his eyes toward the mess nestling in the angle of several trees Parkinson made out a solitary figure leave the building and start walking toward him. Even at this distance it was possible to recognise the measured pace of Lieutenant Cummings.

Intelligent fellow!

But Parkinson knew that intelligence was a trait that rarely came on its own. It was often accompanied by an active imagination. And an active imagination could be a burden to any man out to test his courage. He hadn't asked Whitworth about his flight with Cummings. It was bad for morale to ask one officer about a fellow officer's proficiency. Besides, he would find out all he needed to know in the next hour.

Best to leave it at that.

Cummings walked up to him, fully kitted out in bulky Sidcot, leather helmet and goggles, a bright expression on his face. 'Good morning, sir.'

'Good morning, Cummings. Get a good night's sleep?'

'I did, sir.'

'Breakfast?'

'Tea and toast.'

'Good!' He turned toward the hangars. 'Well, we have a nice clear sky so shall we make a start?'

Two Camels were waiting for them. Parkinson pointed to the nearest. 'I believe that's the one you flew yesterday.'

Cummings checked the tailplane number. 'It is, sir.'

'Any problems?'

'No, Major. It was a smooth flight.'

'Good. Well you can take her up again today.'

'Are we going to the lines?'

'No. Today I'm going to test your responses. When we reach a certain spot I'll break away without warning. Your job will be to keep on my tail and prevent me from getting on yours. Is that clear?'

'Yes, Major.'

'Good. Well, let's get on with it.'

Climbing into his Camel Cummings settled into the wicker seat, hooking his toes into the rudder bar stirrups and fastening the safety straps across his chest. As he tested rudder and ailerons a Sergeant mechanic called up to him, 'We've tightened the wiring, sir. You can be a bit more robust with her today if you wish.'

'Thank you, Sergeant.'

The Major's Camel was already roaring into life as the mechanic swung Cumming's propeller. The engine caught first time, coughing out black smoke as it cleared its lungs.

Time to go.

The Major rolled away. Cummings followed. They picked up speed rapidly over the grass and were soon airborne. Again, Cummings watched the approaching line of trees with stiffening tension, but both machines cleared the upper branches with feet to spare.

****

Heading north, the front was somewhere to their right. Cummings looked in that direction several times but never long enough to fall foul of the lesson he had learnt from Whitworth. Trouble was he wasn't really taking much in.

At this rate it'll take me ages to become familiar with anything.

Then there was the Major to consider. At some stage he was going to breakaway and it would be Cummings task to chase after him, but he didn't give much for his chances. He reckoned he would lose the Major almost straight away.

And shortly after that he'll be hanging on my tail.

But he was determined not to fail through the want of trying. And it was this determination that kept his unblinking eyes fixed rigidly on the rear of the Major's machine.

He'll not slip away without me seeing it.

It couldn't be much longer now. They had been flying in a straight line and at the same height for nearly twenty minutes. Then it occurred to him that he had spent all that time watching what the Major was up to and none on the sky around him.

Idiot! Idiot! Idiot!

Despite his good intentions he had done the one thing he vowed he would never do again; he had become fixated on one thing to the exclusion of all else.

Not bothering to look for Huns creeping up behind me.

It was unlikely there would be any Huns this far from the lines, but that wasn't the point. It was the habit that was important. He had to get into the habit of searching the sky and he had to get into it soon if he hoped to have any chance of surviving the days ahead.

It was then that the Major's Camel barrelled to the left and dipped down beyond sight.

Opening his throttle Cummings followed.

The earth was beneath his portside wingtips, spinning round and round. But his attention was under his top wing centre where the Major's tailplane was just visible.

Both machines were now locked in a furious circle, one chasing the other.

Cummings opened his throttle a little more. More and more of the Major's fuselage came into view.

'Come on! Come on!'

Cummings willed his machine to close the gap. He even squinted along the twin barrels of his guns, hoping to get the Major's rear wing into his sights.

Just a bit more! Just a bit more!

Then the Major's Camel flipped on to its back and dived under him.

Where the hell!

Cummings looked over the side. Nothing!

Damn! I've lost him.

Pulling the stick hard over, he ignored the creaking of his wing spars as the earth flipped above his head. Then it rolled beneath him until the ground was once more under his wheels. But still no sign of the Major.

Where did he go?

Was he still beneath him? Again, he looked over both sides of the cockpit, but all he could see were white fields and country lanes bordered by ranks of desolate trees.

Then some instinct made him look over his shoulder. Still nothing! But as he started to turn back, an upper wing rose into view, quickly followed by spars and bracing wires and the curved cowl of a rotary engine. And beyond the blur of the propeller and the twin muzzles of the machine guns was the Major's grinning face.

177

The grin made Cummings explode with rage. He'd been caught completely unawares for a second time and it made no difference to him that the pilots who had bettered him were more experienced. All he could see was the Major's grin and it seemed to him that he was being mocked.

Wrenching the stick over he banked his machine hard left.

'Well, now we'll see if you can keep up with me.'

****

As they strolled away from the hangars the Major asked, 'Well, what do you think?'

Cummings was taken aback. He thought he would have to listen to the Major give him a stark assessment of his performance. The last thing he'd expected was to be asked for his opinion. Not sure how to reply, he decided his best option was to be vague.

'It's hard to say, Major.'

Parkinson smiled. 'Don't worry. I'm not trying to catch you out. Just give me your general impressions.'

'Well, it wasn't quite a washout. I managed to get back on your tail. I even thought I might get you lined up for a clear shot, but then you did that flip and I lost you entirely until you reappeared behind me. I suppose I was pretty much dead meat at that point.'

Parkinson smiled and nodded. 'But you were very reluctant to accept your fate. You tried your damnest to shake me off and I had the devil of a job keeping on your tail. Not a bad effort all in all.'

This was praise indeed. 'Thank you, Major.'

'Try not to be so hard on yourself all the time,' Parkinson told him. 'You're still at the stage when you have to think through every move you make. Thinking slows you down. You handle your machine well enough. You now need to hone your instincts as a combat pilot.'

'How do I do that, sir?'

'At the end of the day, there's only one way to learn your trade and that's by going out on jobs. Believe me, it's the best training there is.'

'I'm sure it is.'

'Good! Then I see no reason why you shouldn't go out with your flight on their 10.30 patrol tomorrow.'

****

Cummings was disappointed to find the hut empty when he got back. He'd hoped Whitworth might be there so that he could tell him about his flight with the Major and maybe get a friend's unbiased opinion. But as he sat on his bed he realised that there was something that he needed to talk over with himself first.

His flight with the Major had given him an ounce more confidence but it hadn't entirely dispelled his sense of dread at the prospect of going into combat. As far as he could see the question remained.

Am I a coward or not?

All through training he had been eager to get out here and fight the enemy. He saw himself shooting down countless numbers of Huns and returning to base in glory, but now the eagerness was gone. It left him the moment he first looked down upon the front line. In its place was a sense of being in a world that he couldn't comprehend and for which he was not equipped. He wouldn't survive the first proper patrol. He was certain of it. Some unseen enemy would creep up behind him and blast him from the skies.

And the rest of the patrol won't even know I've gone.

The mere thought of such a fate made his hands sweat and his bowels churn. He suddenly felt irritable and unable to keep still. He got up and paced about the hut, but it didn't help. What made it worse was the knowledge that he was no longer in control of his fate. He was now the slave of a greater authority. It had no name and it had no face, but he had to obey it no matter what. And it waited for him behind a door at the end of a long, grim corridor and there was nothing he could do to avoid it.

****

After reporting to the office and recording his flight with Parkinson in his logbook, Cummings wandered back to his hut to change and clean up. He considered going out again, but with little idea where his hut mates might be he finally decided to stay put and try to take his mind off his worries by settling on his bed for a quiet read.

As well as a number of scientific treatises he had also brought with him a couple of works of fiction. One of these was Joseph Conrad's 'Lord Jim'. In the circumstances it seemed appropriate as it was the story of an Englishman disgraced by an act of cowardice.

Let's see how he coped with it.

But he had barely opened the book when the door sprang open and Whitworth bounded in.

'There you are.'

'No I'm not,' Cummings' eyes peered over the top of his book. 'I'm somewhere else entirely.'

'Very amusing. What are you doing?'

'Reading.'

'Do that a lot, do you?'

'It has been remarked upon.'

Whitworth's eyes dropped to the book Cummings had in his hands. 'What are you reading now?'

Reluctant to admit that he was reading a story about a coward he admitted airily, 'Something by Joseph Conrad.'

Whitworth thought for a moment then said. 'Isn't he that Polish fellow who writes tales about the high seas?'

'That's the one.'

Whitworth was delighted. Not only had he guessed correctly but in his world, having a general idea of a book's contents, even if merely divined from the title, was almost the same thing as having actually read the book itself. In this respect, Whitworth was about as well read as it was possible to be. It would be a mistake, however, to see in this the shallow pretensions of a man keen only on raising his status in the eyes of others.

It was more the case that Whitworth was driven by a compulsion to do as much living as he could, but realising that there would never be time enough to do everything he wanted he had hit upon the simple expedient of reducing each activity to its bare essentials. In this fashion, he could spend all the time he wanted doing the things he liked, and hardly any time at all on those things he didn't whilst, at the same time, managing to do both.

'Want to come and feed the horses?'

CHAPTER FIFTEEN

10 DECEMBER 1917

Low clouds and a heavy fall of snow came to the rescue of Cummings that morning, preventing the 10.30 patrol he had been so dreading and any further flying for the rest of the day. Further north on the other side of the Channel the weather was more settled. The clouds were higher and a fleeting sun shone down upon Fancy Willoughby as he cracked his whip in the air above Tracer's chestnut flank. Although spared physical discomfort the sprightly horse knew what was expected and he raised his trot along the country lane to a slightly brisker pace.

Bordered on both sides by high hedges the lane itself was long and pencil-straight and sloped upward on a gentle incline. At the far end of it stood Fancy's destination. It was a large house, with Tudor chimneys, known locally as 'Widdings Folly'. The building was mostly hidden from view by a tall impenetrable bush, which formed a sort of exterior wall. Only the smoking chimneys were visible and the topmost part of the eastern tower, which at this hour was basking in the early morning sunshine.

A gate-sized opening had been cut through the centre of the tall bush at the point where it met the head of the lane. With brisk efficiency Fancy guided the cart through the opening. He then steered it round and brought it to a halt in the shingle drive so that its right side was facing the ivy-fronted house. Putting on the brake he lowered his ageing bones down from the wooden seat and hobbled round to the back of the cart. Here he pulled down the flap of the tailgate and reached in to grab hold of the near edge of a strangely shaped crate.

He guessed from the weight and dimensions that it had to be either a mirror or some sort of framed painting. It was certainly heavy and the wood packaging that encased it made it bulky and difficult for a man of his age to lift and hold. When collecting the item at Antley train station he'd had the muscular assistance of Giles Leaper, the station porter. Between them they'd managed to get it from the platform and onto the back of the cart, but now he was alone and concerned that its weight might prove too much for him.

Fortunately for him, Alice the maidservant had been changing the flowers in one of the upstairs windows when she spotted his arrival. He was a familiar sight as he regularly brought groceries to Widdings from the village so his appearance wasn't that noteworthy. Normally she would leave him to bring in the goods on his own and only interrupt her chores to make him a cup of tea. But when she saw him struggling with the strange looking crate she left the flowers and went downstairs to investigate.

'What you got there, Fancy?' she asked as she came out of the kitchen door.

'Something for the misses,' he wheezed, the crate half on and half off the cart.

'Can you manage it on your own?'

'No, lass. Give us a hand will yer.'

****

How silly of me to behave in such a manner, fainting like some giggling schoolgirl.

Obviously it had been the shock of seeing Colonel Pritchett climbing out of the car instead of her husband. One heard such dreadful things all the time about women who answer their doors only to be greeted by a telegram from the War Office informing them that their man has been killed. But the Colonel had not come to tell her that.

Missing in Action. That's what he'd said.

And she seized upon this slender lifeline, this crumb of hope with such single-minded ferocity it would have required a stout pair of pliers to prise her fingers free. Not that she would have accepted the alternative. She could not, would not believe that her husband was dead. Both her body and her mind refused to entertain even the possibility of such a thing. He was still alive. She knew it. She knew it with a certainty that defied any challenge.

Even the Colonel could not say otherwise.

Her husband's aircraft had crashed. If the crash had been fatal his body would still be in it. But the cockpit was empty. They could not find a body anywhere near the crash site. So, as far as she was concerned the only logical explanation was that William had left his machine and was now somewhere out in the winter stricken fields of Northern France wandering around hurt and alone, confused and unrecognised.

He might even be lying in a hospital bed.

He would be found eventually. Of course he would. It might take days. It might take weeks. It might take even longer than that. Who could tell? But he would be found. Of that she was totally convinced.

And I'll not tolerate any word to the contrary.

In the meantime her first duty above all else was to maintain his home and the running of the household and in such a manner as to not only hold it in readiness for his return but to also confirm the certainty of his existence. As part of this strategy Andrea had taken to doing the sort of things her husband would have done if he had been at home. It was her way of keeping his presence alive. One of the things she had taken to doing was sitting in her husband's battered old armchair.

I can't abide to see it empty.

And when she wasn't able to sit in it she placed on the armrest that day's newspaper, the one her husband always read, trying to make it look as if he had merely gone to some other part of the house and would return shortly. She kept other items of his close to the chair such as his pipe rack, tobacco barrel, Ronson lighter and the small silver pen knife he used to rake out the ashes.

She always made sure that the tobacco was topped up every few days and she continued to do this even though her husband wasn't there to use it. She maintained the charade by every so often throwing away the old tobacco and replacing it with fresh.

He'll expect everything to be exactly as he left it.

The previous day she did a very peculiar thing. As usual she was sitting in her husband's chair with the unfinished scarf and knitting needles lying in her lap. She was staring at his pipe rack when, for some reason, she was overcome by the desire to know what it was like to smoke a pipe. She had never felt this need before. She had always considered smoking unladylike and one of those unsavoury things only men choose to do. Whenever he lit up she always opened a window to keep the air in the room fresh, but now she missed the smell.

Only because it reminds me of William.

Suddenly, it came to her. Why not fill and light his pipe? Why not smoke it? Maybe, by doing something that he did, by re-enacting that ritual and once more filling the room with the smell of tobacco smoke it would be like the burning of some pagan incense. Maybe under its spell she would be able to commune with her husband wherever he might be or conjure into her mind some memory of him, some forgotten scene of domestic bliss that the two of them had shared.

But it was a silly thing to do.

She had filled the bowl of the pipe with tobacco as she had seen him do, packing it in tightly with her thumb. Then, placing the pipe in her mouth, she struck the lighter and held the flame to the tobacco. She drew on the stem of the pipe and her mouth and nose were instantly filled with smoke. She should have had a shrewd idea as to what would happen next, but hope overcame her caution and she paid the price. Her eyes clamped shut and her face exploded into an uncontrollable fit of coughing.

Wait till William hears of it.

She imagined how amused he would be and for the first time in many days a smile found its way onto Andrea's mouth. It was an absent smile, and there was sadness in it, but it was a smile nonetheless. And it stayed there when her head was drawn to the sound of Alice and Fancy Willoughby struggling to get through the front door.

'MAM!' Alice shouted as she and Fancy manhandled the crate into the living room.

Andrea got up from her husband's chair. 'What have you got there, Alice?'

'Something Fancy has brought up from the village.'

'It came this morning, misses,' Fancy explained. 'On the early train from Portsmouth.'

'Well, you'd better put it down over there.'

Alice and Fancy carried the crate over to the centre of the room and eased it down onto the carpet, but held onto its corners so that it would stay upright.

'Do you know what it is?' Andrea asked.

'No, misses. But a letter came with it.

Fancy dug his bony fingers into the frayed pocket of his workman's apron. It took him a moment but finally he pulled forth a long white envelope that was folded in the middle and a little ruffled for being in the pocket so long. He handed it to Andrea and she opened it. Alice and Fancy stood by silently and anxiously as she read the letter and within seconds it was clear from her expression that its contents were having a profound effect upon her.

Finally, she refolded the letter and, without referring to it, put it back in the envelope.

'Can you open the crate?' she asked

Again Fancy dug his fingers into the pocket of his apron and this time produced a claw hammer.

Andrea nodded her assent but felt compelled to add. 'Do it carefully, Fancy.'

****

Why do I always have to be the bearer of bad news?

Knowing that he was the bearer once more Fuchs tried to sound as cheerful as possible when he announced:

'The latest batch of pilots from the east has arrived, Herr Hauptmann.'

Buchner looked up from his desk, lifting his head as if it weighed more than normal and there was little interest in his dull and lifeless eyes. He sighed.

'How many this time?'

Fuchs felt like sighing too. He had given Buchner this very information only the previous day, but then it came as no real surprise. He was finding that the need to repeat things to his Commander was increasing. And part of the reason for this could be seen on Buchner's desk. It was a glass and a bottle of Schnapps. He was relieved to see that the glass was empty and the stopper was in the bottle.

But the presence of either isn't a good sign.

Buchner had started drinking during the day. Fuchs knew this. Like most other pilots Buchner liked a drink in the Kasino whenever a binge was on or just to wind down after a stressful day. But this daytime drinking was something new and it spoke of a troubled spirit. Fuchs knew Buchner was bored and that he was using alcohol to suppress his fighting spirit and thus make his forced inactivity more bearable. At the moment it was no more than the odd glass here and there, but Fuchs feared it would only get worse.

'Just two, Herr Hauptmann.'

'Their names?'

Fuchs could clearly see the list with the officers' names lying close to Buchner's elbow. He felt like pointing to it, but then he decided it wouldn't be a good idea to antagonise Buchner especially as there was more to worry about than a couple of names on a list.

'Leutnant Hoffnung and Leutnant Eulenburg.'

'Well, tell them that I'll see them as soon as they've changed out of their flying gear.'

Buchner couldn't have been aware that with this remark he had precipitated the very moment Fuchs' had been trying to delay, the moment he had vainly hoped to soften by giving the good news first.

'We may have a problem there, Herr Hauptmann.'

'What problem?'

'They didn't come by air. They were driven here.'

Buchner cocked his head enquiringly to one side as his eyebrows came together. 'Driven here! What's happened? Have they lost their machines?'

'Not exactly, Herr Hauptmann.' Fuchs hesitated knowing that what he was about to say would sound absurd. 'It seems they were parted from their machines while they were still on the train.'

Buchner's looked aghast. 'What? Did they fall off?'

Fuchs wasn't sure whether his commander's sarcasm was an attempt to see the humorous side of the situation. But he knew well enough how dangerous it was to make such an assumption.

'No. As far as I can ascertain the freight cars carrying the machines were uncoupled during a brief stop at Stuttgart and then sent off in a different direction. There must have been some sort of mix-up.'

'Mix up!' Buchner slammed his palms onto his desk and lifted himself out of his chair. Then, thinking better of it, he slumped back into his chair and took a moment to expel all the air from of his lungs. 'As usual, Fuchs, you are the master of understatement.'

'Sorry, Herr Hauptmann.'

'Oh God!'

Buchner covered his face with both his hands, but then almost immediately pulled them away and slammed a fist down onto the surface of his desk.

'Of all the fucking stupid incompetence. This is another bloody mess that I'll have to sort out. As if I didn't already have enough on my fucking plate.'

In the face of Buchner's anger Fuchs stood mute. It wasn't that it made him fearful. Not in the way that he felt fearful whenever Hantelmann lost his temper. Hantelmann lost his temper whenever he encountered weaknesses in the system. He felt that things should be better run and felt let down whenever they weren't.

Buchner's anger came from an entirely different place. His anger came out of the resentment he felt at having to do a job he didn't want to do and at having to carry the burdens it imposed upon him. But the anger itself was a sort of burden and he soon tired of it.

And there's no point in saying anything until he does.

'Can you look into it, Fuchs?'

The burden had been shifted to Fuchs, as it always was, but Fuchs knew that Buchner would continue to feel the weight of it.

'Of course, Herr Hauptmann. I'll just get the new pilots settled first.'

****

As Fuchs had surmised Buchner was finding the burden of command, the burden that High Command had placed on his unwilling shoulders, increasingly insupportable. And it was beginning to plague him at night as well as during day. Worse of all was the knowledge that his ineffectiveness as a commander was slowly damaging the unit.

If only I could find some way out of this bloody mess.

Then he had a strange thought. He had heard somewhere that a beam of light only has existence because it is constantly in motion. It has to keep moving. If some incredible device could stop it in its tracks it would cease to exist. Throughout his entire life he had been in constant motion, never pausing long enough to consider the whys and wherefores of anything. But now he had been brought to a stop.

And like the beam of light I'm beginning to feel as if I'm ceasing to exist.

Buchner shuddered. He felt uncomfortable examining his inner soul so closely. Up until quite recently he hadn't even been aware that he had an inner soul. He didn't like it. He wanted to forget it. His eyes strayed to the bottle of schnapps and the glass standing beside it. There lay forgetfulness. But as his hand reached out to take it he heard the roar of aero-engines.

This was the one sound guaranteed to stir within him that part of his old self that had fallen silent. Without even considering what he was doing he got up from his desk and walked through to the outer office. Looking through one of the dusty windows he could see a beautiful day, the sort of acute beauty that only winter can produce. The sky was a cloudless blue, infinite and ravishing. But Buchner saw more than this. He saw a great day for flying, a great day for pulling away from the earth, a great day for climbing into the broad, unheeding heavens.

A better tonic than a shot of schnapps.

And as he stood at the window four machines sped past, lifting their wheels from the ground. The first two were silver bodied and he recognised the one in the lead as the black-beaked Pfalz belonging to Oberleutnant Leintz and the one behind it as Engerhardt's. The trailing machines, their hollow framed bodies still bearing their old eastern front colours of mottled white and grey, belonged to Wülner and Crüger, two of the replacement pilots.

As the four Pfalz climbed away Buchner watched them wistfully, aching to join them. It was an ache he felt every time he watched machines taking off, and that could be as much as five or six times a day. It was not quite two weeks since he last took to the air himself.

But it seems like a lifetime ago.

Yet, despite the ache, some part of him refused to accept that he would never fly again. The war was not over. Maybe it would never end. He still had a part to play in it. Germany still needed him. The call would come again. He was convinced of it.

And I'll be ready.

Despite High Command's injunction that he was too precious to the nation to risk in combat he had told his mechanics to keep his machine, the *Kriegruf,* battle ready, its wires taut, its tanks full, its guns loaded, its engine finely tuned. He had also ignored High Command's order to redistribute the pilots in his Jasta and spread their experience throughout the unit. He considered this unnecessary.

The replacement pilots are experienced enough already.

But he had another reason for not obeying High command. He wanted to keep his Jasta intact so that it would still be there waiting for him when the time came for him to lead it once again. In this way he kept alive the belief that he could take to the air at any moment.

Try as they might they can't keep me on the ground forever.

****

Fuchs, you've become a brazen liar.

How else could he describe himself? Firstly he tells his commanding officer that he's off to settle in the two new pilots when he's already settled them in. Then he tells Buchner that he would deal with the problem of the two missing machines when he had already dealt with it.

But why did I lie?

Despite this searching question he already knew the answer. Quite simply he had lied to gain himself some precious time, time to do the one thing he had been dying to do ever since he got out of bed that morning; he wanted to go and check for himself how work on the old Kasino was progressing. It was important.

The gala opening is tomorrow evening.

So, after taking his leave of Buchner, he headed straight for the ruin of the chateau and walked round to its southern side where the Kasino nestled. Even before it came into sight he could hear the unmistakable sounds of hammering and sawing. And with the sounds came the intoxicating smells of cut wood and fresh paint. As he turned the final corner of the chateau the scene that presented itself was one of seeming chaos. There were men everywhere, working feverishly on a host of different tasks, all driven by the single goal of getting the Kasino ready for the big event.

God, it's cost me enough in bribes and wages. I've even promised the lazy sods a bonus if they finish on time.

Some of the 'lazy sods' now stood at saw benches cutting planks of wood into measured lengths. Others, perched precariously on ladders, were wielding stiff brushes against the exterior walls of the Kasino's long veranda or screwing in the hinges on the weatherproof shutters. Two small lorries were parked near the entrance. From the rear of the nearest men were using pulleys to lower a piano to the ground. From the rear of the other various items of furniture were being removed and conveyed into the Kasino. Fuchs waited to let them pass then followed them in.

It was as busy inside as it was outside and certainly the sound of labour was considerably louder. Much of the heavy construction work was already done. The floors, the walls and the ceiling were in place. And he was pleased to see that a great deal of the interior decoration was complete.

Only the finishing touches remain; the lights, the carpets, the furniture, the mirrors and paintings.

From Fuchs perspective the interior layout of the Kasino looked very much as it had done before it was bombed. What the renovation had brought to it was a sense of elegance, the sort of elegance one might encounter when visiting an expensive club in Berlin.

This is the foremost airbase on the Western Front. Its Kasino should be a reflection of that eminence.

The officers that served in JGN deserved nothing less. They fought bravely during the day and as brave heroes they had earned the right to expect pleasant and comfortable surroundings when they relaxed in the evening. It wasn't just a matter of status.

It's a matter of morale.

This was what Fuchs kept telling himself. He had to. How else was he to justify the entire endeavour? How else was he to justify the money spent, the bribes and the backhanders to officers who had come to do other work on the airbase? How else was he to justify the diversion of labour and resources from tasks that from a military point of view had far greater priority? Most of all how else was he to justify hoodwinking his commander again and again about what he was actually getting up to?

As Fuchs skirted the end of the Kasino's long bar, he recalled that only a day or so previously he had presented Buchner with a number of documents that required his authorisation.

'Not more things to sign,' Buchner had complained half jokingly. 'At this rate I'll wear my name out.'

Several of these had been requisitions for materials.

'What's this one for?' Buchner had asked.

'Timber for the new huts and storage depots,' Fuchs had replied.

'And this one?'

'Glass for the same.'

Despite Buchner's apparent guardedness he had signed both requisitions without further comment seemingly unaware that the amounts ordered were over and above what would normally be expected for the tasks specified. Fuchs didn't feel good about being so devious and underhand nor about any of the other questionable things he'd done but for him the opening of the Kasino had become a matter of paramount importance. It has to be opened and it had to be opened on time.

My reputation depends upon it.

Taking out the bunch of keys that he kept with him at all times Fuchs unlocked the door to the basement cellar and let himself in. After switching on the light he locked the door behind him then descended the wooden steps to the corridor below. The Kasino's stone basement was actually part of the chateau, having been cut out of its limestone foundations. According to the architectural drawings the basement had served the same purpose as it served now, storage. But this hadn't deterred Fuchs from telling lurid tales about dungeons and torture chambers.

Its rough white walls were cool, perfect for the storage of wine and spirits, and proof against any sound except of course the sound of one's own thoughts. And Fuchs thoughts became excited as he made his way along the narrow corridor. The stockroom door was heavy and reinforced and virtually bombproof. It certainly survived the bombing raid almost intact. Again Fuchs sorted through his bunch of keys until he found the largest one on the ring. With this he unlocked the stockroom door and pushed it open.

The interior light revealed endless racks of dusty bottles; wines, Rieslings, clarets, ports and champagnes. There were also piled boxes of cognac, whiskey, Schnapps and other strong spirits as well as the finest Havana cigars. At this point Fuchs would normally have taken out his silver propelling pencil and small stock book to check what quantities were there and what needed to be ordered. But this time he didn't do that. He had something more important to check.

In one corner there were several large barrels of beer lying side by side on a trellis. Sticking out of the front of each was a spigot from which to pour the beer and turning any of them would have produced a stream of best Bavarian lager. One of the barrels, however, was not quite what it seemed. Only the front half of the barrel contained lager. The rear half was empty or leastwise it was empty of lager. It was in this hidden place that Fuchs kept a sturdy strongbox.

Pulling off the rear panel of the barrel he reached inside and removed the strongbox. It was heavy and required some effort to shift, but as soon as it was free he sought out his bunch of keys and soon found the one that he was looking for. This was the moment Fuchs savoured more than any other; the sight and touch of his money and as soon as the lid was lifted he caressed it tenderly as a lover would.

The strongbox was stuffed with great wads of it, notes of different currencies and every denomination. There were Imperial Reichsmarks,

French Francs, Austro-Hungarian Kronen and English pounds sterling. Some notes were crisp and pristine; others were worn, wrinkled and faded. But whatever their condition Fuchs loved them all equally. He loved their blues, their greens, their ruby reds and sepia browns.

To him they were objects of beauty. He had been to art galleries throughout Europe but in none of them had he ever found anything to compare with the divine genius of money. Only in a banknote's richly patterned design and finely engraved detail, only in it's embossed and water-marked texture, it's unique serial number and it's scenes of mythical female figures in flowing robes, could one find the perfect match of beauty and power.

To Fuchs each note represented a cast-iron guarantee, a promise of wealth, luxury and better times. With sufficient quantities one could stay in the finest hotels, dine in the most exclusive restaurants, wear well-cut clothes and enjoy the best entertainment. One could build and own property, command the love of beautiful women and sway the opinions of politicians. One could give orders and not take them.

And that'll be me when this war is over.

CHAPTER SIXTEEN

11 DECEMBER 1917

'I have something for you, my Lady.'

These words from Erich altered everything. They signalled that the pace of events had quickened. Where for a while it looked as if nothing would happen now there was every reason to hope that things were at last starting to come together. Not that Thetis had been idle. Even during the hiatus she had been busy carrying forward the plan of deception and manipulation she had started weaving around Anthea.

Though full of flattery, at its core her letter of 5th December was the private conversation the two of them had had in the Grand Hall. It had certainly taken place, but Thetis' description of the conversation strayed so far from the truth it was little more than pure invention. And the biggest lie of all was her assertion that Anthea had revealed her plans to infiltrate the JGN airbase disguised as a pilot. That Anthea never said any such thing and would certainly deny that she had wasn't really the point. The point was to leave her in doubt as to what she actually did say.

Embedding the idea more firmly in her silly head.

And, if it took hold, it would leave her thinking the idea had been hers all along. There was, of course, the possibility that if Anthea did attempt such a thing it might turn to disaster. Thetis was not unduly concerned. Her letter would not only exonerate her it would also cast her in a favourable light. She would be seen as the person who tried to avert the disaster.

Not as the person who had brought it all about.

So far there had been no reply from Anthea. Thetis had anticipated this. She was certainly aware of the young woman's antipathy toward her and accepted that there was a strong possibility that she might not even reply at all. So instead of sitting idly by Thetis wrote Anthea two more letters, one on 7th December and one on the 9th. Both were short. The first had been a teaser, one guaranteed to grab Anthea's attention like nothing else could.

Injecting the letter with a sense of urgency and using sensational language she told Anthea that she had news concerning the hated Count von Gessendork. According to various sources she had heard that the Count might soon be returning to Germany as part of a military delegation. It was all lies, of course, but Thetis hoped that such news would not only cause Anthea alarm it would also serve as a timely reminder of the secret they shared, thus reinforcing that tenuous bond between them.

Hopefully it'll also incline her to put pen to paper.

Initially, Thetis intended the third letter to be a continuation of the first, urging Anthea to think again about her plans to infiltrate JGN and repeating the warnings she had already given about the pitfalls of pursuing such a dangerous course.

But then I had a change of heart.

It occurred to her that she had been going about the whole business in the wrong way. The stance she had adopted of being the anxious friend had its limitations. And there was a danger too. If she kept sending Anthea admonitory letters it would only be a matter of time before she grew tired of reading them altogether.

I needed to strike out in a different direction.

Her third letter did precisely that. She began it with an apology saying that, on reflection, she now realised that she must have misheard what the Princess had said at the party and as a result had done her an injustice by imagining that she would ever contemplate doing something so silly as to try an infiltrate an airbase. This was an extremely crafty move. Not only had she kept the delicate subject of infiltrating airbases open in Anthea's mind she had also managed to distance herself from any involvement in the enterprise.

But it did much more than that.

With the flourish of her pen she had given herself the freedom she needed to approach the subject more obliquely and less obviously whilst not wholly taking it off the agenda. She could now work on Anthea from an different angle, one that was guaranteed to enthral the Princess and hold her attention more than any other.

Her obsession with the German Air Force.

In the days since her first letter Thetis had gone to great pains to learn as much as she could about the German Air Force, its structure, its machines, its protocols, its administration and its leading personnel. There was a lot to take in.

But it wasn't as taxing as I feared it might be.

Indeed, she knew much already. A great deal of this she had gleaned from conversations with her son during his training and career as a combat pilot and also from her numerous visits to Hermann's aviation factory in Essen. Added to this was what she had managed to learn as an

193

agent of both the British and German governments. And she poured all of this knowledge into her third letter determined to give Anthea the impression that she knew as much as she did on the subject and was just as devoted.

Nothing brings people closer than a shared interest.

And who knows, she thought, if her plan succeeded and Anthea swallowed the bait she might gain her trust and possibly even her friendship. She would then be able to communicate with her as often as she wished, all the while openly discussing aero-engines and warplanes and Germany's valiant Oberkanonen. But between the lines something else would be going on.

Between the lines I'll continue to dangle before her the idea of infiltrating JGN.

As usual she used Erich, her chauffeur and manservant, to deliver all three letters to the Princess through the friendly offices of Helga, Anthea's lady in waiting. When he returned from delivering the second letter she was disappointed to see that he had come back empty handed. And this time when he entered her study her expectations were that he had fared no better. But when he told her that he had something for her she found it hard to contain her delight.

I have her! She's mine! She's mine!

She snatched the letter from Erich's hands and tore it open. Without really reading what was written on the two pages or even taking in the meaning of the words her eyes flashed across the lines and paragraphs, establishing beyond doubt that the letter was from Anthea. Having done this she waited a few moments, gaining control of her breathing and allowing her rapid heartbeat to return to normal. Then she focused on the letter once again this time reading every word with great care.

As Thetis had expected Anthea denied everything, the conversation, what she said and any intention on her part to infiltrate the airbase at Bois de Cheval. And even if she had such things then her words must be taken as nothing more than an idle conceit. Thetis chuckled when she read that.

The seeds of doubt have taken root.

The letter contained little else of interest - Anthea brought it to a close by thanking Thetis for her concerns assuring her that she really didn't have anything to be concerned about – but from its tone and content it was obviously a reply to the first letter. Not that Thetis cared. She was happy enough to have got any reply at all.

Everything is starting to come together.

That was clear. She had made a breakthrough and she knew that it was vital that she acted upon it while it was still fresh. But how? The problem for her was that all this letter writing was taking too much time. She needed to speed things up.

'Erich, I think I need to speak to the Princess on the telephone.'

****

For Anthea it was turning out to be a very strange day indeed. Not that it had started out that way. In fact, it had started out normal enough. She'd got into a heated argument with her mother who was still determined to marry her daughter off to some highborn noble. Knowing from bitter experience that there was no satisfactory method for winning such arguments Anthea decided that escape was her best option. Dressed appropriately she took herself off to the hangars that housed her mother's Albatros BI and her own Halberstadt DII.

After taking to the air it took her less than five minutes to find herself flying over the hard-edged rooftops of Berlin. They were still pristine white but the roads between them were slush-rutted, churned into brown water by thousands of rolling wheels and trudging feet. Anthea flew over the city at chimney pot height. She always kept at that height when flying over metropolitan Berlin.

Any higher and one misses out on the life of a great city and the flow of its population.

She flew east over the Tiergarten along Charlottenburg Strasse then along Unten den Linden to Alexander Platz. Below her she could see boxed trams zipping back and forth, slithering worm-like along their rails. There were motor vehicles and horse-drawn carts and pedestrians hurrying to work or browsing at leisure. The broad pavements were alive with cafes and shouldered hats. And at the shadow of her passage and the buzz of her engine the hats tilted up and she saw faces looking up in amazement. Some waved and sometimes she waved back.

Here, high in the air, was the nearest that Anthea would ever get to humanity. She was with them yet beyond them. Their lives moved beneath her yet she would never be responsible for any of them. She could choose who to watch and who not to watch, who to wonder about and who to ignore. She felt at one with and yet remote from their concerns.

There's just so many of them.

Normally her restless spirit would have kept her above the city for a couple of hours. She certainly had enough fuel. But after only an hour the sky started to darken from the northeast and rather than get caught in the rain she wheeled her Halberstadt round and headed south. Within minutes the tall buildings were far behind her. The suburbs lay ahead. She

195

climbed to a thousand feet and passed through a stray cloud. It wasn't much of a cloud but when she came out the other side she was over the grassy woodlands of the Residenz. After landing she returned to her rooms, moving stealthily to avoid her mother.

'Draw me a bath, Helga,' she ordered, throwing her goggles and gloves onto a nearby divan.

'Yes, my Lady.'

It was at that moment that Anthea's world started to turn strange. It began with the ringing of the telephone.

'Find out who that is will you, Helga.'

Helga obeyed, moving to the small table where the ornate telephone stood. She was somewhat tentative about using the telephone. It was not an apparatus that made her feel comfortable and in consequence she tended to murmur into it. After a few moments of murmuring she placed her hand discretely over the mouthpiece. 'My Lady!'

'What is it, Helga?'

'It's the Baroness von Buchner. She wishes to speak to you.'

For a fleeting moment Anthea felt trapped. She wasn't at all sure that she wished to speak to the Baroness and yet there seemed that there was little she could do to avoid it. Suppressing her irritation she took the telephone from Helga.

'Baroness! What an unexpected pleasure,' Anthea said, infusing her words with some of the false smile that now sat upon her face.

'Please, your Highness, call me Thetis.'

The smile hardened. 'As you wish.'

'I hope you are not angry with me for contacting you like this. My only excuse is that I just had to call you and thank you for your charming letter.'

'Well, after all the letters you have sent me it would have been rude not to acknowledge one of them. Besides you seemed so worried I felt obliged to put your mind at rest.'

'That was very kind of you. As I said I have come to realise that I had got the wrong end of the stick. I should have known that you would never have undertaken such a venture. The difficulties would have been insurmountable.'

Having obtained the ear of the Princess it was at this point that Thetis began to set out in some detail all the obstacles that would have stood in the way whilst at the same time subtly suggesting how they might have been overcome.

'Though you're wonderful costume at the party was utterly convincing and took in not only myself but also the other guests your feminine beauty would have inevitably betrayed you.

Even if you stacked your boots to make yourself taller and practised day and night learning how to speak in a deeper voice your petite form and your songlike voice would still give you away.'

Anthea listened to all of this and as she did so a change came upon her. At the beginning of the conversation she had found her impatience growing. All she wanted to do was put the telephone down and forget this woman who had so forcefully intruded upon her life. But as she continued listening she found the tension in her shoulders relaxing and her grip upon the telephone lessening. And instead of looking exasperated her eyes now became fixed as her ears began to take in what she was being told.

'Think about it, your Highness. Think about all the pitfalls that would have awaited you. For instance, what would you have said if another pilot had engaged you in conversation? What would you have said if he had asked you where you were trained or if you knew so and so at the flying school?'

'Oh, I see. I hadn't really thought about that.'

'You would not have had a sufficient background story to support you in such circumstances. Nor would you have had the proper paperwork or written authorisation. Nor do you have access to such things. As you can see, Your Highness, you were wise to decide against such an undertaking.'

'Yes, I suppose I was,' Anthea agreed as she busied herself scribbling notes on the back of an envelope. 'I suppose I was.'

****

'What will you do if the English bomb it again?'

It was a serious possibility, one that Fuchs had thought about often, but this evening he was too heady with the joy of success to do anything but laugh if off.

'Oh, don't you know,' he replied jovially. 'I've sent them an open invitation. They can come over whenever they like just so long as they pay for their drinks.'

It was the gala opening of the old Kasino and Fuchs stood with Reinhard on the veranda. Though tired he felt invigorated. His dream was now a reality and all memory of the endless expenses, the sleepless nights and the ceaseless effort of the past fortnight was wiped away by the sound of laughter and clinking glasses.

My Kasino is open and doing great business.

Not that it hadn't been a close-run thing. The work of renovation had gone on all through the night and into the early hours. The electricity supply and the new cooker in the kitchen were the last pieces of work to be installed, but it was still dark that morning when everything was finally completed.

The only thing missing was the cutlery.

Now the whole place, outside and in, was ablaze with electric light. The bar was stocked with every variety of alcohol known to man. A cold buffet had been laid out, there were bouquets of winter flowers on every table and a small military band was providing the guests hearty musical entertainment. Everyone was in attendance though there were not as many present as there used to be in the past. Fuchs did a quick head count and reckoned there had to be just over thirty officers in the building. Not all that long ago it would have been packed with well over seventy.

I'm glad Reinhard found time to come.

Normally admission to the Kasino would have been restricted to commissioned officers only, but as this was a special occasion and he wanted the place to look as full as possible Fuchs went to Buchner and asked him if could send out some invitations to local dignitaries.

He shrugged indifferently, but I went ahead anyway.

Everyone that was sent an invitation responded and the Mayors of Senlis and Paillé with their charming wives were among the notables present. To help swell the numbers still further Mimi had agreed to bring over some of her ladies to act as waitresses, though it went without saying that their duties with regard to the officers enjoyed a broader and more liberal remit.

As long as everyone is happy.

Mimi was also responsible for much of the food. The military chef had not turned up as expected, but she had stepped in at the last moment with a plentiful supply of cooked hams, chickens and other delicacies from her own establishment.

Not that she isn't being well paid.

This thought was punctuated by the arrival of Buchner and he looked far from happy.

'Herr Hauptmann,' Reinhard called out in greeting, stiffening to attention as he did so.

'Reinhard! Enjoying your stint at the *Jastaschule*?'

Wary of saying the wrong thing Reinhard chose a diplomatic reply. 'It's different, but I'm not sure I'd want to do it full-time.'

As Buchner nodded his head his mouth twisted into a bitter smile. 'Now there's a sentiment I can appreciate.'

Sensing the conversation was still edging its way into sensitive territory Reinhard tried to steer it in a different direction. 'Fuchs was just telling me that JGN is getting back up to full strength.'

Buchner gave no sign that the subject interested him and his reply only confirmed this impression. 'Yes, we've been receiving replacements transferred from the eastern front.'

'That should make your job much easier.'

'Maybe.' The word came out with flat finality.

Again Reinhard could see where things were heading, but rather than letting it hang in mid-air he decided to confront it head on, 'You seem uncertain?'

'Oh, it's not that.' Buchner's stone façade broke. 'It's just that the place has become full of strangers and unfamiliar faces. I would have it back the way it was.'

'So would I, Herr Hauptmann,' Reinhard said with genuine sympathy. 'But we know that it never will.'

Fuchs listened to this cheerless exchange with increasing irritation. This was to be a night of celebration, his night of celebration and Buchner was spoiling it. He'd had enough of his commanding officer's whining. He didn't want to hear anymore but, not being able to tell him to shut up he decided on an alternative course.

Time to take my leave, I think.

Adopting a polite smile he stepped forward. 'Excuse me, Herr Hauptmann, but I need to check that we aren't running out of champagne.'

****

Seeing Fuchs come in from the veranda Braumfels lifted his glass of Slivovitz and called out, 'Congratulations on your Kasino, Herr Oberleutnant! It's quite splendid.'

Hearing the compliment Fuchs smiled and raised a hand in salute then proceeded on his way to the bar.

'He looks pleased with himself,' Crüger observed.

'And why shouldn't he?' Dessau asked pointedly. 'He worked dammed hard getting this place open and I think the results show that he has a definite flair for such things.'

Crüger looked about him with an air of distaste. 'They do if you like bordellos.'

Dessau smiled. 'I bow to your knowledge in such matters, Crüger. Anyway, I didn't hear you complaining when Fuchs got you that bottle of vodka. '

'Yeah!' Anders added. 'I bet you never thought you'd see any of that after we left Russia.'

This was the first occasion that the new pilot's had been able to get together. From the very start they had been split up and assigned to separate Jastas; Wülner and Crüger to Jasta Leintz, Dessau and Burgmüller to Jasta Reinhard, Braumfels and Anders to Jasta Dostler and Abendroth to Jasta Brandenburg. They settled in quickly and over the days following their arrival their respective Jasta Commanders had taken them out on various flights to familiarise them with both the countryside surrounding Bois de Cheval and their sector of the front.

The early signs were that given time they would soon cease to regard themselves as replacement pilots from the east and come to see themselves as part of *JGN*. This had been the expectation but it hadn't quite worked out like that. Certainly amongst themselves they began referring to each other as either the silver pilots or the bronze pilots depending on which particular group of Jastas they belonged to; *Gruppe Buchner* or *Gruppe Brandenburg*.

But this was only their way of teasing each other. It meant no more than that and certainly wasn't a sign of a division between them or a sign that they were adhering more closely to the identity of JGN. More significantly the unit's rump of original pilots began referring to them as the 'Österfliegern'. It wasn't intended to be an insult but more recognition of their closeness as a group with a shared history and common experience. But in the strange way that these things come about when the replacements learnt what they were being called by the others they were more than pleased to adopt the name for themselves.

There were other reasons slowing their integration. One of them was the fact that they were quartered together in the same two huts. Normally this would not have happened and before their arrival Fuchs had urged that they should be split up but Buchner had overruled him believing that staying together might help them to settle in. Another reason was JGN's lack of manpower. In a unit where only twenty-six original pilots remained it was easy enough for seven newcomers to form a small but significant minority.

'What do think of your new Jasta Commander?' Braumfels asked Dessau.

'Leutnant Greims isn't really our Jasta commander,' Dessau pointed out. 'Oberleutnant Reinhard is.'

'Not until he finishes his stint at the training school.'

'Greim is good. Down to earth but patient and well-informed.'

'Oberleutnant Dostler is like that too,' Anders pointed out. 'He's full of useful tips as well.'

'Not at all like Oberleutnant Brandenburg,' Abendroth lamented. 'You can barely get a word out of him.'

'What about Oberleutnant Leintz?' Burgmüller asked.

'Oh, he's superb,' Wülner nodded enthusiastically. 'I've never known anyone take such care of his machine. And he always checks his ammunition before going out on patrol.'

At that moment Buchner entered the Kasino and all conversation amongst the *Österfliegern* ceased. Their eyes followed him as he walked over to the bar and got himself a drink, wondering who he would speak to first. But he was still at the bar when Fuchs collared him, and the two were soon locked in close conversation.

Still watching Buchner Crüger asked, 'What do you make of our Hauptmann?'

'I'm not sure I know what to make of him.'

'You told us he was a barrel of laughs.'

'He was.' Wülner shook his head in bewilderment. 'Something's changed him.'

'Getting promoted,' Crüger declared. 'That's what's changed him.'

'That and shooting down that English *Oberkanone*. What was his name?'

'Harker!'

'So, he thinks he's the big shot,' Crüger sneered. 'Too big to speak to the rest of us. It happens to the best of them.'

Wülner shook his head. 'No. It's got to be more than that. I tell you, he used to be the life and soul. Now look at him. You'd think he's got the weight of the world on his shoulders.'

****

As the *'Österfliegern'* discussed their commander some thirty-five miles to the east the trainee pilots of the *Jastaschule* at Valenciennes were gathering in their Kasino. But this was no gala opening. Their Kasino was more modest than the one in Bois de Cheval. It had no fancy paintings or luxuriously upholstered furnishings or fine cuisine or a military band providing entertainment. But after a day of risking life and limb on obsolete machines that should have long since been broken up for scrap these young men found their surroundings just as welcoming as any grand establishment.

One general refrain among the trainees was, 'Well, that's another day we've survived.'

'And one day nearer graduation,' was another.

But all too frequently somebody was heard to lament, 'Did you see how poor old Gustav stalled and crashed?'

'According to the mechanic an inlet pipe got clogged and the engine cut out.'

Into this haze of sombre shoptalk stepped the ever-exuberant figure of Oberleutnant Röth. And as soon as he entered the Kasino he was immediately surrounded by trainees, all of them clamouring to buy him a drink. It was no exaggeration to say that both Röth and Reinhard had proved to be very popular additions to the school. Their lectures on combat tactics were always well attended even by those pupils who had no business being there. Yet it was in the informal surroundings of the Kasino that they found themselves mostly in demand.

Whenever either of them appeared they were accosted by those eager to hear about their adventures over the Ste Helene Salient flying with the likes of Buchner, Frommherz, Menckhoff and Hantelmann. The name of Hantelmann was one with which the school was not unfamiliar. Not because the great man had attended Valenciennes but because it had acquired a Hantelmann of its very own. And this particular Hantelmann was no less than the great man's very own son.

Gerard Hantelmann was nineteen years of age. He was as tall as his father, but hadn't yet acquired his facial severity. Nor had the world's cares and disappointments yet worn thin the bloom of his youthful enthusiasm and boundless optimism. And, despite being the son of the illustrious Rudolf Hantelmann, fighter pilot and wounded commander of *Jagdgeschwader Nord,* from the moment Gerard entered the school the other pupils had gravitated to him for his own sake and during his short stay he had acquired many friends. This is not to say that the exploits of his father during the battle of Trois Risseaux had failed to raise Gerard's standing within the *Schule.*

'Have you seen today's newspaper, Gerard?' His friend Ostermann asked.

'No, I haven't. What's in it?'

'An article about your father.'

'Really! What does it say?'

'It says your father has been awarded the Iron Cross First Class.'

Gerard snatched the newspaper from his friend's hands but he had barely started reading the article when someone shouted out: 'The drinks are on Gerard.'

'Why me?' Gerard protested with a laugh as the others dragged him to the bar. 'I haven't done anything heroic.'

'But it's your father we're celebrating.'

'Then get him to buy the drinks.'

Seeing Röth close by Gerard approached him. 'I believe you visited my father in hospital, Herr Oberleutnant.'

'Yes, that's correct. Oberleutnant Reinhard and I paid him a courtesy call a couple of weeks back.'

'How was he?'

Röth smiled. 'He is not a good patient as I'm sure you know. But he's eager to get back to his old command.'

'I've just heard he's been awarded the Iron Cross.'

'And more than well deserved. I take it you feel rather proud of your father?'

'Yes, I do, very much.'

'Good! That's as it should be. And I can tell you that he is very proud of you and given your recent progress he has every reason to be.'

'Thank you, Herr Oberleutnant.'

'You've completed your spot landings successfully?'

'Yes, Herr Oberleutnant.'

'And your high altitudes?'

'Yes, Herr Oberleutnant.'

'Then you should be ready to take your Field Pilot Exam. Two cross-country flights, isn't it?'

'It is.'

'Good. Complete them without any crash landings and you'll be pinning on your Pilot's Badge before the month ends.'

'I hope so, Herr Oberleutnant.'

'Who knows. You might be joining us at the Fighter Unit School by the beginning of January.'

'That would be wonderful, Herr Oberleutnant.'

'Right!' Röth looked around. 'I believe you were about to buy these young men a round of drinks.'

'I'd be honoured if you joined us, Herr Oberleutnant.'

'I thought you'd never ask.'

****

Not to be outdone by their foes the officers of 63 Squadron at Ste Helene were also gathered in their mess. And they had good reason to be there. Captain Ian Hamilton had been granted Christmas leave and the squadron was throwing a binge to celebrate his good fortune. But the English are a strange breed. Steadfast in many respects they possess a singular inability to drink in moderation. Whereas as other nation's drink to the point of jollity the English seem hell bent on drinking themselves into oblivion.

It started as these things usually do with a round of toasts. These were accompanied by witty speeches and anecdotes, which called into question the competence of Hamilton and Parkinson. Both men being present they were allowed to answer. There was laughter all round. Then the toasts got louder and the speeches more and more inarticulate. No one could understand what anyone was saying and this seemed to trigger even greater gales of laughter.

At some point the spoken word was abandoned entirely and song took its place. All the old favourites, the funny ones, the sad ones, the bitter ones, were bellowed at full throttle. Drunken officers, clasping each other's shoulders, swayed from side to side like a choir on the deck of a rolling ship. As Parkinson slipped out of the mess unnoticed someone nudged into someone else. It was an accident. Or was it? There was a general bundle as everyone piled on top of each other. More laughter.

'A Tourney,' someone shouted.

The officers separated into their different flights. Champions were selected. Cummings and Whitworth were chosen for 'B' flight. Holding a broom by its brush Cummings climbed onto Whitworth's shoulders. Musker and Collier of 'C' flight did the same. Everyone stepped to the sides so that a gap was formed for the lists. The two knights and their chargers assembled at either end. They turned about and faced their opponents. Lowering their brooms they charged. At the moment of impact an explosion shook the hut and the lights went out.

A siren sounded. Confusion and chaos followed. Yells and curses filled the air. The darkness was full of unseen motion. There was another explosion, more distant this time. Other explosions followed, each more distant than the last until at last they ceased altogether. An uneasy calm descended upon the darkness. The lights came on. A scene of mayhem was revealed. Officers were lying about all over the floor, some tangled in heaps. There were moans and movement as bodies started to untangle. The door opened and Parkinson entered.

'Don't be alarmed,' he called out. 'There's been a raid. Three bombers. Seems they missed us and hit the farm.'

'Maybe it was the farm they were after,' quipped Ascot of 'A' flight. This raised a roar of laughter.

Now sober the officers slowly got to their feet and dusted themselves off. Only one remained lying on the floor.

'I say, Cummings.' Parkinson joined the others as they gathered around the prone figure. 'Are you all right?'

'I'm not sure, sir,' Cummings grimaced. 'I think I've broken my leg.'

CHAPTER SEVENTEEN

14 DECEMBER 1917

Well, I'll draw my letter to a close for now. I'm sorry that I never seem to have much of interest to write about but as I've said often enough life in the trenches is really rather boring most of the time.
Your loving son.
Thomas

Swain folded the finished letter, which was only a single piece of paper written on both sides, and slipped it into a small pre-addressed envelope that he had to hand. As soon as this was securely buttoned in his breast pocket he took out his mud spattered notebook, removed the rubber band holding it together and started writing.

14ᵗʰ December 1917

Our section had its first casualty this morning and it not only came as a great shock to all of us it also acted as a timely reminder that the difference between life and death out here hangs by a very slender thread indeed. We've been manning Brewer Street trench just over a week now yet in all that time we haven't come to appreciate just how precarious things can be. Despite the dirt and the stink we regarded our situation as more a matter of discomfort than danger.

It's not as if there's bullets flying about and shells going off all the time. There are explosions and the rattle of machine guns. One hears them on most days, but these sounds are always in the distance, somewhere so far away one feels safe enough to ignore them. Then something happened this morning that changed all of that. It happened quite early. In fact it happened just after dawn. It was still dark in the trench but the sky was beginning to lighten and the air was peaceful and still.

Hutchins and Scuttle were up first and they had got the 'Kampite' going for a brew while the rest of us, buried in scarves and greatcoats, stomped around slapping our arms against our sides to get warm. Other than for the odd muttered curse there wasn't really any conversation. There never is at this time of the day. After all, what is there to talk about when you've only just opened your eyes? All anyone is concerned with at such an hour is the first fag and the first brew of tea. Learned discourse on the state of the war and the grand strategy of the General Staff can wait till later.

Not that we regard ourselves as in any way peculiar in this respect. Though we have no evidence to call upon it is our firm belief that the morning habits of Fritzie in the trenches opposite are no different to ours – stomping and brewing and lighting cigarettes. The quietness and general lack of warlike activity at this time of the day seemed to support these assumptions though Shorthouse, who was an authority on everything under the sun, was at great pains to correct us on one small point.

'Fritzie prefers to start his day with coffee not tea.'

'Oh yeah?' came Haggis McLeod's usual challenge. ''Ow d'you know that?'

'I just know that's all,' Shorthouse countered.

But as we stood there this morning waiting for our tea no one gave any thought to the issue. It wasn't long before steam started to come out of the tin on the burner. Hutchins poured the tea into one of the Dixies used for carrying meals back from the rear kitchen. Scuttle then mixed tinned milk and sugar into this and when it was the right colour we all formed an orderly queue in front of him and waited our turn as he filled each of our mess tins.

'Don't forget the Lieutenant, Scuttle,' Dibbs told Scuttle in a wheedling tone. 'He needs his tea too.'

But Scuttle never overlooked the Lieutenant. Now more or less acting as his personal orderly it surprised no one to see that he already had the Lieutenant's mess tin to hand. Without saying a word he filled it with tea and, after mixing in the necessary, headed along the trench to the Lieutenant's dugout.

Scuttle is a big lad. Well over six feet. We often tease him about it because he really stands out especially when on parade. Most of us in the section are short arses being only a few inches over five feet. Even the lieutenant is only about five nine. In a front line trench being a short arse can be a distinct advantage as it isn't always necessary to walk about in a crouch. But for someone of Scuttle's height it pays to keep your head down.

Well, on this occasion he forgot. Maybe it was Dibbs' jibe or maybe it was because he was preparing himself to meet an officer. Whatever the reason he was about halfway along the trench his head held high when his tin helmet suddenly leaps off his head. We all watched in amazement as it flipped and spun in the air and it went quite a distance before it landed somewhere out of sight. Then less than a second later this spectacle was followed by a loud report that made us all duck.

'Sniper!' someone shouted.

We crouched low on our hams for quite a while, tea in one hand fag in the other, and it was some time before we finally felt it safe enough to raise our heads and take a look around. Scuttle was still on his feet but the force of the bullet had spun him round so that he was now facing us. In his right hand was the lieutenant's mess tin full of tea. His left hand was pressed up against the friendly side of the trench as if leaning against it for support.

His eyes were wide, his mouth open as if he had just made an amazing discovery, some deep truth rarely disclosed to mere mortals. And he was holding the side of his head in an odd manner. There was also a puzzled look on his face but other than that he seemed perfectly all right.

'You lucky bugger!' Dibbs exclaimed, voicing what all of us were thinking.

Soldiers are a superstitious lot. They are always intrigued by lucky escapes and Scuttle's survival was certainly luckier than most. Probably hoping that such luck might rub off we advanced toward him. Up to this point he hadn't moved at all. And as we got closer it began to dawn on some of us that something wasn't quite right.

'You all right, Scuttle?' I asked.

He didn't reply. He didn't even look at me. In fact, he wasn't looking at anyone. His eyes were fixed on some point in the distance and the look of amazement had now frozen into a blank and rigid expression. We closed in around him to see if he needed assistance. It was then that Hoon, who was forced by the lack of space to step behind Scuttle, started making a gagging noise. Almost immediately he ran off down the trench with a hand over his mouth.

'What's the matter with him?' Brinkly asked.

'Oh, my God!' Hutchins exclaimed, his voice a mixture of horror and revulsion. He was staring at the back of Scuttle's head and I got in beside him so that I could also have a look. A piece of Scuttle's skull about the size of a man's palm was missing. It had been lifted clean off like the top of a boiled egg. All one could see was his exposed brain underneath and it appeared that the sniper's bullet had damaged that as well.

Lieutenant Leighton emerged from his dugout. The Sergeant was with him.

'What's happened here,' the Lieutenant asked.

'Sniper, sir,' Hoskins volunteered. 'He got Scuttle.'

Entworth, who was standing in front of Scuttle, took a step back. 'My God! He's still alive.'

He was. We could see him breathing and in some strange way this struck us all as more awful than if the poor man had been killed outright. Alive he may have been, but whatever it was that was leaning against the side of the trench it was no longer Private Scuttle and we could all see that it never would be again. It was at this point that Brinkly barged past me and stood facing no-man's-land. Face quivering with rage he started screaming.

'YOU FUCKING BASTARDS! YOU FUCKING BASTARDS!'

****

'So you didn't suffer any serious casualties?' Colonel Pritchett asked his concern evident even over the telephone.

'Only Cummings, Colonel,' Parkinson assured him. 'We thought at first it might be a broken leg, but it turned out to be a wrenched knee. A few weeks rest and it should be good as new.'

'Good! And the base?'

'Only one bomb actually fell within our perimeter and that did no more than dig a hole in the path. Most of the bombs dropped in the adjoining farm. No real damage there either but it rather put the wind up the farmer and his wife. They've decided to evacuate the place.'

'That's a shame. No more fresh eggs for breakfast.'

'Oh, I told the farmer we'd look after the place for him. Keep an eye on the horses and the other animals.'

'How will you manage that?'

'One of corporals is a farmer. He says he knows what to do.'

'Well, as long as it doesn't interfere with base operations. And how are the new fellows?'

'I've put Testeridge in 'A' flight and...' Parkinson paused to consult the sheet of paper on his clipboard '...Hobson and Gooch-Leverton in 'C'.'

'So you're more or less back up to full strength,'

Yes, sir. We're only missing a flight leader for 'C' flight.'

'That's a role you're still playing?'

'Yes, sir.'

'What about machines?'

'We have thirteen Camels with two more expected in a few days.'

Parkinson could hear Pritchett's voice relax at the other end of the line. 'And how's the squadron generally? It's overall morale?'

'It's very good, sir.' Parkinson hesitated. This was the moment he had waited for throughout the conversation so far. 'In fact I was wondering whether it would be possible to spare me over Christmas?'

As Parkinson waited for an answer he stubbed out his cigarette in the empty tobacco tin that Harker used to use when he commanded 63 squadron. Pritchett coughed at the other end of the telephone. This was always a sure sign that he had come to a decision.

'Well, I don't see why not. I was about to suggest you take some leave anyway and my intelligence boys aren't expecting anything major to happen until the New Year so I think we can spare you. When will you go?'

'The twentieth.'

'Do you have any plans?'

'Yes, I shall be spending Christmas Day with my parents, but before that I thought I'd pay Mrs Harker a visit.'

There was a pause then: 'I take it you sent her that portrait of her husband?'

'Yes, Colonel, I did.'

'And how did she take it?'

Parkinson picked an opened envelope from his desk. 'I have a letter from her here. Just received it today. It's quite brief. More a note of thanks than anything else. She says she's had the portrait hung in her living room and that it's presence gives her great comfort.'

'Splendid. Well, I'm sure you know best. If we haven't spoken before you set off enjoy your leave and have a Merry Christmas. And give my kind regards to Mrs Harker when you see her.'

'I will, sir. And thank you.'

It was only when Harker disconnected the call that he was struck by something he hadn't thought of before.

Why did I tell him that? Why did I tell him I was going to visit Mrs Harker?

When Parkinson first contacted Pritchett to report on the bombing raid it had been on his mind to ask for leave. He had been thinking about it for some days, but there had been nothing in his plans about paying Mrs Harker a visit.

So why the hell did I say that I was going to see her?

It hadn't been a slip of the tongue and now that he had said it he realised that somewhere at the back of his mind he had probably intended to do it all along. Indeed, it seemed likely that the decision was made when he sent her the portrait.

But why?

On examination his motives were far from clear. It wasn't as if he had any personal interest in Mrs Harker beyond the fact that she was the wife of his friend. He had never met her and his personal inclination in such matters would have been to avoid coming face to face with a grieving widow. The only reasonable explanation he could come up with was that it was probably no more than curiosity on his part. He was curious to know what she thought of the portrait.

That's it! It's no more than artistic vanity.

But there was something about the speed and readiness with which he accepted this explanation that made him doubt its credibility. It just didn't ring true. There had to be some other reason, but as he thought about it some more he came up against a sense of reluctance to delve any deeper.

Am I hiding something from myself?

And the possibility made him feel uneasy. He had always been brutally honest with himself, especially when facing up to his lack of courage, and he didn't like to think that he might be guilty of self-deceit. It wasn't healthy. Only the truth mattered and one way or another he was determined to uncover it. But now was not the time. His Adjutant, Captain Hargreaves, had entered the office.

'Sorry to trouble you, Major, but you did say you'd like to be informed when the new Camels arrived.'

'Yes, I did. Thank you, Captain. Lead the way.'

****

Being sent to the Residenz to keep a close eye on the Princess made perfect sense. It was the only sure way of ascertaining whether she was responding appropriately to the Baroness' manipulation. Erich knew that and he didn't question it. Nor did he mind having a further opportunity to tumble the beautiful Helga in her wide and spacious bed. All in all as missions went this one was quite pleasurable. But there was a downside.

Having to hide in this damn bedroom.

It wasn't the hiding he found irksome. There had been many times while serving the Baroness when he'd had to keep out of sight, often finding himself pressed close in some dank alleyway or shadowed corner waiting for the danger to pass. Then he had thought nothing of it.

But this bedroom is an entirely different matter.

As one might expect of a lady-in-waiting it was a huge fluffy confection of silks and satins. But what made it a strain on the senses was the colour. Everything was pink. The walls were pink, the sheets were pink, the cushions were pink, the lace curtains were pink, the lampshades were pink.

Even her perfume bottles are pink.

Erich hated pink. It made him feel bilious. It was a sensuous colour and Erich wasn't noted for his sensuality. It was one of the reasons why he detested lying idly about on beds. And it mustn't be forgotten that part of what made him irresistible to women, especially those of noble birth, was not his sensuality but his intense aura of suppressed brutality.

It was not an affected trait, but genuine and Thetis had recognised its usefulness right from the start. Knowing that many high-born women secretly desired being taken by a brute she exploited it, sending him from court to court to spy and, where necessary, to seduce. As Thetis knew only too well from her own experience pillow talk was a highly valuable source of intelligence.

Though she had never succumbed herself to Erich's less than tender charms she had heard other women speak admiringly about his manly prowess. In hushed and excited whispers, they frequently touched upon one of his little methods of seduction, something they referred to as his *ravissante doux.*

The method was straightforward. Pin the woman's hands behind her back, tear the chemise from her heaving bosom then throw her onto the bed. But Erich was not a cruel man. He only pretended to be. He would never force himself upon an unwilling woman. And his grip during *ravissante doux* was always loose enough for her to break free if she so wished.

In this way he not only gave her the thrill of being ravished but also the reassurance that she still had the power of resistance. It was how he had seduced Helga. He recalled how her excited eyes had widened in anticipation as he yanked away her nightdress. From the start it was clear to him that she liked to be dominated and had little time for men who weren't up to the task.

Not that I feel up to it at the moment.

He felt hemmed in, his vitality sucked dry. And intensifying the room's pink claustrophobia was the overpowering heat. Helga, for some reason that Erich could never quite understand, always insisted on keeping it baking hot.

Like a bloody sauna.

Erich's Finnish blood longed to open a window and feel the cold air on his face, but it was something he didn't dare do. The risk of being spotted by someone walking about in the grounds below was just too great. He couldn't take the chance. If he was discovered it would seriously compromise Helga's position.

And put an end to my ability to act as the Baroness' eyes and ears.

His nights with Helga were some compensation for his enforced confinement. She was a passionate and inventive lover and seemingly inexhaustible. But that was only at night. During the day she was in constant demand by the Princess and while she was he had to spend most of his time locked in the bedroom with virtually nothing to do.

She hasn't even got a book I can read.

And when the sun went down, as it was doing now, he had no choice but to sit in the dark. He couldn't turn on the light for the same reason that he couldn't open the windows. And slowly the combination of boredom, heat and growing twilight began to have their effect. His alertness started to give way to drowsiness and his eyes began to grow heavy.

He was about to nod off when he was brought back to wakefulness by the sound of the key turning in the lock. He was about to spring off the bed and hide in the adjoining bathroom when the door opened. The silhouette of a woman stood in the doorway and for a heart-stopping moment he lay wondering who it might be.

'Did you miss me?' Helga's voice asked alluringly.

'More than you can imagine,' Erich replied already stirring beneath the sheets. 'Come here.'

Helga laughed coquettishly. 'Patience, my darling. I need to freshen up first. While you've been lounging about in my bed I've had a busy day you know.'

'That Princess of yours,' Erich called out indignantly as Helga shut the door and disappeared into the bathroom. 'She treats you no better than a slave.'

'Oh she's lovely really especially when you get to know her.' There was a pause as taps were turned on, but as the water splashed into a basin Helga added thoughtfully, 'Although she has been acting rather strangely recently.'

Suddenly alert Erich rolled over on the bed. 'Strangely! How?'

****

The sea was her element. It always had been. Even as a child Thetis had been drawn to its vast expanse, to its mystery and unpredictable violence. It was a monster. But it was her monster. She understood it and she drew strength from it. She could feel its buoyant and unresisting surface supporting her, invigorating her blood and senses as her agile legs and arms powered a brisk crawl through the dark waters back to the waiting bay.

She adored swimming. It was an activity that never exhausted her even when she ventured far out to sea and beyond sight of land. And being the person she was she preferred to swim above its bottomless depths naked and in the light of the full moon. It never concerned her, never even entered her mind that she might get lost and drown. She gave no thought to these dangers. Why would the sea kill one of its own creatures?

Besides, I have an in-built sense of direction that always leads me back to the shore.

It guided her now as she ploughed her way back through the white-glinting waves to the bay. With the assistance of the incoming tide she was soon close enough to the shore's shallow waters to lower her legs and touch the bottom with her toes. Taut-skinned, she rose majestically from the dripping cling of the luminescent surf and, in all her unadorned beauty, strode beyond the lapping waves, her breasts and stomach clothed in shadow, the trim muscles of her bare legs and buttocks frosted in moonlight.

Beside a lit lantern lay some deck sandals, a soft robe and a towel. Standing proud and shameless, she shook her head vigorously from side to side, flinging salty droplets from her hair like a woodland creature shaking the moisture from its mane. She then bent forward and picked up the robe. After slipping this onto her shoulders and tying it at the waist she wound the towel into a tight turban about her dripping hair and placed her slim feet into the sandals. Lifting the lantern from the ground she proceeded with practised ease up the stone steps that were cut roughly into the sheer face of the chalk cliffs.

As she rose to the promontory above she pondered her situation. She had still not heard from her son; he was still refusing to answer her letters and take her calls. Other sources from within Bois de Cheval, however, had revealed to her that his unhappiness at being the commander was growing by the day. Despite this Thetis remained unrepentant. After her son's rampage of vengeance following the death of Frommherz she had been filled with a cold certainty that his own death wasn't far off. And his defeat of Major Harker had only intensified that certainty.

So why should I regret getting him that post?

Nor did she regret telling the British about his appointment. She hoped that by doing so air activity in the Ste Helene Salient would remain low. What she did regret was not being able to speak to her son especially now that her plans regarding Anthea were beginning to bear fruit. Tired of not knowing what was going on she had sent Erich back to the Residenz so that he could be on hand to inform her of any developments.

And if anything should develop it would be useful to have Willi's eyes and ears at my disposal.

The house was empty and exactly as she had left it. All the lights were on and the French windows were open. It was probably for this reason that she caught the sound of the telephone ringing while she was still some distance from the house. It was still ringing when she entered the study.

She lifted the receiver and placed it against her ear. 'Yes, who is it?'

'It's Erich, my Lady.' His voice was almost a whisper.

'Are you still at the Residenz?'

'Yes. And I have news.'

Thetis smiled. 'I'm all ears, Erich.'

'I've just been speaking to Helga and she tells me that her mistress has been behaving strangely.'

'Strangely? Tell me more.'

'Well, for a start she has just taken delivery of a pair of boots.'

'What's so strange about that?'

'Helga tells me that they have stacked heels.'

'How stacked?'

'Several inches I think. And that's not all. Helga also tells me that the Princess has started addressing her in an unnaturally deep voice. Helga asked her if she had a cold, but this only sent the Princess off in a huff.'

Thetis burst out laughing and it took her some moments to get herself back under control.

'Thank you, Erich. Your news is most welcome. In fact, it has raised my spirits more than you can imagine. Go back to your Helga and enjoy the rest of your night together.'

Feeling a great sense of contentment descend upon her Thetis put down the telephone and sat back at her small desk. All in all she was doing as well as she could have hoped at this stage of the game. She had made Anthea her friend and had gained her trust.

All the old animosity is now forgotten.

She could speak to her whenever she wished and at any time of the day. She could speak to her freely and openly and she used that advantage to whisper a persistent message into the young woman's ear, a message of problems and solutions, a message of obstacles and the means of overcoming them.

And she seems to be acting upon it.

Thetis stared thoughtfully through her French windows and off into the distance. It was now more essential than ever to keep up the pressure, essential not to pause or hesitate. Now was the time to tighten the noose, to weave the spell and ensure that Anthea's unknowing feet followed the path laid out for her.

CHAPTER EIGHTEEN

17 DECEMBER 1917

17ᵗʰ December 1917

We lost another member of our section last night. Though, when one thinks about it, we actually lost him a couple days ago. I suppose it was just a case that none of us realised it at the time. It was about six o'clock and we were having our tea when the Sergeant came up and informed us that we were going out on a night patrol. That news cheered us up no end.

Seeing our reaction he reassured us that there was nothing to worry about. It would be a routine patrol and that we wouldn't be going right over to the enemy lines. In fact, we would be doing little more than finding a cosy spot from where we could listen out for enemy activity and try to gauge their strength. This all sounded very pleasant and under normal circumstances we wouldn't have batted an eyelid. But there was a problem.

'Will Hoon be coming with us, Sergeant?'

Shorthouse had asked the question, but in reality it was a matter that was on all our minds.

'Of course he will. Why shouldn't he come with us?'

At this point all of us became very reluctant to say anything. There was a general feeling among us that talking to the Sergeant about another man was just not done. But the issue was an important one and luckily the Sergeant guessed this.

'What's wrong with him?' he asked gruffly.

Feeling the pressure to say something I blurted out, 'He won't talk.'

'He won't talk! What do you mean he won't talk?'

'He hasn't said anything since Scuttle died.'

This was true. Hoon was never much of a talker at the best of times so it took us a while to figure out that something was wrong. But as soon as we did we tried everything we could think of to get him to open his mouth and speak. Nothing worked.

The strange thing about his silence was not just his unwillingness to speak. It was the expression on his face and the look in his eyes. They had a faraway feel to them, staring off into space as if he was a million miles away and not in the trench with us at all.

'It was seeing Scuttle like that with the top of his head off that did it,' Entworth explained.

The Sergeant was still finding it hard to understand what we were on about. 'Did what?'

'Unhinged his mind.'

'Oh, come off it. There's nothing wrong with Hoon. He was never much of a talker. And he still does his jobs. I put him on latrine duty yesterday and he got on with it.'

'But he's not right in the head, Sergeant,' Entworth persisted.

'Just because he's not talking? Look, I wish to God sometimes the rest of you would follow his example. It would make my job a darn sight easier. If he's stopped talking all to the better. At least he won't be opening his gob while we're out on patrol.'

Hutchins stepped forward. 'But that's the point, Sergeant. If he's unhinged there's no telling what he might do when we're out in no-man's-land. He's in some sort of shock at the moment, but what happens if he comes out of it while we're crawling about in the dark? What happens if he has some sort of fit and starts screaming his fucking head off?'

'Then we'd royally buggered,' Dibbs muttered to himself.

This made the Sergeant stop and think. And when he'd stopped his thinking he left us without saying a word. We later learnt that he went straight to the Lieutenant. What he said to him we don't know but Hoon didn't go out on patrol with us that night and later when we returned we found that he had been quietly removed from the line.

****

Conscious that this would probably be the best chance she might ever have, Anthea sprung the hidden catch that opened the secret door to her father's library. Before entering she stood and listened for any sound of movement close to hand. There was none.

This part of the Residenz was more or less deserted. Her mother had gathered all the servants in the Grand Foyer at the front of the house to address them on her plans for the Christmas festivities. More importantly from Anthea's point of view her father was attending a meeting of High Command before making his way to Essen to visit her brother at his factory.

So the chances of being disturbed are remote.

With a light tread she passed through the secret entrance and closed the door gently behind her. Not daring to switch on the lights she turned on her torch and followed its beam across the Persian carpets to the large desk that stood in the middle of the library. Ignoring the startled expressions of her ancestors who were glaring at her from their frames she reached over and took hold of the bronze statuette of the nymph and the satyr that stood on the desk. The satyr was hinged and, by pulling it back at an angle she revealed a hidden space beneath it. In this space was a key. Using this she carefully unlocked one of the drawers.

There were a number of folders in the drawer, but it didn't take her long to locate the ones she wanted, the ones containing blank documents of authorisation. Taking note of their position within the drawer she removed them and placed them on the top of the desk. From one folder she removed a blank *Militärpass,* the sort she would need to produce on entry to any military establishment. From the other folder she took out a blank pilot's licence, the sort issued by the *Féderation Aéronautique Internationale.* This one had Deutschland gold-printed on its leather cover.

In another drawer she located her father's official stamp and embossing pad and for good measure secured some officially headed writing paper. It was at this point that she produced two photographs she had brought with her. Both of them were head and upper torso shots showing her dressed in her German officer's cap and uniform. She persuaded Helga to take them by telling her that she wanted a souvenir of what she looked like in uniform before she grew her hair back to its original length.

Not all of the drawers were locked. From one she found a bottle of adhesive. Using this she pasted the photographs into the documents, the small one into the *Militärpass,* the larger one into the pilot's licence. Taking up her father's official stamp she endorsed both documents, taking care to ensure that the round stamp covered the photograph and the document. Lastly she took her father's pen and, imitating his handwriting, wrote Leutnant Anton Strasser first on the pilot's licence and then on the *Militärpass.*

I can write in the rest later.

As she did all of this she kept telling herself that she merely wanted the documents for her collection, but in this she was deceiving herself and the fact that they had a more serious purpose was set aside. In conscious thought she still considered that purpose the height of insanity. But at some point in time, a moment that would have been hard to determine, her underlying motives had shifted from fantasy to reality.

Somewhere deep within her she had decided to undertake the adventure and infiltrate JGN, but even if she had admitted this to herself the moment of its conception was not something she would have considered anyway. As far as Anthea was concerned all that mattered was the here and now. If she was now determined to do a thing then she had always been determined to do it. The fact that she had once thought otherwise was of no consequence.

Nor did she recognise the influence of Thetis on her actions. Admittedly she had now begun to regard the Baroness as a friend, one who shared her interests and whose thoughts she valued. But because Thetis had made it plain from the very start that she was dead set against the venture Anthea felt justified in regarding her own actions as just that, her own.

I don't need her help anyway.

After all, she wasn't the daughter of Oberstgeneral von Hoeppner for nothing. It was that relationship that now enabled her to identify what she needed. And having obtained what she needed she was about to clear up, but then she spotted something in one of the folders that she hadn't noticed before.

What do we have here?

At first glance it looked like an ordinary certificate or diploma, the sort that might be handed out by a college or university, but it was in fact a blank *Ausweis,* a special permit that gave the bearer the authority to fly a certain model of aircraft. The model was not specified. But there was an empty space on the permit where this could be written in.

Now that could prove very useful.

She endorsed it with the official stamp and slipped it with her other documents between the pages of a book she had brought with her. With everything she wanted now secured she put away the glue and the endorsing pad then placed the folders and the official stamp back exactly where she'd found them, locked both the drawers she had opened and placed the key back under the bronze statuette.

With the same light tread she had used to enter the library she slipped out through its secret door. And all the way back to her apartment her heart was beating violently in her bosom, her breath was coming rapidly and she was feeling almost faint with excitement.

****

'And where did you get to, may I ask?'

Anthea almost leapt out of her skin. She had been on her way back to her apartment with her stolen documents, taking great care not to be seen. The last thing she had expected was to turn a corner and be confronted by her mother and Helga.

'Get to?' she asked tremulously.

'Yes. I saw you slip away from the Christmas meeting.'

'Oh, it was just something I had to do. Nothing important.'

Anyone else would have challenged this rather flimsy excuse, but not Hedda von Hoeppner. For her it was sufficient enough to display her hurt feelings and indignation, to make the guilty party feel guilty. It had to be enough. She knew from the bitter experience of confronting her husband about his affairs that interrogation and weighing up the evidence led to nothing but an impenetrable fog of evasion and denial.

'Well, it was rather thoughtless of you.'

'Oh come on, Mother. I've attended these Christmas meetings ever since I was a little child and I know every detail off by heart. They are always the same.'

'Not this one. There was something very special I wanted to tell you.'

'Something special?'

'Yes. I was thinking of inviting Count von Rüstern over for the holidays.'

'Oh, Mother. Not more match-making, please.'

'And what is wrong with Count von Rüstern? He is young, single and highly eligible.'

'I daresay he would make someone a perfect husband, but I have other plans for Christmas.'

'Other plans!' Hedda's voice had taken on a sharp inflexion of suspicion. 'What other plans?'

Her declaration of having other plans surprised Anthea as much as it had her mother. That she should have said such a thing she could only put down to her desire to thwart her mother's schemes. In reality she had not thought about Christmas at all. But now she had to reveal what those plans were and for a moment she stood before her mother unable to give an answer. Then as she struggled to come up with a credible reply it occurred to her that here was the opportunity she had been waiting for, the opportunity to escape the Residenz for an extended period.

With the sort of smile that only a daughter can give a mother, she informed Hedda, 'I'll be spending the holidays with Hermann this year,'

'This is the first I've heard of it.'

'I did tell father.' As far as lies go this was a safe one. Anthea knew that she would have no trouble convincing her father that he had known about it all along.

But Hedda was still not convinced. 'That seems very convenient to me considering he's not here. Not to worry! I'll telephone him later and see what he has to say about all this.'

Anthea felt her face redden and she was sure that her mother wouldn't fail to notice it. She had forgotten about her father's trip to Essen. She had forgotten about Hermann. Suddenly her lie seemed less safe and she was beginning to regret ever opening her mouth. But it was too late to pull back now. She would have to telephone Hermann and let him know that she was on his Christmas guest list. And she would have to do that before her father reached him. For the moment all she could do was continue to bluster.

'Well, I did tell him and he seemed content so I will be going to Hermann's for Christmas.'

'But surely not on your own?'

'I've spent Christmas there before, Mother.'

'Yes, but your father and I were there with you.'

'I'm old enough now to go on my own.'

Hedda sighed, conceding defeat. 'Well, at least you'll be with us for New Year's.'

Anthea's mouth almost fell open. 'What do you mean?'

'Hermann has confirmed that he and his family will be coming to us for the New Year's celebrations so if you're staying with him for Christmas you'll be coming back here with him for New Year.'

Damn!

Anthea's impromptu plan had hit another unexpected snag. She had hoped that staying with Hermann over the Christmas would give her a chance to figure out what she intended doing next, if anything. Everything else was unclear or at least that was what she tried to believe. In this she continued to delude herself about her true intentions. As far as she was concerned she'd always meant to go to Hermann's for Christmas. The fact that his home in Essen was within easy flying distance of Bois de Cheval was neither here nor there.

At this stage she would have preferred to leave the situation as it was, but this conversation with her mother was forcing her into ever-increasing complications. Getting to Essen was a victory of sorts, but it would remain a hollow victory if she had to return to Berlin for the New Year. She needed to expand her story and she needed to do it fast.

'No, Mother, I won't be coming back with him.'

Hedda's frown was an armoured visor of disapproval. 'Is that so? And where do you think you're going instead?'

Anthea knew that if chose that moment to hesitate the whole enterprise would unravel. But then inspiration came to her aid and much to her astonishment a name popped into her head and out of her mouth.

'I'll be staying with the Baroness von Buchner.'

****

After posing in the cockpit of a spare Albatros for Gunther and his camera, Gerard went to the Kasino for an early lunch. Sausages were on the menu, accompanied by peas, boiled potatoes and buttered rolls. He skipped the desert and settled on a cup of coffee instead.

While he filled his stomach the sky had darkened ominously. Snowflakes had followed and it looked as if he would have to cancel the last of his cross-country flights. Fortunately, the fall of snow didn't amount to much and the dark layer of clouds drifted apart to reveal the blue sky once more.

After waiting ten minutes to see how things developed, he headed over the frozen grass to the hangars. The moment was now approaching, the moment he had dreamt about ever since he was a little boy, the moment he had prepared for, the culmination of endless weeks of lectures, exams, and rigorous training on clapped out and obsolete machines.

My last cross-country flight.

He was nervous and excited. Excited because it was his final test. Nervous because there so much riding on the outcome. If he got it right he would get his licence. If he got it right he would qualify as a pilot. If he got it right he would go on to train as a fighter pilot.

And maybe eventually fly in my Father's unit.

Ahead he could see his instructor, Gustav Bähr, but he was disappointed not to see Röth standing with him. He had hoped he would be there to see him take off. But it was probably just as well. Gerard felt sure that if Röth had been there his nervousness would have been even greater. The last thing he wanted at this stage was to foul up in front of such a renowned pilot.

Most of the available machines, the Rolands, the Rumplers and the DFWs, had been dragged inside to shelter from the snow and Bähr stood at the entrance of one of the hangars looking speculatively at the sky.

'What do you think?' Gerard asked.

By now the sky had opened up even more and the clouds that lingered had their white faces turned toward the sun.

'You should have enough time.'

'Good! I feel ready for this.'

It took two mechanics only a few minutes to roll the compact Aviatik CIII two-seater out into the open air, its straight wings and gently curving back catching the light of the sun. He climbed aboard and got the engine started. A broad road of sunshine lay across the grass as he opened the throttle and trundled forward.

The grip of his wheels felt decidedly sludgy and for a moment it seemed as if the damp earth would slow him, but these impediments vanished as soon as he pulled back the stick. His machine sprang into the sky, bounding over the trees and the clutch of their branches.

He banked left then straightened over the road beside the airfield and followed it south in the direction of Haulchin. For a while it ran in a relatively straight line before curving gently to the west. Then near Thiant it forked and he took the right fork, which brought him back on a southerly heading. From the cockpit Gerard's view was excellent. The only thing blocking it was the exhaust pipe on his starboard side.

Still at a hundred feet, the treetops below him were a rushing blur. A slight pull on the stick and the Aviatik climbed to five hundred feet where Gerard levelled off. The tree-flanked road below him had narrowed into a line and everything on the ground now passed beneath him at a much slower rate. Odd buildings or groups of buildings marched into view. A farmer leading his horse across a field paused to glance up, shading his eyes to watch the single aircraft fly overhead.

Gerard waved, but the farmer didn't respond. Further on, he came upon a hamlet near Haspres where children with a dog waved furiously as they ran along the road in a vain attempt to keep up. Cheered by their exuberance he pulled back the stick and climbed. At a thousand feet he levelled off now nearer the clouds than the ground. Some even blocked his view of the horizon, their shadows moving imperceptibly across the white patchwork of fields and paddocks.

He watched entranced as a small flock of birds flew beside him. They were going in the same direction and it was strange to see them flapping their wings and yet appear almost motionless in the sky. He watched them until they veered away and flew east. Turning to look ahead he almost leapt out of his seat. He was flying straight into a cloud. It was a small one, but up close it looked like a huge recumbent beast. Side-slipping to the right then banking left, he flew around its lower boundaries.

From a distance of several hundred feet, he feasted his eyes on the cloud's brilliant curves and dove-grey shadows, sustaining the illusion that it was solid enough to break off his wings if he strayed too close. After a half circuit he came upon another cloud and this one towered above him like the tallest castle ever built. He climbed its steep walls to its lofty battlements and gazed down upon its glittering peaks.

Now over Villers-en-Cauchies he surveyed a sea of cloud, which now spread beneath him so extensively he could no longer see the surface of the earth. His world was now two endless vistas, one unimaginably white, the other the purest blue, untarnished and metallic, stained only by the light from the sun. Then his attention was drawn to a shadow flitting over the cloud's illusory surface. He smiled. It was the shadow of his Machine. And it seemed to be having such fun. Why not join it?

Pushing the stick forward, he dove down between walls of metamorphic solidity and flattened out in a gorge of pearl blushing crags. Hills of cloud rose before him and he zoomed up their misty slopes, his wheels eddying their uncertain edge. Flying between two towers he spiralled round one, climbing upward, shadow and sunlight lancing his face. Past the pinnacle he continued the ascent, his prop slicing higher and higher until his speed dropped to zero.

For the briefest instant he hung suspended between sky and cloud. Then silently the machine nosed over and fell, picking up speed as it hurtled toward the white savannah below. Judging the moment precisely, Gerard pulled out of the dive and skimmed the surface of the clouds. To hell with the ground and all that crawled upon it; to hell with the streams and bridges, the roads and villages, the churches and steeples. All he wanted was the air and the emptiness of the air.

It was exhilarating. It was intoxicating. It was joyous abandon. His smile was beatific. He felt transported by the freedom and power at his command. He was invincible, capable of anything. All doubt, all anxiety was forgotten. For the first time, he felt at one with his machine. His eyes were its eyes, his thoughts were its thoughts, his hands and feet its will and purpose. Even the lower wings felt as if they were attached to his shoulders. He had evolved into a creature that flew and fed upon the sun.

The Daimler DIII engine coughed politely.

'Scheisse!'

It was no more than a splutter, a misfiring cylinder. It said nothing more. But Gerard tensed, waiting for the roar to hesitate again. It didn't. Like Perseus' thread, the line of mechanical harmony had accompanied him reliably on his outward journey but his hope that it would sustain him on the journey back was now irreparably lost and with it his sense of being at one with his machine. It was once more a fragile thing of struts and wires and consumptive valves. Only one instinct remained; to pray that the engine would hold out long enough for him to complete the course and get safely back to base.

****

'How can you eat those things cold?' Ever since they'd strolled out of the hangar for a snack, Franz Willmanns had watched his friend out of the corner of his eye with a look of mounting disgust.

'They're tasty.' Karl Buckler extended the greaseproof paper wrapper containing the boiled potatoes. 'Go on. Try one.'

Franz moved to the edge of the packing case. 'I'll stick to my tongue sandwiches, thanks very much.'

'You don't know what you're missing.'

With nothing more to say they ate in silence, Franz taking bites out of his tongue sandwich while Karl consumed the potatoes and cold cuts the cook had supplied him with earlier. He had also provided each of them with a thermos of hot coffee, which now steamed in their tin mugs.

Franz surveyed the sky speculatively. 'Clouding over.'

Karl nodded. 'It is that. Who's still up?'

'No one.' Franz lifted his tin mug and gulped down some coffee.

'What about that young fellah doing his cross-country?'

Franz didn't reply, but simply nodded as he took another mouthful of coffee.

'Might need to check his machine over when he gets back.' Karl took out his pipe and started to fill it. 'You know what trainees are like. They lack the gentle touch.'

'That they do,' Franz agreed.

'Oh, by the way.' Karl's voice brightened. 'Did I tell you I got a letter from the missus the other day?'

'No, you didn't.' Franz watched as his friend rummaged in the breast pocket of his overalls.

'The thing's here somewhere.' Karl sounded flustered, but Franz was no longer listening.

'Hold up!' He touched Karl's arm. 'Do you hear that?'

Karl held his head attentively. At first, he could hear nothing, but he had complete faith in Franz who was renowned for his ability to detect distant sounds long before anyone else. And Karl's faith was rewarded. At the limit of his hearing came a sound like the drone of a bumblebee along a summer hedge.

'I make out one machine. Coming from the south.' Karl turned his head in that direction.

'Sounds like the engine's running unevenly.'

As far as Karl's ears were concerned the engine was running perfectly smoothly and if he had been alone he would have thought no more about it. But Franz's ears were legendary. They not only heard machines before anyone else, they also worked out the state of the engine.

'I see it!' Karl rose from the box. Franz may have had sharper hearing, but Karl's eyes were keener. 'Beyond the south end of the field at about 500 feet.'

A speck struggled into view against the horizon, its descent more apparent than its approach. But the roar of its engine grew rapidly in volume. Bert strained his eyes to discern anything that might identify the machine, but as it was coming head on this was not possible.

Franz heard the lowering note of the engine as the pilot reduced throttle. Then he got up from the box and stood beside Karl. 'He'll need it a bit lower than that.'

'Not much lower, I think.' The voice belonged to Röth who had sauntered up behind the two mechanics. He had Instructor Bähr with him.

Karl and Franz snapped to attention, but Röth smiled. 'Relax, Gentleman. Let's watch the landing together.'

Banking west the Aviatik began a circuit of the field, heading north then east before returning to the field's southern end. It was now lower and slower. Skimming over the trees the Aviatik's wheels dropped to the grass, coughing and spluttering as it came to within thirty feet of the four spectators before veering to one side and coming to a stop.

Karl turned to the others and, with the nod of a man who has witnessed many landings said, 'Not bad.'

****

Erich hurried out of the study in what was for him a quite uncharacteristic state of excitement. He had just finished speaking to Helga on the telephone and what she had told him was something that he knew the Baroness would want to hear straightaway.

Realising that as useful as such an arrangement might be Erich couldn't hide in Helga's bedroom indefinitely Thetis had recalled him a couple of days previously. Not that that had ended his association with Helga. She still contacted him regularly on the telephone. Most of what she had to say was merely picking up on threads of gossip established during Erich's confinement in her bedroom. On the whole he found it all rather tedious and frustrating to listen to, but he was astute enough to let her ramble on.

Any attempt on his part to force the conversation to where he wanted it risked rousing her suspicions. To avoid this he listened patiently and, with gentle coaxing steered her toward the subject of importance. In this way he was eventually able to knock on Thetis' bathroom door and say, 'I have news of the Princess, my Lady.'

'Come in, Erich?'

He opened the door to the bathroom and entered. The Baroness was in the tub, up to her neck in steaming water and soapsuds. Upon her head a white towel had been wrapped into a turban. One leg had been raised out of the water and she was currently washing this with a soft flannel,

'You've been speaking to Helga?' she asked.

'I have, my Lady.'

'And what does she have to say?'

'That she saw the Princess slip away from a Christmas meeting the Arch Duchess was holding in the Grand Foyer and head toward her father's library.'

'When was this?'

'This morning.'

'And what was the Princess after in the library?'

'I didn't like to ask.'

Thetis looked up. 'Why not?'

'I thought it might rouse her suspicions about my interest in the Princess.'

Thetis smiled and nodded. 'Quite right, Erich. Besides I think I have a strong idea what she was after. What else did Helga tell you?'

'That the Princess has stopped talking in a funny voice and has put away the boots with the stacked heels.'

Thetis thought about this for a moment. Was it a sign that Anthea had concluded that the whole business of infiltrating JGN was just too difficult to accomplish and had given up on the idea? But then she noticed something she didn't see too often; Erich smiling.

'There's more, isn't there?'

'Yes, my Lady.'

'Don't tease me, Erich. Tell me what it is.'

'Helga was present when the Princess told her mother that she was going to spend the Christmas holidays with her brother.'

'Now that is interesting.'

'There's more. When her mother asked her if she was going to come back for the New Year's celebrations she said no. She said she was going to stay with a friend.'

Thetis allowed her smile to broaden before asking a question to which she was already beginning to suspect the answer. 'And did she give the name of this friend?'

'Yes, my Lady. Apparently it's the Baroness von Buchner.'

Thetis' eyes lit up with delight.

The crafty little minx. She learns fast.

'This news pleases you?'

'Yes it does, Erich. It pleases me greatly. If nothing else it tells me when our little Princess intends to act. She will spend Christmas with her brother. But she won't be coming here for the New Year. I think she has an entirely different destination in mind.'

CHAPTER NINETEEN

21 DECEMBER 1917

'Goal!'

'That was never a goal.'

'Yes it was. Where's the ref?'

'We 'aven't got a ref.'

'Get on with it,' Swain yelled out.

A goal kick was taken and the ball returned to play. Brinkly got it off one of the 'B' section boys and gave it such a whack it hit the brick wall that enclosed the cobbled courtyard where they were playing and rebounded toward Swain who was watching the match from the other side. Stopping it with his foot he kicked it back then continued with his diary entry.

21ˢᵗ December 1917

'A' and 'B' sections always argue during football. It's been the same old story since training. Every tackle and every goal is disputed. But it's a sure sign they're happy. And they have every reason to be. As do I. We were relieved from the line yesterday and we won't be going back until after Christmas.

I'm not sure whether we were surprised or not when it happened. We'd been speculating about it for days. Someone was even running a book on the outcome. Would we be left in the line over Christmas or would they pull us out? Given that we'd only been here for two weeks most thought it unlikely we'd be pulled out so soon. I personally was convinced they'd leave us here so I put half a crown on it. Never was I so pleased to lose two and six.

I'll never forget the moment when the word came. It was the Sergeant who delivered the news though as usual he wasn't giving anything away. He came while we were having a brew and said:

'All right, you lot. You've got thirty minutes to pack your kit.'

This was greeted by a moment's stunned silence during which everyone looked at each other as much as to say what's going on.

'What's it all about, Sergeant?' Lucy asked.

'Well, I'll tell you, Entworth. For some strange reason the officers at Battalion have got it into their heads that you brave heroes deserve a visit from Santa Claus.'

'You mean...'

'Yes. You're being pulled out of the line for Christmas.'

Everyone went cock-a-hoop at this point. In fact we were making so much noise the Sergeant had to tell us to quieten down. As soon as we did we turned to the serious business of packing our kit and stowing away our gear.

'That's it!' The Sergeant chivvied. 'I want this place spotless. I won't have the relief saying 'A' section were no better than a bunch of slovenly louts.'

We did everything we needed to do in well under thirty minutes. Our packs were on our backs and we were standing in line eager to get going. Nothing could stop us now. We were about to leave the trenches and wouldn't be coming back for at least a week. But then it nearly didn't happen. And all because Dibbs couldn't keep his bloody mouth shut. As we stood there waiting for the order to move off some of the lads started talking about our time in the trenches.

'Isn't it strange,' Chippie Feltham observed. 'We've been here two weeks and not once in all that time have we seen a German?'

'That's fine by me,' Unmentionable Heywood concluded. 'I can live my life happy enough if I never ever see one.'

Lucy had begun to look somewhat soulful. 'I can't help thinking of poor old Hoon. He's missing out on all of this.'

'Gah!' Dibbs hawked in disgust. 'All that spineless twerp ever kept going on about was wanting to go 'ome. Well, now he's gone 'ome, and good riddance I say.'

'Shut your fucking gob, Ferret Face,' Windy Hoskins snarled.

'Yeah. And who's going to make me?'

The two men pulled out of the line and squared up to each other. We'd never seen either man fight with his fists so we weren't sure who would come out on top, but we were certainly hoping that Dibbs was about to get his lights punched out. The fight was stopped more or less before it got started. The Sergeant had returned to get us underway and as he entered the trench he was presented with the tableaux of two men frozen in mid blow so to speak, their fists raised and aimed.

'What's all this?' It was a question that didn't need asking. The Sergeant could see for himself what 'all this' was. 'Fighting! Are you two fighting? Because if you are the whole lot of you can forget going to the rear for Christmas.'

Here was a threat we hadn't contemplated and as it loomed over us we all became rigid with dread. It seemed likely that we were about to spend Christmas in the trenches. Fortunately for us Lucy Entworth had a flash of inspiration.

'It's the duelling scene from Hamlet, Sergeant,' he declared.

One of the Sergeant's eyes bulged while the other twitched. 'It's the what?'

'The duelling scene, the one between Hamlet and Laertes. We're rehearsing it for our Christmas play.'

The twitching eye swapped places with the bulging eye and the Sergeant looked fit to burst. But finding nothing suitable to yell about he finally settled on: 'You two! Get back in line!'

Making every effort to be model soldiers we marched with parade ground precision out of Brewer Street and up Caledonian Road. As soon as we got to the rear depot we were assembled with 'B' section, who were also being taken out of the line.

We had to wait there until our relief was led off down the trenches. But we were in for a surprise. The relief had come by narrow gauge train, the train in question being the 'Iron Horse'. Although this meant that we would be spared a long march not everyone was happy. Many still remembered the discomforts of the journey in. But for me it turned out to be a bit of a treat.

While we were waiting I got into conversation with the driver, Corporal Arthur Steadman and when we were ordered to get aboard he invited me to travel with him in the cab. I enjoyed every minute of it. We were taken north to a deserted farm called Le Belle Pâturage, which is close to Ste Helene airfield, and there we were billeted in some old stables. It still smells of horse shit, but none of us really minds. It certainly smells far sweeter than the trenches.

We were deloused and after that it was a long spell in enormous vats of hot soapy water followed by an issue of fresh uniforms and a hot meal. The beds are clean and it makes a pleasant change to settle down for the night covered in warm blankets. Last night I had the first good kip I've had in ages.

****

'What's this I hear about you having Anthea over for Christmas?'

Hermann wasn't sure whether his father was testing him. It was clear from the conversation he'd had with his sister that she was up to something especially when she insisted that he not let on that she had invited herself for the holidays. 'Yes, Father. Apparently she's flying down to Essen on Christmas Eve.'

Von Hoeppner and his son continued to walk away from the airfield where they had just watched one of Hermann's Pfalz DVIIIs put through its paces. The test had been a spectacular one and the pilot had zoomed the machine almost vertically into the sky before pirouetting the wings and putting its nose into a dive so steep it seemed a miracle that the wings weren't torn off.

Though the Archduke had been suitably impressed by every aspect of the sprightly machine's performance he had resolutely held his peace and said nothing. To have done so would have been to praise his son and that was something he adamantly refused to do. Not that Hermann was unduly bothered by his father's lack of response. He knew him well enough to know that a positive reaction was unlikely. He also knew him well enough to know that a lack of response was usually a sign of grudging approval. If he'd had something bad to say he would almost certainly have said it.

'Your mother isn't too happy. She was hoping to get Anthea interested in some young Count she's invited over for Christmas.'

'Not another one!' Hermann allowed himself a short laugh. 'Is mother still trying to get my sister married?'

'Yes. Incredible, isn't it?' As they walked von Hoeppner took out a cigar and lit it. 'But then your mother was always the patron saint of lost causes. You may find this hard to believe but she actually invited someone to Anthea's birthday party ball in the hope that he might be a suitable match.'

'No! Did she? Who was it?'

'Count von Gessendork, the Plenipotentiary to the Court of Austria.'

'Not the one that Anthea insulted.'

'The very same. Your mother was mortified and I feared we might be heading for an international incident.'

'I wondered at the time why Mother looked so put out. And as for the Count I thought he was going to challenge Anthea to a duel.'

'So did I. Fortunately, she was dressed as an ordinary Leutnant and he didn't appear to know her true identity.'

'What happened to him?'

'Oh, he stormed off in a huff and as far as I know nothing has been heard from him since.'

By now they had reached von Hoeppner's staff car. Rittmeister von Abshagen was sitting in the back seat waiting for him.

'How did the trials go, Excellency?' he asked.

'Ah, that reminds me.' Von Hoeppner turned to his son. 'I take it that you'll be preparing a full report on the performance of the new Pfalz?'

'Yes, I will, Father.'

'Good! Make sure you send me a copy. I have good reason to believe your factory will be working at full capacity in the not so distant future.'

'I'll need to take on extra personnel straight away.'

'Well, before you do that you can buy von Abshagen and myself a suitably expensive lunch to celebrate.'

****

Andrea Harker sat in her chair, his chair, facing the portrait of her husband. The focus of her eyes, now red and drained of tears, was fixed on it. Even in the late afternoon light the likeness was remarkable, so remarkable that at times she could convince herself that he was there in the room with her. On one occasion she had even spoken to it. But there was no comfort in the illusion for the face in the portrait was looking away from her much as it had in life. She recognised it, the lingering distraction, the sense that the focus of his attention was always elsewhere.

As if he is here but I'm not.

How long had she sat there with the unfinished black scarf and knitting needles lying in her lap? Maybe days. Who could tell? She remembered a time in the far distant past when her emotions had been a wild orgy of shrieking despair. Her body was no longer her own. It was a mad thing and it had control of her. But then she began to distinguish between the agonies, laying them out like clothes upon the bed; the wild shaking spasms of unbearable grief, the quiet tearful moments, even the moments of tranquil emptiness. That was how she was feeling now.

But it was no longer so tranquil. Somewhere within the emptiness was the dull ache of a new emotion; resentment. Although she struggled against the feeling, seeing it as tantamount to an act of disloyalty to her husband's memory, she was finding it increasingly difficult to hold back her bitterness towards the very notion of his heroism.

It was nothing more than headstrong pride.

The pride of a man always certain that he is right. The pride of a man who would never hang back with the crowd, who always sallied out in front of all the rest and would let no one be as daring as himself.

'Mam!'

Andrea's eyes blinked guiltily. Had her thoughts been overheard? She looked up as if the voice had come from a far distant part of the house. She saw a face she recognised.

'What is it, Alice?'

'There's a gentleman here who wishes to see you.'

'I told you I'm not receiving visitors.'

'But he's an officer, Mam. And he says he knew the Major.'

Andrea focused. 'Does he have a name?'

'Captain Parkinson.'

Andrea looked to the portrait of her husband as if seeking his advice. 'Show him in.'

The man Alice ushered into the room was of medium height and slim build. He had a very young face and Andrea thought that this made his trim moustache look somewhat incongruous. Also, his uniform was impeccable and this confused her for a moment.

She had once met some of her husband's fellow pilots at a dance in the village and, though tidily dressed, there had been a casual quality to their appearance suggestive of the hazardous life they led. But this man

231

was so neatly turned out that at first she assumed he must have been her husband's adjutant.

'My apologies, Mrs Harker,' Parkinson began, his eyes fastening on a strikingly beautiful woman, a woman who by the cast of her features and the steady gaze of her eyes was the true wife of a hero, a woman too lofty and proud for the tastes of ordinary men. 'Normally I would have sent word of my coming rather than turning up unannounced.'

Andrea's gaze held Parkinson for a moment then she inclined her head toward the portrait beside her. 'You painted this.'

This was a statement rather than a question, but either way it wasn't how he'd expected this particular conversation to begin. She'd taken control of it and all he could do was respond. 'Yes, I did.'

'But you didn't sign it.'

Again Parkinson found himself thrown sideways. He had come there to talk about her husband not about the portrait of her husband. Why should it matter whether he had signed it or not? And in an odd way he felt like an artist who has completed a commission and is now being ticked off by the patron for some flaw in the work. Nonetheless, he struggled on hoping that it would come right in the end.

'It didn't seem appropriate.'

Given the pattern of the conversation so far he braced himself for a further challenge, but none was forthcoming. Instead she studied his face and with such intensity he was left feeling that she had found a route into his thoughts and he could only stand there powerless while she examined them at her leisure. Then, having found what she was looking for, she asked:

'Why have you come here today?'

There! She's done it again.

She had asked him something to which he had given no thought and for which he was totally unprepared. And this one was so startling it triggered within him a sense of disorientation as if he had been turned around and was now confronting himself. Yet there was nothing ill-mannered in the way that she put her question. If anything, her delivery was full of grace and eloquence and it was this very charm that robbed him of his defences so much so that he found himself compelled to examine his own motives.

Why did I come here?

To comfort the widow of a friend? To tell her all the good things he could about her husband? That's what he kept telling himself repeatedly throughout the journey from France. And it was the truth. Or rather it was partly the truth. And that was why he was able to convince himself that it was the whole truth. But it wasn't. And he had a horrible feeling that this woman knew it.

The truth, the other part of the truth, the part he had been trying to reconcile from the moment he had decided to make this visit, was an entirely different matter. It was not about the widow. It was about himself. He had come here to make his confession. He had come here to this woman to unburden himself of his guilt.

'Your husband was a hero.'

These were the words Parkinson had practised. He had assumed that his agenda was her agenda and in his rehearsal he had seen himself doing all the talking. The widow's role was to sit and listen attentively to what he had to say. But she hadn't complied. She had gone her own way and now his words sounded trite and hollow.

And she was still ahead of him. She had noticed him swallow hard as he said the word 'hero'. Anyone else would have seen this as a sign of insincerity; a sign that he didn't think her husband was a hero at all and was only saying so out of politeness. But Andrea sensed something else. She sensed that the word troubled him in a way that had nothing to do with her husband.

She looked at the portrait. 'So I have been told.'

This struck Parkinson as an odd way to respond. Though there was no sense of it in her voice it seemed to suggest that she held her husband's bravery with less regard than others. But Parkinson's need to confess was pressing upon him.

'He was brave in many ways and I should know.'

'Why so?'

'He gave me back my life.'

For the first time in the conversation Andrea took a keen interest in the man standing before her. 'How precisely?'

'It was the day that he went missing. A pilot was wreaking havoc on the British retreat. He needed stopping. Your husband ordered me to stop him.'

Parkinson paused and Andrea noticed a smile flit across his mouth. 'Something amuses you?'

'The enemy pilot. The one that needed stopping. He was not a man that anyone could stop. I knew that I was going to my death.'

'Then maybe you were the hero.'

The smile returned. 'Hero is not a word that anyone would use to describe me. But on this day my courage or lack of it didn't seem to matter. I was reconciled to my death and this gave me some comfort.'

'But my husband took your place.'

Clearly, this had to be a guess on her part, but Parkinson was no less impressed by her perception. 'Yes, he did.'

'And you resent him for it.'

She had found it! She had found his guilt. And in finding it she had taken away his need to confess it. 'Yes, I do.'

It was a frank admission and she was grateful that he'd had the courage to say it. She was grateful for his candour, but at the same time it opened in her a sense of injustice, a sense of diminished importance, a sense that the man she had married was a stranger.

Why? Why would he do it? Why would my husband take this man's place?

Again Andrea felt anger that her husband had thought more of this man than he had of her and their son. That the war was of greater importance than the life they shared. The feeling was so intense it seemed to close off her throat trapping the weaning moan that rose within her. And her teeth clamped together.

And in her anger she looked at the man who stood before her and re-appraised him. He was not a brave man but neither was he the coward he thought he was. She knew that she could never care for him. Not as she had for her husband. But at the same time she knew that they shared a common bond, a common fellowship. They both resented what her husband represented; they both resented the hero.

'I thank you for the portrait, Captain Parkinson. It has been a great comfort to me during this uncertain time. Having it here beside me makes me feel that he is close to hand. Would you care for some tea?'

It was then that Parkinson noticed the small round table placed beside her and the pipe rack and tobacco barrel and penknife and folded newspaper that sat upon it and he came to a ghastly realisation. The portrait that he had painted and which now gazed away from his wife was serving a purpose that he had never intended.

Its presence was not only helping her to maintain a sense of her husband in life but also a sense that he was still living. With all the fervour of undiminished hope she refused to believe that he was dead. But hope was the cage in which she had imprisoned herself and that cage was now guarded by her husband's portrait. And while it stood there she would remain trapped by the belief that the man she loved still walked the earth.

****

The waning light had wrapped the evening in stillness and as the chauffeured motor vehicle pulled sedately into the drive, the light from its large headlamps swept indolently across the front of the manor house.

Matthias, the head footman, waited with impassive patience as the staff car came to a halt beside him. When it did he held open its rear door and, with a bow, allowed the passenger to exit.

'It is good to see you again, Herr Hantelmann.'

Anchoring his boots in the snow, Hantelmann stepped out stiffly and, with some effort, pulled himself upright, the fleeting grimace of pain that touched his lips no more than a twitch.

'Thank you, Matthias.' Steadying himself with a hand on the body of the vehicle Hantelmann took time to look around. 'Are the children home?'

'Your son is still away, Herr Hantelmann, but Fraulein Sophie is here.'

Stepping away from the staff car, Hantelmann looked over to the porticoed entrance to his manor house. The door was open and soon its frame was filled with the figure of his teenage daughter, Sophie. Animated by a smile that lit her whole face, she leapt forward, bounding excitedly down the steps and across the drive.

'Father!' she called out as she ran into his arms and with such force it almost carried Hantelmann off his feet.

'Steady, girl.' Hugging her to him he laughed and in a way that he hadn't done for a long time. 'Never one to stand on ceremony, eh Sophie.'

She pulled back and gave him an earnest look. 'How are you, Father? How is your wound?'

'My wound is perfectly all right.' He lifted his right arm so that she could examine it, but when he saw the tremor in his hand he quickly lowered it. 'I hardly ever notice it at all now.'

Pulling back she studied him closely with a serious expression. 'That's as maybe. But it looks to me as if you've some lost weight.'

'Hospital food, my dear. Nothing but thin gruel and raw turnips.'

'You can tease me all you like, Father, but now that you're home we'll feed you up and take good care of you, won't we Matthias?'

Matthias groaned as he lifted the last of the suitcases from the boot of the motor vehicle. 'Indeed we will, Fraulein Sophie.'

Sophie tugged Hantelmann's arm. 'Come, Father. You're room is ready and a meal is being prepared.'

****

It had been quite some time since he had last tasted home cooked food. It was one of the things he had looked forward to during the drive to the house. Yet, despite knowing that the meal he was eating was delicious he found himself struggling against an indifferent appetite. For Sophie's sake he forced himself to clean his plate. She had clearly gone to considerable effort to prepare all of his favourite dishes and was now watching him to make sure he missed nothing.

When he finally placed his knife and fork on his plate she lifted the bottle from the table. 'Some more wine, Father?'

He shook his head. 'Not for the moment, thank you.'

Putting down his napkin Hantelmann rose wearily from the dining table and sought out his favourite armchair by the blazing fire. As he settled down and gazed without thought into the unhurried flames he was conscious of Sophie placing a footstool under his feet. Though gently done the action disturbed his calm.

'Oh, for heaven's sake, Sophie, stop fussing.'

Like a puppy that has been scolded Sophie sprang to her feet and stepped back. 'I'm sorry, Father. I didn't mean to disturb you. It's just that I've looked forward to this moment for so long.'

Instantly regretting his harsh behaviour he smiled and softened his voice. 'I know.'

'With Gerard away I've been mostly on my own in the house. I've had nothing but my own thoughts to keep me company and those thoughts haven't always been happy ones. Some of them have been quite fearful and there were times when I wondered whether either of you would ever return.'

'I know. I'm the one who should apologise. Commanding an air battle group, I'm afraid, has turned me into a bit of a grump. It may take me a while to get back to being my old self. But in the meantime you fuss over me as much as you want. I really quite enjoy being pampered.'

Sophie's gaiety returned. 'Let me get you something, Father. What would you like?'

'Oh, I don't know.' He looked about the room as if trying to find something to choose. 'Why don't you bring me a cigar.'

'Your wish is my command.'

As she skipped off in search of his humidor his gaze returned to the fire. He could not say why but the dancing of the flames seemed to calm his spirit and quell the need to think. Thinking only led to disquiet and anxiety. Not thinking seemed to him the greatest of boons.

'Here's your cigar, Father.'

Deftly she cut off the end and handed the result to Hantelmann, which he took great care to take with his left hand. She noticed this but assumed his wound was forcing him to make greater use of his other hand. Patiently she waited as he rustled it against his ear and held it beneath his nose. Only when he had placed it between his lips did she strike a match and light it.

He puffed on it vigorously several times then sat back in the chair. 'Thank you, dear.'

Seeing the dreamy look in his eyes she asked. 'Would you like to be left alone, Father?'

'No. Stay with me a while.'

Puffing on his cigar he waited until she had fetched a chair to sit beside him.

'Tell me,' he asked. 'Have you had news from Gerard?'

'Yes. I had a letter from him only the other day.' She started to rise from her chair. 'Would you like me to fetch it, Father?'

'No. That won't be necessary. Just tell me what he said.'

She sat back down. 'Well, not a lot really. You know what he's like. As usual it was mostly about his training at the *Kampfeinsitzer Abteilung*.'

Hantelmann paid more attention. 'Oh yes. And how is he doing?'

'Very well. He has passed all his exercises and examinations and has only to complete one more cross-country flight to qualify for his pilot's licence. Then he's off to the *Jagdstaffel Schule* for fighter pilot training. He is very excited.'

'He is a young man and young men are always excited by such things.'

'Yes, I suppose they are,' she said solemnly then brightened as she remembered something. 'Oh, yes. He mentions a man he has befriended. Someone called Röth.'

'Röth!'

'Yes. Gerard has quite taken to him. He runs a sort of training unit for fighter pilots and he has promised to take Gerard under his wing as soon as he qualifies.'

Hantelmann sucked on his cigar contentedly. 'Röth is a good man. Gerard couldn't be in better hands. Did he say anything else?'

'Not really. But he did send you his loving regards and says he regrets not being able to get leave to be here on your return.'

'Never mind. Hopefully he will be here with us for Christmas.'

****

'Shall I put your medal on the mantel, Father?'

Sophie had been studying the Iron Cross in its presentation box for some minutes, reading the citation then running her finger along the medal's metal edges.

'No, Sophie. I would rather you didn't. Just leave it there on the dining table.'

'Very well.' She closed the box and laid it carefully on the table. 'I'm off to bed now, Father. Is there anything you want me to get you before I go?'

'No thank you.'

'Don't stay up too late, will you?'

'No, I won't.'

'Goodnight, Father.'

'Goodnight, darling.'

After Sophie's departure Hantelmann wondered whether he should also retire for the night. He felt tired enough. The trouble was he felt too tired, too tired to even get out of his armchair and climb the stairs to his bedroom. Besides, he was content enough to remain sitting where he was staring into the fire. The flames had by now died down into a steady glow that was strong enough to hold back the room's encroaching darkness.

In this mellow light Hantelmann felt at peace and his domestic surroundings only added to the sense that his life wasn't entirely devoid of blessings. There were his children Sophie and Gerard, his boon and solace in a marriage that gave him nothing but pain.

He smiled when he thought of Sophie.

I haven't really appreciated her as much as I should.

Her sweet nature was a comfort to him. She was still a child in many respects, but at times she could display the level headed common sense of an adult. She was clearly growing up and would soon be a mature woman.

And some fellow will have the good fortune to make her his wife.

No, he didn't have to concern himself about his daughter. She would make her way in life and be happy. But what of Gerard? Hantelmann's thoughts turned to his son. Again he considered himself lucky to have had such a child. Gerard was only eighteen.

But by any standard he is now a man.

When his son had told him that he was joining the Imperial German Air Force Hantelmann had felt both pride and alarm. He was proud to think that his son had chosen to follow in his footsteps and felt sure that he would go on to add further renown to the name of Hantelmann. But that pride was tempered with acute anxiety. He knew from his own experience how perilous the business of aerial combat could be. It was full of risk, there were no certainties and the most dangerous time of all was the period of training.

More dangerous in some ways than actual combat.

There were so many things that could bring a young man to an untimely end and Hantelmann knew all of them. The training schools suffered from a lack of suitable machines. This meant the available aircraft were over-used, reducing their quality and reliability. And aircraft that crashed were continually repaired and to such an extent they became death-traps.

Even the fuel and engine oil is poor quality.

Bit by bit everything was deteriorating, but despite his fears Hantelmann remained optimistic that his son would get through his training and go on to become a famous *Kanone* like himself. He loved his son. And he prayed that he would survive the war and live a long and happy life. But Hantelmann also loved his country and it was his stern belief that the safety of one's country must come first.

We are fighting a war and Gerard has to do his duty like everyone else.

All these thoughts of duty made Hantelmann glance at the wall above the fireplace. Hanging in the shadows was a portrait of Annaliese. But he was not interested in that. His eyes dropped to the mantel and a line of photographs of his children. He could see the frames but he couldn't see the images. It was too dark. But he didn't need to see them. Their faces were imprinted on his mind.

There were about eleven photographs in all. Some showed the children individually and at different ages. Others showed the children standing or playing together. They were all happy photographs, but one of them never failed to give him a sharp pang of anguish whenever he looked upon it.

My daughter Ingrid.

She contracted Diphtheria when she was only five and what made her illness even harder to bear was it coincided with Germany's mobilisation. He was called to arms and, even though his commanding officer, a sympathetic man, had urged him to take compassionate leave, he went ahead and joined his regiment, considering his country's needs to be greater than those of his own daughter.

And while I was at war she died.

Since then he had never for one moment stopped regretting his decision. As he saw it he had sacrificed her upon the altar of his own military ambitions. And for that there could never be any forgiveness. He once asked himself why if the photographs of Ingrid caused him so much pain he didn't just remove them from the mantel. But then he realised that he needed that pain. It was all that he had left of his daughter.

CHAPTER TWENTY

24 DECEMBER 1917

Anthea had been unable to get any sleep that night. She was too excited. It was past midnight and already Christmas Eve and in less than seven hours it would be dawn. Then her adventure would begin. Over the last several days she had been thorough in her preparations, but that didn't stop her from fretting. Nor did it stop her getting in and out of bed repeatedly to check.

I'm sure there's something I've forgotten.

Again and again she pulled the maps from her map case and carefully went over the route she would be taking to Essen. If she wasn't doing that she was checking through the forged documents she kept in a black leather document case. One by one and with minute attention she examined the identification papers, the *Ausweis*, the pilot's licence, the *Militärpass* and the other written authorisations making sure that they were all there and all properly signed.

You can never be too careful.

Her luggage was light. Given the small amount of space on the Halberstadt it had to be. She had limited herself to one medium-sized crocodile-skin suitcase. This contained her carefully pressed German Officer's uniform and black leather boots. This and her flying gear, which she would be wearing for the trip, were all the clothes she would be taking.

I need nothing else.

She didn't. Her brother Hermann kept rooms permanently available for her at his place in Essen and on previous visits she had left there toiletries and also many of her gowns, which were carefully stored for her so that she would always have something suitable to wear whenever she put in an appearance.

The only other things she intended taking with her were Christmas presents for Hermann, his wife Martha and their three young children. Wrapped in colourful festive paper they were piled on a small table by the door. None of the packages were large. All of them had been chosen with an eye to their size and lightness.

Anything heavier and I'll never take off.

As she lay upon her bed thinking of the morrow and her long flight to her brother's home she kept a close guard upon her thoughts. Whenever they showed signs of straying to what might lay beyond Essen she wrenched them back. She insisted to herself that she was merely going to there to spend Christmas with her brother and his family. And that was it. Her plans beyond Christmas remained a closed book.

The uniform and the forged documents would have taxed most people's powers of self-deception, but Anthea even had an explanation for them. She was taking the uniform with her to wear at Hermann's Christmas party, repeating the sensation she had caused at her own birthday party. And as for the documents she told herself that she wanted to show them to Hermann.

And impress him with my forging skills.

But dreams are not so easily fooled and when she finally fell asleep in the small hours it was to slip into one in which she found herself landing in a military airbase, a military airbase that lay in a forest to the east of the Ste Helene Salient.

****

So deep was Anthea's sleep that she may well have overslept. Fortunately, foreseeing such an eventuality she had briefed Helga fully the previous evening.

'You're to bring me my breakfast at six-thirty,' she had instructed her lady-in-waiting.

Helga had looked stunned. 'But my Lady, why so early?'

'How can you say that's early?' Anthea had retorted, her eyes flashing with indignation. 'Don't our brave pilots rise at dawn for their first patrol of the day?'

But her eyes weren't flashing now as she pushed her head from beneath her bedclothes and peeped blearily at the shadowed figure of Helga moving briskly about the still darkened bedroom.

'What time is it?' she drawled incredulously, unable to comprehend what was going on.

'Six-thirty, my Lady.'

Anthea's exposed face told her that the dark was icy cold and her body told her that the bed was enticingly warm. Why would she want to get up? Then she remembered why. She was supposed to be flying to Essen. Wouldn't it be better to put off the flight till later in the day she asked herself? Then she could just turn over and go back to sleep.

But Helga wasn't going to let her get off so easily. 'Time to join our brave pilots on the dawn patrol.'

With some regret, Anthea recalled her performance from the previous evening. Having made such a fuss about Dawn patrols and the hardihood of brave pilots she knew that she would now look rather silly if she didn't get up.

Steeling herself against the first shivering shock she threw back the bedclothes and swung her bare feet onto the floor. A dressing gown thrown around her shoulders she ate her breakfast and with Helga's help she washed and climbed into her flying clothes, which consisted of riding boots and breeches, a thick roll-neck sweater and a brown calf-leather jacket.

'Well, I think I'm ready.' She checked the large-faced wristwatch her brother had bought her when she qualified as a pilot. 'Is the Daimler being brought round?'

'I think so, my Lady. But I'll just go and find out.'

Helga disappeared. Time passed and morning light began to fill the room. As Anthea poured herself a second cup of coffee, a servant appeared and carried away her suitcase and Christmas parcels. After he left she busied herself doing what she had done throughout most of the night; checking her maps and documents. She was still doing this when Helga returned ten minutes later looking agitated.

'What's wrong?'

'The car won't start, my Lady.'

Dear heaven's! I hope this isn't a bad omen.

As if to test Anthea's equanimity further the daylight that had been growing steadily in strength and intensity suddenly darkened as a bank of low clouds moved across the sky. Then it started to snow. Anthea wasn't too bothered by the snow. It was light and the flakes were minuscule. But the ceiling of cloud was a different matter. Staring out of the window she could see that it was far too low to make flight possible. Adding to her misfortunes at that moment was the unexpected appearance of her mother.

'It's not too late to change your mind,' she began as soon as she entered the room. 'You can cancel your trip and stay with us for Christmas. I'm sure Hermann will understand.'

'Stop fretting, Mother. The snow will ease off. I know it will.'

Although there was a confident finality to her words Anthea wasn't so sure that her prediction would have the backing of the elements. And in the end she had to spend four anxious hours at the window before any appreciable change took place. At midday the snow stopped then an hour later the cloud cover lifted.

Either I go now or I don't go at all.

Her fortunes now took a turn for the better. The fault with the motor vehicle had been repaired and her luggage had been put in the boot. With gloves and leather flying helmet she jumped in the back seat with Helga. Both the women were barely seated when the driver let out the break and the Daimler picked up speed, passing out of the driveway and along a path that cut through the western half of the estate.

Several minutes of driving brought them to a large wooden hangar that stood at one end of an open field of grass. It had once housed a couple of gilt-faced horse-drawn carriages, but now it sheltered vehicles of an entirely different sort; Hedda's Albatros BI and Anthea's Halberstadt DII.

The Halberstadt had been wheeled out into the open air and while Anthea climbed aboard and ran through her pre-flight checks Helga helped the driver stow the suitcase, parcels and two cans of aviation fuel into a small lidded receptacle that one of Hermann's engineers had cut into the fuselage.

When everything was ready the driver yanked at the propeller several times until the engine finally fired. Backing off hurriedly from the spinning blade he stood silently beside Helga as she waved her mistress a tearful goodbye.

****

At last! I'm on my way.

This wasn't strictly true, but as Anthea pulled back the stick and climbed through a stray cloud she told herself that she was doing nothing more than travelling along a route she had taken numerous times before, the route to her brother's estate outside Essen. That the real adventure wouldn't begin until the second leg of the journey, the leg that lay beyond Essen, was something she was still determined not to think about. And, whenever it flitted unbidden into her mind she swatted it away as one would a troublesome wasp.

Let's just sit back and enjoy the thrill of flying.

Levelling out the Halberstadt at three hundred metres, she relaxed into the routine of a long flight. Some three hundred kilometres lay between her and Essen. She estimated that her fuel would take her beyond the *Weser* and that she might have to make a fuel stop at Paderborn or Lippstadt. All in all she reckoned that it would take her about three hours to reach her destination.

With any luck I'll get there before it gets dark.

Soon she was beyond the western outskirts of Berlin and flying over the white deserted countryside. Lines of trees stood stark and black against the ground's grey-shadowed floor. Villages were made visible by their regular flat-sided shapes and the helical plumes of smoke rising from their hidden chimneys. And as Anthea flew over them she imagined families huddled round their fireplaces.

Toasting bread and drinking beer.

There was something almost sepulchral about the snow. It lent everything a sort of dismal tranquillity, the sort of timeless tranquillity that arises when all other things are absent; all movement on the ground, all signs of life. Even the wind was in icy slumber, barely raising a sigh sufficient to move the black branches below. And the sky above her was a motionless cover of old and wrinkled skin; its becalmed lines lit silver by the light from a shy and frozen sun.

A great sense of loneliness overwhelmed her, the same sort of loneliness that she always felt on long flights, especially at this time of the year. Feelings such as these would have troubled most people, but not Anthea. To her loneliness was a clarification of who she was and of what she was. At times like these she felt at one with her true self, the person she knew herself to be, the person she didn't always acknowledge.

A feeling that only comes to me when I fly.

****

Just over thirty minutes into her journey Anthea flew over the *Elbe*. She could see it beneath her outstretched wings flowing like a vein of dark, twinkling quicksilver. Shortly after that she passed by the medieval town of Magdeburg, which lay five miles to the south lost to her sight in the static winter mists.

Quarter of the way there.

She didn't need to consult her map to identify the major landmarks along her route. She knew them all. And by her reckoning another fifteen minutes would bring the wheels of her undercarriage above the steeply raked rooftops of *Wolfenbüttel*, a point just under half way between Berlin and Essen.

The wrinkled sky above came with her, as did the feeling that she was the last inhabitant of a world devoid of all human life.

****

The Hanseatic town of Dortmund with its breweries, castles and Wilhelminen houses was behind her and she was not now far from the outskirts of Essen. The winter sun was sinking under its own weight and twilight had started to fall. Objects on the ground were becoming less distinct than they had been before.

Overhead the wrinkled clouds that had kept her company all the way were turning dark grey their crinkled lines interspersed with a deepening pink. She had perhaps fifteen minutes before the light became too dim to see.

At least my fuel tank is almost full.

As she had predicted she had just crossed the *Weser* when her One Hundred and Twenty horsepower water-cooled Mercedes engine gave a polite cough. It wasn't critical, but it was enough to make her glance at her fuel gauge. The needle indicated that her tank wasn't yet empty, but as an experienced pilot she knew that such instruments were hardly ever precise. Besides, it was never a good idea to just fly on until the fuel runs out.

That always happens over a forest or some rocky place.

She flew on for a while, but seeing that she was now skirting the beech-forested foothills of the *Werra* she was now alert to finding a field in which she could land. She found what she was looking for a few miles outside of Paderborn. It was flat and treeless and mostly flattened grass.

Throttling back she reduced her speed and made a gentle landing, her wheels hardly bouncing as they touched the ground beneath the snow. Leaving the engine idling she leapt out of the cockpit and, using her cans of fuel to top up the tank, was soon underway again.

The free Imperial City of Essen with its coalmines coking plants, cast-steel works and weapons factories was soon in sight. Guided by the house lights she flew low but at a height sufficient to avoid any unseen obstacles that might be sticking up out of the gloom like church spires and other tall structures.

By keeping close to the ground she was able to follow the streets to the town hall and from there she located the railway station. It was now a simple matter of keeping to the tracks until she came upon a branch line that ran all the way to Hermann's *Flugzeugwerke*.

The branch line was a short one and she soon caught sight of the sprawling factory building. Beyond it was a large field and she could see that Hermann had thoughtfully placed two lines of ground lights for her convenience. Using these to guide her in she landed with no more than few bumps. Taxiing to a halt she switched off the engine. Silence fell upon her. Pulling off her goggles and leather helmet she climbed out of the cockpit. Hermann was waiting.

'Welcome, sister,' he smiled. 'I'm delighted you were able to accept our invitation.'

****

Swain looked up from his notebook and took in the sight of his trench mates lounging limply around the snowy confines of the stable courtyard. Some stood around the narrow warmth of a burning brazier. Others sat on bales of hay and smoked. All of them looked spent from the day's activities. Shaking his head Swain resumed his scribbling.

Whoever imagines that being taken out of the line means a spell of rest is deluding himself. Our football match on the first morning has been our only period of relaxation. But it didn't last. As soon as we had finished our midday meal we were lined up and divided into work parties.

The rest of that day was spent wandering around the farm filling in craters left by the German bombs. We then had to dig our own dugouts in case the Huns decided to come back for a second go. That went on until the sun went down. The next morning we had to parade at 6.30 a.m. and after that we had kit inspections, foot inspections and gas mask inspections.

By way of variety we spent the afternoon with the rest of the platoon on a five-mile march to the north east where we stopped not to rest but to help with the construction of a new airfield. Then it was a five-mile march back during which Dibbs complained bitterly.

'All this bloody walking!' he growled. 'Why couldn't they have packed us on the train? We've been tramping every inch of the way beside the fucking tracks.'

Everyone agreed with him, but no one said so. Instead, we tried to lighten our exertions by singing a song that seemed appropriate:

> *We are but little soldiers weak;*
> *We only get five franks a week.*
> *The more we do, the more we may,*
> *It makes no diff'rence to our pay.*

And this more or less set the pattern for the next couple of days. We are currently back at the farm resting our aching feet after a long route march. Our boots are off and we are now looking forward to tomorrow, which promises to be a true day of rest.

When we got back to the farm we had a very pleasant surprise waiting for us. Our Christmas parcels from home had been delivered and were standing in a pile inside the stable. These are mostly plain cardboard boxes, but as they contain Christmas treats sent to us by our folks they raised our spirits enormously.

Every one of us got at least one parcel, all of us that is except Coaxie and Dibbs. Coaxie didn't seem all that bothered but Dibbs' rage contorted face was a picture to behold. As usual he was in a foul mood, sniping at everyone and everything. And the

246

sight of the parcels didn't improve he's temper one little bit. He didn't bother looking to see if any of them were for him so he must have known.

Whether we would have felt any sympathy for either of these two was a question left unanswered. It was completely overshadowed by one of those discoveries that take the wind out of your sails. Eager to claim what belonged to us we were like kids sorting through their presents on Christmas morning. Not that we opened any of them. We were determined to save them for tomorrow. But then when all the parcels had been distributed we discovered one that was unclaimed. We looked to see whose name was on the label. But it wasn't addressed to Coaxie and it wasn't addressed to Dibbs. It was addressed to Scuttle.

It is hard to overstate the effect the sight of the parcel had on our feelings especially as it was only the other day that the Lieutenant had informed us at parade that Scuttle had died of his wounds. We stared at his parcel for a long moment not sure what we should do. Then 'Chippie' Feltham suggested:

'Why not give it to the Sergeant? He'll know what to do with it.'

'It's a bloody shame I say,' muttered 'Bookworm' Hutchins. 'A bloody shame! The poor bastard died for no reason at all.'

'It may have escaped your notice 'Bookworm,' Dibbs said and for once there was no sarcasm in his voice. 'But out here we all die for no reason.'

CHAPTER TWENTY-ONE

25 DECEMBER 1917

The clock in the hallway chimed midnight.

This was the signal. Hermann got to his feet and rapped his glass with a spoon.

'Everyone! Your attention please. It is now officially Christmas Day. Please lift your glasses and join me in a toast to the Fatherland.'

The table in Hermann's dining room was not nearly as large as the one at the Residenz, but it was large enough to seat comfortably the thirty odd guests who had been invited to join the family for its traditional Christmas Eve dinner. And unlike gatherings at the Residenz where the guests tended to be aristocrats, diplomats and high-ranking officers those who now sat around Hermann's table were men eminent in the worlds of academia and commerce.

As well as scientists, industrialists and artists there were leading architects such as Hermann Mathesius, Peter Behrens, Theodor Fischer, Josef Hoffmann and Richard Riemerschmid. There were also aviation pioneers and engineers such as Anthony Fokker, Heinrich Focke, Georg Wulf, Karl Jatho, August Euler and Hugo Junkers.

The men with grubby fingernails my father calls them.

But no grubby fingernails could be seen on this occasion. All of them wore dinner jackets, and their wives were decked out in their finest gowns and their most expensive jewels. And as they rose from their seats at Hermann's bidding they lifted their crystal glasses, the candlelight glancing off the polished facets.

'THE FATHERLAND!' was their chorused salute.

The toast over they sat down and conversations were resumed. It was at this moment that Hermann, who was sitting close to Anthea, turned to her and said, 'Seeing you dressed in that uniform of yours has reminded me of something.'

Before coming down to the meal Anthea had struggled long and hard with whether she should put on her uniform or not. Wearing it at Hermann's dinner party had been the reason for bringing it in the first place. Or at least that's what she had kept telling herself.

248

It had seemed a marvellous idea when she first thought of it. But when the moment came for her to change into it she started to have her doubts. Wearing it at a costume party was perfectly acceptable but at a more formal function such as a dinner party it might be considered somewhat *Outré*. Hermann's dark-haired wife, Martha, however, was so enthusiastic Anthea had allowed herself to be persuaded.

'Besides,' Martha had added. 'Hermann has already told everyone you'll be wearing it so you can't let them down now.'

As expected her entrance caused quite a sensation and by the time she reached her seat at the table she was delighted that she had taken the risk. But with Hermann's question she was no longer so sure. Hermann was by nature a mischief-maker. Anthea knew this to her cost and she was now wary of where this reference to her uniform might lead.

'What does it remind you of?' she asked.

'That Austrian fellow?'

It was as she had feared and suddenly Anthea felt as if an invisible hand was gripping her throat. 'What Austrian fellow?'

'Oh, you know, the one in the satin pantaloons. Dammit! For the life of me I can't remember his name.'

'Von Gessendork, dearest,' Martha reminded him.

'Yes, von Gessendork. What happened to him, Anthea? He just disappeared.'

Of all the subjects that her brother could have dredged up this was the one Anthea had dreaded most. And, of course, he had to do it in such a manner as to draw the attention of all the other guests around the table. Every face was now turned in her direction.

'I've no idea,' she replied in a toneless manner, hoping against hope that her supposed disinterest would discourage further enquiry.

'Isn't he plenipotentiary to the Austrian court?' Josef Hoffmann, one of the architects, piped up.

This was all the encouragement Hermann needed. 'That's right! He is. And would you believe it my sister here nigh on challenged him to a duel.'

Karl Jatho almost dropped his glass. 'She didn't!'

'She most certainly did.'

'For Heaven's sake, Hermann,' Anthea pleaded. 'Can't we talk about something else?'

But Hermann showed no sign of desisting. And Anthea cringed at what might be coming next. She didn't fear a description of how she'd insulted the count. That she could easily laugh off. What she really feared was that somehow her brother had learnt how the count had paid her back afterwards, that maybe Thetis, deciding to go back on her word and not keep it a secret, had told Hermann all the lurid details.

And he'd consider it too good a story to pass up.

But as her brother continued to unfold the story it became clear to Anthea that her fears were groundless. Hermann stuck to what he knew, which was no more than what he had seen taking place at the party. And as the guests applauded her actions Anthea relaxed, offering up a prayer of thanks to Thetis.

So the Baroness did keep her word.

Which came as a great surprise to Anthea especially as she knew that if the shoe had been on the other foot she would have found it impossible to keep such a secret to herself and would have told it to everyone she knew without a moment's hesitation.

Throughout Hermann's description of the incident Martha had observed Anthea's increasing discomfort and when it finished she decided to come to her rescue by changing the subject. Addressing the table at large she asked, 'What do you think of Anthea's short hair?'

'I quite like it,' Theodor Fischer said as a servant lent beside him to pour claret into his glass. 'I think it accentuates the beauty of her long neck.'

Anthea was pleased with the compliment. It was the first time anyone had commented on her hair since her arrival at Hermann's Kreuzwerk estate in Essen earlier that day. Hermann had made no mention of it when he came out to his private airfield to greet her, but then why would he? He had already seen the severity of it at her birthday costume ball weeks earlier.

'I thought by now it would have grown more than it has,' Hermann observed as another servant filled his glass with wine.

'I get Helga to keep it in trim,' Anthea told him.

Hermann showed his surprise. 'Whatever for?'

'I think it suits me,' she answered him defiantly.

Sensing a sibling argument brewing, Martha put on a conciliatory smile. 'Who knows, dearest, it may soon become the latest fashion.'

Unconvinced, Hermann addressed his wife firmly. 'It can become what it wants, my dear, as long as you have no thoughts of following it.'

Martha gave her husband a look that said all it needed to say before turning her attention back to Anthea. 'You cannot imagine what a pleasure it is for us to have you here for Christmas, but why can't you come back with us to the Residenz for the New Year celebrations?'

Hermann added his support. 'Yes, why can't you?'

'I would if I could and nothing would have pleased me more, but I have a long standing invitation to visit my friend the Baroness von Buchner at her Rügen estate.'

Hermann almost choked on his wine. 'Friend! I thought you hated the woman?'

'Well you are wrong, dear brother. She extended me a helping hand at a time when I needed it most.'

Hermann frowned. 'Helping hand! Helping hand with what?'

'Never you mind.'

'Yes, Hermann. Stop talking to your sister as if she were one of your mechanics.'

Hermann gave his wife a sheepish look. 'I'm sorry, dearest. You're right, of course. We should be enjoying ourselves instead of bickering.'

****

Christmas morning was as perfect as any Christmas morning could be. Fresh snow had fallen overnight and the air was full of freshly minted sunshine. Everyone rose early and most especially Hermann and Martha's three young children. They galloped down the heavy staircase and into the yellow room where the tree stood tall and proud in its festive decorations.

Beneath the silver streamers, the frosted baubles and lighted candles lay a pile of gaily-papered packages. The children headed straight for them and, knowing which belonged to whom, soon had the floor deeply littered with ribbons and torn wrappings. The adults stood close to the blazing fire, smiling at the squeals and yelps of delight as each gift was revealed. Some of the loudest squeals greeted Anthea's gifts.

'Vielen herzlichen Dank, Tante Anthea,' young Gottfried cried out as he rushed around the room holding aloft his model biplane.

'Vielen dank, Tante.' Young Heinrich chased his brother around the room with his own model biplane.

If Martha and Hermann had expectations that Anthea had bought their daughter, the youngest of the brood, something less warlike they were to be disappointed. Young Mathilde leapt to her stocking feet and chased her brothers with her own model biplane. 'Tausand Dank, Tante Anthea.'

Hermann watched the children as they rushed after each other in a circle and shook his head. 'Seems we have a dogfight on our hands.'

****

251

Dawn broke upon the Western Front and the crisp Christmas air that hung over the farm beside the airfield at Ste Helene Salient had a festive tang to it, helped to no small extent by an overnight delivery of Christmas Eve snow.

'Sort of spruces the place up,' Lucy observed. 'Like a fresh tablecloth laid for breakfast.'

'When did you ever 'ave a tablecloth?' Dibbs asked.

Lucy stared at Dibbs defiantly. 'We had one at Sunday school.'

'Do you think we'll get some Christmas grub today?' Shorthouse asked.

'If we do I 'ope it comes soon.' Hutchins grabbed his belly. 'My stomach thinks its throat's been cut.'

Swain later wrote down what happened next in his diary.

At about nine o'clock Sergeant Worcester came and called us to order. He and Corporal McCleod then marched us out of the stables and into the courtyard where we were stood to with the rest of the company for church parade. We sang the carols like a company of angels but in our hearts we were eager for what was to follow.

Besides the stables was a large farm building and down the middle of this were several long tables groaning under the weight of all sorts of Christmas food. As was the tradition the officers served us, filling our mess tins with beef and pork, roast potatoes and onions and lots of gravy, which was followed by a great beg dollop of Xmas pudding.

Afterwards each of us was given an apple, an orange, several packets of cigarettes and a cigar. There was also plenty of beer and this soon got us in the party spirit. At this point the officers left us to it and we decided to have a bit of a singsong. 'Lucy' knew all the latest Music Hall favourites and we had a fine old time.

Later when the beer had mellowed our mood we retreated back outside. There we built a snowman and christened him General Haig. Dibbs suggested we give him a good kicking, but as this didn't seem to be in the festive spirit we went back to the stables and started opening our parcels from home. These contained all sorts; cigarettes, tobacco, chocolate, homemade cake, knitted socks as well as tins of stuff we don't often see out here.

The opening of the parcels started off feverishly and noisily enough, but soon we quietened down as it began to hit us how much we were missing home. It was then that 'Lucy' asked how we would normally be spending Christmas day. Each of us gave a short reminiscence of how we spent the day. Only Dibbs and Coaxie remained silent.

But we were determined that they wouldn't be left out. Unbeknownst to them, during a period before the meal when both of them were out of the stables, we prised open our boxes and took out enough of the good things to make up two extra boxes, one for Coaxie and one for Dibbs.

'From your mates in 'A' troop,' Shorthouse told them as he handed over the boxes.
'Merry Christmas.'

It was impossible to tell whether Coaxie was pleased or not, but we weren't really concentrating on him. All our attention was on Dibbs. It may have been a trick of the light but it looked as if old 'Ferret Face' had a tear in his eye.

****

'I'm sorry if I embarrassed you with that story about von Gessendork,' Hermann told his sister as, arm in arm, they strolled alone in the garden.

'Why should it have embarrassed me? Besides, it was a rather good story.'

'It was, wasn't it?' He stopped and turned to her. 'Oh, by the way, Martha reminded me to ask you what you would like for Christmas.'

'I hadn't really thought about it,' Anthea answered coyly.

Hermann smiled. 'Well that would be a first. In all your nineteen years I've never known not to think about what you wanted for Christmas and your birthday.'

'Well, as one gets older these things seem less important.'

'So you don't want anything then?'

'I didn't say that.'

'Then you have thought of something?'

'Do you have to be so insensitive?'

'Time is pressing. Christmas will soon be over.'

'Well, I have thought of something, but only just now as we were speaking.'

'Of course. What is it?'

'You'll think me stupid.'

'That would hardly be anything new. Come on! Out with it!'

'My Halberstadt.'

'What about it? If you want it tuned up I've already ordered my mechanics to give it the once over.'

'No, it's not that.'

'What then?'

'I want crosses painted on the wings and fuselage.'

He looked at her askance. 'Crosses! Whatever for?'

Anticipating the possibility of this question she already had her answer to hand. 'Knowing I had them would make me feel safer.'

'Safer! Safer from what?' He paused and gave her a hard look. 'You're not thinking of flying to the front again, are you? Is that the real reason you wanted to spend Christmas with us?'

Anthea's eyes flash defiantly. 'No, it's not. If you must know on the way down I passed an airbase and was buzzed by one of ours. It set me thinking. It's just possible someone on our side could mistake me for the enemy and shoot me down.'

Hermann was still not convinced. 'I can't see that happening. But if it makes you feel safer I'll get somebody onto it.'

'You're an absolute darling, Hermann.'

'So that's all you want then? Some crosses painted on your aircraft?'

'Well, no. There is something else.'

'What?'

'There's one of your machines I'd like to fly.'

1918

CHAPTER TWENTY-TWO

1 JANUARY 1918

Across Europe and the British colonies the New Year was greeted with subdued enthusiasm. Much of it arose out of the relief that a bad year had ended rather than from any real belief that a good year had just started. The horrors of Passchendaele and Cambrai and the turmoil in Russia were memories too painful and too recent for the kindling of genuine optimism.

Ordinary people everywhere thought of the men folk that they had lost fighting for their country. Others prayed for the safe deliverance of those still fighting. Andrea Harker, standing atop her tower watching the village fireworks display offered up such a prayer for her missing husband.

Along the Western Front in the trenches themselves soldiers on both sides took a stoical view of their situation. They had fought long and bitter battles throughout 1917 and it was likely that in the year ahead they would fight many more.

In Brewer Street trench the soldiers of 'A' section, now back in the line, allowed themselves a moment to think of comrades no longer with them. Though ordered not to mark the passing of the old year, they were treated to a sort of fireworks display put on by the Germans. At Midnight a spectacular barrage of star shells of every conceivable colour lit up no-man's-land.

'They're pretty aren't they?' Private 'Lucy' Entworth observed as his enraptured face was bathed in lurid shades of red, green and yellow. 'They remind me of the footlights at the Majestic.'

No one made any comment for beneath the crack and sizzle of the stars shells they became aware of another sound. Across the cratered wasteland drifted the bellowed felicitation *Gutes Neues Jahr!*

Windy Hoskins looked puzzled. 'They keep yelling that.'

Bookworm looked worried. 'What d'you think it means?'

Corporal 'Aggis' snuffed. 'Ask Shorthouse. He's bound to know.'

Bookworm turned to Shorthouse. 'D'you know, Shorty?'

'They're wishing us a Happy New Year.'

'That's nice of them,' Sergeant Worcester said as he entered Brewer Street.

'Ferret Face' Dibbs wasn't slow to see that the Sergeant was carrying something. 'What you got there, Sergeant?'

Sergeant Worcester held up a bottle of Johnny Walker. 'Compliments of the Lieutenant. He wishes you all a Happy New Year.'

In Sassnitz Thetis prayed that the New Year would finally bring peace to the world and that her son would still be alive when it happened.

In Bois de Cheval as he listened to the riotous celebrations coming from the Kasino Buchner prayed that in 1918 the burden of command would at last be lifted from his shoulders and that he would take to the skies once again.

In the Kasino Fuchs watched joyously as the drunken officers spent their money at his bar and he pondered the prospect that 1918 would bring him untold wealth and happiness.

In 63 squadron's mess at Ste Helene Major Parkinson celebrated in the company of all his officers including Cummings and Whitworth. But in his own thoughts he was still troubled by the conversation he'd had with Harker's widow.

In Essen Anthea watched the firework display put on by her Brother, but her mind was excited by thoughts of bold and hazardous adventures.

****

The fireworks display at the rear of the Residenz was the best ever held. No expense had been spared and as the last second of the old year passed into history the black sky above the surrounding parkland exploded again and again with bursts of scintillating light. And accompanying each burst was an 'OOH' followed by an 'AAH' as the assembled guests expressed their appreciation.

Von Hoeppner was delighted by their reaction. Or he was until Hedda suddenly appeared at his side.

'Enjoying the display, my dear?' he asked, sensing trouble and trying to divert it.

'I need to have a word with you.'

The tone of her voice was unmistakable. It was one that he had heard many times before. He knew that she was still upset by Hermann's last minute decision to stay at Essen for business reasons. But her voice told him something else. It told him that he had done something to offend her and now he would have to suffer the consequences.

'Can't it wait?' He knew that it wouldn't but he felt duty bound to ask anyway.

Hedda stood stiffly and implacably beside him her cow eyes fixed unseeingly on the fireworks as she spoke. 'No, it can't.'

Mentally throwing his hands up in resignation von Hoeppner sighed. 'Fine! What's troubling you now?'

'The situation at Bois de Cheval.'

Von Hoeppner barked out a short laugh. 'Now, why am I not surprised?'

Ignoring the derision in his voice Hedda pressed on. 'Putting Buchner in charge of JGN was a mistake. Morale is low and the fighting efficiency of the unit is being undermined.'

Von Hoeppner's voice hardened. 'Look, I've told you often enough before that you shouldn't concern yourself with military matters. It's not your place.'

Undeterred, Hedda turned her gaze upon her husband. 'How can you let an elite unit like JGN go to ruin when you have the perfect man to hand.'

Again the arched laugh. 'Don't tell me. This perfect man. It wouldn't be Hantelmann, would it?'

'Who else? Why have you so taken against him?'

'I haven't taken against him as you put it,' von Hoeppner lied. 'More to the point why are you always taking his side? The man's an idiot.'

'He's not! He's a fine commander, far better than Buchner.'

'Oh, I see! It's all right for you to take against Buchner, but if I say anything against Hantelmann I'm being unreasonable.'

'You are being unreasonable.'

Von Hoeppner had learned over the years that there was never any satisfactory way to end an argument with his wife. She was inexhaustible and was quite capable of going on and on until the sun came up. But for once he thought he might just have something to say that would shut her up.

'This discussion is serving no useful purpose. The question of who commands JGN may well soon become an academic one.'

'What do you mean?'

'JGN is too large and unwieldy. It lacks flexibility and I'm seriously considering splitting it up to reinforce other units on the front.'

Hedda's shocked expression almost made von Hoeppner laugh. 'You can't do that.'

'I can't what?' Von Hoeppner's voice rose to such a pitch it carried above the sound of the fireworks and a number of the nearest guests turned in his direction.

'Excellency?'

It was von Abshagen. He had approached the feuding couple with commendable discretion waiting for a suitable opportunity to announce his presence. Von Hoeppner's climactic bellow seemed like the perfect moment.

'What is it?' von Hoeppner snapped at the interruption but when he saw that it had come from his adjutant his stern expression softened into one of relief.

'I have something you need to see right away.'

Von Hoeppner turned back to his wife. It was clear that she had more to say but she for her part was astute enough to realise that her audience with her husband was over. With nothing to be gained by trying to prolong it she decided on a tactical withdrawal.

'Oh, don't worry about me.' She touched her temple. 'All of these fireworks have given me a headache. I think I need to go and lie down.'

****

With the end of Gerard's Christmas leave and his return to the *Jasta Schule* Hantelmann was left with only his daughter as company. Neither of them felt much like celebrating so both waited up long enough to wish each other a Happy New Year then retired for the night.

Settling in his bed Hantelmann awaited sleep and a visitation from his usual dream. He hated dreams. As far as he was concerned no good ever came from them and his recurrent dream about his near collision at Trois Risseaux did little to improve his opinion. But there was more to his aversion than a mere dislike of nightmares. He hated dreams because they always made him feel powerless. He was not in control of what was going on and to him being in control whether awake or asleep was of paramount importance.

It was one of the reasons he had come to loathe his wife Annaliese. She was a nightmare he had never had under his control. From the very first moment they were introduced she had taken charge. In fact it would be true to say that she was in control of him. Their first words together had established this dynamic and it had persisted throughout the rest of their married life together.

But as he lay alone in the marital bed at his home in Ansbach Hantelmann was no longer troubled by this thought. He was no longer troubled by it because the thought had dissolved into the thoughtlessness of sleep. It came upon him unbidden and as his eyes closed he fell into a dream, a dream so vivid it was unlike any thing he had ever had before.

He knew he was dreaming. He always knew when he was dreaming. In his dreams he seemed to be the spectator and the participant, the observer and the main character. But in this instance the observer noticed that there was something different about this dream. It wasn't the usual one, the only one he'd been having for weeks now. It wasn't the one about dogfights and near collisions.

For this reason he didn't put up any resistance against it. Freed from the dread expectation of imminent death he wasn't coiled and ready to claw his way back to consciousness. In fact, its very difference, its very novelty, made him relaxed and curious enough to want to find out what it was all about and where it might lead him.

As far as he could tell he was standing alone on the gravel driveway of a very large stately building. It was night-time and the windows of the building were ablaze with light. And from somewhere within the building came the sound of high voices and merry laughter.

He stood there for a while staring at the building and its open entrance, which stood atop a number of circular stone steps. Something about the building told him that those living within it possessed great power, a power that dwarfed any authority he had as a living man, a power that made him feel he had no right to be there.

But this was a dream and dreams do not operate by the same rules of logic that apply to the waking world. Whether he belonged or not he knew he had to be there for a reason. He didn't know what it was, but there was only one way to find out and in the end it was the sound of the voices and laughter that compelled him to move forward.

As soon as he took his first step the scene shifted and he found himself inside the building standing in a spacious Grand Foyer with columns and balconies and three crystal chandeliers hanging from its lofty ceiling. And in the middle of its tiled floor there stood a sculpted figure of Aphrodite pouring water into a stone bowl.

Ahead of him was a broad carpeted stairway that led up to a wide gallery. He climbed the stairs and found himself facing two black marble columns and beyond these was a white marble floor on which lay the mosaic of an eagle clutching a double-headed axe in its claws.

The scene shifted once again. This time he was inside a Great hall standing on a raised platform decked out in his dress uniform. Below him was a sea of smiles, elegant and highborn. All the smiles were turned toward him and the eyes above the smiles were lit with the glow of highest esteem.

Sensing that there were others with him on the platform he turned and he wasn't in the least surprised to discover that his companions were the Archduke Maximillian von Hoeppner and his wife Hedda. They were both smiling at him, a regal smile, and von Hoeppner stepped forward to join him at the front of the platform.

To emphasise the occasion's importance von Hoeppner was wearing his dark blue *Friedensuniform* with tasselled shoulder *epaulettes and ponceau* red cuffs and high collar. At the nape of his collar he wore the Grand Iron Cross and on his chest the Württemberg Star. Spanning his broad girth was a belt of braided silver brocade and blue stripes. Over his left shoulder was a sash and on his head he wore the helmet of an Imperial German General with its Guard eagle plate and feathered plumes of white-over-black.

All of the guests clapped loudly, but when the Archduke raised a hand they fell silent. Von Hoeppner then gave a speech in which he praised Hantelmann for his courage and gallantry, referring to him as the perfect German warrior. After the speech von Hoeppner pinned the Iron Cross to Hantelmann's breast then shook his hand. Thunderous applause followed and Hantelmann stepped forward to bask in the adulation.

All of this was rather splendid and it certainly made a pleasant change from the terrors of death, but the part of Hantelmann that was observing the dream couldn't rid himself of a growing sense of anxiety. He wasn't used to good dreams and he feared that whatever conclusion this one was leading to wouldn't be quite so agreeable. Inevitably it would end in some disaster or sudden humiliation.

The scene shifted yet again and now he was amongst the guests, congratulations coming in from all sides. Everyone wanted to shake his hand and clap him on the shoulder and it seemed that there would be no end to it. Then the ArchDuchess Hedda von Hoeppner was standing beside him and the sound of congratulations ceased.

'Come with me,' she said.

The scene shifted one last time and to his complete and utter surprise he found himself lying on top of a naked woman, his hips wedged between the vice-like grip of her thighs. He was thrusting into her like a piston, gritting his teeth into a snarl of rising ecstasy.

He could not tell who the woman was. She had a bolster under her buttocks, lifting her stomach to a level higher than her head and shoulders. But beyond her magnificent breasts all he could see was the underside of her chin thrashing from side to side.

Yet, there was still something familiar about her, something about her wanton abandon that reminded him of his wife Annaliese. Was it her? Was she the bad thing he had been expecting, the bad thing that always happened in his dreams? Damn her! Overcome with a desire to hurt and degrade this woman, the woman he loathed with such intensity, he thrust harder and deeper into her as if trying to tear her asunder.

Bitch! Bitch! This is for never showing me any respect.

But her soft flesh just absorbed him, turning his aggression back against himself as it hurried him to the moment of his release. His spine arched, his head cranked back, his mouth yawned open and a rasping, choking sound stuttered from the depths of his throat as the lust shot out of him in trembling spasms.

When all was spent he collapsed breathless onto the perfumed expanse beneath him and stayed there, not daring to move until the last minor after-tremor had shaken through him. Finally, pulling himself free of the woman, he fell back onto the sheets beside her and stared vacantly at the unfamiliar ornate ceiling.

From the ceiling his eyes wandered downward and he was struck immediately by the bedroom's lush and sinuous forms, by its mauve wall-coverings and its rich, red walnut panelling. Even stranger, on a small table close by was a vase of blue-green, yellow and brown glass depicting dragonflies, plants and flowers and beside it a glazed and iridescent peacock jug, its tail complemented by three feathers that jutted out like sinister flowers.

The woman beside him started moving, removing the bolster that had supported her. He then felt the sheets being pulled up.

'Why haven't you returned?' a voice asked him, but it was not the voice of his wife.

Hantelmann rolled onto his side and stared in utter disbelief at the woman lying beside him, the woman he had just made love to and it was not his wife Annaliese. It was the ArchDuchess Hedda von Hoeppner.

He knew this woman. He had spoken to her many times on the telephone. She had been his champion. She had been instrumental in getting him command of JGN and had helped him out in the matter regarding Buchner. But despite their close association he had never actually met her in person. Strictly speaking he wasn't actually meeting her now. After all this was only a dream. But that didn't alter the fact that the social gulf between them was so enormous she was to all intents and purposes a goddess. And he had just made love to her.

The shock of what he had done and who he had done it to was so great he almost woke at this point. But Hedda's eyes prevented his escape. They skewered him with their intensity, and once again she asked, 'Why haven't you returned?'

Not yet fully in possession of his wits Hantelmann found himself unable to grasp the meaning of the question. He had, however, regained possession of his voice.

'Returned?'

'Why haven't you returned to JGN?'

'Buchner is now in charge.'

'And he is ruining everything you worked so hard to create. Morale is low and discipline is falling apart. If this goes on any longer my husband will step in and break the unit up.'

'But what can I do?' Hantelmann pleaded.

'I got you that command. It's yours! Go to Bois de Cheval and seize it back.'

Hantelmann's eyes sprang open and he found himself back in his own bed. Yet, instead of feeling bruised and exhausted, he felt strangely refreshed and invigorated. And the dream or the memory of it remained vivid and intact especially Hedda's final injunction. Her words had infused him with a renewed sense of purpose. His limbs were galvanised in a way that they hadn't been for ages and much to his utter delight his right hand was no longer shaking.

For the first time in a long time it was clear to him what he had to do.

I'm going to Bois de Cheval and I'm going to take back my command.

****

For a long while von Hoeppner sat looking up at the portraits of his ancestors. This was an unusual thing for him to do. They were such a familiar presence that most of the time he just ignored them in much the same way as he ignored the library's other fixtures and fittings. But now his eyes were regarding one of them with a hard, contemplative stare, the portrait of his grandfather, Siegfried von Hoeppner, a man notorious in his own lifetime for being a hoarder of secrets.

At the height of his powers Siegfried had run an effective network of spies for the Imperial German Government, in much the same way as his own grandson would come to do. But Siegfried came to love secrets for their own sake. Stepping beyond the bounds of political necessity he went to extraordinary lengths to acquire information about his family, his friends and everyone else he knew.

To him secrets were a source of power. As he saw it they not only gave him power over other people, they also gave him power over the world and everything in it. And he held onto those secrets with the iron grasp of a miser holding onto his coins. To his family and everyone who knew him he was known as the Guardian of Secrets.

But how well are you guarding them now?

Von Hoeppner's present concern had come about some twenty minutes earlier when von Abshagen had brought him an urgent message. It was from Intelligence and it stated that there was reason to believe that the British agent known as *Silver Feet* was making a concerted effort to get hold of information about the new Pfalz DVIII. This was especially troubling to von Hoeppner as he had a copy of the trial report on the DVIII that Hermann had sent him, the one that was now locked away in the safe behind the portrait of the Guardian of Secrets, Siegfried von Hoeppner.

After reading the message that von Abshagen had brought him von Hoeppner had immediately opened the safe to check that the report was still there. It was, but seeing it there didn't lessen his concerns. The message about *Silver Feet* had brought to mind other troubling matters that had arisen recently.

Matters that might well be connected.

Only a few days previously he had noticed that certain things in the library had either gone missing or been tampered with. And these objects were not the sort of thing one could easily dismiss as being no more than the usual pilfering or carelessness of servants; the objects involved could be used for subversive purposes if they fell into the wrong hands.

'I'm beginning to think that a spy has taken up home with us in the Residenz.'

Von Abshagen looked up from the lists he had been studying at the Archduke's desk. 'What makes you say that, Excellency?'

Von Hoeppner looked around him as if searching for something he had lost. 'Things have been going missing. Not things lying to hand, but things locked away here in my library.'

Concerned Von Abshagen put down his pen. 'What things exactly?'

'Headed notepaper, the sort I use for writing letters of authority to military units and other senior officers. I always keep a small supply locked in the draw of my desk. Several sheets have been taken.'

'I see.'

'I'm afraid that's the least of it. I also keep a number of blank military passes and pilot licences locked in another drawer. One each of these has gone missing.'

'How can you be so sure?'

'I haven't filled in one for over two months and I always make a note of it whenever I do.'

Von Abshagen got up and walked round the desk. 'This is serious.'

'You're damn right it's serious. It seems that someone in this household can come and go as they please.'

They both fell silent for a moment and during this time von Abshagen considered the situation. Finally he asked: 'Where do you keep the key to the drawer?'

Von Hoeppner pointed to the bronze statuette on his desk. 'It's in a space concealed under the satyr.'

'Does anyone else know that it's there?'

'I'm the only one. I'm certain of that.'

'Can I ask, Excellency, have you taken on any new staff recently?'

'None that I know of though I daresay my wife would know more about that than I would.'

'Do you have any long term guests currently staying at the Residenz?'

'No! The Christmas crowd has long since vacated the premises and after tonight the place will be virtually empty save for my wife and the servants.'

Again von Abshagen considered the situation before asking: 'When did you first notice that these things had gone missing?'

'The Military pass and pilot's licence only the other day, but I noticed the missing notepaper just after Christmas though I thought nothing of it at the time. Besides, there's no way of knowing whether this is a single act of theft or several separate ones.'

Von Abshagen breathed out deeply and decisively. 'We'll need to tighten up security at the Residenz immediately.'

Von Hoeppner turned to his adjutant. 'Do you think this is the work of Silver Feet?'

'It's impossible to say. We'll start with some background checks on the servants.'

'But they've been with the family for years, some literally since birth.'

'It's just a precaution, Excellency.'

'You're right.'

'And while I'm here I'd better take that report your son sent you. I need to put it in a place where we can be sure it is secure.'

Feeling suddenly tired Von Hoeppner sat heavily in the chair at his desk. 'Of course. You do whatever you consider necessary.'

'One other matter, Excellency. That message about Silver Feet.'

'What of it?'

'May I suggest that we issue an urgent notice to all senior commanders.'

'Saying what?'

'That they should be on the alert for anyone acting suspiciously.'

Von Hoeppner's eyes fastened speculatively on the statuette, but now it was no longer the satyr and its hidden key that held his interest.

'Should we mention Silver Feet in this notice of yours?' he asked, his eyes lingering long and hard on the sea nymph.

'I think we should. And I also think we should send a special notice to Hauptmann Buchner at Bois de Cheval airfield.'

'Why?'

'He is the only pilot on the Western Front who happens to have a Pfalz DVIII in his possession.'

****

Standing on the wooden deck of the *Peleus* Thetis watched the sun climb above the eastern horizon, its appearance marking the first dawn of the New Year. Ragged bars of grey and furnace red clouds spread across the vast, disinterested sky and for a moment it was hard to tell whether this was the end of the day or its beginning.

She had been standing at the starboard rail for some hours, watching the crew ready the yacht for sailing, provisioning the galley and scrubbing the decks. She wanted to make sure that the vessel could be got underway at a moment's notice. Given the pace of events there was no telling how fast she might need to weigh anchor. But in the meantime there were still a few loose ends to deal with.

My son and the Princess von Hoeppner.

It was now clear to her that Anthea had become fully ensnared in her own fantasy. First the uniform, then the stacked boots and manly voice and finally the theft of the official documents. She now knew from Helga that the Princess had taken the uniform with her when she flew to her brother's place in Essen.

Supposedly to wear at the Christmas party.

But Thetis knew better. All along she had sensed that the Princess had been struggling with her desires and that as she took each step along the road to fulfilling them she was at the same time denying to herself the ultimate goal of her actions.

Now she has only one more step to take.

And she would have to take it soon. Her brother and his family would be travelling to Berlin in a few days and she would either travel with them or she would head in an entirely different direction.

And she won't be coming here to Sassnitz.

This was what Anthea had told her mother. It was a lie and Thetis guessed that she had lied on impulse. Her reasons for doing so were understandable, but what Thetis couldn't quite fathom was why the Princess hadn't brought her in on the plan.

Maybe I played my part as the voice of caution too well. Maybe she couldn't be entirely sure that I wouldn't betray her.

Not that any of that mattered now. The Princess could execute the last stage of her plan at any time. Indeed, it could already be happening. For Thetis it was essential that she have someone to hand who could tell her what was going on. She had dispatched Erich back to the Residenz to keep an eye on things there. He was also to destroy any incriminating letters between her and the Princess and, if the opportunity presented itself, have another crack at the safe in von Hoeppner's library. But she needed someone inside the airbase at Bois de Cheval.

That's where my son comes in!

What better person could there be? As commander of the base he would know the comings and goings of everyone especially any new arrivals. She knew that he was still angry with her for getting him the command, but she had every hope that by now he would have cooled off sufficiently to accept her letter.

Well, it's on its way now anyway.

She had written it the previous evening taking great care to pour into it all the affection a mother could. She begged his forgiveness for going behind his back and told him that she had been forced to act as she did only out of her concern for his safety. These formed the preliminaries. With them done she turned to general enquiries about how things were faring with him and then, in passing, mentioned a certain Leutnant Strasser she had met at the Residenz in early December. Strasser had told her that he was being assigned to JGN. Had he arrived yet?

With the letter complete she had given it to one of her servants to post in the town. With any luck it would catch the midday collection and reach her son in a couple of days. Then, hopefully, he would call her on the telephone.

And we can begin healing the rift between us.

CHAPTER TWENTY-THREE

3 JANUARY 1918

'Well, what do you think?'

'Oh, Hermann, it looks splendid.'

The upper surfaces of the wings and fuselage of the Halberstadt had been camouflaged in a mottled arrangement of dirty pinks, yellows, greens and blues. Something similar had been done to the under surfaces although here the same colours were augmented by blobs of dark blue. Huge new style crosses, black with white edgings, had been added to the wings and tailplane and two angry eyes and a snarling mouth had been painted over the engine cowling.

'Looks like a real war plane, doesn't it?'

'I don't think I'll be mistaken for the enemy now.'

'No, I suppose you won't. And you shouldn't have any technical problems either. I got my top team to check out your machine from top to bottom. Everything is tight and purring like a kitten. They've also emptied your tank of that war-time muck and replaced it with some of my special reserve.'

'Hermann, you're a darling. But tell me what is that there?'

Anthea pointed one of her heavily gloved hands toward the rear fuselage and the word that had been painted on it in large white letters.

'Oh that. It's a little touch of my own. I thought it was about time that your machine was given a proper name.'

'But 'Aegis'? What does it mean?'

'In Greek mythology it was the shield that Zeus gave to Athene. When she took it into battle no mortal enemy could stand before her.'

'Then it seems I have everything I need.'

'Well, Have a good journey to Sassnitz.'

'Thank you.'

They embraced. Then, as they pulled apart, Hermann gave her a knowing smile and said, 'Make sure you give the Baroness my best wishes when you see her.'

'Er, yes, I will.'

****

The doors swung open and a servant entered the library carrying a breakfast tray. On it was a silver coffeepot and a large cup. He placed the tray on a small table then filled the cup.

'Will you be requiring anything else, Excellency?' he asked when he had filled the cup.

Von Hoeppner, closely wrapped in his dressing gown, looked up from his papers. 'No. That will be all.'

After the servant left von Hoeppner returned to the papers spread across his desk. He had been studying them all through the night and with such intensity that he'd failed to notice the slow dwindling of the fire in the grate, which was now virtually dead. Not that he minded the discomfort. In fact he preferred working in the small hours.

Less interference from busybody females.

With cold fingers and tired eyes he shuffled through the papers. They were mostly communiqués from High Command giving details of the forthcoming offensives to be launched in the early spring against the armies of England and France. But now he was looking for one in particular, a small map that had accompanied one of the communiqués.

Where is it?

It was little more than a sketch, but to von Hoeppner it was of great importance for it included an area to the north and south of the River Lys that was to be part of one of the planned offensives. All it lacked was details of the forces involved as these were still being transported from the former Russian front.

Momentarily giving up the search von Hoeppner climbed to his feet and, on knee joints still aching with morning stiffness, ambled over to the table with the tray of coffee. He lifted the cup and took a welcoming swallow. Then he carried the cup back to the desk, but as he did so his eyes fell once again upon the bronze statuette.

It reminded him of a particular problem he had been wrestling with since the beginning of the New Year. In his conversation with von Abshagen about security and the theft of important documents he had begun to make a tentative connection between the British Agent Silver Feet and the Baroness von Buchner. And in the days that followed as he thought more and more about it the connection had only grown stronger. Again and again he called to mind instances where security had been breached and the involvement of the Baroness could not be entirely ruled out.

It seems my beautiful Thetis might have changed her address.

So far all the evidence was circumstantial, but von Hoeppner had now convinced himself that the case was strong enough to warrant an investigation. Von Abshagen was the man to carry it out. Having made up his mind to act von Hoeppner sat down at his desk and reached for the telephone. But he didn't get to make the call for at that moment the door to the library swung open and in swept Hedda.

What was I saying about busybody females?

A sour comment filled von Hoeppner's mouth but remained there. It was so unusual for Hedda to enter his library and in her dressing gown that he became instantly alert. Their marriage had never been an entirely happy one, mostly due to his wayward behaviour, but during all the years they had been together he had grown to know her moods. And from the obvious anxiety in her cow-like eyes it was clear that her present mood was one not a good one.

'What's wrong?' he asked, trying to expunge the weariness from his voice.

'Anthea's missing.'

****

Erich lay under the cool satin sheets of Helga's bed awaiting her return. He was becoming restless. Before leaving the room she had told him that she was going to get them some breakfast and wouldn't be more than ten minutes, but that had been nearly an hour ago and still there was no sign of her. Left with nothing to do but stare at the walls Erich's thoughts turned once more to the task assigned to him.

The Baroness has given me an impossible job here.

He wasn't referring to sleeping with Helga. That was pleasant enough, but that was not why the Baroness von Buchner had sent him back to the Residenz.

'Take whatever opportunity presents itself to uncover von Hoeppner's secrets,' she had instructed him. 'And most especially any plans he might have for any Offensives planned for the spring.'

He knew that the Baroness had tried to do this herself but had failed and it seemed to him that his chances of success could hardly be any better.

This place is like a fortress.

He didn't mean the Residenz. That was an open house. Every day people came and went more or less as they pleased, treating it like some sort of hotel. And now that he had taken to disguising himself as one of the servants he found that he too could move about with comparative ease.

But the disguise wasn't much help to him when it came to the one place he really wanted to penetrate; von Hoeppner's library. That was the real fortress. When the Archduke was not in it the doors were always locked and the locks were proofed against the cleverest locksmith. The Baroness had told him that there was a secret entrance to the library and it didn't take him long to discover its whereabouts.

But finding an opportunity to get in there unseen is the real problem.

The door to the bedroom flew open and Helga rushed in looking more than a little flustered.

Noticing that she was empty handed he asked, 'Where's my breakfast?'

She looked at her hands as if expecting to see them holding a tray. 'Oh, I forgot.'

'What's wrong? Why are you so agitated?'

'They've found out.'

'Who has found out what?'

'The Archduke and the Archduchess. They've found out that Princess Anthea has gone missing.'

Erich sat up. 'How do you know this?'

'I was there when they rushed out of the library together.'

'The library?'

'Yes. They were in such a hurry they didn't even bother to lock the doors.'

Erich was out of the bed in an instant.

****

Other than passing over a column of waving soldiers the flight to Valenciennes had been uneventful. She had set off at dawn from Essen and covered the two hundred miles in two hours and thirty minutes, but this did include a stop at Mechelen to refuel. Not once along the entire route did her Halberstadt DII give her any anxious moments. It performed perfectly.

Bless you, Hermann.

During the flight Anthea at last admitted to herself the true nature of what she was about to do. It was no longer possible to maintain the pretence and all of the self-deception fell away. She was undertaking an act that though not necessarily dangerous could certainly get her into a great deal of trouble if it went wrong.

As Anthea brought her Halberstadt DII, now decorated with black crosses and fuselage serial number, down onto the brittle grass of the *Jastaschule* she was acutely aware that she was about to face her first major test. She was entering a military facility and as soon as she stepped down from her machine her behaviour would be under close scrutiny.

One slip and my adventure will be over.

A mechanic in blue overalls greeted her on landing and directed her to taxi to the end of a neatly parked group of various aircraft that included Roland and Albatros fighters. He followed her on foot then helped down to the ground.

'Where's the main office?' she enquired in a voice imbued with all the natural command of high birth.

The mechanic pointed to a group of huts. 'Over there, Herr Leutnant.'

Briskly and with the masculine gait she had practised, Anthea took herself to the largest of the huts and entered. It was packed with young trainees gathered round a notice eager to see who would be their tutor for the morrow.

She marched up to the only senior officer she could see and, snapping to attention, announced in the deepest voice she could produce. 'Leutnant Strasser reporting for duty, Herr Hauptmann.'

She rather overdid the voice and all the trainees turned their heads to stare, puzzled as to how someone with such a slight and slender form could produce such a deep sound. Fortunately she was wearing her flying gear and her face was smudged and covered in oil so there was little to give away her true identity.

Ignoring the attention she had drawn she presented the commandant with her forged documents. Doing little more than glancing at them and the letter that said she was assigned as a pilot to JGN he told her that there was no transport going to Bois de Cheval until the following morning.

'And I'm afraid that our billets here are full.'

As far as Anthea was concerned this was another problem solved. 'Don't worry, Herr Hauptmann. If someone can drive me into town I'll stay at a hotel.'

****

As he did on most evenings Parkinson left the mess after a couple of drinks and returned to the office so that he could do a quick assessment of his pilots, weighing up the worth of the news ones and deciding what worth was left in the old ones. The working lifetime of a pilot was a short one. The stress of patrols, even without the added stress of combat, burnt a man out quickly. Parkinson considered it an essential part of his responsibility to spot the early signs of fatigue.

And recommend Home Establishment if necessary.

271

He hadn't done that yet, but knew that when he did he would be haunted by the knowledge that he had nearly met a similar fate himself a few months back. He had been suffering with a loss of nerve and was definitely on the verge of cracking up. It was only the death of his friend, Major Harker that had saved him. The shock had not only banished the fear.

It gave me a sense of purpose.

He never thought it possible that he would take to command as readily as he had. Yet when it happened it seemed to him the most natural thing in the world. Not that it had been much of a challenge. He had been fortunate to take over when things were pretty quiet.

Nothing to compare with the madness of last November.

So far he had been spared the agony of writing letters of condolence to grieving relatives. And he'd been blessed with enough time and peace to settle into the job, reacquainting himself with the pilots and getting to know the new ones, helping them to find their bearings and gently familarise themselves with the needs of war.

Like Cummings.

Parkinson flipped through the small pile of files on his desk and pulled free the one with Cummings' name on it. Besides the usual documents it contained a report on the leg injuries he had sustained during the bombing raid. There was an attachment from the MO saying that Cummings was now fit enough to resume active duty. Parkinson closed the file.

There was something about Cummings that had struck a chord with Parkinson from the very first moment he met him. It was hard to say what it was exactly. The nearest he could come to expressing it was that he saw in Cummings something of himself. There was reserve, but not aloofness. He observed people but not in an over critical manner. His interests were esoteric and somewhat exclusive.

And he appreciates beauty all be it the mathematical kind.

But there was more to it than that. The one thing that had forged an undeclared bond between them was the fear that Parkinson had seen in Cummings' eyes. Parkinson had recognised that fear even when no one else noticed. He recognised it because it was the same fear that he saw every morning staring back at him from his shaving mirror.

Well, tomorrow he will have to face that fear.

****

'Where do we go from here?' Swain asked.

'I knew it,' Hutchins' voice came out of the darkness. 'We're fucking lost.'

'Keep quiet,' Sergeant Worcester growled.

They were about half way across no-man's-land moving at a snail's pace toward Oyster Crater, a large feature that sat athwart the German front line. The crater itself was a relic of an enormous underground mine the British had detonated the previous year. Aerial reconnaissance seemed to indicate that the Huns were busy strengthening the line there and 'A' section had been sent out to find out what was going on.

This was their first proper raiding party in strength. The trouble was that no one, including the lieutenant and the sergeant, seemed to have much sense of direction. They had been wandering around no-man's-land for nearly an hour and had changed direction so often that they couldn't be sure whether they were heading toward the German lines or back toward their own.

'Time to take a roll call, Sergeant,' the lieutenant whispered.

'Yes, sir.'

In a low voice Sergeant Worcester called out the names and everyone answered except for Coaxie.

'Where's Cokeson?' the Sergeant asked.

'Probably done a bunk,' Brinkley offered.

'He better not had,' the Sergeant said menacingly.

'Maybe we've lost him,' Hutchins suggested. 'You can't see sod all out 'ere.'

Just then a lone figure emerged out of the shadows and squatted amongst the others. It was Coaxie.

'Where 'ave you been?' the Sergeant demanded.

'You're going the wrong way,' Coaxie told them. 'That crater you're looking for is over there.'

This was the most that anyone could ever remember Coaxie saying all at one time. By his standards it was a veritable speech and for a moment it held everyone silent. It was the Sergeant who first found his voice.

'Oh yeah. And how do you know that?'

'The stars.'

'What?' Taken aback the lieutenant looked up at the star-filled sky. Then he looked back at Cokeson. 'All right! You lead the way.'

****

'You sure you know where you're going?' Dibbs said.

'Leave him alone,' Swain said. 'He knows.'

273

Coaxie pressed on ahead of the rest. He was like a bloodhound and no one would have been surprised if he had started sniffing the ground. He had been at it for over five minutes and the general feeling amongst the rest of 'A' section was that they were still lost. But then a deeper shadow loomed up in front of them that made them pause. It was a landmark of sorts.

'What's that?'

They had to get up close to make out what it was.

'It's an aircraft,' Swain told the others as he ran a hand over one of its fabric-covered surfaces. 'Its nose is stuck in the ground and it hasn't got its top wing.'

'Is it one of ours or one of theirs?' Brinkley asked.

'How the hell would I know?'

'It's one of ours,' the Lieutenant said as he played the muted light of his torch over the fuselage.

Shorthouse started to get excited. "Ere! I know this one.'

'What one?'

'You know.' Shorthouse struggled to find the right words. 'There was a dogfight between this British Major and that German. Everyone was talking about it.'

'Oh yeah,' Haggis scoffed. 'And who were they?'

'I don't know the name of ours but I think the German was a fellah called Bocher.'

'Buchner,' the Lieutenant corrected him.

'Yeah. That's it! Buchner.'

'Bloody marvellous!' Dibbs exclaimed. 'He remembers the Hun's name but can't remember the name of the poor bastard he shot down.'

'His name was Major Harker,' the Lieutenant said. 'Now I think we've spent enough time with this. I suggest we move on.'

'You 'eard the officer,' Sergeant Worcester snarled. 'Move your arses.'

Sullenly, the men skirted round the snow-covered wreckage and shuffled forward.

'How far to go now, Coaxie?' Swain whispered after a few minutes.

But Coaxie gave no answer. He had stopped and seemed to be studying the ground ahead of him. Though no one could see him he was pressing the toes of his boots down upon a deeper pool of darkness and in this way judged that he was standing on the edge of an incline.

'We're here,' he announced over his shoulder.

The sky lit up and all their shadows glared out behind them. They were exposed with no where to hide and the enemy had seen them. A machine gun started to chatter. Bullets zipped and whistled out of the darkness.

'INTO THE CRATER!' the lieutenant shrieked.

CHAPTER TWENTY-FOUR

4 JANUARY 1918

03.00

An enemy flare whistled into the sky and burst above the men of 'A' section as they lay pressed against the eastern wall of Oyster Crater. A number of them were still reflecting on the narrow escape they'd had when several hours earlier they had been standing on the lip of the Crater and the machine guns had opened fire.

As tracer lanced out of the black night, zipping hither and thither, all thirteen men had reacted with one single instinct, leaping over the edge of the crater and diving headlong into a tar pit of darkness.

Blind and disoriented, they had rolled and rolled down an invisible and seemingly endless incline. Like rag dolls thrown into a toy box their arms and legs had flayed around them uselessly and their bodies felt like so much inert baggage as they plummeted downward. Then they hit the bottom and there they lay sprawled in a disorderly pile, the wind knocked out of them.

'Get to the far slope,' a voice commanded them. 'It's the safest place.'

Although the unrecognisable whisper didn't belong to either the Lieutenant or the Sergeant they still obeyed it, stirring their bruised bodies to scramble across the floor of the crater on their hands and knees. Within seconds of reaching the far slope that part of the crater they had just vacated came under intense mortar fire.

The ground around them shook repeatedly. Blast waves slapped against them. Dirt cascaded upon them. And in their terror they pulled up their legs and pushed their faces into the snow, praying that death would not find them.

For what seemed an eternity the German hate rained down upon them incessantly, and some of the shells came quite close to where they were lying, but after a while the bombardment eased off and finally the darkness fell into an uneasy silence.

For the next hour or so they lay there hardly daring to move or speak in case some stray sound might trigger the enemy into a fresh onslaught.

It was Lieutenant Leighton who eventually summoned the presence of mind to act.

'Find out who's still alive, will you, Sergeant?'

An impromptu roll call established that not everyone in 'A' section had made it. Two were missing, lying dead or injured somewhere in the darkness. One was Private Brinkly. The other was Private 'unmentionable' Haywood.

Nothing much was said after that. Everyone lay where they had dropped, spread around the bottom of the slope nearest the German lines. Their clothes were wet and they shivered in the freezing night air. But as the hours wore on they knew that time was not on their side

'If we hope to get out of this, sir,' they heard the Sergeant tell the Lieutenant. 'We've got to make the attempt while it's still dark.'

'Yes, I know, Sergeant.'

Everyone sensed the Lieutenant pondering what should be done and they felt sure they knew what his decision would be, for no other choice was possible. Finally the Lieutenant gave the word to the Sergeant and the Sergeant passed it to the men.

'When I say so I want you all to start belly crawling back to where we first jumped in. And don't make a sound.'

Everyone got ready and at the signal started crawling across the floor of the crater like a wriggling nest of black serpents. It took them quite a while to get to the other side and when they eventually got there the wall looming above them, though not steep, seemed unusually high.

'Right! Start climbing.'

Digging their fingers and toes into the snow they pulled themselves up the yielding slope inch by grueling inch like snails glistening their way up the wall of a nighttime garden. What made it that much harder was their inability to tell how much further there was to go. The rim of the crater and the black sky above it were virtually indistinguishable.

Soon the lip of the crater was within reach of their grubby nails. They closed their hands upon it. This was the moment. One quick pull, one quick scramble and they would be over the top and into the darkness beyond.

A star shell burst above them, etching them upon the ground, shadow and all. Machine guns opened up, their black anvils tapping out hard tempered rounds. Snow and sod jumped into the air. Tracer hissed and sizzled overhead.

Fingers sprang open. Bodies fell away. Arms and legs rolled back down to the bottom of the slope. And there, panting in the darkness, the thwarted fugitives lay cowed, regretting their bid for freedom.

07.30

It was still dark when Anthea reported back to the camp as instructed. She went straight to the commandant's office. He wasn't there, but his adjutant was. After rummaging through some papers on his desk he found what he was looking for.

'Ah, yes. Leutnant Strasser. You're wanting transport to Bois de Cheval.' He paused a moment and gave her a funny look, but being unable to resolve why he should find the young Leutnant so fascinating he returned to the safety of his papers. 'You're in luck. A staff car is about to leave for Bois de Cheval.'

She hadn't expected to travel in such luxury. 'A staff car?'

'Yes. It belongs to Hauptmann Hantelmann, and he has kindly agreed to take you with him.'

08.15

The sky was beginning to lighten above them and the darkness at the bottom of the crater was no longer so absolute. They could now see each other and they could also see two dark shapes lying motionless at the bottom of the crater's western wall.

'Why do they call it Oyster Crater?' Lucy Entworth asked trying to take his mind off the motionless shapes.

Windy Hoskins shied a small stone at Lucy but missed. ''Cos that's what it looks like, you dope.'

'Yeah! But from where I'm lying it looks just like a bloody great 'ole in the ground.'

'Not from up there it don't,' Shorty informed them.

'Up there?'

'Yeah! Up in the air. They flew over the crater and took a photo of it.'

'Pipe down you lot,' Sergeant Worcester hissed. 'This isn't a ruddy debating society.'

Swain, who was pretending to scribble in his notebook, was actually trying to eavesdrop on a conversation between the Lieutenant and the Sergeant. Although Windy Hoskins lay between him and them he was near enough to get the gist of what was being said.

'I think you're right, sir. It looks as if we're stuck here for the day. We certainly can't make a break for it. We'd be slaughtered before we even got out of the crater.'

'My concern, Sergeant, is that the Germans will open up with those mortars again.'

'I'm not so sure, sir. This crater's pretty big and deep. They can't see us so they can't be sure of hitting us. No, I reckon it's more likely they'll send a force of men to winkle us out. Their lines can't be more than twenty yards ahead of us.'

'Probably. Either way I think we should get the men to make some dugouts on this side of the crater.'

'Good idea, sir. I'll get them on to it right away.'

At this point the conversation ended and Swain stopped listening. But as he readied himself to receive orders from the Sergeant he heard a sound that made him look up. The circle of sky visible to them at the bottom of the crater was much brighter now and beyond the western rim of that circle there appeared nine aircraft.

By now everyone had heard the sound and everyone was looking up. And as the machines move further into the circle a peppering of small smudges suddenly surrounded them as if someone was flicking splats of powdery paint against the sky's quivering canvas. Shortly afterwards the air was filled with sharp barking sounds.

'German Archie,' Shorthouse informed them although all of them knew that already. 'They're shooting at them. They're ours, I think. Camels and Brisfits.'

The group of fighters and two-seaters moved into the centre of the circle of sky until they were almost directly overhead. Then one of the F2Bs coughed and seemed to falter. And as the rest of the group continued on its eastward journey the lone F2B banked around and headed back the way it had come. It disappeared back over the western rim of the crater and once more 'A' section found itself alone.

08.17

Lieutenant Paul Singleton had been having trouble with his engine ever since they met up with their escort of five Camels over Motte de Gazonville. He had tried to sort it out by fiddling with the throttle, but this didn't help at all.

If I take the throttle any lower I'll be dropping out of the sky.

He didn't fancy flying all the way to Seclin and back with a duff engine, but he pressed on as best he could. Then, as the group approached the western edge of Oyster Crater, his engine began to misfire badly.

That's it! They'll have to do without me.

Singleton signalled to his observer Lieutenant Robert Trivers that he intended turning back then began a bank to starboard. His left wings dipped earthward presenting him with a view of the interior of Oyster Crater.

My God! There's men down there!

09.00

'A' flight had taken off at 7.45 to escort F2Bs on a bombing mission to Seclin and now Parkinson was preparing to take 'C' flight out for its morning constitutional. It was then that the telephone in the office rang. Hargreaves, the adjutant was with the armourer so Parkinson picked it up.

'Sixty-three here. Parkinson speaking.'

'Hello, Parkinson. It's Jameson.'

'Hello, Jameson. How's things at eighty-nine?'

'Can't complain. Look, one of my lot was forced to washout from the Seclin job with engine trouble, but as he was turning back he spotted a group of men crouching in Oyster Crater. Seems they're pinned down by fire from the forward German trenches. Battalion believes these fellows are part of a patrol that went missing last night.'

'I see. And I take it Battalion would like us to give them some help?'

'That's about the long and the short of it. If you can eliminate some of the machine gun nests it might give the patrol a fighting chance to get back to our lines.'

Parkinson felt a twinge of the old fear creep up the back of his neck. Battalion was asking him and 'C' flight to carry out a low-level attack on the German trenches, a highly dangerous thing to do.

'Okay, Henry. We'll see what we can do. But it'll take a while to fit Cooper bombs to our machines.'

'Thanks, Bill! I'll let Battalion know.'

09.30

Even the most miserable of individuals have at least one day every now and then when they wake up in a good mood. It may not last very long but while it does it is a free gift from the gods. And so it was with Buchner.

There was no reason why he should feel as he did. It could have been that his natural exuberance, so long suppressed, had at last risen to the surface and reasserted itself. Or it could have been the permanent return of Reinhard to JGN.

It's hard to remain glum with him around.

Whatever the reason might have been Buchner couldn't remember the last time he had felt so cheery and at ease with himself. At long last he had a sense of optimism, a sense that the future still held the promise of things to be done.

And things worth doing.

For the first time in a long time he had taken time to watch several of the Jastas take off. Jasta Leintz left hurriedly at 8.45 to intercept a group of enemy fighters and two-seaters heading for Seclin. Jasta Dostler left at 9.00 on a line patrol and now Jasta Brandenburg had just disappeared over the treetops also on a line patrol.

Silence once again descended upon the field, but Buchner remained where he was taking a moment to enjoy the fresh air and watch as the covering layer of white cloud began to fray and unravel, revealing several patches of gleaming blue sky.

A sight for sore eyes.

But the real boost to his spirits was yet to come. When he returned to the office he found the morning's post waiting for him. Amongst all the usual stuff was another letter from Hantelmann. It was short and sweet but this time it carried news that made Buchner's heart leap for joy.

At long last! Hantelmann's returning to JGN.

The letter didn't give any details as to when this might be, but the clear intimation was that it could be at any moment. What was certain was that he intended taking back his command as soon as he arrived, relieving Buchner of what had been a loathsome burden.

Allowing me to get back into the air once again.

The prospect so excited him that he was tempted to discard the rest of the post and go and check that his machine was still in battle-ready condition. But then, not wishing to give Hantelmann any excuse to criticise how the base had been run in his absence, he decided to finish the post first.

There was only a couple of letters left. One of them was obviously from his mother. Now no longer feeling the same depth of anger he had felt toward her he opened it. And as he read what she had written he felt the last vestiges of his wrath fade away and he resolved to talk to her later on the telephone. But there was one bit of the letter that puzzled him.

'Are we expecting a Leutnant Strasser,' he called out to Fuchs.

'Not that I'm aware of, Herr Hauptmann.'

The last letter was from High Command and the envelope was marked 'Most Secret'. Never having received one of those before he opened it immediately. Inside was a single sheet of paper with three short typewritten paragraphs.

It appeared to be an alert. It began by saying that intelligence had been received that an enemy agent was operating behind the lines. Without going into too much detail it warned all commanding officers to be careful not to discuss operational procedures with anyone not authorised to hear such matters.

It ended by saying that efforts were underway to track down the agent involved. Little could be said with any certainty concerning the agent's identity other than that the person was known as 'Silver Feet'.

What a silly name!

Silly enough to make him smile. Yet there was something familiar about it that made him pause. When he remembered what it was his smile deepened. As a child his mother used to tell him a *Kindermärchen* about a princess called Silver Feet. With the aid of a pair of magical silver slippers she had many adventures flying from castle to castle saving people from all sorts of misfortune.

And while she wore those slippers no one knew her true identity.

The human face has many muscles, but unlike any other part of the body their purpose is subtle, enabling the eyes and mouth to express a thousands shades of emotion, some so fine it is sometimes difficult to assess the exact moment when a person's mood has shifted.

Anyone observing Buchner at that moment would have seen a man indulging in a fond memory. The face was animated by a smile so warm you could have thawed cold hands on it. But the mouth is slower than the eyes and an acute observer would have noticed that it was here that a change had taken place.

Where before Buchner's eyes had been a part of his smile they had now become introspective, apprehensive and full of doubt. His mouth still held onto the smile, but his face had become a grinning mask out of which his eyes now stared with the light of an awful realisation.

10.00

It couldn't have been easier.

Sitting in the back of the open staff car with Hauptmann Hantelmann Anthea reflected on just how easy everything had been. So many obstacles had stood in her way and yet she had overcome them all. Indeed, throughout the entire process despite the occasional odd look no one had given her a second glance.

Turning up the collar of her greatcoat, she glanced quickly at the man sitting beside her. When she first learnt that she would be travelling to Bois de Cheval with Hauptmann Hantelmann she thought she might be in trouble. She knew him or at least knew of him through her mother and feared that he might recognise her. And when she climbed into the vehicle and sat beside him this fear deepened. What if he engaged her in conversation and asked her something that might give her away?

As it turned out she needn't have worried. He began by telling her that he had been visiting his son who was at Valenciennes training to be a pilot. He then asked her a few innocuous questions that she answered easily enough. After that he fell into a brooding silence, which suited her perfectly.

With little else to do she directed her gaze to the passing view. Not that there was an awful lot to see. It was mostly an endless colonnade of tall, imperious poplars walling off the road from the flat white fields beyond. She thought it pretty enough but rather unremarkable.

A country lane is a country lane even in France.

Later on the journey became much more interesting. They were somewhere close to Lille when the traffic on the road became quite congested and soon they found themselves hemmed in by vehicles of every description. There were General Service Wagons pulled by trains of mules laden with cargoes of timber, barbed wire, mortars, machine guns and ammunition all bound for the front. There were lorries with food and medical supplies. Some trailed heavy artillery pieces. Others had soldiers standing shoulder to shoulder in the open backs, laughing, shouting and swearing.

Motor cycles weaved in and out of the gaps, and smart squadrons of cavalry cantered their horses down the middle of the road. And the traffic hadn't all been military. Locked in with the slow moving tenders, lorries and transporters were large horse drawn carts from local farms swaying under impossible loads of winter hay, milk pales, root vegetables or bleeting sheep, all destined for the village market or the slaughterhouse. And over it all had hung the rank smell of horse dung and engine fumes.

Anthea had never experienced anything quite like it before and she had found it both fascinating and exciting. And while it lasted it had made her feel that she was truly part of the vast human enterprise of war. But when they reached the crossroads that led to Auchy-les-Mines it all came to an end. Most of the traffic had turned off in that direction until, eventually, the road became quieter and emptier again. Now there was only the road and the poplars and both stretched into the distance in a perfect play of diminishing perspective.

Fresh pairs of poplars came constantly in to view, joining the ceaseless progression like columns in an infinite colonnade. And wherever Anthea looked, her eyes were always drawn back to the point of convergence on the horizon. There was something hypnotic about it, about the way the moving lines seemed to imprison her vision, dulling the acuity of her attention and weighing down her eyelids. 'How good it feels,' she thought as she closed her eyes, her head nodding forward, its weight surrendering to the gentle cradle of sleep.

'Not far to go now,' Corporal Fulda called out cheerfully from the front of the vehicle, giving his announcement added authenticity by grinding into a lower gear, allowing the whine of the engine to drop as the forward motion of the vehicle slowed.

Not far to go now.

Anthea looked around her expecting to see aircraft and tents and all the other things normally associated with a military airfield. But she could see none of this. Instead her view was a split one with the road in the middle. To the left of it lay fields that stretched as far as the eye could see. To the right of it was a deep and trackless forest.

At first the forest was nothing but trees, but then she could see a village nestling against it, or at least the remains of what had once been a village.

'That's Grand Dessou,' Fulda informed them.

'It looks badly damaged,' Anthea remarked.

Hantelmann turned to her. 'It was in the middle of the British advance.'

Looking toward the fields Anthea could see the carcasses of burnt out tanks and smashed artillery pieces. There were even dark shapes lying partially hidden in the grass that she thought might be the bodies of dead soldiers, but before she could be certain the vehicle took a sudden left turn along a road that sloped upward toward the east.

'Only a few miles more,' Fulda chirped.

Energised by a wave of excitement, Anthea threw aside the greatcoat that she had been using as a blanket and started paying close attention to her uniform, brushing the jacket with her palms, straightening the collar and picking pieces of imaginary lint from the sleeves.

To think that only a matter of minutes now separated her from her goal. It seemed inconceivable. Or at least it had seemed inconceivable all those weeks ago when she first thought up the idea of infiltrating JGN disguised as an airman. Now it was about to become reality.

10.15

Burdened with four twenty-pound Cooper bombs apiece the five Camels of 'C' flight took to the ever-opening blue sky. Major Parkinson was in the lead with Second Lieutenant David Musker, Second Lieutenant Bertrand Collier, Second Lieutenant Charles Medhurst and one of the new boys, Second Lieutenant Maurice Hobson, tucked behind him in a V-formation.

They spent some minutes circling Ste Helene's field, gaining height, before finally pointing their snub-nosed Camels toward the East. Parkinson didn't need to consult his map. The route to Oyster Crater was familiar to them all.

This was Parkinson's first Offensive Patrol since becoming commander of Sixty-three Squadron. It was his first Offensive Patrol for well over a month. He could only hope that he had not become rusty, that he had not lost his fighting edge. He could only hope that his old loss of nerve would not return to hinder him at a critical moment and jeopardise the rest of the flight.

10.25

It can't be true. She can't be Silver Feet.

He just couldn't accept that his mother was a spy! Well, that wasn't strictly true. Buchner knew that his mother had been an agent working for von Hoeppner. He had known that for ages. It was more or less an open secret.

But that had been before the war at a time when all the Courts of Europe had been accessible. He'd assumed that now that most of the counties she had operated in were enemy territory she had been forced to give up her activities.

Anyway, she'd been acting on Germany's behalf.

Not the enemy! She couldn't be a traitor! Besides, how could she have possibly got away with it? He tried to imagine her creeping into darkened rooms searching for battle plans. It seemed ludicrous. Outlandish! A fantasy! A thing so ridiculous it bore as much credibility as the fairy tale she used to tell him when he was only a child.

But then he remembered something that hit him like a sledgehammer. The story she told him about Silver Feet wasn't read from a book. It was a story that she had made up. And if she made it up then she was the only person who could know the name. And if she was the only one who knew the name then she could be the only one to use it. The argument seemed unassailable, but even with such proof he still refused to believe it.

Surely someone would have noticed?

But would they? He was knowledgeable enough to know that spies have many ways of getting what they are after. And he knew that his mother had access to some of the most powerful men in Germany. He also knew that many of them had been her lovers. That must have been how she got her information before the war. Was she still doing it?

Only this time for the enemy?

He read the letter from High Command once again. It said that the suspected espionage had preceded the Battle of Bayonet Ridge. Where was his mother then? Where was she? He struggled to remember. It seemed so long ago. Then he tried a different tack by trying to remember where he was. That was easy. He was under open arrest after his altercation with Hantelmann.

That was when I spoke to her on the telephone.

He told her about the trouble he was in and she promised to help him by having a word with von Hoeppner. He owed her a favour. Von Hoeppner! The Generaloberst! The man commanding German forces on this part of the front, the man who would have been at the centre of operational planning for the Battle of Bayonet Ridge. The evidence against her seemed to be piling up

But it makes no sense. Why would she betray her country?

Then he remembered that Germany wasn't her country. Not by birth. She was born in Scotland, the daughter of the Fifth Earl of Lothgillian. She had only acquired German citizenship through her marriage to Baron von Buchner. And what was the hold that von Hoeppner had over her? He knew she despised him. She had said as much often enough. Yet she was forever visiting him at his Residenz in Berlin.

Are they working together?

With this thought the web of deceit expanded in Buchner's mind. Was it a network of treachery at the highest levels of German society? How far did it reach? He snatched up the telephone on his desk.

'Get me High Command'

No wait! Think this through.

'Cancel that call.'

He put the telephone down. If he reported this it would almost certainly result in his mother's death. He couldn't do that. No he couldn't, no matter what she may have done. She was still his mother. Besides, if this web of treachery was as extensive as he feared it might be then whom he could trust? If he could no longer trust his mother then why would he trust anyone else?

Maybe even personnel at High Command are involved.

Sitting there as he was seemingly chained to his chair holding the letter from High Command in his hands he felt the world of certainty crumbling around him. What was he to do? Who was he to turn to? He couldn't just do nothing. The welfare of his country was at stake. It was depending upon him to make the right decision.

I don't know what to do! I don't know what to do!

He needed to clear his head. He needed time to think and he couldn't do that with Fuchs hanging about. He needed to get away from the office. The phone rang. It was Leutnant Bowski.

'Just to let you know that I'm about to take the Jasta out on patrol, Herr Hauptmann.'

'What? Oh, yes. Fine! Go ahead. No! Hold on! Give me five minutes. I'm coming with you.'

10.35

The freezing slipstream cut through the scarf wrapped round the lower half of his face, numbing his ears and cheekbones. Cummings was also conscious of a runny nose. By jamming the stick between his knees he retrieved his handkerchief.

It was a delicate manoeuvre, especially with the rest of 'B' flight bobbing about in the air currents just ahead of him. They were in formation flying to the front, but there was no telling when something might appear to draw all four of them away from the route they were following.

Ducking his head into the 'office', Cummings hooked down his scarf, blew his nose then pulled his scarf back into place as he lifted his head. Once more in control of the stick, he corrected his position, gently slipping back into place.

This was his first flight since being injured in the bombing of Ste Helene and it was a significant one; his first flight over the lines. He had been placed at the rear of the formation. This was because his sole task was to take in the sights. He was under orders to do nothing else.

'If I signal the others to attack or pursue,' Captain Milton told him. 'You are turn tail for home. Understood?'

His attempt to look crestfallen at these orders had been for his own benefit. By playing the thwarted hero he had hoped to re-invigorate his flagging lust for combat. But it didn't work. The leaden weight of dread was still strapped to his shoulders when he took off.

For the moment, all he had to do was get familiar again with the route they were taking. He had the map that Hargreaves had given him. Not that it was much help. Not at two thousand feet above a thin veil of cloud. All detail on the ground was rendered indistinguishable by the landscape's flat uniformity. One farmhouse looked like any other. The shape of those snow-packed fields looked the same as those fields over there. That church steeple looked like any other church steeple.

The same held for the tree-lined roads, the meandering black streams and the monuments at crossroads that could be seen only by the shadows they cast upon the snow. There were some distinguishing features; the fallen tree lying on the edge of a field or the building without a roof.

The trick was to recognise these things, commit them to memory then join them up in a pattern that formed a mental map. That's what they'd taught him during training. And he'd been quite good at finding his way around. If he hadn't got the main features of a route in his head during the first flight, he'd certainly got them by the second.

But that had been over England.

Here it was different. Here one had to balance map reading with the more pressing need of keeping an eye out for the enemy. Look down. Look up. Look down. Look up. Wait a minute! Didn't he see that church yesterday? The road ran past it before turning sharp right.

Yes! There's the sharp right.

Feeling pleased with himself he fixed the spot on the map with his gloved finger then raised his head expecting to see the pilots in his flight beaming back at him in admiration. But, of course, they weren't. And he was glad that they weren't because he now felt like a complete idiot.

10.40

And now the staff car was turning once again, this time entering a side road on the left that ran along level ground. They had reached the eastern end of Cheval forest and were now heading north toward the JGN airbase.

It was likely that her stay at JGN would be a short one, that the run of luck that had held her true identity hidden would end and that she would quickly be sent home. Given this possibility she was determined to remember as much of the experience as she could.

Then something remarkable happened. While still unable to see any part of the airbase she saw in the distance some dark objects rise from the ground. She knew that they were aircraft taking off on a patrol. She had seen such things before. But what made it so special on this occasion was that their take off should coincide with her arrival.

'Do you see that, Herr Leutnant?' Hantelmann said with a dry smile. 'They must have known you were coming.'

Of course! What else could it be? Somehow they must have known that she was coming and had arranged a fly-by to salute her arrival. Do they do such things, she wondered? She wasn't sure but when the machines roared by overhead she felt a thrill of excitement run down her spine.

At the very least it's a good omen.

Craning her neck as much as she could she tried hard to get her first sight of the airbase. Not that it was unfamiliar to her. She had visited JGN in late November of the previous year, but then the place had been deserted and she had come as herself. Now the place was fully manned and, more to the point, she was in disguise.

It couldn't be very far away now. The road was straight with a wide vista of fields on the left. But the wall of trees on the right were now moving further back from the road, giving way to a widening apron of rough grass. Then she spotted something.

'That's the chateau, isn't it?'

'Yes, Leutnant,' Hantelmann said. 'It is.'

CHAPTER TWENTY-FIVE

4 JANUARY 1918

10.45

Flying through a storm of 'Archie' the five Camels of 'C' flight approached the northern end of Oyster Crater. The machines rocked and shuddered, knocked from side to side by the reverberating blasts.

There was so much smoke in the sky that Parkinson was finding it difficult to see where he was going. Gritting his teeth he pushed his stick forward and led his flight in a steep dive toward the enemy's forward trenches.

God help us!

Tracer materialised before his very eyes and zipped past him. One of the machine guns on the ground had elevated its muzzle and opened fire. Then a second. Then a third. Parkinson's insides hollowed out and a cold sweat shone on the grey skin of his forehead. But even in his fear he could still observe ruefully.

At least they've shown us where to drop our eggs.

Judging the moment with precision he banked sharp right and placed his dangling wheels parallel with the trenches.

10.47

'It's busy up there today.'

The members of 'A' section had turned their heads to the right to watch the five Camels as they flew into their field of view. Everyone had assumed that they were on a patrol into enemy territory and would soon disappear out of sight. But then they were startled to see the five machines suddenly dive toward the ground.

'What are they doing?' Swain asked incredulously.

But the question became redundant when the flight of Camels, dropping through a three-pronged funnel of ground fire, banked toward them.

'They're attacking the trenches.'

'Get your heads down!' Sergeant Worcester yelled at the top of his voice.

10.50

Turning back to the map Cummings traced the route and quickly came up against the waving mass of parallel and connecting lines that indicated the front. He looked straight ahead to see if he could see it, but the cloud cover was making it difficult.

It was at this moment that Captain Milton led the flight in a gentle bank to the left, levelling out only when they were flying north along the trenches. As the five Camels settled into this leg of their patrol, Cummings now cast his eyes to the east. The lesson Whitworth and Parkinson had taught him had taken root.

No one is going to take me unawares a third time.

But the eastern sky remained empty and as the minutes ticked away his concentration began to slacken. Then the flight began a gentle bank to the right and Cummings realised that they were about to fly over no-man's-land.

Oh God! This is it!

For the other pilots this was nothing new. For him it was still a terrible mystery. He became acutely aware that his life depended upon the uncertain reliability of the engine powering his machine and that if anything were to go wrong his chances of survival would be slim.

Now would not be a good time for a broken fuel line.

10.52

With most of the Jastas out on patrol and his own being overhauled Reinhard was feeling at a bit of a loose end. Not sure what to do with himself he decided to a have a word with his friend Buchner. But when he entered the office he found only Fuchs in residence.

'Where is he?'

Fuchs sat back in his chair. 'You've just missed him. One minute he's reading his post the next he's out the door and up in the air.'

'Was something wrong?'

'You're guess is as good as mine.' Fuchs put down his pencil. 'Is there anything I can do to help?'

'No, not really. It wasn't anything important.'

Reinhard was about to leave when the telephone on Fuchs' desk started ringing. As was his habit he lingered to see what the call might be about.

'Fuchs here…No, I'm afraid he's not in the office at the moment…Oh, I see…Yes. Yes. Can you hold on a moment please?'

Putting his hand over the mouthpiece Fuchs looked up at Reinhard. 'It's HQ on the line. They say they need to speak to someone in command urgently.'

With a heartfelt sigh Reinhard took the telephone from Fuchs. 'Reinhard here. What's the problem? …Yes, Herr Hauptmann. When was this? …Flying in what direction? Well, there's no one available except for me. The rest of my Jasta is unavailable…Yes…Yes…Of course, Herr Hauptmann. If those are your orders.'

Reinhard returned the telephone to Fuchs' desk in a less than friendly manner. 'Dammed idiot!'

'What do they want now?'

'Seems a British patrol is attacking our lines near Oyster Crater and they want me to intercept it?'

'What on your own?'

'There's no one else that I know of.'

'That's madness!' Fuchs started to rise from his desk. 'I'll come with you.'

Reinhard's scowl softened into a smile. 'You're a damn good comrade, Fuchs. And there are few others I'd rather have with me, but your leg hasn't healed yet. You stay here. I'll rustle up somebody if I have to kick the cook out of the kitchen.'

And with that he stomped toward the door.

10.54

As the line of huts came into view Anthea took a deep breath and braced herself against her growing nervousness. The critical moment was upon her, the moment she had practiced over and over again in her head, the words she was going to say and the manner of her greeting.

Nothing must go wrong.

The staff car came to a halt outside the office. While Hantelmann waited for Corporal Fulda to open his door Anthea jumped down from her rear seat, straightening her uniform jacket. As she stepped toward the office door she wondered whom she would encounter first.

Will it be Buchner? Or Fuchs?

As it turned out it was neither. Before her hand even reached the handle the door flew open and a clearly agitated Oberleutnant Reinhard strode out. His stern countenance fell upon Anthea.

'Who are you?'

To be standing face to face with her hero wasn't what she'd expected and for a moment she was unable to reply.

'Have you lost your voice?' Reinhard demanded.

Anthea snapped to attention. 'I'm Leutnant Strasser, Herr Oberleutnant.'

'Can you fly a Pfalz?'

'Yes, Herr Oberleutnant.'

'Then get into your gear. We're going up.'

10.55

Von Hoeppner sat staring at his fist as he thumped it rhythmically on the top of Anthea's dressing table. Never in his entire life had he been at such a complete and utter loss. The need to do something, anything, raged within him. Being unable to act upon that need was totally alien to his nature.

Where the hell is she?

He still didn't accept Hedda's hysterical notion that their daughter had been kidnapped. After the doctor had given her a sedative to calm her down von Hoeppner had tried to get more out of her. It seems Anthea was supposed to be staying with the Baroness von Buchner over the New Year. But the Baroness had just called to say that Anthea hadn't turned up.

That doesn't prove she's been kidnapped.

No, something told him that Anthea's disappearance was entirely her own doing, that it was part of a plan she had cooked up and carried out all on her own. Staying with Thetis for the holidays was merely a deception designed to throw everyone off the scent.

She had somewhere else in mind. But where?

Plagued by the suspicion that Thetis was somehow involved in his daughter's disappearance he put in his own telephone call to Sassnitz, but when he got through a servant informed him that the Baroness had left for the day. This only deepened his suspicions.

Maybe the two of them have gone off together.

After that he had turned the Residenz upside down trying to find some clue to his daughter's whereabouts. He had even interrogated the servants reducing some of the women to tears, but nothing was revealed. Yet he remained convinced that no matter how clever his daughter might think she'd been she would still have left some clue that would betray her intentions.

And it has to be in this room.

Before him lay her diary. He had read all the entries, which wasn't many. And all of these were from the middle of December, which led von Hoeppner to suspect that they were made up and written merely to hoodwink any potential reader. The same applied to her correspondence.

Clever girl! She would make an excellent agent.

It was then that he was struck by the horrible notion that she might be the enemy agent they were all looking for, this so-called *Silver Feet*. All of the things that had gone missing. Maybe that was her doing.

She certainly has the means and the opportunity.

Then he just as quickly dismissed the idea. Anthea was too obsessed with flying to become an enemy agent. She couldn't get enough of it, even dressing up as a German officer at her birthday party. And what about that time when she flew to the front with her mother just to get a look at what was going on.

Good God! That's it!

Von Hoeppner stood up so fast it looked as if someone had spiked him from beneath the chair. His face was stricken and his eyes gaped with a horror. He knew. He knew what his daughter planned to do. Suddenly it all made sense. Dressing up in a German officer's uniform. Getting a military haircut. The documents missing from his desk in the library. The picture of Reinhard on the wall and the map next to it of the Ste Helene Salient.

Driven by an urgency that almost made him cry out, he stormed out of Anthea's apartment. Moving like a bear in torment his great frame scattered all before him as he flew along the corridors of the Residenz and down the stairs. Finally he reached the library. Flinging open the double doors, he strode to his desk and snatched up the telephone.

'Put me through to the commander of Jagdgeschwader Nord. This is urgent.'

10.57

Everything in the office was quiet once again. Buchner was out on patrol and Reinhard had just left on a mission to intercept the enemy over Oyster crater.

Giving me a couple of hours of peace and quiet.

Fuchs sat and contemplated what he should do with this period of repose. One option was to remain where he was and have a smoke. Anticipating that this might be his choice he took up his pipe and started filling it with tobacco. Another option was to wander over to the Kasino and count his money.

I wonder how much I have now?

The thought made up his mind; he would stay where he was and dream about his money and what he would do with it when he returned to civilian life. His favourite dream involved setting himself up in a provincial hotel, an idea that had come to him through from having spent so much time with Mimi at her Estaminet in *Senlis*.

But mine will be grander and more exclusive.

The pipe was now lit and in the slowly drifting wreath of smoke that enshrouded his head Fuchs' provincial hotel took shape. He saw guests lounging in beautifully manicured gardens, shaded from the sun as they sipped iced drinks. He remembered a very exclusive brothel he once visited while on leave in Berlin. The interior had been luxuriant with gilt ornaments, mahogany fittings and acres of red carpet. And sitting in the massive lobby entertaining the guests had been a five-piece orchestra.

The hell with it! I'll have the brothel instead.

The door opened and Hantelmann strode in.

Scheisse!

Fuchs sprang to his feet. 'Herr Hauptmann!'

'Hello, Fuchs. Still watering down the beer?'

'I...Err...Why are you here, Herr Hauptmann?'

'I'm here to take back my command.'

Fuchs' attack of stuttering was interrupted by the telephone. Relieved by the distraction he snatched it up.

'Jagdgeschwader Nord! Oberleutnant Fuchs speaking... Yes, I'll hold.'

Who the hell can this be?

During his time as adjutant Fuchs had taken such calls often enough to know that waiting to be put through usually meant the person had to be an officer of senior rank. He had never found speaking to officers of senior rank a relaxing prospect and he didn't now. Nervously he smiled at Hantelmann.

The voice that eventually came through the earpiece not only startled Fuchs it also made him cast an anxious glance at the picture of Oberstgeneral von Hoeppner hanging on the wall behind him.

'Who am I speaking to?' von Hoeppner boomed.

'Oberleutnant Fuchs, Excellency.'

'Where's Buchner?'

'Out on patrol.'

'Who's next in command?'

'Reinhard, Excellency. But he's also out on patrol.'

'Reinhard!'

'Yes, Excellency.' Fuchs was beginning to sense a note of urgency in von Hoeppner's voice. 'Is there something I can assist you with?'

'Who did he go with?'

'What Reinhard? On his own I think.'

'Are you sure?'

'Yes, Excellency.'

'Have you received any new pilots recently?'

'No, not for some days.'

A lengthy silence followed during which Fuchs sensed von Hoeppner struggling to come to a decision at the other end of the line. Then, 'I have reason to believe that my daughter has disguised herself as a new pilot and may well try to infiltrate your airbase.'

'Your daughter?'

'Yes, my daughter. She is using the name Strasser. You are to stop her and detain her and then telephone me back. Do you understand?'

Fuchs voice came out as a squeak. 'Yes, Excellency.'

'You are to stop her and hold her until someone arrives to fetch her, under lock and key if need be.'

'Yes, Excellency.'

'Under no circumstances is she to be allowed anywhere near one of your machines.'

'No, Excellency.'

'And make no mistake, Fuchs, if she comes to any harm, any harm whatsoever, I shall hold you personally responsible.'

The line went dead.

'What was that all about?' Hantelmann asked.

'Please excuse me, Herr Hauptmann,' Fuchs said as he rushed to the door. 'I need to find someone.'

10.58

While flying to the lines the wind had been behind them, increasing their air speed. Now it was behind them again, a westerly breeze that was drawing them rapidly into enemy territory, but Cummings was aware that there was a price to be paid for this natural assistance

It'll be in our faces on the way back.

And this would make their journey to safety a longer one, an unwelcome prospect if they needed to beat a hasty retreat. To take his mind off this growing danger he tried to work out how long it would take to reach the British lines with a ten-mile an hour headwind, but his calculations were shattered violently by a clanging sound.

What the fuck!

It assaulted his left ear, numbing it against the acuity of the world. Then his machine shuddered and swayed, thrown sideways under the impact of a sudden blast.

He turned. Archie! Over shoulder. There! Beyond tailplane! Dirty smudge. Growing large and tenuous.

Another clang! Ahead! Brown stain, high to left.

One to right. Lower! Clang later, like thunder after lightning.

Captain puts nose down.

Flight follows.

Drop fifty feet.

Level off. Two blobs to right, one to left, all high.

Three clangs, one double then one single.

Next two blobs lower. Gunners adjusting elevation.

Sky dirty. Full of smoke.

Captain lifts nose.

Others follow.

Cummings pulls on stick. Shell bursts nearby.

Bus knocked to one side.

Bloody hell!

Stunned. Small fragments rip holes in canvas.

Pass through ball of smoke. Acrid stink!

Ease stick forward. Horizon lifts into view. Then Captain and rest of flight. No-man's-land beneath! German lines just ahead.

Clang! Clang! Clang! Archie bursts all around. Drumming its tattoo upon the skin of the sky.

God! How long does this go on for?

Pull stick. Climb! Push stick. Dive! Up and down. Level out. More bursts. Clang! Clang again! Flinch! Flinch again! Duck with each detonation. Mindless agony! Shrapnel! Large piece! Hot! Smoking! Carbane strut splinters.

Down again! German lines! Shadowed trenches! Something catches his eye. On the ground! Winking light. So small! Winking rapidly. Stops!

How odd!

Starts again! A signal? Now others. Several others! Wide apart! Line of light from each. Broken line! Broken line of flashes! Rising! Curving into the sky like a whip.

Shit!

One line curves toward him. Sears past his peripheral vision. Long lance of cruel flame! Tracer round! Hissing! Punches through upper wing. Flapping Hole!

Machine guns!

Ground fire! Accurate! Flight targeted. Taking damage.

Why are we holding course?

Captain raises hand. He signals! Signals to Cummings! Agreed signal! Enemy Spotted! Attacking. Go home now. Raise gloved hand.

Acknowledge. Bank away. More Archie! More ground fire! Glance back. Back to German lines. Machine-guns still winking. No sign of Camels!

10.59

The appearance of Hantelmann and the telephone call from von Hoeppner had left Fuchs in a state of extreme agitation. But it was the call that was giving him the greatest cause for concern.

The Oberstgeneral had made him personally responsible for the safety and well-being of his daughter, but he had left him powerless to do anything about it. He had no idea where she might be, no description of what she might look like and not the least notion what action to take.

This isn't fair! Why the hell should I be held accountable for the stupidity of his off-spring?

And the more he thought about it the less it seemed to make sense. How could the daughter of an aristocrat slip out of her father's grasp, disguise herself as a German officer and cross hundreds of miles without anyone noticing? Things like that just didn't happen.

Not outside a fairy tale they don't.

His heart pounding he rushed to the main gates and alerted the guards to be on the lookout for a Leutnant Strasser. Hopefully that would stop her getting into the base, but as he was about to return to the office Hantelmann's driver intercepted him.

'Excuse me, Herr Oberleutnant.'

'Yes, what is it?'

'I couldn't help overhearing you mention Leutnant Strasser.'

'What of it?'

'Well, I brought him here with Hauptmann Hantelmann.'

'You did?' Fuchs' stomach felt as if it had just gone into a full-throttle dive. 'Well, where is she...where is he now?'

'I'm not sure, but I saw him take off a few minutes ago.'

11.01

Anthea couldn't believe what had just taken place. With barely more than a few words to Reinhard, without being questioned or even being asked to produce her counterfeit documents, she had found herself pulling on flying gear, climbing into the cockpit of a black-beaked Pfalz and taking off.

Hardly the reception I was expecting.

It wasn't, but as she and what could be called together of Jasta Reinhard headed west through the sunshine, she couldn't help but feel

297

that this was a dream come true, the very dream that for years had excited her every waking hour. She had done it! She had done it all! She had got herself to Bois de Cheval. She had fooled her way into the airbase. She had come face to face with Reinhard.

But I felt sure I would get no further than that.

In her dream she always saw herself in conversation with Reinhard. And after that he would take her to the kasino and introduce her to the other pilots. The dream went through many variations of this but in none of them did she ever see the outcome that she was now experiencing.

My God! I'm in the air. I'm flying a warplane.

And she was heading to the front. For the first time the implications of where she was and what she was doing hit her like a sledgehammer. She was flying to the front. She was flying to the place where pilots attacked and killed each other, where they fought desperate battles high above the hard earth. And if they encountered the enemy she would be expected to play her part.

Oh dear!

Her dreams had been full of dogfights. The idea of diving on to the enemy and shooting him down had exhilarated her imagination. But now she was facing the real thing and for the first time it came to her that she had never actually been trained in any of the skills needed by a fighter pilot. Most men would have quailed at the prospect, but for Anthea such shortcomings paled against the limitless scope of her own self-belief.

After all, how hard can it be?

CHAPTER TWENTY-SIX

4 JANUARY 1918

11.03

Slowly, bit by bit, Cummings was being drawn into the hard business of war. At first he had merely followed the flight on the understanding that if it became involved in a dogfight he was to obey the signal to return to the airfield. He had obeyed that signal and was now returning.

So why am I turning back?

He didn't know why. There couldn't be any good reason for turning back. And even as he continued the turn he kept telling himself that he shouldn't be doing what he was doing. It was madness. He was no longer part of a team. He was alone. And if he were attacked he wouldn't stand a chance. He'd be shot down for sure.

Archie found him and, as if to warn him off, started barking furiously at his heels. Rocked and buffeted and showered with shrapnel he clenched his teeth, terrified that at any moment an exploding shell would disintegrate his flimsy craft into matchwood sending his dead or dying body into oblivion.

Maybe I should climb higher.

That might put him beyond the reach of Archie and above any dogfight involving his comrades. But there was a drawback and he saw it immediately. In his lofty position he would be quite conspicuous. What if the enemy spotted him and came after him?

What the hell do I do then?

This thought accompanied him over no-man's-land and, as he neared the German lines, cold sweat broke out on his forehead and his body went rigid every time a shell burst nearby. Only by will alone was he able to resist the desire to crouch down inside his cockpit.

Go back, you idiot! Go back!

But he sensed that it was already too late. For better or worse he had crossed the lines and was now flying over enemy territory. And the fear became intense, not because the shells were still exploding, not because the streams of angry bullets still hissed and zipped, but because he felt the presence of an added danger.

Scanning the skies around him, Cummings struggled to penetrate the distance for anything moving. What were those dots over there? Did something just go behind that cloud? Are those machines moving across the ground far below? It was impossible to tell. He lifted his goggles to see more clearly, but the slipstream assaulted his eyes so fiercely he had to lower them again.

Then the shelling stopped.

Why would they stop?

He stiffened. He knew why. Ground fire stopped when its own aircraft were close at hand. For Cummings that meant enemy aircraft.

Shit!

Cummings jerked his head from side to side like a man surrounded by a swarm of angry bees.

Where are they?

He saw them, a number of black-beaked Pfalz, at his height and some distance ahead of him. They were flying west toward him. But they were far to port and it appeared that they had other quarry in their sights and were merely getting themselves into the best position to attack.

Who are they after?

He knew the answer even before he saw a flight of Camels far below and climbing. The Pfalz were swinging round in a great circle so that they could come at the Camels from behind.

Anxiously, Cummings looked on, wondering what he should do. The Camels were climbing serenely from the ground seemingly oblivious to the danger above them.

Come on! Come on blast you! Look up!

11.05

Anthea had been to the front before, to this very part of the front. She had been with her mother at the time and they had not ventured beyond the lines, but held back to watch a dogfight taking place over a spot in no-man's-land called Bayonet Ridge. Afterwards, when her father found out he had demanded that they never do such a thing ever again.

What would he say if he could see me now?

The layout of the land below her looked very much as she remembered it except that it was all now covered in snow. Reinhard's Jasta pressed on steadily and she followed dutifully, having no idea where they were going or for what purpose.

But it has to be something urgent.

That had been clear from Reinhard's manner when she first met him. Maybe some enemy patrol was balloon busting and he had been ordered to intercept them. Anthea looked to port and starboard but the nearest balloon was too far away for her theory to make any sense.

And I can't see anything else in the sky.

It was then as Reinhard's Pfalz reached the midpoint of no-man's-land that he dipped his wings to starboard and glided into a banking turn, which Anthea followed. At first the reason behind this manouevre wasn't entirely clear to her, but as they began their second circle it occurred to her that they must be stalking something below them.

Feeling her heartbeat quicken she looked over the side eagerly. The enemy was close, but her eyes were not yet sufficiently trained to discern such things. Frustrated she raised her head and looked behind her and was surprised to see a lone machine shadowing them but apparently keeping itself at a safe distance.

It has to be an enemy machine. It has to be!

She felt certain of it. And she also felt certain that Reinhard hadn't seen it. It entered her head that this single machine could pose a threat and that it was up to her to save the day. More than that it also presented her with an opportunity to prove to the world that even in combat she was as good as any man.

A trained and disciplined war pilot would have flown up to Reinhard and alerted him. But Anthea was not a trained and disciplined war pilot. And even if she had been her temperament would have militated against her acting in such a considered manner. She was a creature of passion and impulse. Cold calculation was not in her nature. Besides, here was a chance to live out her greatest dream.

A chance that might never come again!

Feeling fear like she had never felt it before, a fear that would have made any mortal man think twice, she banked away from the rest of the flight and headed toward the lone machine.

11.06

The cat and mouse game continued. The enemy machines circled the sky waiting for the best moment to pounce on the Camels climbing up from below. Watching the drama unfold Cummings kept himself at a safe distance. Yet all the while an urgent plea was pounding in his head.

Do something! Do something!

He knew that at any second the Pfalz would dive down upon his compatriots. He also knew that it was within his power to avert a disaster. All he had to do was open his throttle and attack the German machines. They appeared to be so intent on the quarry beneath them that they were unaware of his presence.

Giving me the advantage of surprise.

But fear made him hesitate. It seemed likely that if he did attack his chances of shooting down even one of the enemy machines was remote. He'd never used his guns in anger and he doubted his ability to hit what he was aiming at. And if he missed what then? They would turn on him. And he would have to fight them alone. The Camels still had a way to climb and would not get there in time to save him.

But those are my friends down there.

This was the thought that finally shamed him into action. Reaching forward he armed his guns then stretched his hand toward the throttle lever.

Let's do this.

But his decision to take action had come too late. To his utter consternation he watched as the rearmost of the Pfalz suddenly banked away and turned toward him. Instead of attacking he was now being attacked.

11.07

Reinhard was pleased with himself. He had positioned himself perfectly. They were almost directly above the flight of climbing Camels, in a spot where it would be almost impossible for the British to see them. And when they did, as almost inevitably they would, it would be too late to evade or escape the attack.

Then he remembered the newcomer.

What was his name? Strasser!

In all of the rush he had said no more than a few words to him. He had no idea how capable he was or how well he would perform in battle.

Maybe I should wave him out of this one?

He turned and looked back. But where was Strasser?

God! I've lost him already.

No he hadn't! Strasser was still there or rather he was still there but heading away in the opposite direction.

Where the hell's he going?

It was then that Reinhard saw the lone Camel that Strasser was flying toward and he felt anger grow within him. He had ordered Strasser to stay with him no matter what.

And at a most critical moment he chooses to disobey me.

Four Camels were rising into the trap that Reinhard had set for them. He was within seconds of diving onto them and claiming the prize. And now he was faced with a choice.

Do I go ahead with the attack or do I save that blockhead Strasser?

11.08

Feeling like someone who has goaded the neighbour's dog and takes fright when it shows its teeth, Cummings upended his machine, corkscrewing it through the sky until it was speeding away from the rapidly approaching Pfalz.

The manoeuvre achieved its purpose, but cost him vital seconds, seconds that allowed the enemy machine to close the gap and open fire. It was a short burst. Only one bullet found its mark, furrowing the fabric of Cummings' lower port wing.

Oh God! Oh God! Save me! Save me!

The damage was insignificant but the effect on Cummings was dramatic. Acting almost as if the tear in the wing was a wound upon his own flesh he banked violently to the right. Terrified, he looked back. The Pfalz was still in hot pursuit.

11.09

Continuing his sharp turning climb Parkinson finally caught sight of the German machines hanging overhead.

Crafty bastards!

They were about to attack and all Parkinson could do was to give the signal to disperse. But he didn't give the signal and the enemy didn't attack. Instead one of them peeled away and headed in the opposite direction. It had another target in its sights, a lone Camel.

My God! That's Cummings!

What the devil was he doing there? He'd been ordered back to base. Why had he come back? There was no answer to any of this and Parkinson could only watch as the young lieutenant pulled off a strange backwards manoeuvre to turn his machine about face.

The silver skinned Pfalz fired a short burst and Cummings banked away sharply out of the line fire. Meanwhile, one of the remaining Pfalz still shadowing them from above, suddenly chased off after the other Pfalz.

Two against one, eh! Well, there's nothing I can do about it.

11.10

Normally Coaxie gave little attention to anything that didn't involve the immediate needs of survival. A parade of circus animals could appear in no-man's-land, but if it presented no threat to him he would ignore it. It was the way he stayed alive. But for some odd reason he found himself drawn to what was going on in the sky above him.

Things had gone quiet for a while. The attack by the Camels had silenced at least two of the machine guns and the enemy mortars had given up trying to zero in on them. All they had to do was wait until darkness fell. In the meantime, with little to occupy them – smoking was not allowed – they lay on their backs watching the clouds drift by overhead.

But then a flight of high-flying Sopwith Camels had passed over them heading east. What made it notable was that one of them had turned back and the rest had then dived down to where they could no longer be seen, though they could still be heard buzzing around somewhere.

Most of the troop had fallen into a bout of idle chatter, but Coaxie, not being an idle chatterer, continued watching the lone Camel on its journey back to the British lines. It had almost past out of sight when, to Coaxie's surprise, it swung round and flew back over no-man's-land.

What's he up to?

With disinterested curiosity he watched the single machine as it came under fire from the ground. Anti-aircraft fire exploded all around it and he was amazed that it managed to press on unscathed.

Then the entire troop was startled when four Camels, presumably the four that had attacked the trenches earlier, roared over them their wheels little more than twenty feet above their heads.

'Fucking Hell!' Hutchins yelled.

Now everyone was sitting up trying to see what was going on. The four Camels were climbing steeply, the roar of their engines straining with the effort.

But Coaxie was no longer watching them. He had caught sight of enemy machines flying around in a circle high in the sky, and it seemed clear to him that they were waiting to ambush the rising Camels.

Where's that lone Camel got to?

Coaxie looked around the sky and spotted the machine keeping a respectable distance between itself and the circling Germans. But then one of the German machines broke away from the others and headed toward the lone Camel. Seeing itself coming under attack the lone Camel flipped on its tail and fled.

That's it! You make a run for it.

By this time the climbing Camels had come within view and Coaxie waited to see when the German machines would make their attack. But they didn't. There was a sense that they were making up their minds about something. What that something was became clear when another one of them banked away and chased after his colleague.

Having watched the drama unfold Coaxie assumed that the first German had acted impulsively and that the second German, less than pleased with the first, had been forced into doing something he hadn't intended.

This looks like it might become interesting.

11.11

Damn it!

Shooting down an enemy aircraft was proving to be far trickier than Anthea had ever imagined. In her daydreams it had never involved anything more difficult than dropping behind the victim and opening fire.

Of course, her victims always had the good manners to stay still long enough for her to score a direct hit. Not like this Camel pilot. He was tail-skidding about the slippery sky like a skater on an icy lake.

And that's not the least of it.

As well as working her controls continuously to keep on the tail of her quarry she had to constantly adjust her throttle, opening it to keep up and closing it to avoid nosing into the Camel's rear end.

This is going to take forever.

11.12

Having seen 'C' flight strafing the German trenches near Oyster Crater Captain Milton took 'B' flight down to a thousand feet. Then deciding that 'C' flight seemed to be managing quite well he raised the nose of his Camel and proceeded on his original course further into enemy territory.

After a few miles the flight was at its original height and at this point Milton turned them about and headed back to Oyster Crater. Whitworth, who was now in the position vacated by Cummings, had eyes open for everything.

Over his right shoulder he could see a group of machines to the north east. They were heading south west back to their lines along a course that was almost identical to the one that 'B' flight was following.

Must be the group that went out to bomb Seclin.

But they were not alone. They were under attack from what looked like four or five Pfalz. Unfortunately at this distance Whitworth was unable to tell who was having the worst of the encounter.

Then he spotted something closer to home. It was a lone Camel being chased by a lone Pfalz.

Who is that?

The drama was close enough for Whitworth to make out part of the Camel's tail number. Cummings! It was his friend. His friend was in trouble. Without informing his flight leader Whitworth banked right and headed for the Pfalz chasing Cummings.

11.13

Reinhard was still debating whether he should stay in position or go after Strasser. He was inclined to stay where he was. He still had an advantage over the Camels rising beneath him and he had just spotted four Camels approaching from the north east.

But then he saw the rearmost of those four Camels break free from the others and make a beeline toward Strasser. Not a man to argue with necessity, Reinhard signalled to the rest of the pilots in his Jasta to stay where they were. That done he opened his throttle and chased after the Camel chasing Strasser.

11.13

Anthea may have thought that she had enough problems to contend with, but now she had an extra one, a serious one. Someone was firing at her from behind. She had someone on her tail. She looked back. Another Camel, so close she could see the pilot's youthful face.

And he's rather handsome.

Another machine dropped in behind her attacker. A silver-bodied Pfalz. She saw the leader's streamer.

Reinhard!

Come to her rescue. Smile of delight on her face. Turns back to Camel in front. Still there, still wriggling about like a fish on the line. Moves into her sights.

Fire now!

Fingers close on triggers. Eddy of air catches her wings. Spoils her aim.

Damn it!

Bullets whiz past. She looks back. Attacker still there. Reinhard still behind him. Another Camel drops behind Reinhard.

No!

She turns back. Prey in her sights again. Hers for certain. No! Not going to let Reinhard die. Not on her behalf. Kicks rudder bar hard. Banks her Pfalz sharply to right.

11.14

Can't save him! Can't save him! Whitworth knew it. His friend is about to be shot down. All he can do is wreak revenge. Then finds himself under attack. Pfalz behind him. Letting off short bursts. Each burst chews off parts of his Camel.

Then something unexpected happens. Pfalz ahead of him, the one attacking Cummings, suddenly banks to right. Cummings off the hook. Whitworth banks after Pfalz.

11.15

Reinhard is about to fire another burst when he sees Strasser's Pfalz bank sharply to right. Camel pursuing it follows suit.

What's Strasser up to?

Camel behind Reinhard opens fire. Bullets tear fabric from upper wings. Large sheet flaps violently in slipstream.

Reinhard banks right, narrowly avoiding next burst.

11.15

Anthea's banking turn so tight her wings almost vertical to ground. Looks across at Reinhard. Sees Camel firing into his Pfalz.

Line of five machines now four machines chasing each other in a circle. One Camel chases Anthea. Reinhard chases that Camel. Another Camel chases him.

But that Camel is last to join circle. This delay gives Anthea her chance. She gets onto its tail.

Reinhard opens fire on Anthea's pursuer. Reinhard's pursuer opens fire on him. Anthea opens fire on Reinhard's pursuer.

11.15

Whitworth hears crack like sound of a bone breaking. Sheltering shadow of top wing disappears. Suddenly bathed in brilliant light.

Looks up. Top wing no longer there. Only blue sky confronts his horrified eyes. Machine keels over, beyond all control. Earth whirls around him. Resisting ground spreads out its embrace.

11.15

Reinhard sees Camel's top wing fly off. Feelings of triumph pushed aside as his own machine takes further damage.

Smoke from his engine rushes back toward him, filling eyes and nostrils, blinding and choking.

11.16

Anthea sees her burst of gunfire remove undercarriage and tail-wing of Camel pursuing Reinhard. Watches in fascinated horror as pilot struggles to control his rapidly descending machine. Soon it is beyond her sight. She is alone.

Her course was now south easterly. Ahead of her she saw a Jasta of silver-bodied Pfalz flying in the same direction as herself. They were at a greater height than she was and appeared to be oblivious to her presence.

On her starboard side she could see two Pfalz and a group of Camels dog-fighting over Oyster Crater. One of the Camels unexpectedly broke away from the fight and started to climb steeply toward the group of Pfalz she could see flying ahead of her.

He'll never catch them.

She wondered whether she should attempt to intercept him, but by now she had learnt the perils of doing things alone. She looked round.

Where is Reinhard?

At first she couldn't locate him. Then she spotted a trail of smoke. Her eyes followed it down to its point of issue, a Pfalz, Reinhard's Pfalz.

Oh no!

Distressed at the sight of Reinhard's stricken machine Anthea banked round and set off after it unaware of the train of events that she had set in motion.

11.16

It was a minute or so before Cummings realised that he was no longer being attacked. Daring at last to look round he saw that the line of planes that had been behind him were now in a circle some distance away.

He turned his machine back and as the Camel's nose came round he saw Whitworth's machine descending in an erratic fashion, its top wing missing.

Oh God no! Oh God no!

He also saw another Camel flapping about as it plummeted out of the sky without its wheels and tailplane and a Pfalz trailing a lengthening tail of smoke. Another Pfalz was chasing after it.

Cummings was at a loss. What should he do? What could he do in the face of so much death and horror? He watched impotently as his friend's machine grew smaller against the broad earth and his eyes filled with tears.

11.16

'You'd never get me up there in one of those things,' Chippie Feltham said emphatically.

Lucy Entworth shook his head. 'I dunno. I bet the air's a lot fresher up there than down here.'

Coaxie wasn't interested in what his comrades had to say, but he was observing them. What struck him was the rapt attention with which they were observing the dogfight above them.

Every one of their faces was turned toward the sky. Every eye was following one or other of the aircraft. Their mouths were open and they seemed oblivious to everything around them.

The life and death struggle above them lifted them out of the crater and into some different viewpoint that no longer acknowledged their own danger or the close presence of the enemy.

And as he observed the members of his platoon Coaxie made a basic human connection, one that was most telling. The men beside him may have been English, but more fundamental than that they were still human.

The men in the trench some yards away may have been German, but they were also fundamentally human. This was what they had in common. The basic behaviours of one group were essentially the same as the other.

For Coaxie, the process of coming to this conclusion was not an intellectual one nor was it done by logical analysis. It was driven by instinct and it happened in an instant.

He saw the members of his platoon absorbed by the aerial battle and he knew with absolute certainty that the Germans in the nearby trench were doing exactly the same thing. They were looking at the sky.

To analyse one's actions before taking them is to inhibit them. Coaxie never analysed anything. He just did what he needed to do and he did it without thought or hesitation.

Removing his bayonet from his Lee Enfield, he placed it between his teeth pirate fashion then thrust his rifle into the arms of Shorthouse.

'Hey!' Shorty protested.

But the protest came too late. Coaxie was already on his feet. Digging his toes into the side of the crater he scrambled up the slope to the rim and rolled out before anyone even noticed the movement.

Now in the open he crouched and sprinted, covering the short distance between him and the edge of the German trenches in no more than twenty paces.

But in those twenty paces he took hold of a Mills bomb, knuckled loose the pin and lobbed the grenade with blind precision.

Even as the grenade followed its arc ahead of him Coaxie matched its pace, his swift feet bounding over the last trail of wire, his toes landing then springing into the air as he took the bayonet from his mouth and leapt over the edge of the trench.

11.17

Gefreiter Eugen Kalbeck rubbed the back of his sore neck. 'You'd never get me up there in one of those things.'

Unteroffizier Emil Marschner smiled. 'Oh I don't know. It looks quite exciting to me.'

They and their fat comrade Gefreiter Dieter Schock had been standing in their fire trench watching the dogfight for some minutes. This was a rare treat for them, an opportunity to turn their faces skyward and forget about the filth and the stink around them.

Emil was probably enjoying the spectacle the most. He was especially fascinated by flying machines and for some months had been toying with the idea of applying for training in the Fliegertruppen.

I could become a pilot or a mechanic like my brother. I don't mind which.

Like those around him Emil was exhausted by the intense ground fighting he had undergone toward the end of November. He had seen many of his friends killed especially in the counterattack on Bois de Cheval and the long British retreat that followed. All he could think of now was the day when they would be relieved by the arrival of fresh troops.

Then I'll submit my application.

Something registered on the left-hand periphery of his vision. A small dark object flying through the air. But when he turned his head to see what it was there was nothing there. Was it a trick of the light or had he just imagined it?

He turned back to watch the dogfight. But where before his view of the sky had been unimpeded it was now obstructed by something silhouetted against the sky. Something dark. Something cross-shaped like the symbol for multiplication.

Mein Gott!

It was a man! He was flying. Legs and arms outstretched. For one insane moment Emil thought that one of the airmen must have fallen out of his machine and was about to crash into the trench. But that insane moment was his last.

11.17

Even with all the sharp-edged immediacy of what he was experiencing, even with all his senses fired and accelerated Coaxie could never quite be sure whether it was his body that had speeded up or whether it was the world around him that had slowed down.

He was not unfamiliar with the phenomenon. It had happened to him a number of times before. On those occasions he had been fighting for his life in the noisome back allies of London's East End. And in that frozen moment as he hung in the air he was struck by a sense of re-enactment where the past merged with the present.

Father dead in goal. Mother gin-soaked. Kicked out of slum. Street life. Learning to survive. Duck beneath swinging fist. Disable and maim. Endure privation and pain. Hide in plain sight. Dodge coppers and gangs. Run nimble and swift. Shin drainpipes. Cross crumbling rooftops. Drop onto an enemy from above.

As he dropped into the enemy trench his eye was imprinted with every part of it; the boards, the dugouts, the empty boxes. There were three soldiers. Two stood together, the third one, a fat man, was a few yards away.

He was closest to the two standing together. Almost falling directly onto them. He was aware of their startled faces staring up at him. They did not blink. They did not move. And he was upon them before they could draw their next breath.

His bayonet slashed across the throat of one and, in the same fluid motion, the point went into the eye of the other. There was a thud and a scream. The Mills bomb had detonated.

The third soldier, a fat man, stood some feet away. He wasn't sure which way to turn; the explosion or the invader. Wrenching the bayonet from the dead man's eye socket, Coaxie broke into a sprint, throwing the blade as he ran.

The fat soldier took it in the throat. Gurgling and horror stricken his legs buckled beneath him. But Coaxie reached him before they gave and pulled the bayonet free.

As blackness descended upon the fat soldier's eyes the last thing he heard was the sound of Coaxie's boots as they disappeared around a corner of the trench.

11.17

Still clutching Coaxie's rifle as if it were something hot and unsavoury, Shorthouse turned his head and stared up the slope of the trench in disbelief.

'Fucking hell! Did you see that?'

'See what?'

'Coaxie! He just...He just...'

'Where is he?' Sergeant Worcester demanded.

'He just leapt out of the trench.'

'What for?'

'I don't fucking know. He 'ad his bayonet between his teeth like some ruddy Red Indian.'

It was then that they heard the Mills Bomb go off. The sound of the detonation was muffled but there was no mistaking what it was and where it was coming from.

Entworth: 'He's attacking the German trench.'

Hutchins: 'Shit!'

McCleod: 'Come on! What are we waiting for? The fucker can't do it all on his own.'

Lieutenant Leighton pulled his revolver from its holster. 'Okay, men. Follow me.'

In a ragged line the 'A' section scrambled up the side of the crater. Once over the top they ran Helter Skelter toward the lip of the enemy trench, their bayonet-tipped rifles held before them.

Exposed as they were they jumped blindly into the trench ready for close-quarter combat, but what they saw at the bottom stopped them in their tracks.

Three dead Germans lay before them, one with his throat cut, another with an empty eye socket and a third with a bloody gash across his Adam's apple.

'Strewth!' Entworth exclaimed.

It was at that moment that Coaxie appeared around a corner of the trench. He looked unruffled as if he had just returned from a stroll.

'Good God, Coaxie,' Shorthouse laughed. 'You've got the luck of the Devil.'

'Fuck luck! Fuck the Devil! And fuck you!'

Everyone stood silent stunned more by Coaxie's verbosity than his foul language. He for his part seemed unconcerned. He walked round them and straight up the Lieutenant.

'I've dealt with the third machine gun. I would suggest that this is our best chance to get back to our lines.'

CHAPTER TWENTY-SEVEN

4 JANUARY 1918

As 'C' flight continued its climbing turn Parkinson had watched the drama to the north unfold. The pursuit of Cummings. Whitworth and Leith flying to his rescue. The destruction of Whitworth and Leith.

There was at least the comfort of seeing Cummings still alive, but Parkinson's immediate concerns remained the Pfalz waiting for them above. Thus far they had not attacked.

Probably awaiting the return of their leader.

But their leader was not coming back. His machine was descending in a plume of smoke. And it was then that Captain Milton with Gorringe and Rycliffe arrived to chase them off.

And not a moment before time.

'C' flight was now back at the height it had been at before it launched its attack on the trenches. Parkinson now had to decide what to do next course. Top of the list involved joining up with the remnants of 'B' flight and go to the assistance of 'A' flight and the F2Bs who were still fighting off an attack to the north east.

They weren't that far away now, but then Parkinson saw something that made him pause. A lone Pfalz flew past him in a southerly direction. He couldn't be sure but it looked like the Pfalz that had attacked Cummings and shot down Leith.

Parkinson's first thought was to chase after it and give it a taste of its own medicine, but the course of the Pfalz brought to his attention something else. High to the east and heading in that direction was another Jasta.

It struck Parkinson as odd that they had not got themselves involved in either the dogfight that had just taken place or the one that was still going on to the northeast.

What are they doing? Sightseeing?

There were four of them, but it was the one in the lead that caught his attention. It was a Pfalz but of a completely different design. From its stubby snout and wing configuration Parkinson knew it to be one of the new Pfalz DVIII and there was only one man on the western front who flew such a machine.

My God! That's Willi Buchner or I'm a Dutch uncle.

Parkinson was shocked. His understanding was that Buchner had been grounded by his own High Command in order to protect him as a valuable national hero. And yet here he was.

Conflicting emotions raged within Parkinson's breast. Uppermost was fear, the fear a man might feel on seeing a lion. Buchner was a sort of lion. Everyone who went against him died. Parkinson's friend Harker had gone against him and he had died. And this thought brought anger.

I'd love to get that bastard.

But the idea of vengeance brought back the fear for it was likely that the pursuit of vengeance would only result in his own death. Buchner had an aura of invincibility about him. There was no one alive who could harm him let alone kill him.

Why even try?

Besides, Buchner and his Jasta were too high. Parkinson would have to climb after him and by the time he reached their level the Germans would be far in the distance. But by some perverse quirk of reasoning it was the very futility of such an undertaking that swung it for Parkinson.

The hell with it! I'm going to take a shot at that bastard even if it does fall short.

****

From the moment he had led his Jasta off the ground Buchner had kept on climbing, hoping that his ascent would do what it had always done in the past, free him from his earthbound cares. And the care that he was trying to escape now was greater than any he had ever faced in the past.

My mother is a traitor.

Even as the ground fell away beneath him Buchner struggled with this unbearable truth. That she had betrayed her country now seemed to lie beyond dispute. But how could it be? Why would she do such a monstrous thing? Why would she sell out the country that had adopted her, the country that had given her so much?

What makes a person do such a thing?

As he levelled out his machine at three thousand feet he tried hard to find some point of understanding, some formula for making sense out of something that didn't make any sense at all. He couldn't. Nor could he reconcile his own preconceptions of what a traitor was with the woman he knew.

She had always been a loving mother. She had always shown concern for him and his well-being. She had never hesitated to step in and defend him whenever the need arose. She had even spoken to him of her desire to see him with a wife and children.

She deceived me! She deceived me all my life.

More than that she had betrayed him. She had betrayed both her son and her country. And in his outrage at this treachery it came to him that she had only pretended to be his mother. That being his mother was nothing more than another of her cruel deceptions.

Hands and feet moving automatically he turned his machine toward the front. And the members of his Jasta followed, oblivious to the turmoil in the heart of their leader. They could not see the blind hurt in his eyes nor the lack of any outward concentration. If they had they would have been dismayed.

Without any thought to where he was or where he was going he flew on.

****

Please! Please let him get to the ground.

Anthea had never once taken her eyes off Reinhard's crippled machine throughout its descent even though most of the time she kept losing sight of it in the stream of smoke pouring out of it. Nothing else held her attention, not even the fierce battle going on overhead as a group of Camels and F2Bs fought its way back to the front.

Anthea and Reinhard were now down to below a thousand feet and as the ground drew steadily nearer Anthea's anxiety intensified. Reinhard was not out of danger yet. He was clearly still controlling his machine but it could burst into flames at any moment or, just as terrible, Reinhard could succumb to the smoke and lose consciousness.

Sharpening her anxiety was a guilty conscience. She knew that she was entirely to blame for Reinhard's present predicament. If she hadn't disobeyed orders and flown after that British machine none of this would have happened; Reinhard wouldn't have been forced to come to her rescue and he wouldn't have got shot down.

I promise I won't ever do this again. Just let him get to the ground safely.

They were now at five hundred feet. She wasn't sure where they were exactly, but what mattered was that they were still on the friendly side of the lines. She could see the trenches on her left. They were flying parallel to them. On her right she could see what looked like an army supply dump and ahead was an open field.

The perfect place to make a landing.

She followed Reinhard's machine as it cleared some trees. Its wings were level but Anthea was alarmed to realise that it was approaching the ground far faster than it should. She held her breath as the wheels of Reinhard's Pfalz touched the ground. It bounced then dropped again. The undercarriage collapsed and the fuselage ploughed through the snow for about ten yards before it came to a halt.

He's down! He's down!

She landed her own machine close by. Throttling down her engine she left it idling as she unfastened her harness and sprang out of the cockpit. Rushing heedlessly through the smoke enshrouding Reinhard's machine she was at his side within seconds.

He was slumped forward, but, with the undercarriage missing, it was easy enough for her to reach inside and check his pulse.

Thank God! He's alive!

Acting quickly she undid his harness. Then, climbing astride the fuselage behind him, she got hold of him under the armpits and hauled him out of the cockpit. With his upper body now draped over the collar she dropped to the ground and dragged him onto the snow and then to a safe distance away from the smoking machine.

A quick examination revealed that he had no serious injuries. There was an angry red mark above his right eye, but she felt sure that he had sustained this during the crash landing. She would have stayed at his side, but a sound made her lift her head. It was the shouts of approaching soldiers.

I can't be found here. I must get away while I still can.

She laid the palm of her hand tenderly against the side of Reinhard's face and as she did so he opened his eyes. For a moment he seemed confused, but then he recognised the face hovering above him and he smiled. Anthea smiled back and then she did something that startled him. She kissed him on his mouth.

Before he could react she sprang to her feet and ran to her machine. Within seconds she was back in the air.

****

It had been a hard slog, but finally Parkinson had managed to claw his way up to the same height as Buchner's Jasta. As he levelled out his engine stopped protesting and his air speed began to increase.

But the climb had cost him dearly. The enemy was much further on than they had been before. Now their machines were barely more than dots in the distance. The question facing Parkinson was would he be able to catch them.

He did have one thing in his favour. As far as he could judge the Jasta was returning to base at a leisurely pace. They seemed to be in no hurry and with any luck he would be able to close some of the gap between them.

Not wishing to give away his presence he took his Camel down a hundred feet and followed on below the enemy's line of sight. Now it was simply a matter of catching up.

With time on his hands Parkinson started to consider what he was doing. For a start he was flying deeper and deeper into enemy territory. Also he was pursuing a number of enemy machines one of which was piloted by Germany's greatest ace.

I must be stark raving mad.

It was not too late to turn back. No one would blame him if he did. And he was in no position to argue with himself. After all he was a coward of long standing. But then he thought of his friend Harker and of Harker's wife and the scores of men who had fallen to Buchner's guns and he flew on.

The distant dots had now taken on definite form. Given enough time he would definitely catch them up. But he didn't have enough time. If he kept up his pursuit at this rate he would be within firing range when the Jasta reached its home base at Bois de Cheval.

Then I'm a dead 'un.

He had to do something to speed things up. But what? There was no way to get more power out of his engine. It was already at maximum revs. Then he thought of a manouevre that might just work. Trouble was he would only be able to do it once. If he didn't get it right the first time there would be no second chance.

For the time being he just sat and waited patiently as his machine brought him nearer and nearer. He was now close enough to the Pfalz ahead of him that he could make out their individual shapes, but still not quite close enough to do what he intended.

It took another several minutes before Parkinson reached what he considered to be the critical distance. Quickly he assessed his armaments. He had used up just over half of his 250 rounds of .303 ammunition strafing the German trenches. So he had plenty left.

More than enough for what I have in mind.

Casting all further thought from his mind he pushed his stick hard forward and went into a steep dive. The creaking of the wings and the singing of the bracing wires grew louder as the Camel raced earthward. With every second that passed it picked up speed until it seemed that it could go no faster.

Now!

Parkinson pulled the stick back into his lap. The rising earth was replaced by the open sky above him. He was now climbing rapidly at a sharp angle and at the top of that climb were the silver bellies of the enemy machines.

His air speed began to fall away rapidly. He watched the speedometer anxiously. Would he make it? The undersides of the Pfalz drew nearer and nearer, but with every second his rate of approach dropped.

Then he felt his machine start to stall. It would climb no higher. Was he close enough or was he still too far away? It was too late to worry about that now. Adjusting his sights so that they were fixed on the lead Pfalz, Buchner's Pfalz, he opened fire.

A stream of bullets shot out ahead of him covering the distance he could not follow. He managed to get off a short burst, probably no more than thirty or forty rounds, before the nose of his machine fell forward.

****

Despite wrestling with his soul and his conscience Buchner's questions remained unresolved. He knew that he couldn't go on flying forever. He would have to land eventually. The spot where Frommherz died was below them and Bois de Cheval was not far off. But he had no idea what he would do then. Would he hand his mother over to the authorities or would he keep the bitter truth to himself?

It was an agonising dilemma. But on one thing he had resolved. He would resign his commission. He could no longer serve his country knowing what he knew. How could he? He was the son of a traitor

And the son's of traitors cannot be national heroes.

The pain of the decision was etched on his face. Never again would he bask in glory. Never again would he rule the skies. His name and his fame would fade away and he would be forgotten.

This was the unbearable thought that passed through his mind as the bullet passed through his left foot. Of all the rounds that had issued from Parkinson's guns this was the only one that had made it to its target. But it was enough.

Buchner howled in agony as it tore through his tendons. The pain was intense, so intense it momentarily overwhelmed all power of thought. Only instinct kept his uninjured foot pressed on the rudder bar and his hand on the stick.

Slowly and with great effort he was able to localise the source of agony, enough to assess the damage and realise that his left foot was effectively useless. He couldn't move it and any attempt to do so resulted in a fresh wave of pain.

Training and experience told him that although his situation was a desperate one there was still a remote chance that he could bring his machine down safely. And his first inclination was to fight for his life. Why wouldn't he? But then he remembered what awaited him on the ground and he hesitated.

What was there left of his life anyway? His friend Frommherz was dead. He had killed Harker his greatest opponent. Hantelmann was returning to take back his command. His mother was his mother no longer and it was likely that she would have to face a traitor's death.

But then an agonising stab of pain up his ankle and leg reminded him that fate had provided him with the perfect solution to all his problems, one that would take them away forever. A life bound to the earth no longer held any attractions for him. The sky was his domain. It always had been. In his short career he had blazed across it like a meteor.

Now the time has come to blaze across it one last time.

He pulled the stick hard against his stomach and in response to its master's command the Pfalz zoomed away from the earth like an arrow, rocketing upward to punch into the blue heavens above.

Glory is the sun at noon, the wings that make men soar, the golden light for which they kill till glory is no more.

****

As soon as Anthea gained height she took an eastward course, but then she corrected it to a northeast heading. She was not returning to Bois de Cheval. She was returning to Valenciennes. Her priority now was to get back to the *Jastaschule*, retrieve her Halberstadt and fly back to Essen.

She felt sure that by now her parents had discovered what she had been up to and there would almost certainly be hell to pay if she returned home. Her only hope was to seek sanctuary with her brother at least until the storm died down.

The skies around her were once again empty of machines. There was no sign of the Camels and F2Bs she had seen earlier fighting off an attack by a large number of Pfalz and she reckoned that they must have made it safely back over the lines.

But as she took in more of her surroundings she spotted a lone Camel on her starboard side. It was at about her height and heading home in the opposite direction. It was near enough for her to see its flight leader's streamer and she imagined that he was watching her as she passed by, but he kept on his heading and flew on.

Then a little distance further on her saw a strange sight. It was a group of Pfalz. They were also on her starboard side and somewhat lower down, but behaving in an odd manner. They were flying back and forth

320

around the wreckage of a machine on the ground. Her brother had once shown her such a machine at his factory and she recognised the type instantly.

It's a Pfalz DVIII!

It was in bad shape and looked as it must have impacted with the ground head on. The four other Pfalz seemed to be circling it as if shock and despair.

Eventually the spectacle was lost in a ground mist and Anthea thought no more about it. What she could not have known was the identity of the downed pilot or that he was Germany's greatest hero. Not was she aware of the part she had played in his death.

EPILOGUE

CHAPTER TWENTY-EIGHT

11 JANUARY 1918

An offshore breeze pulled at the edge of the German flag revealing a corner of Buchner's coffin. It lay on a bier on the prow of the *Peleus* awaiting the last stage of its long journey.

Thetis stood beside it in silence. She was dressed in black; long black dress, black gloves, black hat with black feather and a black veil drawn over her stricken face. These were her clothes of grief and she had worn them at every stage of her son's journey from Bois de Cheval to Sassnitz.

The journey had started at the airfield from where she had collected her son's body. His old command had already carried out a full military service and out of respect for her the men and officers had kept out of the way. They had even allowed her to collect his personal effects and it was while she was doing this that she discovered the notice about *Silver Feet*.

Did he know?

The shock of such a possibility spurred her into finding out the circumstances of his death. No one really had any idea what to tell her but letters left by Fuchs and Reinhard revealed that on the day of his death the airbase had been on a state of alert following the discovery that an impostor going under the name of Leutnant Strasser had infiltrated JGN.

'He even managed to create a dogfight close to where your son was flying at the time,' Reinhard wrote.

And the moment she read this Thetis knew that Anthea had been instrumental in her son's death. The evidence for this belief was sparse and circumstantial, but she believed it just the same. Anthea had caused his death. And if she believed this then Thetis knew that she had to accept her own part in the tragedy.

I engineered her being here. It was my doing. It was my desire for vengeance that brought it all about.

From Bois de Cheval Thetis travelled with the body across almost the entire length of Germany. The journey had been aboard a black-draped funeral train and Thetis had to endure the outpouring of national emotion at every stop along the way.

Thousands lined the route hoping to catch a glimpse of the train as it slowly rolled past and every town held its own public ceremony in Buchner's honour. Finally the funeral train reached Berlin and here the ceremony was the grandest of them all.

For Thetis all of this was exquisite torture but seeing it as the least she deserved she made no attempt to avoid it. Then she found herself face to face with Maximillian von Hoeppner. It was at an event being held at the Residenz in her son's honour.

While surrounded by guests von Hoeppner had demonstrated great sympathy and he commiserated with her for her loss, but in the privacy of his library it was a different matter. He quickly got to the point.

'You have endangered the life of my daughter in your schemes. You have spied on the country that adopted you and you have betrayed its secrets to the enemy. You have proven that your feet are not made of silver but of clay.

I should have you shot, but the scandal of your trial would not only ruin the reputation of your son but would damage the Fatherland irreparably at this time. You are to leave Germany permanently and take the body of your son with you.'

Feeling as wretched as she did she would have welcomed the executioner's bullet, but she was denied even that. So she took her son's coffin to Sassnitz and now she stood before it on the prow of the Peleus preparing for one last journey. It was almost time to weigh anchor and set sail. All that remained was the setting of the sun.

Lightning Source UK Ltd.
Milton Keynes UK
UKOW08f2014270417
300070UK00003B/149/P